THE
MISSION

THE
MISSION

A Novel

Naomi Kryske

DUNHAM
books

Trade Paperback ISBN: 978-1-939447-70-8
E-book ISBN: 978-1-939447-88-3

Library of Congress Control Number: 2015931050

Printed in the United States of America

BREAKING NEWS

George Bernard Shaw was right: England and America are two countries separated by a common language.

I have honored his conviction in this novel (as I did in *The Witness*) by using British spelling and expressions for the British characters and American spelling for the American characters. Thus you will note "realise/recognise" for "realize/recognize" and "colour/honour/neighbour" for "color/honor/neighbor," to highlight just a few. British English sometimes omits or uses fewer or different prepositions, and their past tenses may be unlike ours: "different to" for "different than" and "learnt" for "learned."

To my sons
Who make me proud

PROLOGUE

The Gold Commander at New Scotland Yard could not believe what he saw. His twenty-seven years of experience with London's Metropolitan Police had taught him to maintain outward calm regardless of inner turmoil, but this afternoon he was finding it difficult. As Gold, he had developed the strategy and allocated the resources for dealing with the considerable number of demonstrators at Europe's largest defence exhibition, being held today at the London Docklands. Further responsibility included being on the alert for any indication of violence by monitoring the bank of screens which covered the crowd. Now, however, his attention was directed away from those screens. The ones displayed on the lower left showed an aeroplane exploding as it flew into a towering skyscraper in New York City. Was the crash intentional? Had someone found a novel way to kill himself? Certainly no capable pilot could miss the World Trade Center! He watched the replay. No, the skies were perfectly clear, and the plane looked too large to be a private craft. Dear God, what was happening in America? Mass murder? He forced himself to concentrate. Then a second plane hit the second tower, and all hell broke loose.

There wasn't an officer in MetOps who didn't have the same emotional discipline as he, but none of them had dealt with an act of violence on this scale. Voices were raised in shock and disbelief. Terse phrases were spit out as individuals attempted to communicate what they were seeing. Frustration erupted as they realised they were powerless to assist their neighbours across the pond in any way. Their brief was to make London safer for its citizens, but loss of innocent life anywhere in the world hit them hard. Britain had been the target of IRA attacks for years, but the landscape of American law enforcement – including her security forces – was now irrevocably changed. The use of suicide bombers was a Middle Eastern phenomenon. If these evildoers came from the Middle East, the entire world had changed in the space of a few minutes, because a dangerous precedent had been set. More attacks would come.

The Commissioner of Police was in the air over the mid-Atlantic, on his way to confer with Bob Muller, the new head of the Federal Bureau of Investigation. The Gold Commander rang the Commissioner's office and was told by his personal assistant that he had been informed of the crisis. Because American air space was now closed, his plane had been forced to turn about and would be returning home.

"The Pentagon, sir," an associate behind him mumbled thickly. "An aeroplane has hit the Pentagon in Washington, D.C."

"That makes three," he responded. "How many more? When will this slaughter from the skies end?" He thought of his wife and children and felt a desperate need to ring them and assure himself of their safety. As quickly as the thought arose, however, he quelled it: Individual needs must be set aside. Seeing to the security of the many must take priority over personal concerns. He had not become a policeman to protect one life at a time; he had always hoped he would prove worthy of a rank high enough to affect the safety and well-being of many more.

By now the visual images would have been seared into the minds of all who had seen them. Because of the United Kingdom's close alliance with the United States, London could be the next target. People were spontaneously evacuating high-rise buildings and crowding the streets. To prevent panic, he must supply mental pictures to reassure them. Uniformed police were a symbol of stability in a country ruled by law. The public looked to the police for protection. They must be seen to be on the Job. He ordered all leaves cancelled and made arrangements for every available officer to report for high visibility duties. He summoned his deputy, whose stricken face had aged him. "Contact our counterparts in Kent and the other neighbouring counties. We'll need manpower from them to assist us."

The news must have got round the demonstrators at the Docklands. The screens showed the mass of people splintering into groups which huddled together briefly before dispersing. Excellent. He could reduce the quantity of officers assigned there and increase the number on London streets. He rang the Silver Commander, the senior officer in charge at the scene.

There may have been British citizens on the hijacked planes, but regardless of nationality, every seat had held a human being. When had the passengers known their fate? How had parents controlled their fears and comforted their children? He was put in mind of his early days on the Job. In his two probationary years he had seen more human tragedy than most experienced in a lifetime. Road accidents, train wrecks, bodies battered beyond recognition. In some cases he'd had to notify the next of kin and watch their desperate disbelief replaced by despair as facts crowded out the last slivers of hope. Some screamed; some went silent. Eventually, determination to carry on, to honour the dead, to see justice done, prevailed.

MetOps was now crowded with officers straining to see the drama being played out on the screens. Gasps and exclamations from them joined his own. One of the World Trade Center towers had collapsed, the ash mixing with dark billowing smoke in a cloud of horror. Without a doubt British citizens had worked in the World Trade Centers. Many would have been killed along with their American colleagues. The lucky ones had died instantly. Still others could be missing under the thousands of tonnes of steel and concrete still being shown. And the loved ones they left behind would be devastated with grief.

He looked about. Not unlike many offices in the World Trade Centers, MetOps was an interior room, artificially lit, located in one of New Scotland Yard's two-tower buildings. Occupants would have no warning of an approaching threat. Mercifully, however, MetOps was on Victoria Block's second floor, an unlikely target for an insidious attack of this sort. Fortunately smoking was not allowed. He could not have tolerated the sight of even a wisp of smoke.

He returned to the screens. "Four," he whispered, his concentration so complete that he was unaware he had spoken aloud. In Pennsylvania a fourth plane had crashed. Still the nightmare continued. The second tower fell, then parts of the Pentagon. He felt again the shock, then the grip of despair, and resolved that he would not give in to either. Determination was the order of the day. His mission: take steps to do everything within his considerable power to deliver the best security to Londoners that his force could provide. He knew he'd be on watch indefinitely. He reached for his phone.

PART ONE

SEPTEMBER, 2001

The battle has been joined on many fronts.

— George W. Bush

CHAPTER 1

Jennifer Sinclair's serene September day was shattered by a phone call. It was her husband, Colin, a detective chief inspector with London's Metropolitan Police. He often called during the day, but this time his voice was terse and strained. "Jenny, turn on the telly. Your country's been attacked. New York and other places. We're all on alert here. I don't know when I'll be home."

"Colin, you're scaring me!"

"Jenny – remember that evil cannot win. There are more of us fighting it than those participating in it."

"I still wish you were here."

"I know. I love you."

All the news channels were covering the events. Over and over she saw planes flying into buildings, the skies raining flames, smoke, papers as thick as snow, glass from shattered windows which would have sliced into the faces of bystanders below, and – *people*. People had jumped to their deaths from the burning towers. Fortunately there were no closeups, an unusual mercy on the part of the media, who must have felt that no further sensationalism was necessary. She didn't mind the repetitive nature of the reports; it helped the unthinkable to sink in. Terrorists had attacked her country and murdered hundreds of her people. She imagined her nation uttering one great collective scream before the silence of shock muted her.

The memory of her rape resurrected itself with alarming intensity: the terror she had felt, how helpless she had been. But her attacker hadn't known or cared that she was an American, only that she was the right size and sex for his violence. Then when he discovered she was still alive, he had sent others to kill her. Colin had placed her in witness protection, but she had endured months of fear until her attacker had been convicted. Like her country, she had lost her innocence through violent acts on a beautifully clear fall day. And as she had, tomorrow all Americans would wake to a new and frightening world in which the rules of engagement were forever changed.

Over the pounding of her heart, she heard her mobile ring again. This time her hands were shaking when she answered.

"Are you all right, love?" a voice she knew well asked. One of the Met's specialist firearms officers, Sergeant Simon Casey had been in charge of her witness protection team. Everything about him had frightened her at first: his stern expression, his uncompromising manner, even his icy blue eyes, which had dared her not to meet his expectations. Prior to joining the police, he had been an elite Special Forces operative until an injury required him to retire from military service.

"Simon, what does it mean?"

"Your country's at war. Unless I miss my guess, we'll be in it with you. And I'm in the wrong bloody uniform."

"At war? I don't understand. Didn't the terrorists die on the planes?"

"Jenny, someone sent them. It was a complex and coordinated attack. They were well trained and well equipped."

"Simon, I can't stop shaking."

"Breathe. Focus. Like I taught you."

"Is it over? Will there be more?"

"It's too soon to know, but your people will find out who is behind it. Don't panic. You're safe with us."

"Thank you, Simon." She closed her phone. Safe. She had been safe ever since Colin had become a part of her life. He had made sure of it. She returned to the news coverage. She saw again the fireballs when the planes hit their targets. She knew how fragile people's bodies were, how easily skin split open and bones broke. Had their blood burned, those passengers who had flown into eternity? Passengers – my God, there would have been women and children on those planes! What kind of monster planned to murder *children?*

Lines from Longfellow's poem, "The Building of the Ship," flashed through her mind: "Sail on, O Ship of State! / Humanity with all its fears, / With all the hopes of future years, / Is hanging breathless on thy fate!" The British named their warships after courageous qualities: HMS *Dauntless*, HMS *Resolute*, and HMS *Invincible*. Gilbert and Sullivan had poked fun at the practice by placing sailors in one of their operettas on HMS *Pinafore*, named for a girl's article of clothing, but seamen on the real ships were proud of their legacy and wanted to prove themselves worthy. Now America was like the Titanic, a ship touted as unsinkable but vulnerable nonetheless to an insidious threat.

She shivered. Their flat in Hampstead, a suburb northwest of London, was difficult to heat, but she suspected she was chilled more by the fear in the air. She made some tea – the British palliative – and again dialed her parents' number in Houston, Texas, where she had grown up, but only the busy signal answered, and she felt lonely and defenseless. In witness protection the officers assigned to her had provided a constant, reassuring presence. PC Danny Sullivan, not much older than her brothers, was an inveterate practical joker who had kept the atmosphere light. Even today he would have found a way to pierce the dread and make her smile. PC Brian Davies, a huge bear of a man whose wife Beth was now one of her closest friends, had been an outstanding cook. Maybe if the flat were filled with the aroma of one of his dishes, she would feel less alone. Even Hunt, the irreverent PC Alan Hunt, would remind her not to take life too seriously. And, of course, the ginger-haired thirty-something Simon, who had treated her tension with regular doses of physical exercise and challenged her to face every adversity. She respected his dedication and focus.

"Colin, I want to go home," she said when he called again.

"You'll have to wait for a bit. All planes are grounded in the States, and no international flights are allowed into American air space."

"But I can't reach my family!"

"They'll be all right, Jenny. Texas is out of the line of fire. Open a bottle of wine. I'll be home before too long. I have something for you. Wait there for me."

It would take at least thirty minutes, she knew, for him to walk to the Embankment Station, take the Edgware branch of the Northern Line to Hampstead Station, and traverse the Hampstead streets that lay between the subway and their home. She washed her face, ran a brush through her hair, and found the corkscrew, all the while wondering what he could be bringing her.

It was an American flag.

CHAPTER 2

The next days passed in a blur, Jenny unable to tear herself away from the September 11 news coverage for very long but desperate at the same time to escape it. The horror of the news was matched by her hunger for it, because she feared another attack could be imminent.

Meanwhile she wanted to *do* something, anything, to alleviate her feeling of helplessness. She inquired about donating blood but was told that her travel outside the UK and her insufficient weight made her ineligible. Frustrated, she went to the library to learn how Londoners had survived the Blitz in World War II. Southern England, she discovered, had been the principal target for German bombers. People had used the subway stations for shelter. Hampstead was the deepest in the underground network, reaching 192 feet below the surface. That alone would have been daunting, but "Keep calm and carry on" had been the watchwords then and seemed just as appropriate now.

Colin had taught her how to use the subway – what he called the tube – system. Although she had loved the open roads in Texas, she had been tentative about driving in the UK, and the ease and efficiency of public transportation meant that driving was not a necessity.

"Each train is identified by its end point. Simply check to be sure your stop is on the way to the final destination.

If you need to change trains, follow the Way Out signs after you deboard the first. You'll be directed to the next line and platform."

The British were extremely well-organized, and after a while it all made sense. She felt like a native and even liked the genteel reminders to "Mind the gap between the train and the platform" and the posh female voice that announced each stop beforehand by directing the passengers to "alight."

"At Hampstead you'll always take the lift down to the platforms," he had continued.

She had laughed. "Shouldn't lifts always go up?"

He had teased back. "Elevators go both up and down, don't they?"

The lift was unusual. People entered on one side and exited the other. Jenny learned to use her Oyster card, a prepaid travel debit card, and to stand on the right side of the escalators that negotiated the levels between platforms. If a tube station closed without warning, however, she couldn't change trains where she had planned. In that case she gave up and took a cab home.

Always she thought about the nineteen men who had hijacked the planes. They had apparently come disguised as normal people, their dark skin not remarkable in a country that prided itself on being a melting pot. Through their actions they had stepped into every living room in America, their teeth bared in malevolent snarls. Colin acknowledged that these terrorists were a new breed: IRA bombers had wanted to live to fight another day. Most had not chosen to die with their victims.

When Simon called on Friday, the anniversary of the assault on her in central London, she felt that only a single thread separated her from the traumas of her past. "I wasn't crushed by imploding buildings or consumed by jet fuel," she told him, "but this attack brought back memories of my experience – the shock, the terror."

"It's been three years, love."

"Sometimes it seems like it was yesterday."

"You overcame it then. You can do it now."

His confidence cheered her a little, and she smiled.

He and the rest of her witness protection officers had continually encouraged her to believe in herself, to move forward. "Thanks for remembering. Have you been busier than usual?"

"A big one came off today. It had been in the works for some time; we had to wait until the suits were sure of their intel."

"Were they terrorists?"

"No, love. Just ordinary criminals who didn't take a holiday."

"Simon, your work is so dangerous. Is everybody okay?" She knew that Brian, her friend Beth's husband, was on Simon's team.

"We were awake and alert. They weren't. That's why we go early. And it didn't hurt that they'd been drinking the night before. Arrests made, firearms and drugs confiscated. A good result all round."

He rang off, and she returned to her musings. She usually paid scant attention to British politics, but she noticed and applauded Prime Minister Tony Blair's show of support for President Bush. In addition, the Queen had ordered that the American national anthem be played at Buckingham Palace, and there was a memorial service scheduled at St. Paul's. Jenny immersed herself in British history, reading about how Winston Churchill's warnings of a German menace had fallen on deaf ears. But America hadn't had a Churchill to wake her from her naïve sleep. Instead, she had been preoccupied with prosperity and had ignored the growing peril. The '93 bombing at the World Trade Center hadn't changed her outlook; the bombings at the U.S. embassies in Africa in 1998 hadn't; the attack on the USS *Cole* in 2000 hadn't either.

When Colin came home from work, she was still pensive and somewhat surprised when he suggested that they visit the Hampstead restaurant where they had celebrated their engagement. Now, as they sat across the table from each other at La Gaffe sipping wine and waiting for their rocket salads to be delivered, she smiled at his gentle questions.

"Jenny, why did you rearrange the furniture?"

That was kind. She had taken all the pictures down, too, and rehung them in different places. "Because 9/11 has made me feel different. I thought the flat should reflect that. I hope you don't mind."

"Not at all. And your new hairdo?"

She had pulled her long hair into a ponytail, exposing instead of concealing the scar she still wore on her right cheek. "My country has been scarred. I'm proud of where I'm from, so I don't care if my scar shows."

"I'd hoped we could focus tonight on life, not loss."

She smiled at his way of reminding her that their lovemaking had an added purpose. Not long after their marriage, Colin had spoken to her about children. They'd made love and were still holding each other when he introduced the subject. He didn't want to pressure her, he said. Being a father was important to him, but she would carry the child in her body, and she had to be willing to accept all the changes that would result. He'd asked her to have a think on it. "I'd like to focus on life, too. Colin, we've been trying for quite a while, but I haven't gotten pregnant. That's the life I want to focus on – having another Sinclair to love. I want to see your sister's doctor, her gynecologist."

The excitement that welled up inside him was tempered with concern. "Brilliant, Jenny! But are you certain? I expect that sort of exam won't be easy for you." The severe abuse she had suffered during her sexual assault, combined with her small size, had engendered a host of protective feelings in him from their first meeting. The only surviving victim of a serial killer, her information had been critical to the Met's investigation. During the interviews he had been charmed by her Texas drawl and the fact that she was educated, a recent university graduate. Establishing rapport with her, important to do with potential witnesses, had been easy, and he had discovered that rapport was a two way street. Laughter was a precious commodity in policing, and she had made him laugh.

As the investigation progressed, he had admired her courage and determination, and it had been increasingly difficult to keep his personal feelings in check. By the time her role as a witness ended, he had known he was in love with her. She had gone home to Texas, and the light had gone out of his life until he had persuaded her to return to London. Now she sat before him with a new commitment to making the love in their life grow. He raised his wine glass, realising as he did so that he would have felt light headed even without the wine.

She finished her salad and inhaled the aroma of the braised lamb the waiter had just set in front of her. "I'm a little nervous about the examination – well, more than a little – so I wondered if you would go with me. I feel safer when you're around." At 6'2", he was a foot taller than she. His embraces enveloped her.

"Yes. Jenny, yes."

"Colin, you haven't touched your Dover sole."

He set his fork down. "I've lost my appetite for anything but you." He hailed the waiter. "We'll take our food with us."

She laughed softly and prepared to leave.

CHAPTER 3

Originally proposed by the Home Secretary, Project Sapphire was the Met's attempt to remedy the way sexual offences were investigated and to improve the care of victims. Colin Sinclair was pleased when he was tapped to lead the day-to-day operations of the new unit. From his office, he could see a lamppost on the tree-lined Victoria Embankment and beyond, the calm waters of the Thames. These were tangible symbols of what he wished all rape victims could experience: light and peace, understanding and healing.

His deep commitment was not shared by all officers, however, and he faced an uphill battle in implementing the programme. Many considered rape a low priority. According to studies, only one in ten victims reported the crime. Others were afraid to do so, fearing that the police would not believe them or that they would be made to feel that the attack was their fault. Rape victims were psychologically fragile; even a raised eyebrow by an officer could cause a woman to change her mind about continuing the interview. A substantial number of those who did contact police were not willing to go through the legal process, frightened of what the court experience would be. Fear was the common thread – fear when the crime occurred and fear of everything that followed. Less than five percent of rape allegations were successfully prosecuted.

Another complicating factor was the frequent lack of forensic evidence. Some rapes were downgraded to less serious offences, and many defendants were acquitted because physical injuries did not exist in their victims. Sinclair understood the seriousness of the charge and the need to eliminate reasonable doubt, but psychological injuries, though more difficult to demonstrate, were often more lasting and severe. How could juries not recognise rape for the assault that it was? Others considered only stranger rape to be "real rape" and discounted sexual assaults by anyone known to the victim. In Sinclair's experience, the traumas from both were deep and enduring, and some victims were affected for the rest of their lives.

Other legal problems existed. Prosecutors had to resort to plea bargains in cases where the victim would not make a credible witness, denying individuals their day in court. In no other crime was the credibility of the victim assessed first, but in an overwhelming majority of cases, acquaintance rape pitted one person's word against another's. Investigators needed to look for ways to prove or disprove a victim's account of the event and particularly for evidence prosecutors could use beyond DNA.

In many boroughs Criminal Investigation Department (CID) officers dealt with robbery and burglary as well as rape. Each borough needed a dedicated Sapphire unit, a full complement of specialist officers trained to interview victims of sexual assault. In addition, emergency operators and front desk staff needed to have training since they were the first to have contact with victims. Sapphire was a strategic team. They had no powers of enforcement, nor could they mandate any new policy. Borough chief superintendents had to be won over to the Sapphire policies.

Sinclair was indebted to his junior officers and passed on "well dones" to them whenever he could. His sergeants were energetic, capable, and creative, focussed on the result and more concerned with getting others on board than with receiving credit. Indeed, they were often able to set out policy in such a way that the borough officers they visited ended up believing they had thought of it themselves.

Sinclair's experience with Jenny's case had given him a unique understanding of the issues rape victims faced. He wanted to furnish as non-threatening an environment as possible for the interview and medical procedures, ensure that the victims were treated with gentleness and respect, and offer them continuing support and reassurance. These factors had first been established at The Haven in Camberwell, a clinic which had opened in June the previous year. Forensic examinations were given there, medical care was provided, and counselling was offered, ending the customary long periods of waiting in police medical suites or hospital emergency rooms. Often the victim was accompanied by a specialist officer who gave the doctor the details of the offence so the victim didn't have to do. A crisis worker, a nurse, obtained the victim's consent for the procedure and described what to expect. A curtain hid the examination table from view while the doctor took the patient's medical history. When the examination did take place, only one part of the body was viewed at a time. Shower facilities were supplied. Victims were always encouraged to return for aftercare and support services through a separate entrance and waiting room.

Sinclair glanced at his watch. Visitors from Canada were due to arrive soon. Indeed, Sapphire's international reputation had brought law enforcement officers and prosecutors from around the world to meet with him. Everyone expressed curiosity at the name, smiling when he quipped that they'd thought of designating their unit "Amethyst," but no one could spell it. Their intent had been to adopt a name that didn't use the word "rape" and thus maintained the private nature of the calls they received. He'd been told that the title was appropriate: Sapphires symbolised truth, sincerity, and good health, which he hoped all victims would regain.

Jenny had progressed a great deal in recovering from her trauma. He'd never forget the first time he had seen her, how small and defenceless she had looked in the hospital bed, unable to breathe without assistance, unable to speak. She'd had a long and difficult recovery. Her life had been in jeopardy, and on more than one occasion he had feared he'd lose her. After the villain who assaulted her had been convicted, her personal trials had continued. Love, counselling, and her own determination to overcome her fears had been the keys to her recovery. She had eventually trusted him enough to enter into an intimate relationship. She had become his wife. And recently she had taken an even bigger step, consulting a doctor regarding their struggle to conceive.

She was still a bit tentative when meeting people for the first time, so he had accompanied her on the first visit. Knowing that questions would be asked concerning her medical history, he had brought a copy of her record. It detailed the violence of her attack, the severity of her injuries, and the surgeries that had been required to preserve her life. He would have been uncomfortable verbalising such personal information, and she would have been acutely embarrassed if he had done. Also, the medical record would spare her from having to explain her multiple scars.

Dr. Hannaford had seemed to take it in stride. He had informed Jenny that he'd be making a brief preliminary examination and had allowed Sinclair to wait in his office. Sinclair had paced the room, too concerned to think of anything but his powerlessness to protect her from the invasive nature of the examinations that lay ahead. When she returned, pale but struggling to smile, he had been too overcome with pride, love, and relief to speak. He had hugged her on the spot, and she had returned his gesture with an equally tight hug of her own and then reported the doctor's initial advice: "Take your temperature to determine time of ovulation, select a position that will use gravity to assist the process, and spend more intimate time together. And we'll need to test your husband, of course."

If she conceived soon, he would not be a young father at age thirty-nine, but the zest and humour she possessed at twenty-six made him feel young. On a recent trip to his mother's home in Kent, she had stripped off her shoes and socks, rolled up her jeans, and waded into the duck pond. "Don't you want to feel the mud between your toes?" she had asked, holding out her hand to him. He hadn't done that since he was a boy, but that day he had joined her. The water and the mud had been cool, but the embrace his petite, dark-haired wife had given him had been warm.

A crisp knock on his door brought him back to the present.

"Sir, your visitors have arrived," Sergeant Bridges informed him. He took a last sip of Sapphire's substandard tea and made a stab at organising the many piles on his desk. Lack of time, lack of space, and lack of manpower characterised policing everywhere. Their only surfeit was paperwork because records had to be kept of everything. In his unit, of particular import were the statistics concerning how many victims came to the Haven, the disposition of their cases, and the unit's progress with cold cases. He stood and welcomed the opportunity to discuss Sapphire's mission, procedures, and success with his Canadian counterparts.

CHAPTER 4

The briefing rooms used by the Met's specialist firearms officers were devoid of windows. Instead, filing cabinets and whiteboards crowded the walls. All designed to keep their minds focussed on the upcoming ops, PC Brian Davies thought. When team leader Sergeant Simon Casey suspended the briefing, Davies and the other officers sighed in frustration. A few uttered quiet but choice expletives. Not only was there nothing to occupy them while they waited, new intelligence could require looking yet again at their planned manoeuvres and possibly revising or even delaying them. Davies knew that Casey was as eager to get on with it as the next man, but his unusual discipline would never allow his face to reveal it. The one thing his discipline could not tame was his love for Jenny.

Of course, when they had first met her, it had been their responsibility to protect her. Six other women had been raped and murdered. Somehow Jenny had survived, and the Met was determined to hear her testify against the villain who had done it. She'd had a rough go of it. She'd come to depend on them during the rough patches, and Davies had liked that. It was clear evidence that they were helping.

She was a pretty little thing. Eye candy, one of the officers had called her, and he hadn't been wrong, but Davies thought it was her ability to overcome the trauma and setbacks in the recovery process that had caused Casey to take notice. During the witness protection assignment, Davies had begun to suspect that Casey's feelings for her were more serious than he let on, but all junior officers knew that becoming entangled with a witness you had been tasked to protect would not be forgiven. Casey was a sergeant, but it had been clear that the supervising officer, DCI Sinclair, fancied her as well. Casey had set his feelings aside, contenting himself with maintaining a close but platonic friendship with her. Still, Davies thought that Casey's subsequent women were divided into two groups: Jenny and all the others, whom Davies lumped together as, "Not Jenny."

Casey was an effective team leader, and Davies had learnt a lot from him. The mental battle must be fought first, Casey was fond of saying. "Getting your mind straight," he called it. But Casey hadn't been able to do it when Jenny married Sinclair. The witness protection officers whom she had considered friends had been invited to the wedding in Texas. They had attended, eager to see at least part of the state they'd heard so much of. All except Casey. He had invented an excuse and had drunk the city dry while they were gone. Davies knew because he had called by Casey's flat when he returned. A forest of empty bottles had greeted him. Clearly Casey wasn't particular about what he drank. Or what he wore – his clothes looked slept in, and he hadn't shaved in days.

"What's this about?" he had asked.

"He's bedding her. He's having her," Casey had replied in a thick voice.

"Nothing's changed, mate. They've been together for some time."

"She's wed. She's lost to me."

"She'll be ringing you when she comes back. It won't do for her to see you like this. Besides, she's happy. It's what we wanted, isn't it? After what she went through? You'd rather see her happy with another man than see her unhappy, wouldn't you?"

Casey was silent.

"Jenny's parents had a do for us the night before the

wedding, dinner at a steak restaurant. I had the 18-ounce prime rib. With shrimp. Sinclair was gracious; no senior officer attitude at all. And some of Jenny's friends were lovely."

"How'd she look?" Casey asked.

Davies handed him a photo. Jenny's wedding had taken place in the afternoon. She had not worn a white dress. Her jacket, blouse, and skirt were more the colour of the champagne in the glass she held in her hand, with long sleeves, pearl buttons, and pearls around the collar and cuffs. A strand of pearls was woven into her dark hair. And, as always, she wore around her neck the pearl cross the protection team had given her. The scar on her cheek, although faint, was still visible, yet she had faced the camera head-on, unveiled, smiling.

"She had a professional photographer. He even made Hunt look good."

"Even Hunt," Casey echoed with a slight smile, remembering Jenny's nickname for the protection officer whose aggressive ways had initially unsettled her.

"You should've come, mate. She missed you. She'd have had a snap taken with you."

Davies watched Casey close his eyes briefly and turn the picture face down. "Listen to me, mate. It's time to get on with it."

Casey's voice was bitter. "Just what we told her on more than one occasion."

"True then and true now."

Slowly Casey nodded.

Since that day Davies had never referred to Casey's lapse. Casey had returned to duty, quieter and more focussed than ever. Now he addressed the waiting officers. "New intel didn't change anything. It's a go," he said.

CHAPTER 5

Jenny's entire fall was punctuated with breaking news reports. Were terrorist incidents around the world occurring more frequently or just being reported more fully now? Expecting to hear of another terrorist act became the norm, and days with stories only about the economy, crime, or the latest celebrity divorce were the unusual ones. The Commissioner of the Metropolitan Police had acted immediately, however, launching Operation Calm, in which extra officers were assigned to patrol possible target areas. He was taking steps to increase the size of the anti-terrorist squad, and Simon had reported that all specialist units were undergoing additional training. Unfortunately, none of these actions completely reassured her.

The planes had flown into the towers on days when the skies had been clear and blue, so forecasts of cloudless skies worried her. She wanted dark, stormy days to fill the calendar, days on which air travel was curtailed or cancelled. Heavy thunderstorms and high winds spelled safety. Colin often had to remind her that the most important things in life stayed the same: faith, hope, and their love. Her parents also emphasized the positive, speaking of a new American camaraderie which the events of 9/11 had birthed, a wordless compassion that strangers in their community shared, instances when the individual experience and the universal fused.

Still under the cloud of 9/11, she lay on the examination table waiting for Dr. Hannaford to come in and wondered how many babies had been born on that date, babies whose parents would struggle in future years to separate the joy of their child's birth from the sorrow of the national loss.

She hadn't felt much compassion from the doctor; he never gave her as much information as she wanted, and his manner was abrupt. Why, she wondered, had he chosen this branch of medicine if he weren't willing to deal with women's feelings? Colin's sister Jillian, who had recommended him to Jenny, hadn't mentioned his brusque personality, but Jillian had conceived without difficulty and had had two normal pregnancies.

He hadn't found any medical reason to explain why she hadn't conceived. She was young, healthy, and "nonspecifically infertile," as he put it. It seemed so unfair! Each visit he simply recommended another test. It was hard waiting for him. Why were his patient rooms so stark? Unlike her dentist's office in Houston – which had a TV screen in the ceiling and a remote so the patient could change the channel – these surroundings had nothing to distract her from what lay ahead. Her bottom half was covered by a sheet, but she still felt exposed. I love Colin, she told herself. He'll be such a good father, patient and gentle. Maybe the baby will have his blue eyes.

The door to the examining room opened. "Let's get started, shall we?" the doctor said. He folded the sheet back and adjusted his light.

She closed her eyes and took a deep breath. She heard him make a comment to the nurse and felt a sudden, sharp pain in her stomach, so strong that it made her dizzy. She cried out and gripped the sides of the examination table. The other tests hadn't hurt like this! Why hadn't he told her what to expect? Instead of calling it "discomfort." Discomfort was when you bumped your knee, not when it felt like something had torn inside! "What are you doing to me?" she gasped.

"Your uterus is contracting," the doctor replied. "It's a

normal response."

Great, she thought. I had a labor pain without a baby.

"I'm through for today," the doctor continued. "See the appointments secretary before you leave."

Leave? Jenny didn't think she could raise her head. And where was Colin?

CHAPTER 6

In a flat in far northeast London, the door was stuck again. Alcina Michalopolous pushed against it, hard, knowing her shoulder would be sore the next day as a result. She smiled bitterly at the irony: She had to try hard to enter a flat she wished she could leave. It was neat enough, of course. She had too few possessions now for it to be cluttered. But it was dark and small, the curtains smelled, and the rug was so threadbare she was surprised she hadn't got splinters from the wood that lay beneath.

They hadn't lived in this flat when they first came to the city. Tony had been hired by a man from England who paid handsomely for his services, and she had been eager to come. The farther from her family the better. Tony didn't talk about his work much, which suited her fine. All work was dull, and they had much more interesting things to share. They had a large, airy flat, fancy, and she had taken the job at Kosta's Taverna just for something to do during the day. They didn't need the money. Tony bought her jewellery and all the clothes she wanted, colourful clothes which complemented her thick black hair and olive skin and made Tony proud when they went out together. Of course, waitresses at Kosta's were required to wear black. Tony had called those her "widow's weeds." Had that been an omen? Because the bad times had come, and now, although Tony wasn't dead, she wore the colour that the widows in her native Greece wore.

Seven years fat, seven years lean – that was in the Bible, but she knew that Tony could be gone much longer than seven years, and she was already thin. She'd had to move from the fancy flat and sell most of her jewellery, only keeping the pearl ring that the buyer had told her wasn't worth much. She worked nights now as well as days. The tips were always better at night, but she needed even the meagre income from her day shifts.

As she kicked off her shoes, she counted the money. She always tried to guess which patrons would be generous, those smug men with their mezedes and ouzo, their pastitsio and retsina. Sometimes she could win over those who might give less by swinging her hips when she walked by or brushing up against them.

She hated everything English: their weather, their food, their pale skin. Their false politeness: Give them a chance, and they stabbed you in the back, like they had Tony. Their snobbery: They thought their ways were best, but their system of justice was a travesty. How could that jury have convicted Tony? She had been so angry when she heard the verdict she thought she would choke. A curse on all of them: the police, the prosecutor, all those who had given evidence. That man Scott, who had employed Tony, had been convicted of horrible crimes, but Tony hadn't known about them, he had told her so. The man who'd worked with Tony had run. The stupid English police hadn't been able to find him, of course. He could have vouched for Tony, she was sure of it. Tony had never run from anything.

The only thing their precious evidence proved was that he had been in that house. Not when or why. The real evidence had pointed to others. Why should Tony suffer because he had been with the wrong crowd? He had sworn to her that he had done none of it.

It would take all of tomorrow, the trip to and from the prison. She hated the trains.

CHAPTER 7

Casey and his team waited in the van for the Go! Go! Go!
from the senior firearms officer. They were all suited and
booted, their Fives ready. His eyes travelled over the group.
Davies was solid, steady, and surprisingly quick on his feet
for a big man. As stick man, he would force compliance if
any of the suspects were slow to obey commands. Aidan
Traylor, the newest and youngest team member, had scored
exceptionally well in training, but the lean, affable, soft-
spoken man would never say so. Performance on the Job
was what counted, and he had yet to prove himself. Because
their ops required rapid but not sudden movement, less
experienced men could struggle to control the surge of
adrenaline that was necessary for energy, quick strength,
and alertness. Others might baulk or hesitate, so Traylor
would be among the last to make entry. Fortunately he'd
already learnt not to waste energy. A vein throbbing high
in his forehead was the only sign of tension that showed
through his dark, close-cropped hair.

Casey couldn't recall Watkins' first name. Predictably,
the fanatic weightlifter who was their method of entry man
was called Moe. Dancer, the wiry Welshman with dark
eyes and darker brows, had tripped on a training exercise
– only the once, but it was sufficient to earn Brice Dermott
the name. Donny Miller, or Sleepy, known for his ability to

zone out during down times, was heavy lidded even now, his dirty blond hair slightly rumpled.

Casey was certain they had names for him less flattering than Doc. He had been the team medic before becoming team leader, although all of them knew some first aid and carried not only field dressings but, in case of burns, clingfilm to cover the affected area. He pushed them hard during training and practices, knowing that in times of stress, individuals did not generally rise to meet an unusual challenge but sank to the level of their training. There must be no missed signals, no missteps. Even in training, injuries were always possible, and this morning's exercise was no drill. These early morning spins carried no guarantee of success. Sometimes intelligence was faulty. Once the suspects had still been awake from the night before. The speed of their entry allowed no time for assessment, yet they needed to be perfect every time. He'd not like to lose anyone.

Many of his mates were married or had partners, like Clive Hewlett, an ex-smoker who would have a wad of gum in his mouth even now. Their loved ones worried. Jenny said she did; he wondered how much. Or Amanda, his latest flame. He thought not, but they got on well. He played hard when he was off duty, and Amanda kept up with him. A few drinks and she'd be running her fingers up his thighs and asking if he were willing to "share." He liked her long hair, dark like Jenny's, and her long legs, particularly when they were wrapped round him.

"Go! Go! Go!" he heard through his covert earpiece. He relayed the command through the microphone secreted in his body armour. The team exited the van quietly and quickly in the thinning dark that preceded dawn, their black uniforms and gear providing further cover as they approached the target area. Not a word would be spoken until they'd made entry. Noise travelled too well at night, and they had no intention of telegraphing their arrival.

Davies' long legs covered the distance easily. Moe, carrying the enforcer, his preferred tool for gaining access, was followed by Hugh McGill, the Scotsman, who would assist him. Ross Pilner, also known as Pilsner, was a true lager lout but the unflappable ex-Army bloke was reliable on the Job, as was Marty Dyer, who muzzled his constant chat with difficulty until the raid was done. The rookie Traylor chugged along behind them. In moments all had reached the stairs. Not far now.

They were in. The suspects were jarred from a dead sleep by the full-throated screams of "Armed police! Armed police! Hit the floor! Hit the floor! Now! Now!" Because the barrels of their MP5s were only inches away, the baddies were too stunned to resist. Sudden extreme noise was a very effective way to take control fast.

In seconds it was over. The bad guys were down. Not a shot fired. Once again stealth, speed, and surprise had given them the necessary edge. They plasticuffed the occupants of the squalid flat and withdrew from the scene. It was secure for the locals to sort out. Their work was done. Good job all round. Time to return to base and put on a brew.

CHAPTER 8

Jenny and Beth were lunching at the Hampstead Tea Rooms, a fixture on South End Road for over thirty years. Business must have been good; its peach-tinged walls were covered with watercolor paintings the owners had never found the time to adjust from their odd angles. Jenny always had fun with Beth, who was closer to her own age than the wives of Colin's colleagues. Slightly taller than Jenny, she had bouncy dark curls that matched her light-hearted, bubbly personality. Brian adored her.

"Ice and slice?" the waitress asked Beth when she ordered her still water.

"Lemon, yes," Beth answered. "And I'll have the club."

"Salad with that?"

Beth nodded, knowing that she would receive lettuce, tomato, and cucumber on her sandwich, not a separate bowl of greens with dressing.

Jenny ordered orange juice to go with her omelette instead of still or sparkling water.

"Have you heard the latest about Simon?" Beth asked as their food was delivered. "He broke it off with his girlfriend. Somehow his relationships never last very long! But he already has another: Amanda. That almost sounds posh, doesn't it? She's rather wild, though."

"I wish he'd find someone and settle down," Jenny answered. "He's a good man. He's been calling more frequently since 9/11, which means a lot. He doesn't talk much about what he does, though, privately or professionally." She tasted her ham and cheese omelette.

"Usually Brian doesn't tell me about a raid until it's past, but I worry all the same. He's such a big target! I don't know why he's not in crowd control or something. And his hours are terrible – so many early mornings." She cut her club sandwich in half and took a bite. "Love this baguette," she mumbled. "Better than bread. Jenny, you're lucky. Colin has regular hours, and he's never in the line of fire. What does the doctor say?"

That was Beth: changing subjects like quicksilver. "Not much. And Colin hasn't been with me since the first appointment."

Beth laughed. "I don't expect so! Blokes don't like that sort of thing. I don't know how you got him to go even once."

It was too wet to sit outside, and because of the personal nature of their conversation, Jenny was glad they were at one of the tables in the recessed nook instead of near the large front windows that looked out onto the street. "He certainly likes the rest of it – the frequent sex the doctor recommended. I do, too, but I'm beginning to feel used. Sometimes I think it isn't about me, I'm just the means for getting a baby."

"He's good to you, though, Jenny. He's thoughtful, and he never tells you to watch what you spend, like Brian does me."

Jenny took another bite of her omelette. "That's true," she mumbled, chewing quickly. "He's generous. It's just that he seems to think sex is the solution for everything. Better than tea."

Beth chuckled.

"The other night we had a real fight," Jenny continued. "Since 9/11 and the doctor visits, I've needed more reassurance from him, and he comes home late and then is tired when he gets there. Not too tired for sex, of course, but too tired to romance me much. Then he tells me I shouldn't be so dependent."

Beth nodded. "Sometimes Brian wants me to depend on him, and sometimes he doesn't. I can never predict! He wants me to be able to make decisions without him but not to tell him what to do. But I thought the sex was better when we were trying to have a baby." She ate some of the fruit that came with her sandwich. "We're thinking on having another. Wouldn't it be keen if we were pregnant at the same time? I know it's difficult now, but you'll love being pregnant. After the morning sickness passes, that is. And when you're pregnant, you can't get enough! Brian was over the top! Compensation, I guess, for the time after the baby's born when sex is off limits for a while. But don't think about that now," she laughed. "Enjoy yourself!"

"Usually I do," Jenny said, wrapping her croissant in a napkin to take home with her. "We're really still newlyweds. I'm learning things about him even now. Did you know he was a hostage negotiator?"

"No! What about his work at Sapphire?"

"They support him. He's only on call several weeks a year. Anyway, last night he came back from a hostage incident, an armed robbery in a jewelry store that didn't work out the way the robbers hoped. He said that SO-19 officers were on the scene. Did Brian mention it?"

Beth's mouth was full, so she shook her head in response.

"Evidently there's some overlap between negotiating techniques and the interview techniques Colin learned in his detective course, and one of the functions of a good negotiator is to gather information. Honesty is important because lying destroys trust. If he has to lie about something, he has to make sure he isn't found out. Then he explained some of the principles that govern good negotiation skills. For example, if the parties are far apart, a good negotiator tries to find some areas of agreement to narrow the gap. Do you want to know what I did?"

"Of course," Beth said with a curious smile.

"I moved closer to him on the sofa. He was still very serious, talking about how giving is required on both sides and it isn't smart to give in to a hostage taker's demand without requiring something in return."

Beth's smile broadened.

"When he said that urgency should be avoided, I kissed him and told him I was feeling very urgent about something I didn't want to avoid. He caught on pretty quickly, kissing me back and adding that when the negotiation process is complete, the negotiator should congratulate the other side."

Beth laughed aloud.

"I wasn't sure which side I was on, so after we'd spent some time – well, you know – not talking, we congratulated each other."

"I'm glad you're happy, Jenny. Brian and I are. I always thought we'd end up together, but I wanted to see if the grass was greener before I committed myself."

Jenny raised her eyebrows. "Was it?"

"No!" Beth exclaimed, bursting into giggles. "My Bri was always the biggest and the best!"

CHAPTER 9

When their cab pulled up to Buckland Manor, Jenny's spirits lifted, because the sun lent an optimistic golden glow to the façade in spite of the near-freezing temperature. She had been low since her last doctor's appointment, when Dr. Hannaford had spent an inordinate amount of time trying unsuccessfully to force gas through her Fallopian tubes. She remembered nearly passing out the month before, and she had dreaded the visit. "Either there's an obstruction, or you're excessively tense," Hannaford had finally concluded. "I rather favour the latter." Colin had been unhappy with the news, which Jenny felt was unfair. She was the one who would suffer the consequences, because the lack of results meant there would need to be another test. At the hospital, the doctor had said. Jenny wondered if they'd anesthetize her. She hoped they would; wasn't that what hospitals were for?

She and Colin had taken the Jubilee Line tube from Finchley to Baker Street then changed to the Bakerloo, which ran to Paddington Station. An above-ground train from Paddington and then a cab delivered them to the elegant Cotswold country house in time to feast on scones and champagne at tea. The grounds were breathtaking, and the historic hotel (Was there anything in England that wasn't historic?) was exclusive – only thirteen rooms, and theirs was one of only two with a four-poster bed: a beautiful place to celebrate their second wedding anniversary. Since they'd married in Texas and honeymooned in Bermuda, she had no wedding cake to put in her freezer. Colin had therefore suggested that she wear her tailored satin wedding suit each anniversary, promising to take her somewhere very special every time. Last year, their first, they had dined at Claridge's. This room recalled their honeymoon, however. In Bermuda they'd also had a spacious room, one with a private balcony with an ocean view. When she had asked Colin what he'd like to do first, he had answered, "Make love to Mrs. Sinclair." So the pink beaches had waited, and to the sound of the surf, they had celebrated their union.

Now it was December 8, a date they had thought was appropriate for their marriage since the day that followed the bombing of Pearl Harbor in World War II had initiated the alliance between America and Britain. They made reservations for dinner, where Colin ordered a bottle of Bordeaux rosé to accompany her lamb and his fish. "Bottled poetry," he said, quoting Robert Louis Stevenson. Their candlelit meal was unhurried; the service was unobtrusive; and no contentious topics were discussed. She felt herself being courted all over again, and the combination of Colin's charm, his deep blue eyes, and the wine began to relax her. Wishing they were already alone together, she decided against the rich dessert and the after-dinner liqueur.

Back in their room, she showered and donned new lingerie – long, lacey, and black – while Colin started a fire in the fireplace. He caressed her with a special tenderness, and when they finished, she rested her head on his chest and wished they could feel this close all the time. "Colin, I love you so much. I'm sorry I've been short-tempered. I know how important having a family is to you. I'll see this through. I'll schedule the next infertility test after the first of the year."

He didn't respond immediately. Then, softly, he said, "No, Jen. I've been unpardonably selfish. The sort of tests you're undergoing – they'd be difficult for most women, but for you – unbearable. And I've provided little support. I'll not ask you to continue with this. Shall we take what comes?"

"What if nothing comes?"

"Then we'll have each other, without any tests."

"I didn't know how bad they'd be, or how weak I'd be. I wanted to think I had gotten over everything. I was unfair to you. You didn't ask me to see the doctor; I pushed myself to do it."

He shifted his body, wanting to communicate face to face, to read her expressions and allow her to read his. "Jenny, I never meant to imply that you were not enough for me. You are."

"But Colin – we can't just suddenly stop wanting children!"

"No, but I'd consider adoption. If you would."

"Are you giving up on me?"

"Never." He kissed her. "When we married, I felt that God had made us something more than we had been when we were apart. If – if we become parents, we'll be something more then as well. But Jen – it's your body, so it's your choice. I'll stand with you either way."

- -

It was wintry in the Cotswolds. In the morning Jenny and Colin bundled up, Jenny in one of the many sweaters Colin had given her when they first married. He knew she wasn't yet accustomed to the damp cold in London, so he bought her turtleneck sweaters, sweater-jackets, even sweatshirts with hoods and pouches in front to warm her hands. Too cold for tennis or croquet, they walked the grounds, finding the waterfalls and wondering how far the temperature would have to fall before the cascading water froze in place. They consumed warm soup and hot tea, and Jenny read some of Elizabeth Barrett Browning's love poetry from the collection Colin had given her as an anniversary gift. He took her photo with his new camera, promising to frame the best ones as Christmas gifts for her family.

Strange – once the burden of proceeding with the medical tests was removed, their estrangement seemed to disappear, and she felt more capable of continuing with them. The frosty air and the lush landscape that grew within it paralleled their ability as husband and wife to flourish in spite of the difficulties that threatened them. They renewed their commitment to each other and to a shared future, whatever that might hold.

CHAPTER 10

Not long after Colin and Jenny's idyllic respite in the Cotswolds, the holiday season erupted with news of further terrorist incidents. The December 21st London *Daily Telegraph* reported that a cargo ship called the *Nisha* had been boarded in the English Channel by anti-terror police. BBC News also carried the story. A Scotland Yard spokesman insisted there was no danger to the public, but Jenny wasn't so sure. She called Colin, who knew no more than she did.

"Outside of SO13, the Anti-Terrorist Branch, only the most senior Yard officials would have been informed," he said. "But be reassured: The action took place in international waters. The ship wasn't allowed to enter the Thames."

Over dinner, she picked at her food while Colin spoke of lighter things, but afterward he made another attempt to set her mind at rest. "We've a good deal of experience fighting terrorists. The IRA was a thorn in our side for years, and we learnt how to respond." He put his arm around her shoulders. "You're safe here."

She snuggled closer. "I don't think a terrorist will come to our door. I'm just worried about something bad happening somewhere else."

Instead of answering, he kissed her, and she stopped

thinking about terrorism completely.

The next morning her fears returned with a vengeance. The *Telegraph* had a followup report, and other newspapers also carried the story. Officials were concerned that the ship may have had terrorist material on board. When Simon called, she asked him what that meant.

"The *Nisha*?" One of his Special Boat Service "Shakyboats" mates who had been on the assault team had had more than a few choice words for the bitterly cold and windy weather.

"Simon, are terrorists using ships now instead of planes?"

"Since 9/11, I'd guess that the intelligence services have been monitoring all major types of transport and their routes. Assault teams are always on standby."

"Didn't the ship see them coming? They might have been shot down."

"Jenny, helicopters aren't armoured, but they would have gone early in the morning and flown without lights. They can navigate with night-vision goggles and instruments. They'd have had gunships with snipers to cover the boarding parties who would have hit it hard and fast. Neutralised resistance. Taken control of the ship, then handed it over, the ship to Royal Navy blokes and the contents to the experts."

"What was on it? What qualifies as terrorist material? They wouldn't have boarded it just for guns, would they?"

Her multiple questions revealed her anxiety. "Even if I knew, I couldn't tell you. The important thing to remember is that the ship was stopped."

"Simon, do you miss it? Being in the Special Forces?"

"Some, but there's baddies here as well for me to go after."

"What is it like? Are you scared? Please tell me."

He paused. "Briefly," he admitted. "Then you review your role in the mission and you get excited. You check your equipment. Make sure you have a round chambered. By that time you're settled and confident. Ready to jump or hit the ropes." His mate had been rather proud of how they had managed to fast-rope down onto a vessel under way.

"You slide down a rope?"

"We call it fast-roping because you're down in seconds.

That's why it's so effective, but it takes a bit of upper body strength. And satisfactory gloves."

His understated humor made her smile. "Thanks, Simon. And sorry for the interrogation."

After they hung up, she realized she'd never given him a chance to say why he'd called, a fact she forgot when the news broke about Richard Reid. He had tried to destroy an American Airlines plane in flight with a bomb in his shoe but had been subdued by passengers and flight attendants.

Terrorism was insidious, she thought. An attack could occur anywhere and anytime, requiring only one individual who was willing to die. And Reid had been born and raised in Britain. For those living in the UK, the threat could come from within.

An airplane again – and her parents and brothers were scheduled to visit for Christmas. Throughout the afternoon and into the evening she tried to talk herself out of calling Simon. And lost.

"Simon, I know we just spoke this morning, but I'm really afraid now," she began. "This Richard Reid thing. I need to hear your no-nonsense voice. My family is flying in soon. Is it safe? Or should I tell them not to come?"

She heard a woman's voice in the background. "Wait one, Mandy," Simon said sharply.

"Oh, I'm sorry. You're with someone, and I disturbed you."

"Not to worry. Jenny, listen to me. Reid wasn't successful. Security procedures are better now in American airports than they used to be and certainly better than in Paris, where Reid's flight originated. I believe your family will be all right." Out of the corner of his eye he saw Amanda get up for a cigarette.

"Promise?" Jenny asked.

"You know I can't do that, love."

"Will you pray that they'll be okay?"

"I'll hope for it."

"Simon, I have a little Christmas something for you, but we'll be in Kent until after New Year's."

"Shall I ring you then?"

"That'd be great. Sorry I interrupted you, Simon. Merry Christmas."

When he closed his phone, Amanda's full lips were set in a pout. "Who was that?"

"A friend. Am I not allowed to have friends?" he asked lightly, hoping to dispel her mood. She hadn't bothered to cover herself when she came back to bed, and he liked what he saw.

"Not if it's a woman!"

"Things are going well between us, aren't they?"

"But you're planning to see her."

"I was one of her protection officers. Some while ago."

"Why do you still keep in touch with each other then?"

"I've given you no cause to distrust me, Mandy."

"Your voice changed when you spoke to her. I heard it."

"Are you questioning my integrity?" he pressed, evading the question.

She stubbed out her fag angrily. "Are you cheating on me?"

"Amanda, don't do this," he said, each word quieter and colder than the last.

"Damn it, you are, aren't you?"

He swung his legs to the side of the bed and reached for his trousers. Amanda wasn't the first to question his relationship with Jenny. She wouldn't be the last. He'd have a pint down the pub. More, actually.

CHAPTER 11

Alcina hated everything about Christmas: the lights, the music, the cheer. She particularly hated the romantic adverts about the gifts couples could give each other, because she and Tony could not give each other anything. Worse, Christmas this year fell on a Tuesday, one of the prison's nonvisitation days, so she'd had to choose between seeing him before or after the holiday. At least going after Christmas had eliminated any expectations she might have had.

For over two years she had caught the train from Victoria Station to Maidstone East in northern Kent and then walked the short distance to the prison. Early arrival was the rule, but she still had to wait sometimes to see him. She and the other prison widows. Some had children with them. Thank God she and Tony hadn't had any.

She hated the prison guards. She was the victim in this relationship, but she was treated as if she had also committed a crime. The officious guards searched her every time she entered and left, a demeaning, humiliating process which she was sure they enjoyed. They still perused her passport as if she were a stranger. They recognised her — after all the times they had patted her down, she was certain they did — but when on one occasion she had forgotten the precious VO, the Visiting Order Tony had sent her, she had been refused admittance and sent away with a stern reminder to obey the rules, no sympathy and no regret on their wooden faces. She wanted to look her best for Tony, but she couldn't even freshen her lipstick because her handbag was placed in a locker before she was escorted to the visitors' room. And their time together was limited to one short hour.

On the two previous Christmases, she had requested and received permission to bring Tony a photograph of herself. Not this year; she was no longer the same girl who had attracted his attention. She had been the prettiest of the Castellanos sisters, everyone had said so, but the hardships of the months since Tony's conviction had aged her. Her clothes hung on her thin frame. She hated seeing her reflection; her face was gaunt and drawn, with new lines appearing from nowhere, and even her hair had lost its lustre. Perhaps that was why Tony was short with her.

At the beginning Tony had been the one who had hated everything. Because he had been convicted of a charge involving rape, sex offender counselling was required, part of the prison's "resettlement" process. He had refused to cooperate, doggedly maintaining his innocence. Nor would he participate in any of the instructional programmes. During one of her visits, he'd complained so loudly that the guards had cut their time short, roughly wrenching him away from her. Were they afraid of him? What did they think he could do with his bare hands? They were the ones with the weapons.

On her next visit she had urged him to comply, frightened that his continued resistance could result in disciplinary measures or transfer to a prison farther away. "Don't you want to get out of here?" she'd hissed. "Do whatever they want you to do! You don't have to mean it!"

The train would reach the Kent station in a few minutes. It was bitterly cold; she would be chilled through in no time. What would his mood be today? Would he be glad to see her? She was tired, hungry, lonely. Christmas was a hateful holiday.

CHAPTER 12

Jenny spent the entire Christmas season wishing she were pregnant. After all, Christmas existed because a baby, a particular baby, had been born. In Kent, where Joanne, Colin's mother, lived, she was surrounded by family, both Colin's and hers, and she reflected that there would be no families if couples didn't have children. She and Colin, both the firstborns in their families, had spring birthdays, so their mothers had been pregnant over Christmas. She hadn't told her mother or Colin's about her infertility problem, and she knew Colin wouldn't. That was one good thing about being married to a policeman: She never had to worry about him revealing confidential information.

The Kent estate had been in Colin's family for generations. Colin always slowed when he guided the car up the long, wide drive, perhaps as a way of finally leaving the hustle and bustle of the city behind. It gave Jenny a chance to absorb the peace that graced her when she visited, much the way the dark ivy grew on the creamy red brick, a felicitous color combination for Yuletide festivities.

Joanne's years of accompanying her husband on his foreign service tours had made her a consummate hostess, and as she guided Jenny's family through the social rooms on the ground floor, up the wide staircase to the adult bedrooms and baths on the first, and finally through the children's rooms on the second, Jenny enjoyed seeing the easy rapport Joanne had with her parents. Not burdening any of them with her worries was like presenting them with an unspoken gift.

She watched Colin showing her brothers how to use the camera she had given him for their wedding anniversary, and she thought about what a good father he would make. When his sister Jillian and brother-in-law Derek Horne arrived with their children, he had greeted nine-year-old Malcolm and six-year-old Becky with open arms, and they had both vied for his attention.

On two occasions, Jenny managed to set her feelings aside completely. On Christmas Eve, they bundled up in coats and scarves and attended the midnight service at St. Alban's, the little Anglican church where Father Rogers was the vicar. He had known Colin's family for years and had officiated at the memorial service for Colin's father. The church was lit only by candles, and on the stroke of midnight, Father Rogers stopped his homily in midsentence and exclaimed, "Our Saviour is born! Rejoice!" The ushers intoned, "Hear! Hear!" Then Father Rogers announced that as his gift to the congregation, he would not resume his homily. Several called out, "Hear! Hear!" Many chuckled, and Father Rogers, his cheeks as round and rosy as Santa's, sent everyone home with what he called good words for good people: Love one another, and do everything in your power to make love grow.

Jenny also forgot her concerns on Christmas morning when Colin opened a gift from her and laughed because she had given him jeans. His closet was filled to overflowing with tailored suits; he never seemed to buy casual wear like she did. "Not jeans, 'luxury denim,'" she insisted. "That's what they called it at the shop on Rivington Street. Besides, you'll look so good in them." Of course, she gave him more than jeans: an Armani stainless steel sport watch with a blue dial and a myriad of functions she was sure he could decipher and a year's subscription to the Wine of the Month to begin in January. He gave her a 24-carat gold charm bracelet with each charm wrapped separately: an emerald, her birthstone;

her initial in diamonds; an eagle with a sapphire eye for her "country of origin," as he put it; and a ruby heart for each of their years together. "I'll add to it," he promised.

Since their anniversary, Colin had not mentioned her infertility. They took long walks, holding hands. Often in the house he came up behind her, put his arms around her, and kissed her.

Joanne had given her a Scrabble game and explained the "adult" version, so she asked Colin if he wanted to play some serious Scrabble.

"I recall playing it as a child," he said, "but we were never very serious about it."

"After you and Jillian went to bed, your parents were," she smiled. "Low word counts meant short kisses, and high word counts meant long kisses. Your mom said it was a good system, because no matter who had the most points, they both won."

He nuzzled her neck. "I don't believe we need the game," he whispered.

The New Year heard Jenny's sigh of relief: Her family had arrived home safely after their holiday. It was good to know that people who traveled by air did still reach their destinations without incident, but she doubted that anyone in these post-9/11 days boarded a plane without a prayer.

She returned to her routine. When she married Colin, her visa status had changed, making employment possible. She worked several afternoons a week at Hollister's, a Hampstead used book shop, and, because she didn't really need the money, volunteered at Beth's school on other days. Beth taught at a junior school, the equivalent of grades two through six in the American system. Jenny helped the children with informal tutoring in the core subjects, with field trips, and with supervised exercise. She liked their spontaneity and unending energy.

Often she wondered if her baby would become as good a sprinter as Rory or as slim and self-possessed as Gwyneth. Would her child need tutoring in math? Both she and Colin enjoyed reading, but neither had excelled in math or science during their schooldays. None of the students she met had cerulean blue eyes, a Sinclair trait, but she loved the shy smiles they wore when she complimented them on improved assignments.

She was no closer to making a decision about continuing

with her infertility treatments. Needing more information, she called the doctor's office and asked Dr. Hannaford's nurse the name of the test. Hysterosalpingogram, an x-ray, the nurse said. That made it sound easy, but the name alone frightened Jenny, and the cold and clinical information revealed from her internet search scared her even more. The HSG evaluated the uterus and fallopian tubes. A speculum was used in the vagina. Dye was injected through a cannula in the opening of the cervix and an x-ray taken. Just reading the description of the procedure made her feel faint. But there were side effects, too. Patients often felt light-headed. Heavy cramping could occur during and for several hours after the procedure. Spotting was expected for one to two days. Anxiety on the part of the patient could increase the side effects. Anesthesia wasn't mentioned. The only good news: The weeks following an HSG offered the best chance for conception.

Not for the first time, Jenny raged against her body because she could not make it behave. In the past, it had helped to set her thoughts down on paper, so she made two lists: *Reasons To Do It* and *Reasons Not To Do It*.

Reasons To Do It: 1. It might make it possible for me to get pregnant. 2. It could be the last test I'd have to have. 3. It wouldn't be for several weeks, so I'd have time to psych myself up for it. 4. Colin would be proud of me.

Reasons Not To Do It: 1. The test is done in the hospital with people I don't know. 2. It's invasive. 3. It'll probably hurt a lot. 4. It will remind me of my rape. 5. I'm too afraid. 6. Colin said I didn't have to.

It didn't look good. *Reasons Not To Do It* outnumbered *Reasons To Do It*. And the reasons against could all be boiled down to one word: fear.

She set her lists aside, grabbed a sweater and her umbrella, and headed out to meet Simon for lunch at Café Rouge, a long-standing Hampstead eatery on the High Street only a ten-minute walk from the flat. Usually he arrived on time and she a little late, but today she didn't spot him when she entered. She was seated at a small table with wicker chairs and smiled at the whimsical designs painted on the walls. Hearts and stars alternated with trailing floral vines dotted with leaves and flowers. A much more interesting décor than wallpaper, she thought, and the butternut squash yellow background seemed appropriate for an establishment that served food. She had never adjusted to the bitter coffee, so she ordered a pot of tea, congratulating herself on her assimilation. When Simon came, she waved away his apology for being behind the time. They exchanged belated Christmas gifts while waiting for their soups and baguettes to be prepared.

"Open yours first," she encouraged him. She had given him two books: *River* by Colin Fletcher and *Into Thin Air* by Jon Krakauer. "They're both about outdoor adventures, so I thought you might like them."

He assured her that he did, then handed her a narrow rectangular package.

"You even used Christmas paper. Did you have your girlfriend wrap it for you?" she teased.

"Nothing like that."

"Oh – chocolate! And so elegant. Thank you, Simon." Two rows of dark chocolate shells filled the box.

"Taste one," he suggested.

She smiled in mid-bite. "They have liqueur in them! Yum. And having dessert before the meal – I love that. You try one."

The waiter interrupted with their food, and Jenny set the chocolates by her purse.

"Simon, I need to ask you something." She paused, trying to summon enough courage to raise a frightening issue. "How – how do you handle pain?"

He felt his stomach tighten, knowing she was asking for herself. What pain was she expecting? He wanted to ask but if he couldn't prevent it, he didn't want to know. "The normal human reaction to pain is panic. If you know that, you can anticipate the reaction and control it. You can't let pain control you. You have to take the fear out of it. Fear can cloud your thinking, and if you're in pain, you need your mind clear."

She hadn't touched her soup. "But pain can kill you.

How can you not be afraid?"

"Pain doesn't kill you. Injuries do, if they're serious enough and not treated. You can live with pain for a time. Sometimes you have to do."

Just talking about it was scary. She tasted a spoonful of the cream of mushroom soup and, trying to relax, held it in her mouth for a minute before swallowing. Simon was nearly through with his potato bisque. "How? I need to know how."

"By facing it, giving it a sense of purpose. Put it in the context of your mission, whatever that may be. The mission is more important than your reaction to it. Focus on the mission, and you can put exhaustion, fear, and even pain in perspective."

"I think I'll focus on finishing my soup." She asked the waiter for a box to take her sandwich home in. Most of her appetite had deserted her.

He had to know. "Are you in pain, Jenny? Can I help?"

"You just did," she said. Her mission was to have a baby. That meant signing on for labor pains, and she wasn't afraid of those. Maybe she should be, but they were an inevitable part of the process. Perhaps she could accept pain earlier on, too. Colin thought she had courage. Simon had told her once that it was all right to be a little afraid. If she didn't proceed, she'd feel relieved, but how long would that relief last if she didn't get pregnant?

"What's this about then?"

"A decision I have to make. And I think I've just decided not to be a victim."

Damn. She had set a boundary when he wanted her to need him. He knew he shouldn't press her further, but he had to try once more. "Jenny – "

"Simon, I'll be okay."

That was his dismissal, but she had taken his hand and still held it, an indication that she had not yet conquered her fear.

Another wasted day. The guards at the prison had kept her waiting, with no explanation. You couldn't react or they'd bar you from the visit altogether. She knew because she'd protested once, objecting only mildly by saying, "But I've come from London!" and been told she was too "unstable" to enter. Today she had inquired politely and been met with a wall of silence.

So arbitrary. A not-so-subtle reminder of where they stood in the pecking order: at the bottom. When she and the other visitors had finally been admitted, Tony had blamed her for the delay and sulked nearly the entire time.

Everything about her prison visits angered her. She was angry at the way she was treated; angry at the dull clothes she had to wear or endure the guards' glances; angry at Tony's diminished standing; angry at the dull-witted, hardhearted, petty thickheads who controlled her contact with Tony.

She railed against them all the way back to London, scowling at everyone on the train as well as those she passed on the street. She was no less angry when she entered the flat. Opening the door and seeing the worn, tired furnishings never ceased to be a shock. And an insult.

She was hungry. Hungry for all the delicacies she and Tony used to enjoy, foods she could not afford to buy now. Hungry for a lifestyle that included rest instead of continual labor. Hungry even more for the prestige and authority and deference they used to receive than for the sustenance she needed now.

CHAPTER 15

Being in a service profession often meant long hours, but no matter how tired he was, Colin's steps quickened as he neared home. He knew Jenny would be waiting for him. Although part of the London Borough of Camden, Hampstead was quite a commute from his central London office. Despite the invasion of some chain stores, it still maintained its quiet hilltop identity, and he'd always liked the village ambiance and narrow tree-lined lanes. Most nights he arrived too late to see the carefully tended front gardens that lined his street, so he marked off the front doors as he passed. White door, green door, black door. He spent his days trying to stem the tide of evil things that people did to each other, and his job was made easier because he came home to a woman who made his heart light. Yellow door, blue door: home. The flat was dark. "Jenny?" he called as he mounted the stairs.

"Colin, I'm so glad you're home."

He heard the sob in her voice. She was in bed, and she didn't get up to greet him. "Are you all right? Do you need a doctor?"

"That's the last thing I need," she sobbed. "I had a test today, at the hospital, and it was awful."

He sat down on the edge of the bed and wiped the tears from her cheeks. "Today? Why didn't you tell me?"

"Because you said it was my choice. Because if you

knew and couldn't come," she was crying in earnest now, "I would have been so disappointed, and that would have come between us, and right now more than anything I need to feel close to you."

He gathered her in his arms and kissed her. "But this is a joint effort, Jen. Will you tell me what was done?"

She described the procedure in halting phrases. The purpose, the method. She had been so frightened the nurse had had to help her walk from the dressing room to the table. Her chest had been tight, and she had been unable to take the deep breaths that would relax her. The radiographer had pushed on her stomach. He had made her turn on her side with the instruments still inside her. Then the cramps had started. She had tried to imagine holding her baby and failed. She had cried on the table, and the radiographer had impatiently asked, "Didn't your doctor tell you to take a pain reliever?" He hadn't. And no amount of analgesic would have lessened the indignity of it all.

He saw her amethyst watch on her wrist, the one with the purple hearts he had given her long ago when he had wanted her to know how courageous he thought she was. He realised she must have worn it during the procedure, and he nearly cried himself.

"The dye makes sure my tubes are open, Colin, so the test could help me conceive. But I'm spotting, and now I'm too sore for sex. I'm so sorry."

"Don't worry about that," he soothed. "There'll be time for us." He held her until she calmed, brought her a glass of wine, and ran her a bath. When she felt well enough, she nibbled some of the cheese and fruit he prepared for dinner.

"Jenny, no more of this," he said while she ate. "Let's have a serious talk about adoption."

"Not yet," she begged. "This test could help. And if I don't conceive soon, the next test will be surgical. If they put me to sleep, I don't care what they do to my insides. Piece of cake."

He held her until she slept, his usual practice since his protective feelings were still strong. In the days ahead there would be time for lovemaking.

A rare event: Simon Casey's team was spare, with the assurance that they'd not be called in. He didn't believe it; promises could be given but retracted on a moment's notice without guilt if the need for a firearms team arose. However, with several hours to kill, he hoped, he rang Jenny. When he couldn't reach her, he phoned Davies to ask whether Jenny was with Beth. "No," Davies said, "Jenny's off. Had a medical at the hospital yesterday."

"What sort?"

"Infertility testing, Beth says. She had a difficult time. Don't know more than that."

Casey rang off. That, then, was the cause of her fear. But what sort of test required a hospital setting? He needed to know how she was. He headed for the tube station.

There was no answer when he rang the bell. Concerned, he knocked loudly and called out her name. When she opened the door, she wasn't dressed, wearing only a dressing gown above bare feet.

"Simon – I wasn't expecting you."

"Are you all right? Davies said you were at hospital and why." He followed her in and sat down next to her on the sofa.

"Still a little sore and shaky."

"Why didn't you tell me?"

She sighed. "Oh, Simon – it's too embarrassing."

He took her hand and began to massage her palm. "Tell me now."

It was the voice no one said no to, embarrassment notwithstanding. Still, she hesitated. He had been her medical officer when she was in witness protection, but she felt shy nonetheless.

He continued to rub her hand. "Talk to me," he said softly.

She couldn't look at him, so she focused on his hand and the gentle rhythm of his fingers. "The radiographer – he – forced dye into my fallopian tubes and then took x-rays. He was rough. It was rough."

There was only one way he knew of to reach a woman's tubes without surgery, and he didn't want to think on it. "Bad news?"

"No, no news, which is worse. Simon, they never find anything wrong, so they have to keep testing. And if one more doctor tells me to relax, I'll scream."

"You've had other tests?"

"Yes. Some are painful, and all are invasive."

"Was Sinclair with you?"

"No, I didn't tell him until afterward. He can't stand to see what they do."

She had protected him. He understood why, but he didn't like it. "Is Sinclair making you do this?" he asked.

She looked up. It had been a long time since she'd heard that hard, cold edge in his voice. "No. He wants to know what the problem is, of course, but I do too. I wish they'd find something they could fix! Have I always been – infertile? I hate that word! It sounds so final. Or did the monster do this to me, Simon?"

He knew she was referring to the man who had attacked her. He had beaten her so severely that she had required surgery to correct internal injuries. Her spleen had been removed. "I can't answer that, love. What does the doctor say?"

"Not much." She shifted her weight and closed her eyes briefly at the discomfort.

"Shall I brew?" he asked.

"Yes, thanks."

She smiled when he returned with their cups. He'd found the lemon cake in the kitchen and put a slice on her saucer. He was indifferent to sweets but knew she wasn't.

"You could adopt, Jenny," he said.

"I don't want to adopt! Women have been having babies for millions of years. I don't know why I can't join that club."

When she made up her mind about something, she didn't quit. He respected that but tried anyway. "You could help a little sprog."

She nodded. "I helped one the other day. A little boy at Beth's school. His teacher couldn't get him to sit at his desk, so I took him aside to talk to him. And he told me how sore his bum was. When I touched his thigh, he cringed, so I thought he got more than a spanking. The school nurse discovered bruises from the waist down. I seem to attract the wounded ones." Her tea was cool enough now to sip. Simon had finished his. Was his throat made of asbestos?

"Did she report it?"

"Yes, and I kept thinking that if he were mine, he wouldn't be hurting like that. Hurting and ashamed. Loving his mom and afraid of her at the same time. There's no dad, you see." She paused. "Would you ever want children, Simon?"

"With the right woman and at the right time, yes." And he now knew with certainty that it wouldn't be with Jenny. She and Sinclair were happy. They wanted to start a family. It was time for him to be open to a serious relationship. He hadn't gone out with anyone since he'd broken it off with Amanda. He'd keep in touch with Jenny – he'd always want to protect her – but he needed to let go. "Let's have a walk," he suggested. "Nothing strenuous. It'll do you good to get out. I'll wait while you dress."

She sighed. He believed exercise, like tea, could cure almost anything. She climbed the stairs to the bedroom, pulled on jeans, a pink and white striped oxford cloth shirt she didn't bother to tuck in, and a dark cardigan. Downstairs she laced her tennis shoes and picked up her umbrella.

They ambled through the narrow residential streets, he

adjusting to her slow pace and she searching for a subject. Hampstead was replete with austere Georgian homes, each with a small lawn facing the street, so she pointed out the ones with multiple chimneys and dormer windows. "There were four King Georges in a row," she said, realizing when she saw his frown that her comment sounded like a *non sequitur* and she'd have to explain. "They reigned for almost 100 years, and culturally it was a rich period. Handel in music; Jane Austen in literature; the painters Gainsborough, Turner, and Constable; and the Romantic poets all lived then. Try to look interested," she teased. "What else? The American Revolution, the French Revolution, and – "

"The police," he interrupted. "Sir Robert Peel created the Met."

"And ice cream was invented!" she concluded. "The history books say that George Washington loved it."

They continued their walk, but when they passed a young mother pushing her baby in a pram, Jenny's smiles dissolved. He saw the longing on her face and wanted to comfort her. Not my place, he reminded himself. Nonetheless, it was going to be more difficult to discipline his feelings for her than he had thought.

CHAPTER 17

Alcina rarely missed her family, but her birthday was an exception. She could recall the gifts her parents had given her, and she would never forget how they had made her feel on her special day: like a princess. Her mother had prepared her favourite foods for every meal, culminating in a candle-lit dinner. She wore a new dress then, a real treat because nearly all her clothes had been worn by her three older sisters before they came to her. She had wished for birthdays more than once a year, because the rest of the time she was disregarded, dismissed, and ignored.

She had been jealous of her older sisters, Lara, Eliana, and Cecilia, of the makeup they were allowed to wear, of their freedoms, of their private conversations. Lara and Eliana had been born a year apart, almost four years before Alcina. She hated being left out, hated being the baby, hated being fat, and hated the way they patronised her. Cecilia had been closer to her age but had wanted to spend more time with the older girls.

She had had her revenge, however. Even now thinking about it made her smile. At Lara's engagement party, she had bumped into her, causing her to spill her red wine on the bodice of her dress. Lara had been furious, insisting that she had done it on purpose. Alcina had, of course, but she had cried so hard in apparent regret that her parents had not believed it of her.

There had been other occasions, but although her sisters were suspicious, complaining that she got away with everything, they had never been able to prove her cunning. She had withheld their telephone messages, misplaced their keys, and poked holes in their socks. When Eliana's favourite blouse had been laundered with bleach, the maid had been blamed and consequently let go.

Tony had flattered and spoilt her at first; perhaps that was why she had fallen in love with him. They had met when he came into the travel agency to pick up tickets for one of the patrons at the club where he worked. He provided extra services for them whenever he could, and he made good money. He was well dressed, ambitious, and older than her sisters' husbands, a man of the world who could show her the world. She was just a clerk, too new to the job to have much responsibility, but he had noticed her, probably because of the way she dressed. Ever since she lost weight, she had spent her earnings on herself, for clothes and beauty products. She wasn't selfish; living at home was just practical. Her sisters had married and sprouted babies like seeds sown in a greenhouse, but she had worked hard to get a slim figure and fully intended to keep it. She had played hard to get with Tony at first, but she had always been interested in him.

Her parents had expressed reservations about the marriage, but she was strong willed. When she got something in her mind, nothing – not discipline, reason, coaxing, cajoling, even outright bribery – could make her change it. From the time she was a toddler, her primary expression had been a pout. Over the years her mother had shaken her head in exasperation at her, but her father had called her – not without a little pride for he had no sons – his little bulldog.

This year she wouldn't celebrate with female friends. She hadn't any. She had always got on better with men. The couples she and Tony had known, however, had dropped her when Tony was convicted. If the tables had been reversed, she would have done the same. She wasn't cut out for social work. Would her parents call with birthday wishes? Perhaps. Her sisters neither wrote nor called; they had been glad when she and Tony moved to London. She would never move back to Greece. She would not hear from Tony.

CHAPTER 18

On Valentine's Day Jenny and Colin walked up Heath Street to dine at their favorite Hampstead restaurant, La Gaffe, which had come about in an unusual way. Bernardo Stella, an Italian who worked in a French restaurant in London, fell in love with the young Cypriot Androulla and decided to open his own establishment. Neither their relationship nor their joint endeavor was a *gaffe* – a mistake – and their business had grown to include a family run hotel on the same premises. Being greeted by their son, the current manager, always made Jenny feel welcome, and over their tricolor salad and minestrone soup, she sipped her first glass of wine, knowing she would need warmth inside and out to counter the frigid temperatures they would encounter on their walk home.

"If I order the veal in lemon sauce, I'll have room for dessert," she told Colin. "But may I taste your lamb?" Over the *dolci* – tonight she chose *crème brulée* – she suggested that they continue their celebration when they returned to their flat. "I love London winters – cold, not too humid, dark early. Let's light a fire in the fireplace and remember all our special times."

On their way back through the up-and-down Hampstead streets, she took his arm and asked, "When did you know you were in love with me?"

"When I realised I'd do anything to see you smile. And you?"

"It took awhile. You were so austere at first – so serious about the investigation – but you placed such a high premium on my safety that I began to trust you. And then you romanced me with such respect and restraint that I fell in love with you – with a tall, elegant man who was a citizen of a foreign country! Imagine that!"

"And I never expected to be swept off my feet by a young, petite Texan. After my first marriage ended, I thought I had closed off my heart."

They had reached the flat. He set about preparing the fire.

"Remember the first time you kissed me?" she asked as they listened to the music the fire made, the crackles and soft hiss when the kindling caught the flames. "I still felt so damaged from the attack that I was amazed that someone wanted me. Then I realized how much I enjoyed being with you, and when you hadn't visited the protection flat in a while, I missed you. I'm still sorry that when I knew for sure that I loved you, I was too scared to do anything about it."

He put his arm around her. "I knew what you'd been through, Jenny. You fought so hard not to stay a victim."

"If anyone had told me that I'd end up sharing my life with the senior detective on my case, I wouldn't have believed them."

"It's a good thing, then, that we don't know what the future holds," he said.

She snuggled closer. "I wish I could stop time. Stay in this moment."

"Even if I make the next moment better?" he teased, kissing her, caressing her chest, and feeling her heartbeat increase. He led her to the shower before they had finished removing each other's clothing then laughed as she frantically stripped off the remaining items. He stroked her with the bath sheet and soap and closed his eyes while she stroked him. After they turned off the water, he rubbed her all over with a warm towel.

In bed his startlingly blue eyes softened and his smile

widened. She pulled him to her. "Maybe this time, Colin," she whispered. "Maybe this time I'll conceive."

"There is no one like you in all the world, Mrs. Sinclair," he whispered. "I love you."

"Colin, I love you so much. Please don't stop."

"Just starting." Knowing where she liked to be touched and how, he enhanced her sensations. He heard her cry out, and a few moments later he called her name.

She wrapped her arms and legs around him to keep him in place. She didn't ever want to be separated from him. She fell asleep wishing for some way to preserve what they had, the way artists preserved their perspectives with oils or pastels.

CHAPTER 19

Colin had a busy morning. Following his briefing to his staff, he received a fax from law enforcement professionals in New York, requesting a visit in three weeks' time. He instructed Bridges to make the arrangements. In addition, since he had pledged to begin a review of cold cases, he spent some time setting aside those he would bring to the attention of solicitors and scheduling meetings with them. Between phone calls, he updated his calendar and thought about his wife.

Recently they had attended a do for Mark Twichell, who had retired after thirty years on the force. He had been Colin's supervisor when Colin completed the detective course and was first assigned to detective work. A barrel-chested man who had not needed a microphone to address the large gathering, Twichell had made brief comments about the ways in which policing had changed. "More violence, more drugs, more guns, more knives, and more young people involved in every aspect of crime. I never thought I'd say this, but I'm glad to leave it to you lot."

All the toasts offered on Twichell's behalf notwithstanding, Jenny had been the star of the evening, stunning in a long black skirt, bolero jacket, and white high-necked blouse. She had worn the high heels he preferred, and heads had turned when they entered. All the senior officers had found an excuse to greet her, the youngest and loveliest woman present, and he had felt more than fortunate that she was his wife.

Only a week had passed since their Valentine's Day celebration, and they were still in the honeymoon period after her last medical test. He had scheduled a time for his visit to the doctor. Their lovemaking had new joy and hope, because they felt that each encounter could lead to the creation of a precious new life in their family. He smiled, thinking of her tousled hair and the particular little frown she had when she was concentrating on her pleasure. He wanted to surprise her with a special gift, new earrings that would show against her dark hair and move when she turned her head. He had found a pair in a shop not too far from the Bond Street station – teardrop emeralds wrapped in diamonds and suspended on tiny gold chains. If he collected them on his lunch hour, he could present them to her tonight. He grabbed his coat and left for the tube.

PART TWO

My grief lies onward and my joy behind.

— William Shakespeare

CHAPTER 1

The uniformed officer at the door already had his warrant card out. "PC Parker, Mrs. Sinclair. There's been an incident, and DCI Sinclair has been injured. I have a car waiting. If you'll just accompany me, I'll take you to him."

"What happened? Where is he? How is he?" Jenny's voice rose.

"St. Mary's. May I suggest a coat? It's quite cold."

"A hospital? How badly is he hurt? Is he going to be okay?"

"I'm afraid I don't have any details," Parker replied. "Chief Superintendent Higham will brief you when we arrive."

Chief Superintendent Stuart Higham was Colin's boss. Why would he be at the hospital? Jenny took the first sweater she saw when she opened the chest of drawers, anything to cover the old knit pullover shirt she wore. She hadn't planned to go out but didn't want to take the time now to change. She grabbed her purse and followed Parker downstairs. A police sedan with a driver was waiting for them, not one of the easily recognizable black-and-white panda patrol cars that criss-crossed London streets. Parker installed her in the back seat then joined the driver in the front. No one spoke, but the siren was wailing as the driver accelerated through the narrow streets. Colin has a desk job, she thought, trying to control her surging fear. This is not happening. She closed her eyes, held her sweater to her chest like a shield, and tried not to imagine the worst.

Almost before her dazed mind could register it, the driver had pulled up to the hospital's Accident and Emergency entrance. When she opened the door, Parker was there, extending his hand. The first set of double doors opened automatically, and he guided her through the second and down a long corridor. Near the end she saw a number of well-dressed men gathered in twos and threes, some with familiar faces, some not, but all with somber expressions. David Andrews, "amiable Andrews," who had been Colin's detective sergeant on her case, wasn't smiling now. His normally cheerful face showed shock and – sorrow? He took a step toward her and opened his mouth but did not speak. She became correspondingly mute, afraid to ask any of the questions that were crowding her mind.

Barry Bridges turned in her direction, his eyes empty of the twinkle that usually brightened them, his boyish smile smothered. He now worked with Colin at Sapphire, but he had been able to guide her through the most difficult parts of her formal interviews when others had failed. She recognized Chief Superintendent Higham, a stocky man with a thick mustache and tweedy hair. Tension lined his face.

"Mrs. Sinclair," Higham said, stepping away from the group. "I must speak with you privately." PC Parker moved away. "There's been an incident, as you know. Your husband was severely injured. Ambulances were called to the scene, and he was treated and transported immediately, but – Mrs. Sinclair – I'm sorry to tell you – I'm afraid he's gone."

Had she heard correctly? No, it couldn't be! She and Colin had barely begun their life together! Just this morning they had made love, Colin providing warmth in the chilly early hours. She heard a roaring in her ears, and Higham went out of focus. Her knees turned to jelly, and she sank to the floor.

"Mrs. Sinclair – " " – Jenny – " " – Are you all right?" Multiple voices penetrated the fog, and she felt hands guiding her to a sitting position.

"I want to see him," she whispered.

"Mrs. Sinclair – "

"Where is he?"

David and Barry helped her stand, neither wanting to release her to what lay ahead.

Higham tried again. "Mrs. Sinclair, would you like someone to accompany you?"

"No. I want to see my husband alone."

"Mrs. Sinclair, I must insist."

"No. Please."

"Are you certain? We are here to help."

How could they help? "No," she repeated. "I want to be alone with him."

With reluctance he gestured to an innocuous hospital door, several yards down the corridor. "Last door on the right."

They stood back, watching as she reached out to steady herself against the wall.

The door was heavy. She pushed against it with her shoulder, desperate to enter but afraid of what she would see. Empty of hospital personnel, the room was still small. Machines that would have provided life support were now silent against the walls, and there were no windows except the one to the next world. A body lay on a bed, fully covered by a sheet. That's it, she thought, relief flooding her. It's a mistake. It isn't Colin.

She approached the bed and folded the sheet down from the person's face. Oh, God – it *was* Colin. Her relief evaporated, her legs felt suddenly weak, and she leaned against the bed to keep from falling. No, no, she wanted to scream, but her throat was too tight for even a moan to escape. Colin, her beloved Colin, but he didn't look the same. His eyes were closed, and it was immediately clear to Jenny that he would not wake. Something was missing that had been a part of his expression even in slumber, an essence so tangible that its absence made his face slack, as if his blood vessels had contracted slightly when his spirit had left. The bandage covering part of his temple looked like a foreign thing, and she removed it. The wound was nasty, far worse than the one which had scarred her cheek, and this wound would never heal. His color wasn't right, and there were smears of blood from the scratches on his face. No one had cleaned him up. He would hate looking such a mess. She straightened, found a paper towel, and dampened it. Gently she stroked his nose and cheeks, and then his lips, though it was not necessary. She kissed him, her silent tears cleansing his face further.

The hospital sheet still covered the rest of his body. She moved it aside and then was sorry she had. His shirt had been cut away, and she closed her eyes briefly against the horror. Blood-soaked bandages covered his chest and abdomen. In times past she had rested her head on his chest, sometimes for comfort after a bad dream but more often to prolong the closeness she had felt after they'd made love. His hands were cold. She rubbed them but couldn't make them warm.

It hit her that never again would she lie next to him. Stifling a sob, she climbed onto the hospital bed and nestled beside him, her head on his shoulder and her arm across his chest in a last embrace. So many times he had held her, and she had been reassured by the sound of his heart. Now, although his shoulders and chest were still warm, the only heart beating was hers. He didn't even smell the same. To counter the strange metallic and medical odors, she tried to find the place behind his ear where he splashed his aftershave. A trace lingered, and she began to talk to him.

"Colin, where are you? I can't find you! You can't be gone! I love you so much. I need you. How could this happen to you? How can I go on without you? I'll always need you!"

A sob escaped her. "I'm sorry for the times I hurt you, the times I wasn't patient. The times I resented how much time your job took. I take it all back. I know your work is important, really I do, and I'm so proud of you.

"Colin, I wish I'd told you more often how much your love means to me. I wish – " She began to cry in earnest, because always before he had responded to her wishes. He had listened, he had done his best to make them come true, and even when he couldn't grant them, he had respected her feelings. Wanting to shut out the sight of the soulless equipment that surrounded them, she closed her eyes and gripped him more tightly. She had never thought that the last bed the two of them would share would be in a hospital.

- -

A nurse approached the group of officers in the corridor. The number had grown since word had got round. "We need to take him," she said to no one in particular. "But Mrs. Sinclair is still with him."

No one answered at first. Andrews realised that Higham didn't know her well. "I'll speak with her," he said. He followed the nurse to the door, but when he pushed it open, he could hear Jenny's soft voice and left without disturbing her. "I couldn't do it, sir," he reported to Higham, "but I believe there's someone here who can." He gestured at Casey, who had arrived with Davies and another firearms officer. Higham agreed, and Andrews explained to Casey where Jenny was and why.

Casey swore under his breath.

"We have a car and driver on standby," Higham added.

Casey nodded grimly then gestured to Davies to accompany him. Through her sobs, Jenny was speaking, but not to them. "We shouldn't be hearing this," Davies said.

"Jenny," Casey said, interrupting her. He cleared his throat. "It's time to go."

Why did he sound so rough? She pushed herself up on one elbow.

"He's gone, love. Say good-bye."

It was an order she did not intend to obey. She and Colin never said good-bye to each other. Good-bye was too final a word, and she had hated the idea of separation that was inherent in it. *Hasta la vista* or any of the other equivalents for "until I see you again" had been their practice. Good-bye? *Good-bye?* Panic rose in her chest. "No! If I leave him, I'll never see him again!"

Casey's tone was a bit gentler. "Come with us. We'll see

you home." He and Davies approached the bed, their eyes drawn to the tears on her cheeks and the smudges of blood on the front of her clothes. She was wearing Sinclair's wounds, his blood like patches of faded poppies on her shirt. Casey held out his hand, but she didn't take it. It was Davies who put his arms around her waist and helped her down.

Forensics officers would be coming to examine Sinclair's body and the Coroner's Office to collect it. Casey wanted to spare her those sights, at least. "The nurses will look after him now," he lied.

She was trembling. "Colin, I love you. Colin, I don't want to go! Colin – "

Casey leant toward her. "Jenny, shut off your mind. Just breathe."

"No! No!" she wailed. "I won't leave him, and you can't make me!"

Casey stepped forward and put his arms around her, crushing her to his chest. He felt her struggle to free herself, and he hated what he had to do. "Jenny! Listen to me! Breathe! In. Out. In. Out."

She fought him. "I can't," she gasped.

He relaxed his hold on her a bit and felt her take a shaky breath. "Again," he commanded. "Deeper."

"I'll faint," she objected.

"No. It'll calm you." He stepped back and nodded to Davies to open the door. Before he guided her through it, he allowed her one last look in Sinclair's direction. Davies had covered him.

She swayed slightly. Casey put his arm around her waist and waited for her to regain her balance. "Walk with us."

She didn't move. Casey's repeated instruction seemed to startle her. "One step at a time," he said.

Davies held the door while Jenny exited, Casey beside her. The large crowd in the corridor became suddenly and unnaturally quiet at the sight of her. Casey and Davies' footsteps echoed in the silence as they escorted her to the waiting car.

CHAPTER 2

Jenny felt numb. She didn't know whether the drive to Hampstead took two minutes or two hours. If the driver used his siren, she didn't hear it. Nothing registered except the rhythmic motions of Simon's fingers on her palm. Somehow her legs carried her from the car to the flat, but she had lost the fine motor coordination necessary to unlock the door and had to give the keys to Simon. Entering, she felt the weight of exhaustion cover her like a mantle, and without a word she crept upstairs to the master bedroom to lie down.

Davies checked the fridge. "Not much useful here," he informed Casey. "We'll need some food. I'll ring Beth, and I'll be back."

Casey nodded. "I'll deal here." He scaled the steps and called to Jenny from the bedroom door. "Would you want some tea, love?" No answer. He tried again. "Before you get your head down, you need to ring your mum. Sinclair's mum. Possibly others."

She stirred. "My mobile's in my purse."

He retrieved it.

She sat up and punched in the number. "Mom – " Her voice broke. "Mom, I need you. Colin – Colin – Simon, I can't!" Her hand shook, and the phone fell into her lap.

He picked it up. "Mrs. Jeffries, Simon Casey here. I'm afraid I have news of the worst sort." He hesitated. "Sinclair was – " He realised he needed to rephrase. "Jenny's husband was killed today in a terrorist attack. You'll need to make travel plans immediately."

Jenny could hear her mother's exclamations and Simon's responses. "No details are available yet, but he's gone." A pause. "You'll let us know when you have reservations? Good." Another pause. "She's in shock – like someone's run her over." He listened. "No, ma'am. We'll not leave her alone. I can promise you that." He ended the call.

Jenny took a deep breath and called her mother-in-law. "Joanne, it's Jenny. I have some awful news about Colin. He – he – "

Again Simon had to deliver the news. "You saw a report on the telly? No, the Met won't release his name until they're certain all family members have been notified. You'll ring his sister? Yes, I'll tell Jenny you'll be arriving first thing tomorrow." He turned to Jenny. "Anyone else?"

She was trembling. "Father Goodwyn. Will you do it? His number's in my call list."

Goodwyn, a former Royal Army chaplain who now worked for the Met, had counselled Jenny during her time in witness protection. Simon rang the priest. "He's on his way," he reported.

CHAPTER 3

The next twelve hours passed with only odd moments lifting Jenny above the fog. Beth arrived and gently suggested that she change her clothes.

"Why?" Jenny asked. She looked down, and in a flash saw what Beth saw: spots of dried blood clinging to her shirt and sweater. Even her jeans were stained. She hugged herself tightly. "The blood is Colin's. It's all I have left of him," she managed to say.

"We'll not wash them," Beth soothed. There was fear behind the compassion in Beth's eyes: Brian's job was more dangerous than Colin's. "I'll help you choose something else."

She opened the wardrobe, but Jenny couldn't decide about anything she held up. Finally she chose a silk blend blouse because it was one of Colin's favorites and a clean pair of jeans. They walked downstairs.

Simon rarely left her side, even when Father Goodwyn arrived. The priest sat down across from her and took both her hands in his. "Jenny," he said, "I received a call about Colin. I'm so very sorry."

When she didn't respond, he added quietly, "I'm reminded of the first time we met. You were being protected by police, but you had become ill and filled with despair. Colin brought me to visit with you. I'm afraid this trauma won't pass as quickly or be as easily treated as that previous one, but I want you to know that I'll walk with you for as long as you need." He paused. "Can you tell me anything about the events of this day?"

Again there was no response. "I'll just sit with you then," he said, "until you're ready."

After a few minutes he released her hands, rose, and walked toward the bookcase where the music system rested. He selected a Mozart CD then returned to Jenny. "Silence can be oppressive sometimes, can it not?"

"She's not hearing it," Simon noted.

"Perhaps not consciously," Goodwyn agreed. "But I found during my time with the Royal Army that music did more than shield us from the sounds of warfare. When I played it in my tent, it lifted me out of my surroundings for a bit. Made me feel less alone. Provided a respite from what we were facing. For some, music brought a sort of peace, because it spoke of happier times."

Again he addressed Jenny. "Were you taken to see Colin? Were you able to say good-bye?"

"I was," she whispered. "But he wasn't."

Goodwyn would have taken her hand, but Simon was already holding it, stroking her fingers.

Brian, in the kitchen making spaghetti, was glad for the music. Although usually confident in the kitchen, he had felt self-conscious breaking the silence by opening cabinets, using utensils, even stirring the sauce in the pan.

Jenny frowned slightly, unable to focus on either the music or Brian's movements. In witness protection, when she had been waiting to testify at the trial of the man who had attacked her, he had done most of the cooking. She hadn't known Beth then; she and Brian weren't seeing each other regularly. But Colin had been alive. At first he had come by with questions about the case or to keep her informed of their progress. Later he had come for her company, romancing her with poetry and wine, because his integrity had kept him from expressing himself physically. She remembered her surprise when he had admitted his feelings for her; how flattered she had been; how touched by his patience; and the joy they had shared when she told him she loved him.

Brian's spaghetti sauce needed only to simmer. He set the water to boil for the pasta. Casey and Beth were sitting near Jenny, but Brian didn't think Jenny heard any of their conversation. Sinclair's death had knocked her for six. It wasn't like her to be so still and quiet. And the blank look she had on her face – she wasn't seeing anything either. He never wanted Beth to be in Jenny's shoes. Tonight when they got home, he'd reassure Beth about his safety, how careful he was. Give her a cuddle. More.

Beth's voice interrupted Jenny's reverie, jarring her back to harsh reality. "Dinner's ready."

The CD had ended, and the meal was quiet. After Father Goodwyn's blessing, no one spoke except Beth, who tried from time to time to encourage Jenny to eat.

When the meal was complete, Goodwyn started another CD then had a word with Jenny. "I'd like to pray with you before I go." He began to repeat the Lord's Prayer, hoping she would find some comfort in the familiar words.

Goodwyn's voice seemed far away, but when she heard the phrase, "Deliver us from evil," she cried out. "No! Stop! God didn't deliver Colin from evil! Don't say any more!"

The priest had intended the prayer for Jenny, not for her husband, but he did not correct her. "Of course. I understand," he soothed. "I'll see you tomorrow."

Night seemed to come early. Jenny showered and then wondered why she should put on a nightgown that Colin would not see. The jeans she had worn during the day were clean enough, and a sweatshirt would cover her sufficiently. In bed and exhausted, she found she couldn't sleep. She and Colin had never slept apart in their marriage, and now she didn't even know where his body was. Simon heard her gasping cries and brought her tea which he had spiked. Through the blur she could feel his arm around her, and the presence of a warm, living body and the brandy lulled her into slumber.

On Saturday Goodwyn visited again. "Jenny, I'm aware that things must seem very dark to you just now," he said.

"I would encourage you not to run from the darkness. If we do that, we let the darkness win. I prefer to stay in the darkness but bring a light to it."

What light is there? she frowned. The flat was fraught with dark shadows, and the table lamps shed only small pools of illumination.

"Jenny, I'm referring to the light of understanding, of fellowship. That's why I'm here," Goodwyn said, hoping to engage her, but she did not reply.

Later Simon admitted the Family Liaison Officer, who brought the newspapers with her. He glanced at them. "Met Officer Killed in Blast," one headline read. "Terrorist Attack on Bond Street," said another. "Bomb Takes Life of Police Officer," screamed a third. "Heroic Action by Met Policeman Saves Many" was a gentler rendering of the event. "She shouldn't see these," he said.

"Of course not," the FLO replied. "She's likely in a daze now, but later she'll want them." She introduced herself to Jenny. "Mrs. Sinclair, I'm PC Compton, a Family Liaison Officer. I've come to help you however I can."

A specialist officer, Jenny thought. That means she knows what to do. Police always know what to do. Automatically she thought of Colin and how proud he was of the training given to members of the Metropolitan Police. She missed the rest of PC Compton's introduction and wondered if the young officer had asked her something. She blinked and tried to focus. PC Compton had sympathetic brown eyes, but no one, she argued in her mind with Colin, no one with cherub cheeks could know anything about death or grief, the quality of her training notwithstanding.

"I'd like you to call me Tracy."

She had short hair, too short, Colin would have said. Colin. Colin. Jenny felt the first stirring of panic rise like a wave from her stomach to her chest.

" – Mrs. Sinclair?"

"Jenny," she replied automatically. Colin had begun calling her Jenny early in his investigation. Was that something all officers were taught? To achieve rapport quickly, use first names?

" – checklist."

Jenny frowned. Checklist. The word had no meaning. Was she supposed to make a list of some kind? Colin would want her to be courteous, but he would understand her shock and grief. She could not smile; should she admit she didn't understand? She looked at – she'd forgotten the officer's name.

"We'll have to wait for the coroner to issue a temporary death certificate, thereby authorising burial."

Death certificate. Burial. "I can't," Jenny gasped. "I can't do this. Simon – Father Goodwyn – make her stop."

"Perhaps a postponement would be wise," Goodwyn suggested.

"Of course you're upset," the FLO replied softly. "I'll make some tea, and we'll have a chat later on."

Time passed. She was aware of nothing until Simon touched her shoulder. "Your tea," he said, nodding at the tray. The other cups were empty. "Have a taste before it gets cold."

She stared at him. Her husband was dead, and they expected her to drink tea? *Tea?* She wanted to laugh hysterically – or cry hysterically – but couldn't decide which. Dead. She had seen his blood, his lifeless body. She began to tremble. She felt Simon take her hand. His fingers were kneading her palm. She closed her eyes and concentrated on his touch. She didn't want him to stop. If he let go, she'd drift away like an astronaut severed from his lifeline. She turned toward him and gripped his arm.

The knock on the door startled her. The FLO answered it, and when Jenny saw the anguish on Joanne's face, she sobbed so hard she thought she would choke. Was it her imagination, or were the streaks of gray in her mother-in-law's hair more prominent now? Joanne was the first to regain control, thanking Father Goodwyn for his presence. After accepting a cup of tea, she spoke to Simon and then conversed with the FLO in tones so subdued that Jenny could not hear them.

"I'm cold," she said to Simon. "I can't get warm." He wrapped a blanket around her. She rested her head against his rough cheek and felt his pulse throbbing in his neck. Colin's pulse was silent. Was he cold? In a brief moment of lucidity, she recalled Dante's concept of hell as cold. But Colin wasn't there. She was.

CHAPTER 4

On Sunday, February 25, The London *Daily Telegraph* read:

Metropolitan Police
Detective Colin Sinclair

Colin Thomas Dowding Sinclair, who died on 23 February at age 39, acted heroically on that date in his effort to deter a suicide bomber, thereby saving the lives of many civilians near the Bond Street, London, tube station. Detective Chief Inspector Sinclair, although authorised to carry a firearm, was unarmed at the time he confronted the attacker. After identifying himself as a police officer, DCI Sinclair attempted to calm the agitated individual whilst simultaneously warning shoppers and pedestrians of the potential peril. DCI Sinclair stood his ground, suffering injuries from the explosion that proved fatal.

Sinclair's action caps an illustrious police career, which began 17 years ago after his graduation from Cambridge and Hendon Police College. Early assignments included Bromley, where he was initially sent to patrol streets. Showing an early interest in and aptitude for detective work, at each stage he passed the detective courses and requisite examinations. He maintained a steady rise in rank from Sergeant to Detective Sergeant at Bexley, Detective Inspector at Southwark, and Detective Chief Inspector at Islington.

From Islington he was seconded in 1998 to New Scotland Yard, where he joined Operation No Mercy. His involvement in the celebrated "Carpet Killer" case led to the apprehension and conviction of serial rapist and murderer William Cecil Crighton Scott. Following this case, he was placed in charge of the newly created Sapphire Unit of the Metropolitan Police Service, a unit dedicated entirely to improving the treatment of rape victims and the conviction rate of rapists in the London area.

He was born at Ashford, Kent, UK, on March 20, 1962, the eldest of two children of Cameron James Rhys Sinclair, a foreign service officer. In 1986 he married Violet Ashleigh Dalton. After six years of marriage, he and his first wife divorced, and in 1999 he married, secondly, Jennifer Catherine Jeffries, of Houston, Texas, USA. He is survived by his wife, his mother, Joanne Sheffield Sinclair, his sister and brother-in-law, Jillian and Derek Horne, and his niece and nephew, Rebecca and Malcolm Horne.

- -

The Sunday *Telegraph* printed a picture of Colin next to the article. His name was beneath it: Colin Thomas Dowding Sinclair, 1962 – 2002. His knowledge, his commitment, his values, his love, his smile, his touch, his whole life, reduced to a dash. Jenny's tears made the newsprint run.

CHAPTER 5

Alcina recognised Sinclair's face: He had testified at Tony's trial. She scanned the paragraphs. The newspaper had highlighted the case of Cecil Scott – Tony's employer – but hadn't deemed Tony's worthy even of a mention. She ripped out the page, intending to destroy it, but another name jumped out at her: Jennifer Catherine Jeffries. Sinclair's wife? She had been single when she was called as a witness at the trial. She had married a police detective. No wonder she had testified against Tony! Now she was a widow. Scott had been killed in prison. This policeman had been killed in the street. Perhaps those who had wronged her Tony were being struck down.

And he had been wronged. She'd never forget the morning when they had come for him. They had entered the flat before daylight, their voices deafening, jarring Tony and herself from sleep. They had come into the bedroom where she was clinging in fright to Tony and wrenched him from her arms. They had been rough with him and barely civil to her while they cuffed him and bundled him into their car. That had been their last embrace, hers and Tony's.

His arrest had only been the beginning. She had been certain he would be vindicated, but he had been charged, tried, convicted, and incarcerated, each step driving nails further into her heart. Where had justice been? She would never forgive them.

Tony would want to know about Sinclair's death. Instead of

discarding the article, she folded it carefully and set it aside. She would show it to Tony on her next visit to the prison.

CHAPTER 6

Police Commissioner Hugh Peterson was accompanied by Chief Superintendent Stuart Higham. "My deepest sympathy for your loss," Peterson said to Jenny. He nodded briefly at PC Compton, who closed the door after them. Peterson had thinning hair and a myriad of fine lines around his eyes. Thick braid nearly covered the brim of his hat, his epaulettes and lapels were heavy with the symbols of his rank and achievements, and his stature seemed twice hers. "May we come through?"

Jenny felt tongue tied in front of London's top cop, and she wished she'd followed Joanne's recommendation to change into less wrinkled clothes, because her attire seemed dismal and drab next to the heavily-adorned senior officer. She gestured for both men to make themselves comfortable and sat down in one of the armchairs across from them. "I make a terrible cup of tea," she stammered, looking pleadingly at Colin's mother.

"Tea would be very welcome," Peterson said

"I'll make it," Compton, the Family Liaison officer, said. She headed toward the kitchen while Joanne found a place to sit near Jenny.

"Jenny – may I call you Jenny?" Peterson continued. "We are devoting every resource to the investigation of the case which claimed your husband's life, and based on witness statements and CCTV footage, we believe we have a fairly clear picture of the events that took place on Friday last." Peterson paused. "First, however, I'd like to reassure you that everything was done to save your husband. After a bomb explosion, our first priority is not to seal the scene but to preserve life. Your husband was attended to and removed in an emergency vehicle before any investigative steps were taken."

Higham looked steadily at Jenny but did not speak.

"Once the members of the emergency services had ascertained that your husband was the only victim, a bomb-scene manager was designated from the Anti-Terrorist Branch. No two bomb scenes are exactly the same, and our purpose is to recover as much evidence as possible as quickly and as thoroughly as we can. That involves the establishment of inner and outer cordons, the services of a police photographer, the resources of a large forensic team, and the formation of a communications network. Of course all officers are required to wear protective clothing, not only as a form of identification but also to ensure that the scene is not contaminated in any way."

Colin was the one who had needed the protective clothing, Jenny thought. "I want to know what happened," she said.

"Of course," the Commissioner nodded. "Witnesses report seeing a semitic-looking individual on Davies Street near the small entrance to the Bond Street station. He was clutching his coat closed, not unusual behaviour on a cold day, but we believe that his agitation – he was continually looking about, with a wild expression – aroused your husband's suspicion. Your husband was closer to the station entrance than the suspect, and he identified himself as a police officer and requested a word. When the suspect backed away, hugging his coat more tightly, your husband began to wave people away and again tried to engage the suspect." He paused. "I'd like to emphasise – it was evident that your husband endeavoured to establish a dialogue with the suspect."

Of course he did, Jenny thought. He was a negotiator.

Higham appeared to listen attentively to the

Commissioner's recitation.

"Your husband acknowledged the suspect's nervousness and asked if he could be of assistance. In response, the suspect became even more agitated. Your husband implored him to stay calm. He then ordered the suspect to keep his hands away from his chest. At that moment the suspect screamed a foreign phrase and ignited the device. Fortunately Davies Street is narrow and not nearly as crowded as the main entrance on Oxford Street. The cold weather caused patrons to forgo the outdoor tables at the Hog in the Pound, just across the way, and eat indoors, thus keeping them out of range of the explosion. "

PC Compton had waited for the Commissioner to finish speaking. She now served the tea. Jenny accepted a cup, wishing Simon were there to add brandy to it. Compton poured her own cup last and settled just outside the circle.

"The mechanism was rather crude," Peterson continued. "A home-made explosive perhaps, certainly not a very sophisticated one."

Jenny found her voice. "It was effective enough!"

Higham looked pained.

"I'm afraid so," Peterson agreed. "The bomber, a Mr. – "

"No!" Jenny exclaimed. "Not his name. I don't want to know his name."

Higham and Peterson exchanged glances. "As you wish," Peterson said. "I can tell you, however, that he was British born. Mixed parentage. He may have thought he had to prove himself." He sipped his tea. "The investigation will continue until we have either satisfied ourselves that he acted alone or have identified his co-conspirators."

The shock waves from 9/11 have reached us, Jenny thought, and she felt a sudden kinship with the September 11 families. She knew now how it felt to have a loved one ripped from your life in an abrupt and totally unforeseen act of violence. Had Colin known he was going to die? Had he been afraid? "Did he suffer?" she asked.

"He never regained consciousness," Higham answered, speaking for the first time. "I reached the hospital shortly after the ambulance, and the attendants assured me that he did not."

"You didn't answer my question," Jenny objected. "The bomber was probably killed instantly, but Colin may not have been. Did he know he was going to die?"

Joanne stepped forward and rested her hand on Jenny's shoulder. Jenny grasped it.

"Mrs. Sinclair – " Higham began.

Interesting. To the Commissioner, she was Jenny. To Higham, she was Mrs. Sinclair. The Commissioner must want something.

"Witnesses tell us – and indeed, the cameras confirm – that events transpired very rapidly. Your husband could not have known – or felt – except for the briefest time."

That question had haunted her. "Thank you," she told Higham.

"It is our considered opinion," Peterson resumed, "that your husband lost his life in the line of duty, and I can therefore report that I am recommending that you receive his death-in-service benefit plus pension for life."

Jenny blinked. PC Compton hadn't mentioned any formal compensation when she discussed Colin's finances.

"Jenny, your husband had no weapon, no radio, no backup. His was an extraordinarily courageous action. Had he not intervened, many, many more would have been killed." Peterson paused. "He is a hero. As a result, we would like your indulgence on a very important matter. Would you allow us to hold a memorial service in his honour here in the capital? Chief Superintendent Higham would be at your disposal, to assist you in any way with the planning of the event."

"I'll be available to help also," Compton added.

Jenny had forgotten that the liaison officer was present. Now she looked at her earnest face and then at her mother-in-law's. Joanne had predicted that the Met would want to use Colin's sacrifice as a way to bolster their image and had helped her decide what her response would be. "That would be a media circus," she said. "A spectacle. I really think that Colin has given you enough of himself."

"Jenny, I beg you to reconsider. Your husband deserves

the accolades he will receive."

Jenny suddenly felt very tired. "That's true, but memorial services are meant for the living, not for the dead. It is my intention to take my husband home. The service will be held in Kent. You're welcome to come. I would like a Force flag to be draped over his coffin. I'll liaise with Chief Superintendent Higham, but my mother-in-law and I will plan his service. I mean no disrespect – I appreciate your visit very much – but that is all I can bear to face today. I'm sorry."

Both men stood when she stood.

"I'll be honoured to attend," Peterson said.

With appropriate farewells, Joanne showed them out.

- -

That night Jenny dreamed about Colin for the first time. They'd planned to meet for lunch, and when she neared the restaurant, she saw him remonstrating with a man in the street, a shadowy figure in a bulging coat. Colin, however, was in high definition, his blue eyes unusually bright, the extra wrinkle on the left side of his mouth contracting and relaxing as he spoke. His arm was outstretched, and at first she thought he was welcoming her, but then she realized that he wanted her to stay back. Out of nowhere uniformed policemen surrounded the shadowy man, and Colin came forward and smiled at her. "All clear," he said. "All clear." She felt his arms around her, felt secure, felt loved. A husband, not a hero.

When she woke, her initial thought was that the dream was real and her other life – and Colin's death – were a cruel, misleading vision. But she was alone in her bed. Joanne had suggested that she sleep on Colin's side, that she use his pillow. And that was proof positive that the nightmare was real.

Jenny sat between her family and Colin's, listening to the organist's prelude and remembering the last time their families had gathered in St. Albans. It had been on Christmas Eve, when the warmth of their Christmas joy had mitigated the winter cold. At Christmas, however, they hadn't been seated in the front rows; Jillian's children had been present; and Colin had been next to her, holding her hand. No reporters and cameramen had waited for them outside, and the pews had not been crowded with uniformed policemen, their uniforms such a dark blue that they looked black. St. Albans, the first British Christian martyr, had died on A.D. 283. At Christmas they had gathered in his church to celebrate a birth; death had brought them together on this day.

Jenny had hoped for at least a semiprivate time with family and friends at the memorial service honoring Colin, but the presence of Commissioner Peterson, although as an attendee only, had eliminated that. Other senior officers were there, too: Detective Superintendent Graves, Colin's boss when he worked at New Scotland Yard, still tense and spare; Detective Chief Superintendent Woulson, next in the chain of command, his jowls giving him a truly mournful look; and Colin's current supervisor, Stuart Higham, who had given her a small black box containing Colin's personal effects. Several of them had spoken of Colin, as had officers who had served with him earlier in his career. Jenny was hungry to hear his name spoken, and she devoured every word. Gordon Harvey, who had been Colin's supervising officer when he was a rookie, was now heading toward the pulpit. He'd put on weight since the last time he'd worn his uniform, and his uniform appeared to be protesting. She focused on his round, ruddy face as he spoke.

"Sinclair. Well. I remember one call we made – after he'd settled in – to check on an elderly woman. Her neighbours hadn't seen her about, you see. We made Sinclair force the door to the flat, because we wanted to see if he'd developed any muscle at university, and we found the woman deceased. It was the first body Sinclair had dealt with, and his eyes were streaming. We all thought he'd gone soft already, and we set about preparing a few choice nicknames for him, but it was the cats. Allergic to them, he was! As it turned out, the deceased had kept seventeen of them." He paused. "He was educated, Sinclair was, that was clear from the off. Some of us were a bit put off by it at first, but he only ever treated us as equals. He had a way with people. Got more from witnesses than the rest of us ever did. I always thought he'd go far." He looked at Jenny. "Things just shouldn't have ended for him the way they did. My respects, ma'am."

Another of Colin's favorite hymns followed, the sonorous bass notes of the organ providing an undercurrent of grief in the music. Jenny hadn't known which were his favorites or which colleagues should be asked to say a few words. Joanne had guided her through all the preparations. She had stayed with Jenny, cleaned the flat, gone to the market, done the laundry, and selected clothes for her when she stood paralyzed in front of the closet unable to decide what to wear. When Jenny's family arrived, she visited every day, often sending Jenny's brothers on errands to relieve them of the awkwardness they felt in the flat and with the liaison officer. Simon had come daily, too, looking tired, staying only briefly, but hugging her each time before he left. Men's hugs were so different from women's: Women's hugs gave comfort, but men's spoke of strength. Jenny needed both at this time in her life. She had implored Simon to sit with them at the service, but he had not agreed. "You have your family, love."

The next speaker was Sergeant Roger Fulford, a chunky man with prominent brows and a dark mustache but no beard to hide his extra chin. "He had a temper," he began. "I know, because I was on the receiving end a few times, with good reason, I'm sorry to say. 'I'll not tolerate sloppy or incomplete policing.' That's what DCI Sinclair said at the start of every investigation, and he meant it. I learnt a good deal from him." He paused briefly. "He well and truly believed that coppers should be held to the highest standard of integrity. Anything less was a betrayal of his trust and the public trust and deserving of ire. It's fair to say that any officer who broke the law ceased to be an officer in his mind. He became a criminal, and DCI Sinclair had no difficulty pursuing evidence against criminals.

"Injustice made him angry. Cruelty made him angry. Senseless death made him angry." Fulford bowed his head for a moment. He was unable to keep the bitterness from his voice when he continued. "Senseless death angers me also, more than I can express in this setting. My sincere condolences to his family." He moved heavily from the pulpit, and Detective Sergeant David Andrews, Colin's colleague at Islington and New Scotland Yard, took his place. He had corralled his wavy hair, and his broad, friendly face was solemn.

"Colin Sinclair had an unusual understanding of people. He recognised an officer's individual strengths and abilities and tried to assign jobs accordingly. He believed in teamwork but didn't require everyone to fit the same mould. The best officers, in his view, weren't the ones who never took risks and consequently never made mistakes but those who learnt from their mistakes. On any new investigation everyone began with a clean slate.

"He covered it well, but anyone who worked with Colin Sinclair for any length of time became aware of his impatience, particularly as it related to evidence. He always saw further ahead than the rest of us, hence his four-step test for determining the sufficiency of evidence. First, is it sufficient to identify the wrongdoer? Second, is it sufficient for an arrest to be made and charges to be laid? Third, will the CPS – the Crown Prosecution Service – consider it sufficient to proceed? And fourth, will it give the desired result: conviction. His record of success was outstanding. We have indeed lost a champion.

"I can't conclude without mentioning the love he had for Jenny, his wife. He didn't speak of it; he didn't have to do. When she rang him, he always took her call. He wasn't impatient with her, he was impatient to see her. At the end of a long day when we were all knackered and showing it, he still had a spring in his step because he was going home to her. I respected him as a police officer. And as a man. I – " his voice wavered, and he stopped. The assembly waited quietly. After a moment he shook his head and left the pulpit.

Jenny couldn't contain her tears, and her mother leaned over and patted her hand.

The service of Holy Communion began with family members served first. When she returned to her seat, Jenny watched others coming forward, many of them strangers to her, people Colin must have known but whom she had never met. Occasionally Joanne would whisper a name to her and a brief explanation. When one couple moved forward, however, Jenny heard a sharp intake of breath from her mother-in-law. The man, wearing an expensive dark suit, was accompanied by a tall, model-thin woman whose blonde hair nearly touched her shoulders. She was wearing a black cashmere sweater with a single strand of pearls, and her black skirt reached her ankles but didn't hide her high-heeled fashion boots. "Mr. and Mrs. Richard Denham-Ross," Joanne murmured, adding, when she saw Jenny's puzzled look, "Violet. She left him! She's here just to show off. How could she?"

Colin's ex-wife: stunning, somber, but to Jenny's eye, not sad. Jenny shared her mother-in-law's anger but felt something akin to wonder, too: She, Jenny, small, dark-haired, and casual in her manner and dress, was nothing like that elegant woman, yet Colin had loved her.

Father Rogers then read the John Donne quote she had given him: "All mankind is of one author, and is one volume; when one man dies, one chapter is not torn out of the book, but translated into a better language; and every chapter must be so translated..." Hearing his words made her feel still connected to Colin. Her eyes rested on the cross that represented Jesus' sacrifice. Colin had died for people he had not known. What was his icon? She could imagine him saying, "That's what coppers do, Jen. They serve, and sometimes they lose their lives while serving. No symbol necessary except the badge." What was her icon? A weeping willow? What a pathetic panegyric!

She gripped the railing in front of her, knowing the service was coming to a close and she would somehow have to find the strength to stand. Father Goodwyn had joined Father Rogers in front of the altar. Together they intoned the final blessing. It was time to go to the cemetery. How would she be able to? Half of her knew she must, but the other half wanted to run the other way.

- -

When Jenny saw the casket for the first time, it looked alien. She hadn't wanted anything fancy; her preference was for something strong, so strong that it would resist time and the elements and prevent the dirt from ever touching him. She hoped her final gift to him was inside, held in his hand as she had requested: a copy, in calligraphy, of Elizabeth Barrett Browning's famous poem, "How do I love thee? / Let me count the ways." It concluded with a declaration of love: "I love thee with the breath, / Smiles, tears, of all my life! — and, if God choose, / I shall but love thee better after death." It had been her wedding gift and her promise to him, an indication of how enduring she considered her love for him to be.

The Sinclair family cemetery had a number of graves, and Joanne saw to it that all were tended regularly. Trees lay just beyond, their bare branches reaching for the sky, as if they too wanted release from the cold, confining ground where Colin would lie. Jenny wished for a distraction to draw her attention away from the gleaming box and the gaping maw in the earth that would swallow it. She needed an animal to amble by, a bird to sing, or a sudden wind to drown out the sound of Father Rogers' voice, but there was nothing.

Someone from the funeral home removed the force flag from the casket, folded it, and placed it on her lap. Even folded, she could see its intense blue, darker than Colin's eyes, and a portion of the same symbol of the Queen that had been on his warrant card, which was held in a folder as black as her skirt. "Do I have to wear all black?" she'd asked her mother. With the assurance that she didn't, she had finally chosen a pale gray blouse with dark vines embroidered around a pink velvet heart because Colin had always smiled when she wore it. Her throat tightened, and because she couldn't say it aloud, she had to think the words of the farewell she had planned: "Good-night, sweet prince..." There was more to the quotation, but she couldn't remember. What was it? What was it? If only she'd written it down! But her eyes had misted over, and she couldn't have read the words if she'd had them.

Around her, people rose to their feet. The service must be over. Her brothers, younger than she but much taller, shifted their feet, not knowing what to do. "It's time, Punkin," her father said. "I'll walk with you," added her mother, cradling her elbow.

She felt strapped to her chair, and anger tightened her throat even further. Why did she have to leave him again? "Not yet," she managed to whisper. Colin, she thought, why did you have to go so soon? When we were happy? When I had overcome so much to be with you? She began to cry. Colin, I want you to come home to me!

The trees that surrounded the cemetery were tall and stark, their branches bald and black. The breeze didn't register when it ruffled her hair, and although the sun dazzled with a rare winter display, it did not disperse the clouds in her heart.

In the end her family stayed with her, Colin's mother with them, but she felt more connected to Colin than to her living relatives. She was as cold and still as he, except for her shaking shoulders and searing sobs. She folded her chilled fingers into fists and pressed them into her lap but could not contain her sorrow.

Joanne put her arm around her shoulders and whispered, "When Cam was buried here, I stayed for the longest time. I still come often. It helps to know where he is. But there's no rush. I'll wait with you, we all will, the way Colin did with me, until you're ready."

CHAPTER 8

Jenny hadn't anticipated the crushing silence. Since she had returned to Hampstead and her family had left for Texas, the flat was as silent and still as a tomb, reminding her of her last moments with Colin. Now, since he had been her most frequent caller, her phone rarely rang.

Outside the world seemed to be going on as usual. She could often hear sirens from ambulances taking people to the Royal Free Hospital, and occasionally she'd catch snatches of conversation as individuals passed by on the street. The normal sounds she made – her footsteps on the kitchen floor, setting a teacup on the counter, using her hair dryer – seemed unnaturally loud, and at first she was afraid they'd keep her from hearing Colin's footsteps on the stairs or his key in the lock. Sometimes she wondered if she should slam the cabinet door or scream at the top of her voice to cover up the fact that he was not coming home, not ever. Finally she turned on the radio and let it play constantly, because the voices, although disembodied, belonged to living beings.

She hadn't anticipated the unrelenting emptiness. The flat seemed void, not just of Colin, but of everything, even air. She wasn't even sure she could take a breath. If she struck a match, would it burn? She dressed, although even lightweight clothes felt heavy and suffocating.

She hadn't anticipated the all-encompassing loneliness.

How could Colin be gone and all his things be in their usual places? His suits, his ties, his shoes? Her body was lonely for him. Making things worse, her period had started, causing a new despair. She had hoped against hope that he had left a part of himself behind and that she could count the days until she could embrace his son or daughter. She recalled a succession of intimate moments: Colin, confessing not long after their wedding that he wished they'd have a family sooner rather than later; Colin, so moved with joy he couldn't speak when she told him she wanted birth conception, not birth control; the gentle, almost reverent way he made love to her that night; the intensity of their union, when she felt they were participating in an act far greater than just the two of them because there was a purpose beyond their own pleasure. Now she was mourning the death of a dream and two lives instead of one.

She hadn't anticipated her need for consistency. She wanted – no, *needed* – to find reassurance in routine and solace in the utter sameness of the flat and its furnishings. She didn't change anything. If she opened his closet door, she needed to see all his clothes in their usual places. She found a piece of paper and wrote two titles across the top: *Things That Are the Same* and *Things That Are Different*. His clothes should be in the hamper, his aftershave in the air when she woke, his tea cup in the kitchen sink. At the end of the day she should hear the front door opening and his voice calling out to her. She did not put pen to paper; it was too depressing. Only one thing remained the same: her love for him.

She finally opened the box of Colin's personal effects. Inside was an inventory of the items, printed neatly on Metropolitan Police Service letterhead. She knew what to expect: his wallet, with driver's license, credit cards, and cash. Assorted change from his pocket. Keys, which made a jarring sound when she set them on the table. She wondered suddenly what the bomb had sounded like, if it had deafened him. If he had died in silence. She picked up the keys again and jangled them to rid her mind of the thought. What else was in the box?

No warrant card; he had been holding it at the time of the blast, so it probably hadn't been found. No handkerchief, although she knew he would have had one. The last item was a surprise: *One diamond and emerald drop earring. Only shards (not enclosed) recovered from the second earring.* One earring whole, one shattered, but two lives shattered, she thought. The surviving earring was beautiful – the emerald, outlined in diamonds, was in the shape of a tiny teardrop. Why had Colin bought them? No important anniversaries lay immediately ahead. It didn't matter; it was a gift from beyond the grave, and she treasured it.

The knock on the door startled her. Colin? – no, he didn't need to knock, he had a key. And he was gone. Gone, she reminded herself. It must be Simon.

He held her mail in his hand. The entrance to her side of the building was on the ground floor, but the front door to her flat was on the first. Cards and notes of sympathy continued to be delivered through the letter box, and no matter how brief or trite, she cherished every one. They were all she had the concentration to read, and like the refrain from a favorite song, she pored over them again and again. Today, however, there was also something from Dr. Hannaford. She opened the envelope. A bill! He was charging her for the visit Colin had scheduled and not kept! Didn't they know why he had missed the appointment? Didn't his death count for anything? She tore the statement in half and put it in her pocket. "Your accessories match," she said to Simon, trying to keep her voice light.

He glanced from his brown leather jacket to his brown boots. "Dressed for the weather," he shrugged. She seemed smaller somehow, even her voice lacking its usual resonance. "You're wearing yesterday's clothes, I see."

Even jeans and sweatshirts wrinkled if you slept in them, and her Dallas Cowboys sweatshirt was so old that the letters across the front were cracked. "They're clean enough. Tea?"

"I'll brew." He cocked his head. "Why is the radio switched on?"

"It was too quiet."

"Where's the liaison officer?"

"I sent her away. I was uncomfortable with her, and I think she was uncomfortable with me."

"Was that wise?"

Simon's question indicated that he didn't think so. Jenny sighed. Compton had suggested gently that Jenny's judgement had been affected by grief. "She meant well, but she hovered around me all the time. After a while she felt like an intruder."

She leaned against the counter and watched him set the water to boil and place teabags in their cups. Amazing. Men who couldn't cook anything else knew how to make a good cup of tea.

"I have a mission today," he said. "Davies and I – we want to know if you'll be staying in London and if you need any help."

"Nothing can help."

"I meant, help to stay here."

It took her a minute to realize that he was talking about money. "Colin had a will," she answered. "After we married, he bought this block of flats, so I'll have rent from the other tenants. He had a life insurance policy, and I'll receive a monthly allowance from his estate. I don't know how much. I've been putting off seeing the solicitor. The Commissioner said I might get his pension and a death-in-service benefit. I'm waiting to hear from someone in Financial Liaison Services."

"And the property in Kent?"

"That stays in the family. Jillian's children will inherit it when they are of age."

"Still enough to live on, then."

"Yes, more than enough, if I'm careful, but my visa status has changed. I'll have to apply for an indefinite leave to remain. I hope they'll grant it on compassionate grounds."

They took their tea into the living room.

"Simon, I've been thinking a lot about the man with the bomb. He must have been angry! So angry that he didn't care how many people he killed, including himself. And now *I'm* angry. Angry that the bomber is dead. Angry that he took Colin with him. I'm even angry at the people who came to Colin's memorial service. It's so unfair! Every one of them had known him longer than I had! Was I a stranger in my husband's life?"

Her hands were shaking. Simon took her cup.

"You've just put my teacup on the coffee table. No one drinks coffee here. Why isn't it called a tea table?" Her half smile dissolved, and she began to cry.

He put an arm around her shoulders and thought about his dilemma. The woman he loved was even more bound to Sinclair in grief than she had been in happiness.

The flat was quiet when Jenny woke. However, instead of thinking for a brief moment that Colin had left for work and then experiencing his loss all over again, her chest felt heavy, because she knew she was alone. Only her London policeman teddy bear, a gift from Colin's colleague Barry Bridges long ago, rested on the pillow.

She forced herself out of bed, her limbs as sluggish as if she were wading through deep water. She had overslept but still felt exhausted through and through, her mind as well as her body. Was there no remedy? No respite? She dragged herself into the kitchen. She needed something to help her focus. It didn't matter what she ate, but tea – or anything with caffeine – was essential.

She set one cup and saucer on the counter, removed one spoon from the drawer. One: It all came down to one. Thousands had been lost on September 11, but those numbers were made up of ones, of single individuals mourned by their families. She was one wife who had lost one husband, and her sorrow was unbearable.

She now had two companions, Guilt and Grief, who took turns assailing her. "You didn't love him enough," Guilt said. "He deserved better." "He's gone forever," Grief added. "Your life will never be the same." It was true, all true. She and Colin had been two parts of the same equation. Now she was one number, a constant because she was alone.

She tried to discipline herself to think about the support she had received. Barry, now one of the officers at Sapphire, had told her how much Colin was missed. "Your case gave him a unique perspective on the work we do," he had said. "The next DCI's not likely to have that." His words had helped her to feel briefly that she wasn't grieving alone. Simon had kept her company, and Colin's mother had grieved with her, sometimes embracing Jenny when she cried and other times being embraced by her. Colleagues of Colin's, some of whom she had never met, had either called or sent cards or flowers. She had acknowledged their expressions of sympathy, but she needed to talk about him to someone, talk about that awful day, and there was no one to tell. With a tinge of regret, she realized she could have spoken to the liaison officer, but she was gone. And since she hadn't known Colin, it would have been a one sided, less than satisfying conversation. Writing it down didn't help; she had tried. The black ink on the white paper looked cold, sterile, and final. Colin had been warm, loving, and committed to protecting and saving lives.

The dining room table still held copies of the newspapers whose headlines covered the news of the explosion which had killed Colin. She hadn't been able to read past the first sentence or two in each one and didn't know if she'd ever be capable of reading the complete articles. She didn't want to discard them, however; in a strange way they connected her to him, as if she had been beside him when the tragedy occurred.

She peered out the window. She would have to dress. Maybe if she wore something colorful, Father Goodwyn wouldn't notice her gray mood. No, nothing but clown makeup could disguise her pale and drawn face. She pulled on jeans and the first blouse her fingers touched. He was scheduled to come by before lunch, but he was late, and no wonder: It was raining hard, the precipitation pummelling the pavement. She liked Neil Goodwyn. He reminded her of Colin, not in his looks, because Colin had been younger and taller with blue eyes instead of brown, but in his manner, his gentle regard for her. And he never used platitudes. Sometimes he just kept her company, helped her consume leftovers from the fridge, or watered the many potted plants people had sent in sympathy. During his time as a Royal Army chaplain, he'd been subjected to all the elements and stresses that his soldiers had – exhaustion, sandstorms, and extreme cold – hence his weathered face. He had seen men injured and killed and claimed that each loss had added another grey hair and another wrinkle, thus giving him a permanent way to remember them. His faith had somehow survived it all, and she reminded herself that she didn't have to pretend to be strong with him when she wasn't. She had asked him once why he came to see her so frequently. "The Bible tells us to 'rejoice with those who rejoice; mourn with those who mourn,'" he said. "I don't like to think of you grieving alone."

Today he came in with a smile, some digestive biscuits, and an offer to make tea.

She should have made a fresh pot already but had been too preoccupied. "All of Britain considers tea a miracle drink," she told him. "Maybe if you make it, it really will be. And digestives – is the name supposed to make me feel less guilty for eating cookies?"

"Yes," Goodwyn smiled. "Tell yourself they're good for your system." They retired to the sitting room with their snacks and cups. "Jenny, people often try to process what they've seen by focussing on one image above all others. Often the worst. Have you?"

Her throat tightened. "I wish – I wish I had amnesia!"

"It's unlikely that you'll ever forget what you saw, but over time other memories – more positive ones – will be stronger. For now, it may help to share what shocked you so much."

She took a deep breath. "The blood. I think that image is burned into my brain. They had cut away his shirt, you see."

He nodded. He had been shocked the first time he had seen a severely injured soldier with his uniform stripped away.

"He had blood on his face, too, on his forehead and cheeks and nose."

"And you wiped it away."

"Yes. It was silly, I guess, and useless. It didn't help him in any way."

When Goodwyn replied, his voice was soft. "Jenny, there are times when the human touch is holy. I believe that was one of those times, because love motivated you." He waited while she wiped her eyes. "You're in a sort of war zone. I think having some leave could help."

"What does that mean exactly?"

"You're alone still. I'd like to think that you were experiencing fellowship of some sort."

"It's hard to feel connected to other people. Time seems to swallow me." She took a bite of the digestive: good oat flavor but it would have tasted better dipped in chocolate.

"Perhaps we need to speak about your choices."

"What choices?"

"Isolation or companionship. Isolation may feel safe, but it's not. In God's world, healing can't take place in isolation. We are meant to be connected with each other. That was one very positive thing about my time in military service. The men I served were part of a unit, a community. When crisis came, we supported each other. All personalities, all differences, disappeared."

"How did you stand it? So much death, so much grief?"

"Because I saw hope as well. And courage was there, and honor, trust, and love. Colin was courageous. When I conducted memorial services, I often quoted John 15, verses 12-14: 'Greater love has no one but this, that he lay down his life for his friends.' It's as appropriate for Colin as it was for those young soldiers."

"Was he – was he – "

He waited.

"Afraid," she whispered.

"In my experience there's often no time for fear. Events happen too quickly for us to absorb anything other than what is most urgent."

Unable to respond, she nodded her thanks.

"Today, Jenny, my focus is on you. You and your healing."

She swallowed hard. "I don't know what healing means. I wouldn't mind feeling less tired, but I don't see how I can be happy. And even if I could, I'd feel too guilty."

"My purpose is not to make you feel happy when you're not but to encourage you to experience life even while you are sad. You see, time does not heal by itself, particularly in the case of emotional wounds. Time simply gives us the chance to allow healing to take place, much as soil allows seeds to root, sprout, and grow. Healing requires an action on our part."

"Like the farmer who plants the seeds."

"Exactly, yes. And there's another element. Healing doesn't occur in a vacuum. Seeds are planted in a specific environment. Your healing environment needs to be an experience, and that means involving others."

"But I still love Colin," she objected.

"Yes, and he still loves you, but I'm not speaking of finding a substitute for him. Love can come from many sources. I want you to know how much love still exists in your world, and in order to do that, you'll have to stop hiding yourself away. I believe your family hoped you'd go back with them to Texas for a bit."

She shook her head. "I couldn't. I would have been too far from Colin." She tried to explain. "This flat – it reflects him. The high ceilings, because he was tall. The books on the bookshelves because he was educated and had an inquisitive mind. Even the bay window, because he always wanted to know what was going on in the world. And his things are here. This flat is my home. I'm safe here. And I was loved here."

"I'm glad you still consider it home. I'd not like you to take any major decisions at the minute. I know, however, that Colin's mother would welcome you for a visit."

She hesitated. It would take energy to pack and travel, but Joanne's country home in Kent had always been a place of renewal. She had loved visiting with Colin, but she had also visited sometimes without him. Maybe there she wouldn't look for him in every room, and Joanne wouldn't expect her to be cheerful. "Yes, I could go to Kent."

Father Goodwyn nodded his agreement, finished his tea, and after a short prayer, left her to make the arrangements. She rang Joanne first, then Beth, and last, Simon. As she packed her suitcase, she thought about the things she would not miss: the emptiness she felt when visitors departed; washing clothes for herself and not for Colin; making meals for one.

Three was an important number, Alcina thought. When she and Tony had married, they had swapped rings three times during the ceremony. They had worn crowns of flowers and exchanged them three times. Tony had thought the white blossoms beautiful on her dark hair, and she had laughed, laughed in the middle of the ceremony, to see fragile flowers on his thick locks – she knew what sinewy strength he had. They had drunk three times from the cup of wine. Then they had begun their journey into marriage by walking three times around the altar. She sighed, thinking of where their steps had taken them since that happy day.

The number had a new significance for her now: Three years it had been, three long years, since Tony had been sent away. Since she had been forced to work to survive. Someone should pay.

Scott, her husband's employer, had been killed in prison. He had paid. It gave her a measure of satisfaction to know that the man who had led her husband astray was dead. *Ena*: one. And the police detective who had been killed by the bomb. Someone had made him pay, not for his part in Tony's conviction, but it had been payment nonetheless. *Duo*: two. But there needed to be *tria*: three. Perhaps the detective's wife, the one who had testified against Tony, that weak fount of tears who had swayed the jury, could be struck down.

Three lives lost for the injustice done to Tony? Only one of the three remained unscathed, but she could change that. They had exchanged no vows at their wedding, she and Tony, their presence in the church speaking for itself, but she made one now: I will avenge you.

She felt lighter, freer, stronger. Her anger, like a laser, was now focussed. She smiled, remembering the literal meaning of her name: "strong-minded." She would have to be, but she had always been good at payback. Of her three sisters, Cecilia had been the worst. Alcina had never been far from her sharp tongue and constant criticism. So when Alcina had lost weight and begun to attract attention from boys, she'd seduced Cecilia's fiancé. The sweet part hadn't been the sex – he was an inexperienced and ineffective lover – but knowing that she could destroy Cecilia's world any time she chose. That gave her power she relished.

What would Tony think? He'd not try to dissuade her. He had always had his own ideas about right and wrong.

CHAPTER 11

Jenny traveled to Kent in a daze. At the station in West Hampstead she had turned the wrong way off the lift and been puzzled by the barred passage until someone had touched her shoulder and redirected her. She had then tried to pay better attention, locating the right platform and taking the train through St. Pancras. Colin's mother, Joanne, had met her at the station in Ashford.

The first few days in the cocoon that was Kent were peaceful. It was comforting to be where Colin had been. "I'm here when you're ready to talk about him," Colin's mother, Joanne, said when she arrived. She hadn't wanted to talk, just to wander through the grounds, remembering earlier visits when Colin had walked with her and named each type of tree. He had known them all. Now only the members of the pine family maintained their greenery, the stately Douglas firs like captains of the forest leading a scraggly team. Winter had robbed the deciduous trees of their leafy personas, but she recognized the oaks from their bark and low branches. Hawthorns were smaller, the sweet chestnuts' shiny dark green leathery leaves had yet to appear, and the statuesque walnuts, which came into leaf later than other species, were still awaiting their spring flowers. Poplars? Sycamores? They were there, but without Colin's discerning eye, she couldn't identify them.

Otherwise Kent promised the bloom of spring. When she walked to the duck pond, she passed the honeysuckle adorning the arbor. Mallards and mandarins enjoyed the quiet water, their feet moving so gently under the surface that ripples could scarcely be seen above. She wished that she could glide through life as easily; for her even the simplest things were difficult. She could only sit still; but when she did, rabbits came to the water's edge.

Paths led to the pond, but she couldn't see where they trailed away. The forest was uncharted territory, as was the life that lay ahead of her, and she found herself in a kind of paralysis. If she made a cup of tea, it grew cold before she remembered to drink it. If she brought a book with her, not a page was turned nor a word read. She had no plans for the future and couldn't conceive of any except to dress, eat, shower, sleep. It was winter in her spirit, cold and inhospitable to development of any kind.

If she stayed away from the cemetery, it was easier to deceive herself, to think that Colin was involved with a case in London and couldn't be with her for a while. She slept in his room. It was a man's room, with dark paneling covering one wall and framing the windows on the other. Bookshelves which held mementos as well as books. Some had been pushed aside to make room for something Colin had brought with him, his mobile phone or car keys. Now only the space remained.

When she opened the wardrobe door, a few dress shirts and ties peered out at her; not his preferred ones, or he would have taken them with him, but still his. She was glad Joanne hadn't disposed of them. Fresh towels lay in a neat stack for the bathroom down the hall, and a man's long terry robe was folded next to them.

In the evening over dinner, she confessed that she still expected Colin to come home.

"That's what I missed most at first," Joanne answered, "after Cam died. He'd always find me straightaway, kiss me, and then announce: 'Joanne kissed me!' It was a paraphrase of a Leigh Hunt poem." She laughed lightly. "It embarrassed the children, but that didn't stop Cam. He had such zest."

Jenny listened, wondering how Joanne managed to talk about her husband without crying. Waiting for her own tears to stop was like waiting for drought in rain-soaked London.

"The day came when he seemed much weaker than usual. I bent over and kissed him, and he whispered those three words: 'Joanne kissed me.' They were the last he spoke to me. Then he slipped away." She paused. "For the first time I'm glad Cam is gone, because he didn't have to bury his son."

"I've wondered – if Colin thought of me at the end. Or if he died too fast. And then I wish that he did die too fast, so he didn't feel any pain or fear. I'll always wish I'd been able to tell him one more time how much I loved him. In the hospital, he was already gone when I saw him, but I talked to him anyway." She dug in her pocket for a Kleenex. "I wish I'd been better to him."

"It's normal to have some regrets, but Jenny – he was so happy with you."

"Happier than with Violet? I'm afraid of the answer, but I have to ask."

"He and Violet had more unhappy years than happy ones," Joanne said. "The happiness he felt with you was a result of mature love. You shared the same values. You wanted the same things in life. He was looking forward to everything that lay ahead for the two of you. I understand what you mean, though. I wanted to see his hair turn grey."

Joanne's salt-and-sand hair was held loosely in place by a barrette at the nape of her neck. "He wanted children so badly," Jenny said. "He wanted to be the kind of father for them that his father was for him. We were trying to start a family. Maybe if we'd had more time – "

"Oh, Jenny, we're all Goldilocks when it comes to time, aren't we? Either we have too much of it or too little. It's never just right. But I like to recall Cam, his expressions, his laugh. It helps to remember."

Jenny sighed. "I think it hurts to remember, because mostly I remember Colin's death. I can't seem to focus on his life."

"That will come," Joanne said, "but you can't rush it, and

you can't fight it. Let each day bring what it will."

That night Jenny dreamed that it all happened differently. The young officer who took her to the hospital wasn't silent, uncomfortable, devoid of details. He was talkative and encouraging. "DCI Sinclair's been hurt, but it's all minor," he said. "He'll be fine, really. You'll see." And at the hospital, Colin was sitting up and smiling when she entered the treatment room. He had lots of scratches and was polka dotted with small bandages. She cried with relief.

In the morning she wanted to hold onto the dream, not face the reality. She snapped at Joanne over breakfast and then burst into tears when she should have apologized. In the afternoon her sobs chased the chatty squirrels away, and at dinner she dropped one of Joanne's china cups. Instead of fussing, Joanne put her arms around her and cried with her. It was Colin's birthday.

CHAPTER 12

Simon Casey had had a bad feeling about this raid from the off but hadn't been able to put his finger on why. The team was ready. All were experienced. Each man knew his job. The suits in CID had given him what appeared to be good intel and free rein with the plan. His men were fully briefed. He rechecked his Five to be sure that the mags were loaded and seated.

There had been reports of gang activity in the area. They were going after two gang members with guns and ammunitions in a third-floor flat. They'd done this sort of dig-out many times. He tapped his mag again.

He'd been up since 3:00 a.m. The team had left Leman Street at 4:30. Suspects should be asleep when they hit the door. He was tired, but the adrenalin was pumping and would keep him alert.

The stairs creaked under Davies' weight. They'd recced the plot and knew the entire estate was in disrepair. Broken glass, empty cans, and cigarette butts littered the pavement, and the steps were sticky in spots. Everything reeked of old rubbish no one had bothered to bin. Entry wouldn't be a problem. Sometimes a Hatton round, a 12-gauge shotgun round, was used to shoot locks and hinges off locked doors, because it disintegrated on impact instead of ricocheting like a bullet. This morning, however, the enforcer would do nicely.

The staircase would have been dark even in daylight. When Casey's boot hit the step, it gave way, turning his ankle. An exposed nail beneath the step caught his calf above his boot. Pain raced up his right leg. Bloody hell! When he grabbed the railing to pull himself up, it came out of the wall. Cursing under his breath, he dragged himself to the landing, swept the broken bottles out of the way, and propped himself against the wall.

The sound of the enforcer splintering the paper-thin door told him the entry was under way. He heard the members of his team bellowing, "Armed police! Armed police! Don't move! Don't move!" Then screams which seemed to last forever. He knew none of his team had fired; the suspects must be frightened. To a man his team were large, heavily armed, and clad in black. Helmets covered their faces when they made entry. Their own mums would be afraid. Shouts of "Clear! Close! Out!" echoed.

Clenching his teeth against the pain, he inspected the damage. Between the probable sprain and the sutures he would require, he'd be out a while. He slapped a field dressing on the laceration and gracelessly struggled under the four-and-a-half stone of gear to stand on his good leg.

The team had followed through as they should have done. Pilner, who was ex-Army, had been in front of him. He understood that the mission came first. Once the momentum was under way, there was no stopping or slowing until the mission was complete. He was always amazed by how fast and fluid their maneouvres were.

"You all right, Doc?"

"Nothing that can't be fixed," he growled but pleased nonetheless that McGill, the team medic, was on the spot. He leant on him and hopped into the flat. Usually his gear kept him warm enough, but the flat was unheated, and with shock possibly setting in, he felt the cold. Twin girls – who couldn't have been more than twelve – were huddled together crying and shivering in their nightdresses, dwarfed by the officers who stood by bristling with gear. Their two brothers had gang tattoos, the 15-year-old looking a bit shaken, but the 17-year-old sullen. All, even the girls, were plasticuffed.

"Firearms and ammo were found in the girls' room," Davies reported.

Casey understood. Kids under sixteen were often recruited by gangs because they got lighter sentences. The investigators would have to sort out what the sisters knew, if anything. "No parents?" he asked.

"Their mum works nights," Traylor said. "No father."

Casey hated to see children involved, and these days gangs were using younger and younger ones. He wondered if anyone would address or even acknowledge the trauma these girls had experienced. Suddenly tired, he leant against the wall. "Somebody find a blanket for those two," he said.

CHAPTER 13

"No fracture," the doctor at the hospital Accident & Emergency reported. He finished suturing the tear in Casey's calf and left the nurse, a leggy blonde with hazel eyes and a nice smile, to instruct him in posttreatment care.

"You know all this, I think," she said after a moment.

"Yes, but I like hearing you say it," Casey told her.

"Your police training?"

"Something like that."

She gave him an appraising look. "What then? You had no anxiety about the procedure, and you didn't flinch. Most of the patients I see have curiosity at the least. You looked like you knew what the doctor was going to do before he did it and then watched to be sure he did it right."

She was direct and perceptive. He liked that. And the long legs. "I could explain over a drink. When your shift ends."

"You're willing to wait another two hours?"

"I'm going nowhere fast on this ankle." And Jenny was in Kent. "But I'll need to know what the 'M' stands for, Ms. M. Collier."

"Marcia, and you'll have to lose your bodyguard. Unless I'm going to need him."

He laughed. Davies had accompanied him to the hospital, but he would be glad to head home.

They found a pub nearby. Casey noted that Marcia drained her pints nearly as fast as he did.

"Dilutes the stress, doesn't it?" she said. "So? Where'd you grow up? Where'd you learn about emergency medicine?"

Responding to her prodding, he told her a bit about his childhood in Penzance and his subsequent medical training with the Royal Marines. "Some of my training took place in civilian hospitals. My mum's a nurse. She lives in Portsmouth now, where my brother Martin – a Royal Navy sailor – is based. Penzance is a good place to live if you fancy fishing and bird watching and don't mind the smell of the sea. Growing up I could never escape the smell of sea air. Later I'd no desire to."

"But you wanted more."

He nodded. In his experience nurses weren't shy, and she was a bit of all right. "I'd like to see you again. What do you do to relax?" he asked.

"Listen to music. I'm not terribly athletic, and I'm on my feet close to twelve hours a day, so I'm not keen on anything that requires me to walk or stand for long. And with that ankle, neither should you."

"I can suggest some activities that wouldn't require either of us to stand at all."

"I'm not interested in moving too fast," she objected, lifting her chin.

He felt a tug at his heart, remembering Jenny doing the same when she intended to be stubborn about something and stand her ground. He had liked seeing it, even when he was the one she was challenging. It took him a moment to recover himself. "I was thinking of dinner and a film," he said. "Tomorrow?"

She laughed. "If that's true, I accept," she said. "I share a flat with my younger sister, Abby. I'll give you the address."

CHAPTER 14

March 31, 2002: Easter. Jenny sat next to Joanne and listened to Father Rogers' homily about resurrection and how Jesus had foretold it: "You will grieve, but your grief will turn to joy." St. Albans was ablaze with light, and pure white lilies dotted the aisles and the altar. Everyone in the small choir smiled when they sang. It wasn't fair, she thought. The disciples had grieved for only three days before Christ rose.

"You seem angry," Joanne observed over lunch. "I was angry after Cam died. I was angry at him, actually. Of course he didn't ask to have cancer. Irrational, but there it is."

"What did you do?" Jenny asked, her heart nearly stopping in midbeat at Joanne's disclosure.

"Jillian wouldn't have understood," Joanne answered. "She idolised her father. Colin would have worried about me." She smiled. "So I started doing my own gardening. I ripped out weeds. I trimmed shrubs. To the ground! Have you noticed that the west side of the house is a bit bare of greenery? That's my doing. I went too far, and some of the plants never came back."

"I am angry," Jenny confessed. "Angry at the terrorist who killed him. At the doctors who couldn't save him. Please don't hate me, but I'm angry at Colin, too. I know it wasn't his fault and wouldn't have been his choice, but I keep wondering how he could have let it happen. He should have been thinking about me, about protecting me. And then I think about how selfish that sounds, and I feel guilty."

"I have something that might help," Joanne said. "Wait a moment."

She returned with a stack of ceramic plates. "I've been meaning to take these to Oxfam – they're old and some are chipped – but now I think you might have a better use for them. Come with me."

Together they went outside. "The west side of the house would be best, I think," Joanne said. "It's shielded from the road, and because of me, there aren't any shrubs to cushion the blows." She gripped a plate, took aim, and smashed it against the brick. She handed a plate to Jenny. "Now it's your turn. Throw it as hard as you can. If you don't, it won't break, and then it won't be satisfying at all."

Jenny's first plate didn't break. She retrieved it, stepped a little closer, and threw again, harder. This time she was more successful. She knew the plates were a metaphor – because she was the one who was broken – but the effort it took and the sound it made released something inside.

Joanne stood back. "They're all yours," she said.

Jenny threw even harder and faster, reaching the bottom of the pile in no time.

"Good job," Joanne said. "How do you feel?"

Jenny was panting. "Better. Calmer. Not as angry. But I've made a real mess."

"Not to worry. We'll leave it for now."

The morning service, the physical activity, and the effort it took to be social had exhausted Jenny. Since it was too bright in the conservatory, she dragged herself upstairs to nap. Neither the rest nor the light supper Joanne served revived her. "Joanne," she asked when they were clearing the table, "now that Colin is gone, am I still related to you? I don't think I could stand it if I lost Colin and you, too."

Joanne put her arm around her. "I'm so glad you came to me," she said. "I consider you my daughter. I have no intention of letting you go. Perhaps you should call me Mum."

Jenny hugged her back and for a few minutes couldn't speak at all.

When she took the train back to Hampstead later that week, she was wearing a bracelet that Joanne had given her. "A friend gave it to me after Cam died," Joanne had said. "I wore it round the clock; that's why some of the letters are a bit worn. I wasn't able to follow its instruction for quite some time." Jane Austen's prayer was engraved in the silver: "Teach us...that we may feel the importance of every day, of every hour, as it passes."

CHAPTER 15

Simon Casey was looking forward to the weekend. He and Marcia had plans on. He'd seen her several times since his injury, and so far things were going fine. She liked to have fun. She made him laugh. She wasn't put off by his unpredictable and demanding schedule; hers was time consuming as well. As a child, she'd always bandaged her dolls. Her parents had hoped to send her to medical school, but they didn't earn enough. Her dad was a Royal Mail postman, and her mum worked for an accountant. She hadn't come from a privileged background, and neither had he.

Her nursing experience had given her an easy confidence, and she was forthright about her likes and dislikes. The sort of films she preferred – fantasies, romantic comedies – weren't his cup of tea, but he wasn't particular about his entertainment. She wasn't much for cooking, so they ate out.

They'd been to the karaoke bar in her neighbourhood. "I'm not a singer," she said. "I just enjoy watching other people having fun trying. Some of them are quite good, and the rest are just funny. A few good laughs, and I'm less tense. Helps me to unwind." He would have preferred the pub, but the drinks were just as good in the bar.

She kept the conversation light, although she had told him that her long-standing boyfriend Adrian had broken it off with her recently. He was an actor – rather self-absorbed, she admitted – who had got a part in a New York play and left abruptly. Hadn't invited her along. Their two years together hadn't warranted even a discussion about his priorities.

Her sister, Abby, was an accessories buyer for a London department store. Simon had only met her once. Younger and a bit slimmer than Marcia, she had been on her way to a dinner meeting. Fortunately Marcia didn't wear that much makeup or dress that fancy.

Their physical relationship needed improving. The one time he'd suggested picking up some takeaway and going back to her flat, she had told him she wasn't ready for what she thought he had in mind. He and Amanda had slept together quite quickly. Marcia was more cautious, and he didn't know what she wanted or expected from him. He'd had to curb his impatience by reminding himself that she had lost a loved one. Not in the way Jenny had done, but suddenly nonetheless, and she was still smarting from the humiliation.

Davies was having a barbecue at the weekend, and he'd invited her to go. She kept pressing him to tell her more about himself, and perhaps meeting some of his mates would satisfy her questions.

He could make time for Marcia; Jenny was in Texas.

CHAPTER 16

Jenny had forgotten how hot it was in Texas. Even in mid-April, Houston temperatures exceeded those in London by twenty-five to thirty degrees. No wonder Texans liked their drinks cold! Unlike London, where a glass held little or no ice, the amount of ice in Texas glasses left little room for the beverage.

She went shopping with her mother for shorts and tank tops and then wondered why she should buy clothes that Colin would never see. She had thought she would miss him less in Texas, but when they went places he had never been, she ached for him all over again, wishing he were there so they could experience them together. He was a part of her, a part she would not excise even if she could, and her parents' urging her to move back to Texas fell on deaf ears.

She walked through her parents' house, noticing that her mother had already replaced the heavy winter bedspreads with striped, combed cotton seersucker ones for the summer, a different color in each bedroom. The aqua and blue covers reminded her of the blanket Colin had given her long ago, because he knew she was cold in the witness protection flat. He had been thoughtful, and now he was gone.

She looked for herself in the familiar surroundings but found reminders only of a stranger, the innocent child she had been. She was a grown woman now. Under the spell of sorrow, however, sometimes she felt helpless as a child.

She was delighted and a little relieved to hear from her college friend, Emily Richards, a fiery redhead with a personality to match. Emily had teased Jenny when she heard that Jenny planned to marry a British man, calling it the Sean Connery Syndrome. When Jenny had told her that Colin was a police officer, not a spy, she had laughed aloud at the idea that someone with a college degree would marry a cop. Her tune had changed when she met him. "Four stars," she had decided. "He's charming, elegant, has a sexy accent, and is handsome too. He should be in the movies."

Although Emily knew Colin had been killed, Jenny could count on Emily to keep the atmosphere light, and attending her cocktail party would give her a respite from her parents' earnest concern. Emily and her husband, Morgan, hadn't started a family yet, Emily still focused on her teaching and Morgan working long hours at a Houston law firm.

Two Jennys stood in Emily's split level living room, the exterior Jenny smiling, conversing, and sipping her drink. Large-paned double doors led to the patio and pool, where some guests had congregated. She spoke to several other college friends and was introduced to a number of people who worked with Emily or Morgan.

"Jenny went to school with me, but she lives in London now," Emily said, and Jenny parried the questions about her life in London by talking about what a wonderful city it was. Those who knew of Colin's death moved on quickly, however, as if Jenny's bad luck were a contagious disease they might contract if they got too close to her. Those who had attended her wedding had seen the scar on her cheek and understood its significance, but the new acquaintances seemed to be conspicuously not looking at it. Jenny had finally gotten so used to it that she often forgot it was there and disliked the surreptitious glances which reminded her.

The interior Jenny watched and didn't feel a part of the alcohol-induced merriment. She remembered the last party she had attended: to celebrate the retirement from the police service of one of Colin's colleagues. She had been dressed up, with a long coat to keep the London winter at bay, not in tonight's casual lightweight clothes. Colin had been by her side as they listened to the congratulatory speeches, instead of – What was his name? Ted? – who hovered at her elbow now. When the evening was over, they had gone home and made love. Three weeks later he was dead. The outer Jenny accepted a refill on her drink while the inside Jenny wondered if she could swallow it with the tightness in her throat. She wished herself back in her solitary life in London, where she did not have to pretend.

Laughter erupted in one corner of the room, Emily no doubt at the center of it, her capacity for carefree fun making her seem so young. Because her life was unfolding just the way she had planned, she believed she was in control of it. "Watch out," she teased as she breezed by Jenny on her way to the kitchen. "That's Ready Teddy who's plying you with liquor."

"What are you ready for?" Jenny asked the young man with a tan almost as dark as his brown eyes and hair.

"To entertain you," he answered smoothly. "If you like baseball, that is. I work for the Houston Astros, and I have tickets for Saturday's game. A group of us will be going. Will you join us?"

She had always liked baseball, even scoring some of the games, but she didn't have the concentration to do that now. The cocktail party was much shorter than an evening of baseball, and she was already exhausted. The fine line between the outer Jenny and the inner one was narrowing. Ted had been courteous and gracious, holding up more than his side of the conversation, but soon it would be evident that she was not functioning as well as others thought. A relationship was out of the question. She would visit her grandmother as scheduled.

"Thanks, but I won't be here then," she said as sincerely as she could and excused herself to say good-bye to the Richards.

"Thanks for coming," Emily effused. "I knew you wouldn't be dreary."

Jenny bit back her anger. She wasn't healed and whole. Why did everyone expect her to be? Later, trying to fall asleep in her room at her parents' house, she made a mental list: *Things I Know and Wish I Didn't*. *My grief has set me apart* was the first entry. *Friends can be cruel* was the next.

CHAPTER 17

Jenny was most relaxed when she stayed for several days with her maternal grandmother, whose husband had died when Jenny was in high school. Grandma Ellie's home in Clear Lake, southeast of Houston, smelled liked lavender, which Jenny found soothing. She resolved to buy some lavender soap when she got home.

Grandma Ellie's single-level house was large for one person, with multiple bedrooms and bathrooms, an in-house atrium and porch, and an open kitchen that folded into the dining and living areas. She hadn't let anyone talk her into moving, however. She wanted to be where Grandpa Ed had been, to work in her garden, to maintain her network of friends. She and Jenny worked jigsaw puzzles, played cards, and watched the birds at the birdbath. In spite of the shade provided by the trees, it was too hot to spend time in the hammock, but they made cinnamon bread, the only recipe worth using the oven for in hot weather, Ellie said.

"I feel disconnected, separate from everyone," Jenny told her. Ellie's auburn hair had faded to gray and then to white, but her gnarled hands were still strong, and she kneaded the dough with practiced ease. "And I don't think Mom and Dad understand. How did you stand it after Grandpa Ed died?"

"Everything was in a jumble for a while. You have to find

your own way, and it always takes longer than you want it to."

"Did you lose things? And then spend an inordinate amount of time looking for them?"

"Yes," Ellie laughed, "and then I'd find them in the most unlikely places!"

"How did you and Grandpa meet?"

"We'll set the timer to let the dough rise, and then I'll tell you," Ellie said. She filled Jenny's glass with ice and poured lemonade for both of them. "I was in nursing school," she remembered. "Ed had just come back from the war and was taking engineering classes on the GI Bill. We studied at the same library. I noticed him because he was tall, like your Colin."

Ellie and Colin had met on one of his Texas visits, and he had been charmed by her resemblance to Jenny in her stature and her smile.

"The other nursing students and I had a system for rating boys. We called it the R Factors: RT, RC, RS, and RN, for Real Tall, Real Cute, Real Smart, and Real Nice. We didn't go out with anyone who was just one R; two or more Rs we'd give a try." She laughed. "We always said that a 4R was MM: marriage material. We were all very silly and immature, and in the end I married your grandfather because I loved him and felt at home with him. Ed and Elinor, but he called me El. Of the four I think the Real Nice factor was the most important for an enduring and happy marriage, although if he hadn't been Real Smart, he couldn't have gotten the job at NASA."

Colin had been all four and more: real sexy, real strong, real tender. And he alone had called her Jen. "You can talk about him and laugh," she said wistfully.

"We had our disappointments. We both wanted a big family but had just your mother. We were married almost forty-five years, but in his later years his heart disease kept us from traveling the way we had hoped after his retirement."

"Colin and I wanted a large family, too."

"I'm so sorry, dear," Ellie said. The timer dinged. "Time

to roll out the dough and season it."

Jenny found the brown sugar and cinnamon in the pantry and watched while her grandmother added them to the flattened, buttered dough and rolled the dough into loaves. She nibbled the brown sugar crumbs that spilled out the edges.

"When the dough has risen in the loaf pans, we'll put them in the oven."

Thirty minutes rising in the pans, thirty minutes cooking, and ten minutes cooling before they upended the pans and rested the loaves on sheets of foil. Jenny's grandmother gave each of them a thick slice and took the butter out of the fridge. "Now we receive the reward for our hard work," she said with a smile.

Jenny took one bite and sighed with satisfaction. "Colin would have loved this. I wish I'd known how to make it."

"Now you do," Ellie said briskly. "Another slice? I'm having one more."

"Of course! It's too good to resist."

Ellie cut two more pieces. "We'll let the other loaves cool while I take my nap."

When Grandpa Ed had been diagnosed with heart disease, he had begun resting for an hour every afternoon. After he died, Grandma Ellie had continued to nap, saying it was a habit. Now Jenny suspected that she had wanted to keep doing the things they had done together. She wandered into the den and scanned the book titles on the shelves. Many referred to space and the solar system, which she expected, but an unusual number of others focused on the famous thirteen-day siege of the Alamo in 1836.

The Alamo's defenders, over two hundred of them, had fought to the death against General Santa Anna's 1,500 troops. The battle had been an inspiration to other Texans, and Texas, led by General Sam Houston, had won her independence just weeks later at the Battle of San Jacinto.

"Who was so interested in the Alamo?" she asked her grandmother when she woke.

"Your grandfather," Ellie answered. "It was always said in his family that they were related to one of the men who died there. As far as we know, only two of the Alamo defenders had children: William Daniel Hersee from England and Thomas Jackson, who was Irish. Ed was never able to confirm or disprove it, however."

"Then I might have some British blood in my veins," Jenny exclaimed. Colin would have been intrigued.

That night after her grandmother had gone to bed, Jenny thumbed through one of the books. Twenty-six men from Britain had died at the Alamo. They had been young, most in their twenties, the oldest only forty-one. Why had they left the cool temperatures of home for the heat of Texas? Why had they fought for someone else's independence? Was it significant that they had died fighting? Or just that they had died? Colin had been killed trying to keep others safe. RP: real protective.

On her flight home the next evening, a loaf of cinnamon bread in her carry-on luggage, Jenny thought about her trip. High temperatures, high humidity, but not a drop of rain. Colin would have missed the rain.

CHAPTER 18

Not long after Jenny returned from Texas, Beth invited her for dinner. Brian was on late turn, so Jenny came to their home in Rickmansworth, or Ricky, as the residents called it, northwest of London. The weather was beautiful, so she decided to take the tube from the Finchley Road station. With no sign of rain in sight, the longer walk from the flat didn't discourage her, and she could take the Metropolitan line straight to Ricky.

After their marriage, Brian and Beth had lived first in a flat on Nightingale Road while they waited for a house they could afford to become available. "Ours is the smallest on the street," Beth laughed, "but at least we're on the street!" True, the walkway behind the privet hedge to the front door left little room for grass, but the back garden was large enough for Brian's cookouts. The red brick trim that arched over the entrance was cheerful against the white stucco, and the first-floor bay window in Brian and Beth's bedroom gave a broad view of the quaint street. Their daughter, Margaret Lynne, whom they had nicknamed Meg, was almost a year old and already walking. Used to being the center of attention in her family, she was noisy, curious, and full of life.

"You've repainted," Jenny said. The living room walls were now a creamy blue with flowered print curtains over the windows and the dining room pale green with a floral border. Because of Meg, Beth was serving dinner in the kitchen, where the numerous windows let in the light and the pale yellow walls looked like the first rays of the rising sun.

"I wanted to bring some of the outdoors in. And make the rooms look bigger!"

Their families had given them most of their furniture, and the worn look made it cozy, but the coffee table was bare. "Where are your family pictures?" Jenny asked.

"I moved them to the mantelpiece. The less Meg can reach, the better." She took a chicken pie from the oven. "Promise you won't tell Brian?" Beth asked. "When he's not here, I give Meg prepared food. I don't cook from scratch, the way he does. How was your trip to Texas?"

"Strange. My friends are either advancing in their professions or raising their families or both. I spent a lot of time with my parents, but sometimes I got the feeling that they were at a loss to know what to do with me. And I couldn't get any UK news, except a brief report on the Queen Mother's funeral with a shot of all the people lining the streets. Nothing of much importance was reported in the Houston newspaper, just numbers that showed attendance down at the Astros baseball games and stories about other cyclists trying to implicate Lance Armstrong in drug use." She paused. "Some funny things happened, though. We went to a country French restaurant, and the waitress welcomed us by saying, 'Bonjour,' with a Texas accent and then asked, 'Do y'all want a menu or the buffet?'" She watched Meg bang her spoon on the highchair. Beth fed her with another spoon. "My mother made all my favorite foods: sugar cookies seasoned with nutmeg and rolled in powdered sugar, homemade Oreos, and lemon cake with lemon custard between the layers."

"All your favourites are sweet!" Beth laughed.

"Lots of Mexican food, though. Tacos, tamales, enchiladas, fajitas. All with guacamole."

"When I've finished feeding Meg, we'll have our dinner: leftover shepherd's pie that Brian made. Hope that's all right."

Jenny smiled. "My dad had shepherd's pie recently. We went to the Black Labrador, a pub in Houston, if you can believe it! It was fancy on the outside, with a red British telephone booth near the parking lot and a red door, but my kind of casual on the inside: bargain basement tables and chairs, no two alike. The food was terrific, though."

"Good girl, Meg," Beth said. "One more bite for Mummy."

"I had bubble and squeak, and it made me homesick for Brian's cooking. The first time he made that, I objected to the cabbage, and he said, 'Trust me. You won't taste the cabbage. It just holds the mashed potatoes together.' And I didn't. Their wow-wow sauce was good, too, but not as good as Brian's."

"Did they have British beer? I'll be ready for one when I get Meg down."

"Yes, I had a Boddingtons and then wondered why Colin liked it."

Beth looked up sharply. It was the first time Jenny had mentioned him. "Are you doing all right?" she asked. "We're worried about you."

"I miss him so much, and it doesn't go away. And I'm not sure where I belong now. I belonged here because I belonged with him, and now that he's gone, I don't know what to do. I feel lost."

"You still belong here," Beth said firmly.

"Everyone's moving on with their lives," Jenny commented, "even the wives of Colin's colleagues I used to shop or lunch with. My brothers, too. Matt's a sophomore in college now, majoring in computer science, and BJ's in his first year of law school. My family and friends seem to lead such innocent lives. I attended one of my dad's lectures on American history, and that made me sad. So much of history involves conflict, and that means fear and death for some and loss and grief for others."

Meg had spit out her last bite, and Beth wiped her mouth. Somehow Meg had gotten food in her hair. "It'll all come out in the bath," Beth laughed. She lifted Meg out of the highchair. "Let me give her a quick wash and a bottle and then we'll have our meal."

"I'll clean up here," Jenny said. She rinsed the tray on the highchair, swept the floor beneath it, and threw away the extra napkins Beth had used while feeding Meg. She found the shepherd's pie in the refrigerator and put it in the oven to warm. As she set the table for two, she remembered that at her flat, she only needed dishes and cutlery for one. Then she opened the small bottle of wine on the counter and poured herself a glass.

Beth brought Meg into the kitchen. "Give Aunt Jenny a kiss," she said.

Jenny hugged the little girl in the zoo animal pajamas and then gently handed her back to Beth.

"Back in two ticks," Beth said. "It doesn't take Meg long to get sleepy when her tummy is full of milk." When she returned, she looked at Jenny thoughtfully. "You're good with children. We miss you at school. Summer term doesn't end until July. Are you coming back?"

Jenny had enjoyed her time with the children. Hearing them speak had caused her to realize that her child – hers and Colin's – would have a British, not an American, accent. She had been delighted. Now there would be no baby. "I'm not ready yet. What's the news here?"

"I've got to know my neighbours," Beth answered while serving their plates and opening a bottle of beer. "The couple next to us – the ones in the pebble-dash house with trellises on each side of the front door – are empty nesters. The wife offered to watch Meg from time to time, and her husband gave me the history of the housing development. I didn't know I lived in Metroland!"

"Even Brian's leftovers taste good," Jenny said. "Metroland? I've never heard of it."

"In the late 1800's, the Metropolitan Railway – that's above-ground trains – extended their line out this way. In the early twentieth century, they set up a company to create housing and shops along the line so they'd have more customers. It was supposed to be a mixture of countryside and suburbia. Of course, we're served by the Metropolitan Underground now, but the name still fits. Poems have even been written about it."

"None that I studied," Jenny admitted. "What else is new?"

"The latest gossip? Simon has a real girlfriend. An A&E nurse, very outgoing. He brought her to Brian's last cookout, and we liked her. Reminds me of you in a way, some of her expressions. Tall and blonde, of course. Sometimes I feel we brunettes are the last to be noticed. He met her at hospital, when he was injured."

"I didn't know he was hurt. I've really been out of it," she said, trying to swallow her last bite of shepherd's pie past the constriction in her throat. "Is he okay?"

"You'd never know if he weren't! Brian says he's tough as nails. I don't think they're sleeping together yet, Simon and Marcia. That's her name: Marcia. They're relaxed with each other but still a bit reserved, if you know what I mean. More pie?"

"No, I'm replete. I'll have a little more wine, though."

Later Jenny wondered if she were always going to be doomed to experience happiness and sadness at the same time. She'd been happy to be with Beth and happy when Meg climbed in her lap, but so sad that she and Colin hadn't had a baby. She was happy that her brothers had a sense of purpose in their lives but sad because she couldn't imagine anything giving her that enthusiasm. She was happy that Simon had found someone, if he really had, but for some reason that made her feel more alone than ever.

CHAPTER 19

When Brian Davies saw Beth coming out of the loo, he smiled and propped himself on one elbow to get a better look. They both initiated sex, but wearing her black nightdress was one of her ways of letting him know she was interested. The other was chatting while they cuddled. She said it helped her to reconnect with him. He didn't need helping; he felt connected to her the moment he came through the door. On his ride home, the tensions from what he saw on the Job – guns, knives, drugs, children who were casualties of the choices that adults made, all the bad – fell away. Once home, he rarely referred to them. And a chat before lovemaking was only ever a bother if Meg woke and interrupted them. He liked feeling Beth's breath when she spoke, smelling her perfume, and thinking on what lay ahead.

She stretched out next to him. "I wish Jenny would come back to school. The children liked her, and she was good with them, but she says she's not ready."

He and Beth had known each other since they were children. She'd been his first love and he, hers. When she went to university and he to the police, he had thought it was over between them. He was as busy with the Met as she was with her courses, and upon graduation, she had returned to Norwich to teach. Some years passed before she found a teaching position in London and got in touch with him. It hadn't taken them long then to realise that they were still in love. She kissed his chest, which he liked. Not as much as when she kissed him other places, but he would never tell her to stop. He held her closer.

"Jenny had this and lost it. There's been no pleasure in her life since Colin was killed."

He recalled hearing the news. "Bad one today, boys," the duty sergeant had said. "Bomb near Bond Street Station. An unarmed officer tried to stop it but couldn't. Bomber dead. Don't know about the officer." Fortunately it had been on a week when Casey's team was spare, and three of them had headed to hospital as soon as they heard that the officer was Jenny's husband.

"That was a rough day," he said.

"Bri, if you were hurt or – or – "

She rarely brought it up, but he knew she worried. Since Sinclair's death, she had risen with him on even the earliest mornings and sent him off with a kiss. When he came home at night, she was unable to hide her relief. "Not going to happen, Bethie," he soothed. "Casey keeps us sharp. Makes us practise. We've got full kit. We're ready for most anything." On many operations the unexpected cropped up, but they were all experienced enough to adapt quickly. He never disclosed the problems to Beth, however, just the successes.

"I'd still have Meg, though, and that would keep me going. I wish Jenny had been pregnant when Colin died."

She'd regained her shape after Meg's birth, except for a slight roundness near her navel. She didn't like it, but he did. It put him in mind of what they'd done together. He put his hand under her nightdress and rested it on the spot.

"She can't have his baby now, but I can have yours," she whispered.

They had already decided to try for a second child, but because her life would change more than his, he had left the timing down to her. Now, as he thought on it, his heart skipped a beat. "Now? Tonight?"

She gave him a long kiss. "Yes. I love you, Bri."

She could still take his breath away. "Sshh then," he said. There was no more chat.

CHAPTER 20

Alcina had a new routine. When the lull came between lunch and dinner at the restaurant, she read the newspaper obituaries and drank ouzo. Just a swallow, of course, so Kosta wouldn't miss it. Sundays she was off. She bought the newspaper, but there was no ouzo.

So far her searches had not been fruitful. She had to assume that Sinclair's wife was still alive, but she had no idea where. She was an American. What if she no longer lived in London? Where had Sinclair lived?

She thumbed idly through the paper. Engagement and wedding announcements were listed, and many named the city where the groom lived. According to Sinclair's obituary, he had married Jennifer Jeffries in 1999, but she hadn't been married when she'd given her testimony, so the wedding must have taken place later in the year.

The library would have back issues of the newspaper.

On her first visit she covered May, June, and July. Her second visit yielded many marriage announcements in the months of August and September, but not the one she was seeking. Her lack of success irritated her. Having to use the library for her research irritated her as well. She had a computer, but the last time it had crashed, she hadn't had the money to repair or replace it.

On her third visit she found it: *Mr. C.T.D. Sinclair and Miss J.C. Jeffries*, the headline read. *The marriage took place between*

Colin Thomas Dowding Sinclair of Hampstead, son of the late Cameron James Rhys Sinclair and Mrs. Joanne Sheffield Sinclair, and Jennifer Catherine Jeffries, daughter of Mr. and Mrs. William Austin Jeffries, on...

She didn't read the rest. *Of Hampstead.* He had lived in Hampstead.

CHAPTER 21

The doorbell startled Jenny. She was expecting Simon, but since she'd been alone, every noise unnerved her. Father Goodwyn had told her that loneliness and anxiety were normal after the death of a spouse, but she hadn't expected to feel insecure in her own flat.

"You look nice," he said.

It was the first time a man had complimented her since Colin's death, and she was surprised the comment came from Simon. "You like my denim?"

"It's ruffly."

Flowers were sewn in stripes down the front, and there were ruffles around the neck and sleeves.

He held out a package. "For your birthday."

All day she'd heard a refrain in her head: widow at 27, widow at 27. She knew she was only one day older than the day before, but without Colin to celebrate it with her, age had become a weight. She set the package aside. "Simon, ever since Beth told me you'd been hurt, I've been afraid for you. Are you okay?"

"No limp. I'm healing."

She put her hand on his arm. "Are you sure? Could I see?"

He sat down on the sofa and pushed his jeans above his calf. To his surprise, her eyes filled with tears.

"Simon, if something happened to you, I couldn't stand it."

Her upset surprised him, and the irrational spark of hope he felt irritated him. "Jenny, I'm all right. The sutures have already been removed."

She smiled in spite of herself and wiped her cheeks. Anyone else would have called them stitches. "What happened?"

"Stepped on the wrong stair. The rotten one instead of the solid one. On a raid," he explained. Wanting to dispel the memory, he suggested that she open her present.

It was a book with blank pages, stark white. How could she soil them with black ink and black thoughts? "Thank you," she said, "but Simon – I need a book with instructions. A book that tells me what to do."

He accepted the beer she offered him. "You know what to do, I think."

"Are you going to tell me to get past it?"

He set the beer down and took her hand. "Jenny, the battle you're fighting – I've never fought it. And your mission isn't time bound. Don't you remember? Sometimes there's no quick fix."

"If my mission is to learn how to live without Colin, I don't want to."

"You've no other choice. We've all got to play the cards we're dealt. The only question is how."

"No kidding," she said with bitterness.

"Look forward, not back. There comes a time when looking back doesn't hold you back. Until then you've got to trust that it will be all right."

"I trusted Father Goodwyn. He wanted me to maintain social contact, so I went to Kent and then to Texas. But none of my Texas friends have even lost a grandparent, much less a husband. I felt more isolated with them than I do when I'm by myself."

"Jenny, you have the ability to pick yourself up and carry on. I've seen you do it again and again." He released her hand and drained his beer.

"Psychological stamina. That's what my old shrink

would call it, but I don't think I have it now."

"Resilience, yes. And I believe you do have."

"Simon, did you kill people? When you were in the Special Forces in the Gulf War?"

Her sudden change of subject surprised him, and it was a moment before he replied. "I did what my government asked me to do."

"Yes, but did you kill anyone? Was anyone in your unit killed?"

"Jenny, it was a war," he said slowly. "I used the weapons I was issued. The enemy used theirs. The winners woke up the next morning."

She sighed. She knew he had done brave and dangerous things, but getting a straight answer from him was like pulling teeth. "I'm trying to make sense of Colin's death. I didn't worry about him very much, not the way I worry about you. He didn't carry a gun. He didn't patrol the streets. He had an *office* job. He sat at a desk and talked to people or called them on the phone. I never expected him to be in any danger at all. I never expected him to die, and knowing who killed him doesn't help at all. Anyway, I wondered if you ever got used to it. Death, I mean."

He'd lost mates, and he wanted to lose this conversation. "I don't see how my experience can help," he frowned. A postcard on the table caught his eye. "Who's sending you NASA postcards?" he asked, picking it up.

"Simon – "

Dear Colin, it read. *I wore your shirt today, the blue one that matches your eyes.* He knew he shouldn't keep reading, but the sinking feeling in his stomach propelled him. *I still have all your clothes, except the suit you were buried in. It was my favorite, and I hated to let it go, but I wanted you to look your best. Love always, Jenny.* Mute, he looked up at her.

"Simon, stop looking at me like that. You're – x-raying me."

He had stared, that was true. He tried to soften his gaze. "What's this?" he asked, the anguish in his voice unmistakable.

"I want to stay connected to him," she whispered.

He shook his head. "Not like this, love. Not like this."

"Another beer?"

He refused to be diverted. "Use the book, Jenny. I can't be with you as often as I'd like now. As team leader, I have admin duties as well as planning and ops."

"And a girlfriend, Beth says. Simon, I'm glad. I wish you the best." She couldn't decipher the emotions that crossed his face. He hadn't hugged her, and she missed that, but he had remembered her birthday.

CHAPTER 22

During the summer Jenny tried with varying success to become better acquainted with the tenants on the other side of the building. Wilfred Stanley, the military historian, had bushy eyebrows that drooped over his horn-rimmed glasses. Rumpled, dull, and shy, he would speak a sentence or two and then correct himself before continuing. She imagined him storing in his chipmunk cheeks the tidbits of information he gathered. Gavin Baker was a BBC producer. A fashionably slim man in his forties, he wore expensive jeans that were the epitome of sloppy chic. He raised his eyebrows when he saw her, making her self-conscious about her t-shirts and worn denim. The pharmaceutical products salesman was rarely home. The others were too busy to make a dent in her time.

British Summer Time made the days seem interminable. Sometimes dark didn't cover the landscape completely until almost ten in the evening, and Jenny often saw children buying ice cream cones from the truck that traversed the main streets. Unlike Texas, however, it was never too hot to walk. The trees on the Heath shielded and shaded those who passed beneath.

Once, while walking through back streets on her way to the Heath, a vast, natural park near Hampstead with fields, forests, and ponds, she passed Fenton House, a seventeenth century private home now a property of the National Trust. She paid the nominal fee for admission and was surprised by the number of antique musical instruments displayed there, harpsichords, clavichords, virginals, spinets, and even an eighteenth century grand piano which didn't seem grand by current standards. Fireplaces must have been the only source of heat, because the attics were the only rooms without them. Almost every room had at least one window seat with a view of the garden below. She suppressed a giggle when she saw what the curator had placed on each chair that was not meant for visitors to use: a pine cone! She hadn't seen a pine cone since she had left Houston.

Her admission fee covered tours of both the house and the garden, but in the future, if she wished to see only the garden, entry would require just a deposit of two pounds in the honesty box. The garden alone was worth far more than that; there were holly trees, apple trees, and a plethora of flowers and flowering shrubs, all beautifully arranged in the landscape. Because it was in bloom, she recognized the lavender. She rested on one of the benches surrounded by yew hedges and decided that she could postpone her Heath visit. She had occupied more than enough time at Fenton House and had felt less lonely there than she often did on the Heath.

She found a grief support group at a nearby church and attended several sessions, although she didn't receive much comfort from them. The other widows had been married for many years before their loved ones had died. They had children, and most had grandchildren. When they told her that life had more in store for her, she thought they were insensitive to her grief. Weren't her feelings of loss and devastation at least as painful as theirs? She stomped home, too angry to be hungry, and started a new list, nearly stabbing the paper with her pen. *Why I'm Angry,* she titled it.

1. *Because someone killed Colin.*
2. *Because the world didn't stop when it happened.*
3. *Because Colin and I will never have a family.*
4. *Because the people who should understand, don't.*

5. *Because grief hurts.* Sometimes her throat and chest felt tight. When she cried for Colin in the night, her tears burned, and the muscles around her rib cage ached. Her head pounded.
6. *Because I'm so lonely.* She had lost more than a husband; she had lost a friend, lover, protector, companion, sounding board, cheerleader.

She returned to her work at the bookshop. She liked Esther Hollister, the proprietor, an ebullient gray-haired woman who considered each book a personal friend. Jenny kept the computer files up to date and helped with shelving new purchases, but the wailing of the sirens as they approached the nearby Royal Free Hospital interrupted her concentration and reminded her of her trip to St. Mary's on the day Colin had died. Esther lent Jenny a copy of C.S. Lewis' *A Grief Observed,* and told her to keep it as long as she needed. Jenny took it home but didn't open it. She was living her grief. She wanted to get away from it, not study it.

Somewhat against her better judgment, she acceded to Beth's requests and spent some time each week assisting at her school. Since her current energy level could not match that of the children, however, she was forced to limit the hours she volunteered.

Her family visited over the July 4 holiday to get away from the blistering Texas heat, so unlike the cool, wet days the British summer provided. The World Cup had just ended, and both England and the U.S. had lost in the quarter finals, but her brothers had watched the soccer games in spite of the odd hours of the broadcasts. They all joined Joanne, Colin's sister, Jillian, her husband, Derek, and their children in Kent. An Australian won Wimbledon, but Jenny and her family celebrated Texan Lance Armstrong's fourth Tour de France victory. Between meals too sumptuous for Jenny to consume and sports coverage on TV which held her attention only sporadically, Joanne took her aside to visit the graves of their husbands at the family cemetery. Colin's granite headstone had been delivered, and Jenny cried when she saw it. *Beloved husband of...*it read, but not *Beloved father,* and she grieved again her failure to conceive. A broken column had been carved in his father's stone, to symbolize his early death. Colin's bore a broken sword, because his life had been cut short. She and Joanne sat for a long time, shoulder to shoulder, hands entwined, neither wanting to leave her husband's resting place. "I like to think of them being together," Joanne said. "It helps."

Jenny began to use the journal Simon had given her. Her first entry was a list of things she missed about Colin.

1. *His physical presence.* Father Goodwyn could talk all he liked about Colin's spirit, but that didn't occupy the other side of the bed. Colin had held her, their bodies coming together, then parting. Sometimes they had walked hand in hand. The embrace of grief was too tight, and there was no warmth in it.

2. *His love of travel.* He had wanted to show her his country, so they had taken day or weekend trips to Cambridge, to Wales, and to the stone houses in the Cotswolds. In Scotland he had chuckled at her struggle to understand the accent. He had promised future holidays in Switzerland and France.

3. *Trying out new recipes on him.* "You're my guinea pig," she had said, and he had responded by informing her that because it was against the law in the UK to experiment on human beings, he would be forced to arrest her. She had not resisted.

4. *His smile.* His face lit up when he saw her. Now she studied the photos of him, wanting to memorize his features, the fine, straight nose, startlingly blue eyes, wide brows.

5. *The sound of his voice.* A deep baritone. He should have been a singer, she had told him.

6. *His thoughtfulness.* She still wondered why, on the day of his death, he had bought earrings for her.

7. *The sound of his heart beating.* It was the soundtrack when they made love: rapid and pounding, then slowing as it returned to its normal rhythm.

8. *Watching him dress.* He was such a handsome man and always so elegantly clothed.

9. Watching him undress. He was such a handsome man...

She sighed. She missed the future they would not share, too. He would never grow old with her. His wrinkles would never deepen, and his steps would never slow. Shakespeare had said, "Each substance of grief hath twenty shadows." She looked at her list and thought, Only twenty? She was just getting started.

The weeks passed, Jenny trying to deal with her new reality, but nothing she did changed anything in any meaningful way. She opened his drawers, seeking a connection with him, but seeing the cufflinks, coins, and sunglasses in one and the socks and underwear in another, accomplished nothing. His closet was filled with dress shirts, shoes, sweaters, ties, and suits. All she knew was that she wasn't ready to let any of it go.

The bed with the new spread was not where Colin slept, and the sweaters and jackets she bought stayed on their hangers while she wore the ones he had given her. No matter when she ate or what she cooked, he was not at the table. She tried to read but after starting the same page five times, set the book aside. When she watched TV, she remembered times when Colin had been more interested in her than in the program, and she had laughed when he put the remote out of her reach.

She tried to play cards, shuffling a deck and dealing a hand of solitaire. Solitaire, solitary, solitude; she put the cards down, never beginning the game. She opened one cabinet after another in the kitchen and stared at the contents but removed nothing. What next? The bedroom, where she lay down to wait for something, anything, to happen. For the day to turn into night. She felt like making a mark on the wall to keep track of the passing days, the way prisoners did who wanted to document their confinement. She had days when she didn't cry but no days when she didn't feel that her heart had been cut in two. She thought of grief as a fist that held her so tightly that its knuckles were white.

Simon came by occasionally. They often took walks on

the Heath, where Simon and Brian had taken early morning runs when they had been part of Jenny's witness protection team. She still remembered Colin outlining the Gunpowder Plot of the fifth of November, 1605, in which Guy Fawkes and his co-conspirators had attempted to assassinate King James I by planting gunpowder beneath the House of Lords. They then reportedly gathered on Parliament Hill to watch the Houses of Parliament blow up. Fawkes was discovered, however, and tortured until he revealed the details of the plot. He was then drawn and quartered, and citizens celebrated the King's safety. Jenny thought it was a particularly gory episode of English history, but effigies of Fawkes were still burned on bonfires every November.

Fortunately Parliament had resisted the efforts of developers, who, over the years, had wanted to build cottages and other types of housing on the Heath land. She had always loved the Heath, from the first time Colin had shared it with her. Now, however, the light high clouds and oceanic sky that spoke of carefree days mocked her – she who knew that hopes were destroyed as easily on sunny days as on dreary ones – and the lush landscape didn't enrich her. The poet Leigh Hunt had thought of the Heath as "silently smiling," but she thought the frequent showers washed away any smiles, the Heath's and hers.

The canopies of foliage were so thick along some of the paths that the sun could barely peek through, giving the horseback riders and bicyclists cool outings. Below the highest leafy branches, however, spots on the trunks testified to previous decay or damage from high winds, reminding her that she was not the only battered one. Families spread blankets on the fields near the ponds and picnicked. The voices of children, excited to see a butterfly or to play with their dog, carried on the light breeze. Other than those around the bathing ponds, there were no fences, which she liked, and countless benches. Her new mission: locating every bench and choosing her favorite.

"It's hard," she told Simon, "because there are so many, and because sometimes I walk right by them. Their presence doesn't register unless I force myself to say aloud,

'Look right. Look left. Look for the bench.' See? Here in Pryors Field they're spread apart. Some overlook the ponds, and others are quite a distance from the path. Many are memorial benches." She held his arm while they crossed the muddy, uneven ground and showed him the dedications, some with letters nearly worn away. "Sad, isn't it? This bench memorializes a young woman who died when she was 26."

Sometimes they talked the whole way, and other times they were quiet, but she felt calmer from the exercise. Once she asked about Marcia. She knew he was still seeing her. "Do you love her, Simon?" After a long time he said, "I fancy her."

CHAPTER 23

Everything Alcina learnt during the summer months made her angry. Her visits to Hampstead ignited it. The cars people drove, the flats they lived in, all looked luxurious. The women's handbags and shoes were expensive, and they shopped in the posh boutiques for more. Tourists with cameras and colour in their cheeks strutted up and down the streets, laughing and chatting in their loud voices, their arms heavy with carrier-bags. All with fancy clothes, worn without a care. What did they know of poverty? Of doing without? Of working to exhaustion and still not having enough? They ate their fill in the restaurants and cafés, while some days she had to sneak morsels from the kitchen at Kosta's to take the edge off her hunger.

Her anger grew and made her stronger. It sent the blood rushing through her body. It brought energy to her every step. It gave her purpose. It fuelled her. She liked the taste of it in her mouth.

She needed her anger. So far she had been unable to locate her prey. Hampstead was a larger community than she had expected, with street after street of residences. Her travel on the underground, although not at the peak travel times, ate into the few hours between the end of her lunch shift and the beginning of her dinner shift. Only on Sundays was she able to devote significant hours to her quest.

Where? Where? she stormed, her anger increasing the pace of

her steps. Would her prey shop at the Sainsbury's near Finchley Road? Or would she frequent the High Street? There was so much ground to cover between them.

Her energy flagged. Were all her efforts in vain? Perhaps her quarry no longer lived in Hampstead.

Determination, she screamed silently. She slapped her cheeks to make her blood rise and swore to herself that she would not quit until she had investigated every avenue, every possible place, every destination. She could not let doubt prevail. She would not.

Marcia didn't exercise, so Simon was glad for the walks he took with Jenny. Sometimes she cried on those walks, and he held her hand.

"I have a pulse," she told him, "but I feel more broken than alive. My concentration's still shot. And the sadness – it comes over me like a flash flood. Other times I feel like I'm stuck in quicksand and fighting not to go under." Always he wanted to comfort her further but felt Marcia wouldn't understand.

Someone needed to look out for Jenny. Most days she walked alone, and she wasn't as alert to her surroundings as she needed to be. The Heath Constabulary policed the area, but the twelve of them were too thin on the ground to maintain the safety of any specific individual. He should see her more often – her lack of awareness made her an easy target – but after his long hours on the Job and his time with Marcia, little was left.

On one visit the flat was a mess, all the furniture pushed to the middle of the sitting room and all the books and paintings on the floor. "I wanted a change but couldn't decide what," she said, "and I couldn't figure out if the pictures were askew or I was."

It made no sense to him. She shrugged when he offered to help her straighten up. "I don't know where I want anything. Anywhere but where it was, I guess." The sofa ended up on one wall, the two armchairs next to the bookcase, and nothing facing the fireplace. She left the walls bare, the naked picture hooks the only décor. She tried to make a joke of it – "Are we playing house?" – but neither of them laughed.

Once he found that the fruit in the bowl on the dining room table had moulded. "Artists paint arrangements like that," she said. "They call them 'still life.' Get it? It's an oxymoron. Still. Life."

Her bitterness surprised and disturbed him. Sometimes he found her mail unopened. Old dishes crowded the counters in her kitchen because she'd bought new ones and didn't have room for both. When he made tea, he discovered the milk in her fridge had gone off. She hadn't many tins in the larder. "Are you eating?" he asked.

"Are you the pantry police?" she had retorted. "I just don't have much appetite."

"Perhaps you should see Dr. Knowles."

"See a psychiatrist because my pantry isn't stocked to your satisfaction? I don't think so," she snapped.

He tried another approach. "You're taking Sinclair's death hard. It's worrying. You'd be worried about me if I were in your situation, wouldn't you?"

"If you were grieving because your husband had died, I'd have been worrying about you for a long time already," she responded, steel in her voice.

"Damn," he muttered. Women's emotions were a minefield.

She sighed and sank into a chair. "Simon, I'm sorry. I shouldn't belittle your concern. But – he was my *husband*. His death was sudden. I loved him, and I miss him terribly. I'm sad and tired, but that isn't crazy. I'm pretty sure it's normal."

He left it.

On another afternoon, he vented his frustration about the Job, and she opened a bottle of wine and drank with him. "We take as many baddies off the streets as we can, but more take their place. We've raided different locations and found the same scum we cuffed before. They've been bailed or not convicted or not even prosecuted. We're not making a difference."

She refilled his glass as well as her own.

"It's like a mutant octopus," he said, "with tentacles everywhere. We hack away at them, but they just grow back." He drained his glass. Wine went down easily. "The suits add the numbers up," he continued, "and the numbers show that crime is rising, so we must not be doing our job. It's rubbish. Bloody rubbish." Marcia wasn't much for serious chat, and it felt good to get things off his chest with Jenny.

"Simon, give me your hand." She held it, palm up, and rubbed her fingers across it.

He had done that for her many times. Had any other woman done, he would have kissed her. Wrong thing to do, he told himself. Wrong for her. She still wore her engagement and wedding rings. Wrong for – Marcia.

CHAPTER 25

Success, Alcina thought. Was it too early for her to think of her mission in terms of success? No, because success was built step by step with small achievements leading to a glorious and gratifying conclusion. Her first success was learning of Sinclair's death. It had required little effort on her part, but she would take credit for it nonetheless. Second, her focus and dedication had led to her discovery of his city of residence. Next – she smiled with grim satisfaction – as a result of her perseverance and resolve, she had seen her quarry.

Her quarry had been alone and seemingly unaware of the presence of others on the pavement. Her hair was longer and she was thinner, and at first Alcina hadn't been certain of her identity. Then the breeze had blown her hair, and she had seen the scar on her cheek and known she had found the one who had spoken lies and destroyed her world. A chance encounter? No, it was meant to be. An important piece of the puzzle had slipped into place: Her quarry was alive and living in Hampstead.

Success never came singly, but Alcina knew she would not have come this far if she had not been determined, if she had not persisted in her quest. She smiled again. What wonderful qualities she was cultivating in herself, qualities that were certain to move her forward.

Now, however, she must plan. She needed to spend more time in Hampstead. She didn't earn much from the lunch shift at

Kosta's. She would continue to work the dinner shift there, but she would look for a day job in Hampstead.

CHAPTER 26

Summer turned into fall, and with it came the anniversary of September 11. The Queen attended a service of remembrance at St. Paul's Cathedral, and at the U.S. Embassy in London, the American flag flew at half mast. Jenny wondered if she should describe herself as "flying at half mast."

She remembered the shock and horror of that day, and no matter how many times she saw the twin towers crumbling, she was still moved. The two one-minute silences observed across Britain to mark the times when the hijacked airplanes hit didn't seem long enough for the scope of the tragedy. And why silence? Was silence the way she should honor Colin on the anniversary of his death? If so, she honored him already, because the flat was always silent.

She now shared the heartbreak of the families of the 9/11 victims. They of all people understood how deep and enduring was the suffering caused by sudden death and the injustice when innocent people were struck down. Were they healed after one year? Seven months since Colin's death, and she wasn't. Did they also feel that nothing worse could happen to them than already had? Did they feel guilty for being alive? Were they angry at the unfairness of it all?

The newspapers were full of articles about terrorist alerts. Clearly both the British and American governments expected an incident to occur, and fear rose in her throat. As she knew from Colin's death, it took only one crazed fanatic to cause panic and anguish. Was that why the hairs on the back of her neck stood on end sometimes as she walked the Hampstead streets?

The anniversary of her attack came, and with it, Simon's call of support, which touched her, because no one else remembered. It had been four years, after all, and although she still bore the scars, its consequences no longer ruled her life as they once had. Those dark clouds had been replaced by others, her grief for Colin the most constant and intense.

When he was alive, it had never occurred to her how large the flat was, but now it seemed as titanic as her sorrow. Shortly after she and Colin decided to have children, he had purchased the apartment building, or block, as the Brits called it, where they lived. The flats on the east side were smaller than those leased by the tenants on the west, but remodeling had customized the floors to suit Colin and Jenny's needs. Colin's car was parked in the basement, and the ground floor held two guest bedrooms, both en suite, and the utility room. An expanded kitchen, dining room, living room, and guest bath filled the first floor. The second floor was home to a spacious master suite and two smaller bedrooms, intended for the children, with a bathroom in between. All the rooms had wainscoting separating wallpapered and painted walls, except the kitchen, where Jenny had wanted pale blue paper with branches bearing tiny red apples from floor to ceiling. The public rooms were shades of ivory, but other pastels had been used in the bedrooms.

Every room reminded her of her loss, so she spent as little time there as she could, increasing her time at the school where Beth taught and at Hollister's Books. After school she stomped past the four-story buildings on Heath and Hampstead High Streets, no longer noticing their varying shades of red or taupe brick. In some places the sidewalk was wide enough for the cafés to set a few outdoor tables and chairs, but she did not stop. She was still angry at everyone who had hurt Colin, including herself. Up Spaniards Road and through the Heath she went, all the way to Spaniards Inn. Other times she trudged up South

End Road, the walkway darkened by plane trees, and through South Hill Park. When she walked past the ponds, she watched raindrops blend and disappear on the surface, much as the world absorbed her grief without a ripple.

Once she wandered down Church Row past the succession of Georgian houses, their brown bricks reminding her of rye and pumpernickel toast. Each window was trimmed with the orange red of apricot preserves. At the end was the parish church of Saint John-at-Hampstead, its clock tower and Roman numerals reaching toward heaven and the building surrounded by a cemetery shaded by the branches of ancient trees. The atmosphere was cool and peaceful, but Jenny felt a pervasive sadness. Many of the gravestones were tilted, no longer straight and proud, and their inscriptions were nearly worn away. Others were covered with moss or nearly lost in the underbrush. Joanne would never allow Colin's grave to look so neglected, so forgotten.

Colin had liked Hampstead, partly because the name came from the Old English word for homestead and also because the trees and ponds on the Heath reminded him of his boyhood home in Kent. He had introduced her to it early in their relationship.

She also liked the Heath. Like the feelings of grief she could not curtail or control, the park was wild and unmanicured. The seasons came and went, but outside the natural cycle, time stood still there, captured among the trees. When she had been confined to the witness protection flat, Colin had encouraged her to look beyond its walls, explaining that freedom was found in one's spirit, not one's surroundings. Now she was free to go anywhere she pleased, but her spirit was imprisoned by sorrow. No matter how far she walked, she did not find release, and returning to the flat meant passing numerous Georgian houses with chimneys on both sides of the roofs and shutterless large symmetrical windows on the main floors. Seeing those homes irritated her, because she was unable to attain the balance or equilibrium in her own life that the architectural design reflected.

Their work done, Casey's team hit the pub. Today's specials were listed on a chalkboard to the right of the bar, but they hadn't come to eat. They needed to release some of the tension that built up on the Job. Regulars by now, they didn't have to tell the barman what they drank. He filled glasses from the array of bottles on the wall and handed them over. No table service was offered in the small rooms, so Davies collected the first round, Moe the second, and Traylor the third. When the others topped off and headed home to their families, Casey moved to a stool by the curved bar and drank alone, not so much from thirst as from a need to fill the time. Marcia was on at hospital until late; they wouldn't see each other tonight. His flat? He was not drawn to it.

Lately he and Marcia had rented films, Marcia having decided to fill in the gaps in his entertainment education. Most were chick flicks she liked. No matter – it was worth it for what came after. Watching the girl get the guy made her happy. Probably a message there, because she wanted him to meet her parents. He'd put her off, not certain he was ready for that. At a nod, the barman pulled him another pint. On the other hand, it couldn't do any harm, could it?

He recalled the first time they'd made love. She'd worked extra hours and confessed that she was so tired of being on her feet that she'd taken a cab home. He'd removed her shoes and massaged her feet, then her calves. She had leant forward and kissed him. "I promise not to let your feet touch the floor," he had told her. "Sounds good to me," she said. He thought it had been good for both of them.

He took another swallow and looked about. Framed football posters covered every inch of space and made the pub feel crowded even when it wasn't.

He hadn't told Marcia about Jenny. Nothing to tell, really; he hadn't kissed her. And it had been some time since he'd seen her. He rang her mobile and told her he wanted to call by.

"I'm not home. I'm walking. I just left the Heath."

"Jenny, it's after dark. Not safe."

And raining, but gently, a rain that distorted the landscape, elongating the limbs of the trees and making them look as ungainly as she felt. She wanted rain that would sting her face, rain that would cause an external pain to counter what she felt inside. "It gets dark too early, and the flat is as empty and quiet as the North Pole."

His in Ruislip as well. When he'd first moved to the London area, he'd taken the first flat available, planning to find a better one when he had time. But as the months passed, he'd discovered that since he used it so little – just for stowing his gear and getting a little kip – upgrading made no sense. It was still as small and stark as when he had let it. "Go home, Jenny. I'll meet you there."

He arrived before she did and waited outside on the stoop.

"The street lights make the wet pavement shine, but it's poor compensation for always having to carry my umbrella," she said.

"How far away were you when I rang?" he asked as they went in together.

"The farthest I've been. I didn't have anything to hurry home for, so I explored the West Heath. It was nearly deserted, but the Hill Garden and pergola were beautiful."

He raised his eyebrows.

"I had to look it up in the dictionary after I read about it," she laughed. "A pergola is like an arbor, but large enough for you to walk beneath the arches. The one on the Heath has an elevated walkway, with roses and wisteria hugging the stone columns. The view is beautiful, quite a contrast with the wild woods around it."

"You walked all that way in the rain?"

"The rain stopped and started, but it was dry when I reached Golders Hill Park. There were more people there, because it has a bandstand – no music today, however – and a small zoo. And a pub nearby with a typical British name, the Old Bull and Bush. They have a big bar, of course, but what caught my eye while I drank my coke was the wallpaper – bulls in all kinds of action poses. Reminded me of Texas. Would you like a beer?"

"Coffee will do."

"I read an article recently that made me think of you," she said as she made coffee for both of them. "Something about the Special Boat Service having its image brought up to Special Air Service standards."

He laughed shortly. "To qualify we had to pass their selection and then ours. We never felt we were second class citizens. And we never sought the limelight. We didn't need others to recognise us to be proud of what we did."

"Did you jump off a diving board blindfolded? Wearing all your equipment?"

"Where'd you get that?"

"The newspaper, Simon. It also said you had to swim for two miles, canoe five miles at night, and then march for thirty. Compared to that, being a policeman must be easy."

"We carry firearms, love. And face low-lifes who do also. There's risk."

She watched him finish his coffee. He always took it black. "Do you miss it, Simon? The SBS?"

He paused. "I've been a copper a while now, and what I do is useful."

She set her cup aside, having barely sipped any of the coffee. "I miss Colin. At night the most. I miss having someone to talk to when I'm afraid."

"What are you afraid of?"

She shrugged. "Nothing specific, but sometimes when I'm running errands and stuff, a creepy feeling comes over me, like something bad is about to happen. It isn't a sudden fear, more a sense of something not being quite right. I just feel like I should get out of there, wherever I am. So I come back here and then feel suffocated and head out again."

She was jumpy now, clasping her hands in her lap and then unclasping them. He joined her on the sofa. "Jenny, the anniversary of 9/11 wasn't too long ago, and the danger's not yet over. It wouldn't surprise me to hear that many Americans living abroad feel the need to look over their shoulders." She crossed her legs, and he noticed that her socks weren't matched.

"It feels more personal than that, but maybe it isn't. I spent months being afraid of the man who attacked me, so maybe I'm more easily frightened than most people. And I know it sounds crazy, but being married to a policeman made me feel safer. Now the only police officer protecting me is the teddy bear Barry Bridges gave me. Remember? The one in the constable's uniform. It's silly, but holding onto him helps."

She'd closed her hands into fists. He took one, uncurled the fingers, and laced his through hers. "If you see someone suspicious, you'll ring me?"

She smiled. "Thanks, but I can't go running to you every time I feel afraid. I have to learn to take care of myself."

In the past he would have approved her desire for independence. Now, however, he felt a pang of regret.

A dilemma. Look for a job on Finchley Road or the High Street? Alcina visited both. Finchley had larger commercial establishments and might be more likely to have job openings, but the High Street was more posh. Sinclair had had four names and sufficient income to live in Hampstead. She chose the High Street.

A challenge. She walked up one side of the High Street, up Heath Street, and back. Many posh boutiques, but she couldn't apply for a job at any of them. Their closing hours would not allow her enough time to arrive at her evening job at Kosta's. Also, she would be confined to the shop for long periods and thence unable to continue her reconnaissance.

Where then? Again she marched up one side of the street and down the other. Cleaning establishments would need few employees. Restaurants might have openings for an experienced waitress, but her target would be unlikely to dine alone and thus might not ever enter. A bookshop? She had always been too impatient to read, so she had never developed skills that would qualify her for employment at a bookshop.

The newsstand: one worker. The chemist? She saw two, both elderly but robust. Post office. No. Charity shoppes? She smiled bitterly. She was more suited to be a customer there than an employee. Florist? She had never arranged or sold flowers; in her better days she had received them. The retail shop which sold primarily kitchen items was so crowded with merchandise that she would not be able to watch the street.

She had time for one more circuit. Restaurant, cleaners, boutique, restaurant – no, not a restaurant. A bakery. Bakeries opened earlier in the morning than other establishments and closed earlier in the afternoon. There were several bakeries in Hampstead. She must remember to smile when she applied.

CHAPTER 29

During October, Jenny continued her exploration of the Heath and its hundreds of benches. Some were in need of repair, with slats missing that allowed the wind to caress her back. Some showed the wear of frequent visitors, the movement of a multitude of feet preventing the grass from growing nearby. Others were clearly not used, because the overgrown blades that surrounded them nearly obscured them. Memorial benches with epitaphs like "So many happy hours spent here" saddened her. Leaves crackled under her feet as she walked. The reds and yellows were the most recent casualties of the season, too new to have begun the process of decay.

The Heath attracted all kinds of people: birdwatchers, landscape photographers, athletes, artists, even swimmers, or as the British called them, bathers. Naturalists looked for mushrooms or catalogued types of trees. In some seasons a croquet club held games, and art or amusement fairs occasionally occupied a portion of the park.

One Sunday she passed people engaged in tug-of-war games. In another area she saw a gathering with individuals holding dark brown objects hanging from strings. Conkers, she was told, another name for the seed of the horse chestnut tree. No tampering was allowed: It was against the rules to boil, roast, or alter the conker in any way. The competition appeared to be purely offensive, since one player had to let his conker dangle while the other swung his and tried to crack his opponent's.

She surveyed the faces of the contestants and saw tension and anxiety, absorbed concentration, and sudden, wide smiles when an attack was successful. All ages were represented, and even the spectators were having fun.

She tried to remember the last time she had done something light-hearted and playful and couldn't. Colin would have known all about conkering, or whatever the game was called, and would have laughed with her when she teased him about the odd pastimes of his countrymen. She walked on.

Once she passed a bench where a little boy, ten years old or a small eleven, sat with an older woman, perhaps his grandmother. She had never seen a child so dejected or so still. The kids at Beth's school were always in motion, swinging a foot or twirling a lock of hair, even during silent reading or exams. She paused, curious but not wanting to intrude, as the grandmother took his hand and coaxed him to walk with her by the ponds. "The ducks will be there. You always liked the ducks, didn't you?" The boy, his blond hair so light it was almost translucent, looked up, showing eyes as blue as Colin's, but his face was blank, and he didn't answer. He stood stiffly and walked with halting steps, and Jenny wondered what could make a child so lost and so sad.

She stayed away from Parliament Hill; she and Colin had shared too many afternoons there enjoying the panoramic view of St. Paul's and other London landmarks. Instead she wandered down the wide trail that led to the Viaduct Pond, or as the locals called it, the Red Arches, because red brick had been used to construct them. Ducks with green heads and others with multi-colored plumage barely disturbed the surface of the water, and no one seemed to notice that she perched on the bench for long periods without doing anything. She had no dog, no human companion, and no reading material, only the ruminations of her mind. Could external peace bring internal peace? Why had no one told her, as Oscar Wilde had written, that "the brain can hold /

In a tiny ivory cell / God's heaven and hell?" Where were the birds she could hear but not see? She occasionally found a feather. Birds, unlike people, could lose a part of themselves without pain.

She watched the skies weep and wondered if the ground beneath her feet would begin to shudder as it had in Manchester, where fifteen earthquakes had been reported in a twenty-four hour period. Her mood was unsettled, too, the chilling gloom in her spirit matching the news bulletins describing the IRA's resistance to peace and the victims of a serial rapist who was still at large. When it rained, she shielded herself with her umbrella but didn't leave her bench. In the States benchwarmers were extra players who didn't get into the game. Was she doomed to spend her life on the sidelines?

She started her walk back to the flat. The rain was cold, falling gently but unceasingly. Some parts of Britain had experienced storms so severe that people had been killed by falling trees. At least Colin hadn't died that way, she thought, as she zig-zagged around the puddles on the gravel path. She wished the downpour would dull her senses the way it dulled the surroundings. When the rain stopped, stray drops, like residual tears, fell from the branches as she passed by.

Not far from Heath Street, she heard a child crying, and his sobs threatened to shatter her fragile composure. Was it the blond boy with his grandmother? No, he had not walked in this direction. She took a deep breath and looked for a distraction. Ah – a bakery. Surely it wouldn't matter if she indulged her sweet tooth occasionally by purchasing a chocolate croissant or cookie, and it would calm her. Nevertheless, her conscience must have bothered her because her stomach felt queasy as she stood by the counter. The owner, who was round all over, packaged her selections quickly, while his equally rotund wife served as cashier. A tall woman, thin and somber as Jenny, brought trays of fresh bread and rolls and placed them on the shelves for the customers.

She continued her walks, not caring whether the sky

was sunny or cloudy, but always weighed down with her umbrella. Sunshine in the morning was no guarantee of a rain-free afternoon. The British sun didn't stare, the way it did in Texas; it blinked. Some days the breeze was mild; on others crisp gusts of wind nipped at her cheeks. People walked their dogs in all kinds of weather, but clear days were needed for the kites. Until Colin's death, she had liked watching families fly kites. Now watching shared fun – and seeing kites soar when her life had crashed – hurt. The snatches of conversation she heard reminded her that others were not alone, and the laughter and happy chatter of children saddened her because she had no children.

A vague sense of uneasiness kept recurring, like a candle she couldn't blow out. Was it the knowledge that she was on her own that made her feel so vulnerable? Colin had always known what to do, and she had even teased him by saying that he wouldn't have made detective if his reassurance quotient hadn't been so high. And now he was gone and the reassurance she needed was gone with him.

Streets which had once had a gentle slope now felt steep to her leaden feet, and the sun, that deceptive orb, gave no warmth. Coming down the High Street one Sunday afternoon, lost in thought, a pedestrian bumped into her, hard, knocking her to her knees. Usually Londoners were solicitous in these situations, but this individual didn't stop or even slow, much less apologize.

"How rude!" said a young woman pushing a stroller. "Are you all right?"

"Yes, thanks," she answered, feeling ruffled and ridiculous as she picked up her purse and gathered the contents which had spilled out. She couldn't even have described the person: someone tall in a raincoat and hat was her only impression, and when someone her height described a person as tall, it wasn't very useful.

On other walks she felt a nervousness that ebbed and flowed like a tide. Sometimes walking faster helped. Once she stopped and looked at the people on the street: more women than men, and none of the men seemed to have any interest in her. In the evenings she watched smoke from the chimneys rise into the sky. Sometimes the wind dispersed it the way a child blew out a birthday candle; other times it hung over the houses like a shroud.

One particularly dark evening, the flashing blue lights of police cars lit up one of the larger, more upscale residences several streets away from her flat. As she walked closer, she spotted several officers in the lane. "Danny?" she said. "What are you doing here?"

One of the men turned and smiled. "I'm on IRVs now – immediate response vehicles." It was PC Daniel Sullivan, a former member of her witness protection team. At age 22, he had been the youngest as well as the most lighthearted and least officious policeman she had met. "Two adult males in hooded sweatshirts accosted the female resident as she locked her car. One grabbed her handbag, and the other demanded her jewellery. She's shaken up but all right. What are you doing out after dark?"

"Passing the time, Danny."

"I'll walk you home. Back in two ticks." He spoke to another officer and returned. "We've had several calls to this area. There's concern that the frequency and force will escalate. I wouldn't like to be called to your flat, Sis."

She smiled upon hearing the nickname and asked about his real sisters.

"Samantha's still working as a hairdresser. She has a partner, but she tells Mum and Dad that they're engaged. Gemma finished secretarial school and has a job at one of those fancy financial offices. My younger sister, Gwennie, works at a library. A shy Sullivan, if you can believe it! I told her she'd never meet any blokes there – all the men in libraries are either old or dull."

"Do you have a girlfriend?"

"Lots! No one special, though." His smile dimmed. "Sis, I want you to promise that you'll not walk alone at night. It's not safe."

Simon had said the same thing, but she hadn't paid any attention. She liked the embrace of darkness; a cruel embrace but an embrace nonetheless. "Danny, I have so much time on my hands."

"Rent films then. Stay home and lock your doors."

She noticed that he wasn't armed. "Where's your gun?"

"I'm not an authorised firearms officer anymore, Sis. I decided I didn't want to carry a firearm so I didn't keep up with the training."

"Because of what happened to us?" When she had been shot at the courthouse prior to her testimony, he had been, too, and his injuries had been far more serious.

"I saw what guns can do, and I don't want any part of it. Unarmed policing is a bit of fun. I'm better suited to it." They had arrived at her door. "Now promise."

She promised and hugged him.

In the days that followed, she limited her walks to the daylight hours and rented movies as he had suggested. They helped to pass the time, because she still didn't have the concentration to read. She had tried books set in a different time or place, but reading about fictional characters didn't help her, because their lives all seemed to follow a plan, while she felt aimless and unmoored. On Simon's next visit, she told him about Danny's advice. "I don't rent romances or anything with a Pollyanna ending."

"Some of these I wouldn't mind viewing," he said, picking up *Saving Private Ryan, Courage Under Fire,* and *The Matrix.*

"I haven't gotten to those yet. I liked *Billy Elliot. G.I. Jane* I couldn't watch – she was raped. In *Castaway* Tom Hanks was stranded on an island. I have all the creature comforts, but even in his deprivation, he seemed more alive. That's my life now: pause, rewind, stop."

He saw a bed pillow and rumpled blanket on the sofa in the living room. "What's this?"

"I sleep here most nights now. The bed upstairs is too big for one person. And lonely, hence my teddy bear."

He looked up sharply. Was that an invitation?

She gave him a sheepish smile. "I guess I'm feeling a little sorry for myself."

"You've a right."

"Maybe so, but I don't want to be that way. I just can't seem to stop missing him, though."

Damn. First because she still missed Sinclair and also because he still cared. We're cut from the same cloth, he thought. Both wanting what we can't have.

CHAPTER 30

Alcina's appetite had been whetted. Her one encounter with her quarry – who hadn't even seen her coming! – had been satisfying, but she wanted another. Wait, she told herself. Biding her time would make her stronger. Delay is not defeat. Time would only make her object even more complacent. Alcina would use that false sense of security against her. She could do it. Their collision hadn't been planned, but it had taught her that she could improvise, that she was capable of acting on the spur of the moment. An important quality to have. Hadn't someone said that battles rarely went exactly as intended?

She had also confirmed that her target was weak. It had taken only a bump to bring her to her knees. She wished she could have witnessed her target's distress, but allowing herself to be seen was dangerous. Attracting attention was not wise. It was too soon, much too soon, to reveal herself. She must give no clue about who she was and what lay ahead.

CHAPTER 31

Simon's evening with Marcia's parents got off to a slow start. She had warned him that her dad might be a bit gruff; he was more protective of her since Adrian's desertion. "He'll introduce himself as Walt and my mum as Frances, but he'll be reserving his judgement."

"Not to worry," Simon said. "He's doing what he ought."

Simon brought flowers for her mother, something that Adrian, even with his flair for the dramatic, had not done. Frances, neither as blonde nor as slim as her daughter, placed the bouquet in a vase in the sitting room where it provided a bit of colour in the otherwise neutral space. The muted green sofa and patterned armchairs were comfortably upholstered, and Simon, who had dressed conservatively in khaki slacks, a dress shirt, and a jacket, accepted a beer but waited to seat himself until Marcia's mum had done.

"You and Marcia met at hospital," Frances began. "Do injuries occur often?"

"Not as often as you would expect," Simon answered. "Our work is inherently dangerous, but our training is the best, and we're well aware of the importance of safety procedures."

"Don't like firearms," Walt said abruptly, shifting his bulk to be more comfortable in the chair across from Simon.

"They're needed on some ops," Simon responded in his

usual terse way and then seemed to realise that a fuller answer was called for. "We're mindful of the fact that we carry loaded weapons. Show-offs or officers with a complacent attitude don't qualify for our unit."

"Not satisfied with being a regular copper?"

"I like a challenge, sir," Simon said evenly. "Mars and I both do."

Marcia liked the nickname Simon had given her, although they weren't as close as the affectionate appellation implied.

"Fond of films, are you?" Walt asked in a brusque tone.

"Dad!" "Walt!" Marcia and her mother objected almost simultaneously. The last thing Marcia wanted was for her dad's demeanour to drive Simon away.

"Not a problem," Simon said, placing his hand over Marcia's. "Sir, I'm not much for films. I've very little recreational time."

Frances, relieved that the conversation had not escalated, headed for the kitchen. Walt nodded a grudging approval at Simon. He had never been sold on Adrian's charm or choice of career. "He's not on stage here," he'd grumbled. "Ought to tone it down. Damn firefly. Only ever loves himself."

"My hours may look reasonable on paper," Simon continued, "but if a call comes in, we're obligated to answer it regardless of the time we've already spent on duty. Marcia's the same: If she's needed beyond her shift, she stays. I respect that about her."

Adrian had always downplayed the importance of her work, Marcia recalled. Only his world of make believe had been real to him, and she had never been certain that his romantic declarations were true or if he simply wanted to hear himself recite the lines. She had been so flattered when he had drawn her into his circle; now she wondered why he had. Had he valued the stability she provided? She had been an emotional as well as a financial anchor for him. No, she thought bitterly, her gullibility had been the key. She had given him power over her self-esteem, and his sudden and heartless departure had destroyed it. Perhaps that was why she still hurt. The tortoise and the hare: Simon, the cautious and steady one, and Adrian, rushing headlong without thought or care.

Simon rose to his feet. Was he leaving? Had her dad's bristly demeanour offended him? No, her mum had just entered the room.

"We'll eat in the dining room," she said.

Perhaps the more restful ambiance in the dining room – wood paneling with a soft peach tint above – would soothe her dad's feathers, Marcia hoped.

"Fisherman's stew," Frances announced. Marcia had told her that Simon always ordered seafood when they went out.

"*Cioppino,*" Simon exclaimed. "My favourite. My mum used to make this, but she never used as much seafood. Scallops and clams as well as fish – you have outdone yourself, Mrs. Collier."

"Do you speak Italian?" Marcia asked, surprised by his use of the foreign term.

"I know a few Italian words. *Buon appetito.*"

They laughed, but knowing his tendency to understatement, Marcia suspected that he had quite a vocabulary and resolved to ask him more about his facility with languages later on.

The stew was accompanied by a salad of mixed greens and thick, crusty bread. Over the meal, Simon continued to allow himself to be interrogated. He answered Frances' queries about growing up in Penzance and mentoring his younger brother. Walt wanted to know about Simon's days in the Royal Marines.

"Were you in combat?" he asked bluntly. "In dangerous spots?"

Simon paused. "Sir, we've women here. I'll just say that when I'd finished reviewing in my mind what would be expected of me and how I would respond, I thought on other things. We were outdoors. Often the nights were clear. I lay under the stars and learnt to recognise the constellations. It helped to focus on things that could last."

As the dinner progressed, Marcia watched Simon give his full attention to her mum and then to her dad, which Adrian had never done. He had sought attention, not shared it, and sulked when he didn't receive it. Why had she been so enamored with Adrian? He had been tall and handsome, with a magnetic personality, but Simon was courteous and patient. Worthy of trust. She wished she could love him without reservation, but Adrian had taught her how dangerous that was.

Before they left, Walt, nudged by Frances, shook Simon's hand.

"You'll be careful, won't you?" Frances asked.

"I will that," Simon answered, giving her a quick kiss on each cheek. "And thank you for having me."

On their way home, Simon seemed preoccupied. "Nice family," he finally said.

"My dad was rude to you!"

"He didn't shoot at me," Simon smiled. "I'd be glad for a father like yours."

Marcia put her arm through his and leant her head against his shoulder. Simon rarely spoke of him, but she knew that Simon's dad had left his family. She and Simon had both been abandoned by someone, she realised. Simon might be slow to commit to a permanent relationship, but when he did, he would mean it. She could afford to wait.

CHAPTER 32

Wasted. Another day wasted. Alcina's job at the bakery had not yet begun, so she was still working both shifts at Kosta's. Although she could not afford to do it, she had taken the entire day off. How could she not? It was her wedding anniversary, and she had wanted to spend it with Tony. What an exaggeration – she hadn't spent the day with him. She had spent most of the day travelling to see him and returning. She and Tony had only had an hour together. Together? If she weren't so angry, she would have laughed. How could you consider yourselves to be together when you were in a prison's public room with others all round you? When you couldn't touch without incurring the intervention of the guards? When you couldn't exchange gifts? Or share champagne? Or do anything that would be considered a celebration?

She had married Tony because he was good in the bedroom, he made good money, and he showed her a good time when they were together. All good. Now everything had been taken away. What did they have to celebrate now? Their happy times were in the past.

She had wanted to wear something special to remind Tony of their wedding day, so she had tried on her going away dress. She hadn't worn it to see him, however. It no longer fit her the way it had, caressing her curves so well that Tony couldn't keep his eyes off her. She'd smiled to herself then, a new bride with a confident, carefree smile, wondering how long he could wait. Would he kiss her in the taxi? In the elevator on the way to their hotel room? Before he had even locked the hotel room door? She had loved having that effect on him.

Now she was thin, and the dress didn't complement her. Too thin, Tony would say. The only extra weight she carried these days was on her shoulders, although he didn't ever acknowledge that. What did he recognise? That she had lines on her face now that others her age did not, damn him.

The final insult? Tony had not remembered the day. And if she had expressed her anger to him, the guards would have forcibly removed her. Perhaps she should have told him how furious she was. Perhaps she should have let Tony see her outrage. Perhaps then he would have seen how impossibly difficult life was for her instead of whingeing constantly about his situation. Perhaps then he would have recalled that he was married. Wedding anniversary? A day set aside to celebrate your marriage? She cursed aloud. What kind of marriage was this?

As the days grew shorter and the nights longer, Jenny continued to struggle with her grief. Father Goodwyn, whom she now called Neil, visited regularly with words of encouragement.

"Life is so unfair," she said.

"Sometimes it doesn't make sense," he admitted. "Crying can help. Releasing any feeling actually. I'm not unused to tears; in my Army service I saw many soldiers weep."

"Is that what you said to Colin after his father died?"

"I listened more than I spoke, as I recall. And I learnt to be alert to nonverbal cues. Grief wears a number of guises. This morning, for example, you look tense. Are you having other physical symptoms?" Her shirt looked lopsided, as if she hadn't fastened the buttons properly, and she hadn't tucked it into her jeans.

"Nightmares occasionally. I dream that some part of my body is gone, and when I wake up, I know that it's Colin. Sometimes it's easier to sleep during the day than at night." She heard a two-tone siren and wondered if Danny were responding to another robbery call.

"Are you eating well?"

She shook her head with a smile. "Is that why you always bring food with you when you come?" Today he had brought banana nut muffins, which they both sampled.

"Food helps us relax. So does prayer. 'More things are wrought by prayer than this world ever knows of.'"

She recognized the Tennyson quote.

"Sometimes, in addition to food and prayer, I indulge in a shot of Laphroaig. That's Scotch – a strong, earthy single malt."

"Are you prescribing alcohol?" she laughed.

"Only in moderation," he smiled. "But I would prescribe exercise."

"I walk on the Heath, but I don't see how that helps anything."

"Jenny, I assure you, being in good physical condition can help us deal with all sorts of other demands. Motion affects emotions. When I first joined the Army, no one told me chaplains needed to be fit. I felt so inferior, being out of shape when everyone else was leaner and tougher. I played a lot of football, to lose weight and to establish relationships. I still try to stay active." He paused. "Jenny, I want you to know: I see courage in your despair. And in your honesty. Nothing can be healed without honesty."

She disagreed. "There isn't anything brave about it! I didn't have any choice."

"On the contrary. You choose to see me. You choose to face your sorrow. You choose to keep fighting." He smiled. "There's a part of you that wants to heal, an unconscious part as well as a conscious part. Psychologists believe this life force comes from your brain, your mind. I prefer to think of it as the God-given desire to live He placed in your heart."

"My heart is either broken or dead."

"Jenny, you're wounded, but my faith teaches that despair is not the end. You may stop there for a night, but joy comes in the morning, metaphorically, at least."

"Despair is my middle name," she said bitterly.

"It takes time to adjust to new situations," he observed, "but in time I believe you will. When I first returned to England after my military service ended, I counselled a number of young soldiers who had completed their tours of duty. Many felt lost, without purpose. They had brought baggage home with them, because they had all lost something in combat, some part of themselves, perhaps physical, perhaps emotional."

"Like my dreams," she murmured.

"Exactly so. In combat, as in trauma, one's feelings are heightened, and it can be difficult finding meaningful ways to spend one's time. The most important thing I could do was to let them know I cared. And that God did."

"If God cares, His way of showing it is too subtle for me."

He nodded. "Sometimes God seems to be silent, but even during those times, I had strength beyond my own. So when He wasn't speaking, I believe He was working with other means."

"Did you have trouble adjusting?"

"In some ways. I did find it difficult sometimes, after serving in a combat zone for a number of years, to believe that I was safe. That may be one reason I moved from serving God and country to serving God and the police. It is a haven of sorts."

Maybe that was why she felt uneasy. Her time in witness protection had become a haven, surrounded by police officers pledged to protect her. Now she was alone. "I'm a boat without a rudder. I have no husband, no children, no career – sometimes I even feel like I don't have a country."

"Share those feelings with God, Jenny. He is big enough to handle them." After a short prayer, he left, but not before kissing her on both cheeks in the British fashion. His gentle affection was the only physical contact she received from anyone.

She started another list in her journal. *Grief is:*

1. *Silence.* She still had so many things to tell Colin, things she couldn't speak into the empty rooms. Even if she could, her words would only breach the silence briefly, not banish it.
2. *Amputation.* Part of her had been cut away when he died. She now realized that she didn't even know exactly when that was. She knew the day, of course – she'd never forget it – but not the exact time. Had it been mid afternoon when she was driven to the hospital, or earlier? Was he already gone then? It

was light, but it had been dark when she had left the hospital with Simon and Brian.

3. *Darkness.* Because grief was the black hole of the universe, sucking her in and crushing her, like the dark earth that pressed against Colin's casket. Before her rape, she had been drugged. She had regained consciousness in a dark, cold room. She had been afraid of the dark ever since and still slept with a nightlight. She hated thinking of Colin alone in the dark.

4. *A prison.* With endless remand, because there was no trial date and therefore no possibility of acquittal and release.

5. *Being colder inside than the weather outside.* How could her frozen heart produce warm tears? She looked out at the gray sky and wondered if nature grieved. Did the flower mourn the loss of each petal, the tree the loss of each leaf?

6. *Anger.* She wished now she had asked more about the terrorist who had killed Colin. What did he look like? How tall was he? Did he have any distinguishing features? Was his hair long or short? Colin had been tall, elegant, educated, tender – he deserved to live! What right did anyone have to take him away from her? Neil Goodwyn had told her once that Royal Army chaplains weren't permitted to carry weapons. Had he been angry at what he saw? Had he ever wished he had a gun or a knife?

7. *Endless.* People were mortal. Why wasn't grief?

8. *Capricious.* Her ups and downs were as sudden as a see-saw's.

9. *Remembering.* Two formal remembrance services had been held recently, a requiem Mass for deceased officers held by the Catholic Police Guild and a memorial ceremony organized by the Met for all officers killed that year. Joanne had accompanied her to both of them. A color photograph of each officer had been included at each event, and seeing Colin's blue eyes had reminded her of the sad little boy she had

seen on the Heath. It had been a school day, and he had been the only child she'd seen on her walk. Was he mourning someone, too?

She contemplated her entries. Was nervousness a part of grief? Fear? She didn't think so, but even in broad daylight she was wary. And at dusk the shadows behind the trees unnerved her. She set the journal aside and went into the kitchen. She wasn't very hungry; leftover soup would be enough.

After dinner she looked for something to read. She removed the National Trust's book on Chartwell, Winston Churchill's home, from the shelf and thumbed through it. She had read about Churchill during her time in witness protection and had been impressed by what he had accomplished in spite of his depression. Because it would have taken trips on both the tube and the overland train to reach the site, Colin had driven from Hampstead to Kent when he took her there. She had been surprised to see a parking lot on the premises. Of course it hadn't been there in Churchill's time but became necessary later to accommodate the thousands of visitors.

She had seen bookshelves from the floor to the ceiling in most rooms and in some rooms, even above the doorways. Churchill had had two desks in his study, one with a chair and the other taller, because he had often worked standing up. Preparation for his speeches in Parliament? She supposed so. At the time she had been struck by how peaceful it felt in the house, with wide, tall windows in many rooms that overlooked the property. What a welcome respite from the pressures of London it must have been for him!

Some of Churchill's paintings were shown in the National Trust book, but there were no photographs of the many gifts he had received during his time in political office and afterward. Thinking about them now made her sad, because so many had known and honored Churchill during his life and mourned him upon his death, while there were so few to remember Colin. She replaced the book on the shelf.

What else? Not a novel – she hadn't the concentration to

follow the plot. Poetry, then, beginning with her old friends, Shelley and Keats. She also read a few selections by Louis MacNeice. Something was missing: anger. She recalled the Siegfried Sassoon poems Colin had brought her long ago, when she was in witness protection and he wanted to help her pass the time. Sassoon had become a vocal opponent of World War I, and some of his work more closely reflected her feelings. In "How to Die," his words saddened her, because he wrote of actions Colin had not had time to make: "He lifts his fingers toward the skies / Where holy brightness breaks in flame; / Radiance reflected in his eyes, / And on his lips a whispered name."

It was in Wilfred Owen that she found a voice with rage enough to match hers. He wrote about the gas, the cold, the dread. At least Colin had died quickly. When she read, "Red lips are not so red / As the stained stones kissed by the English dead," she remembered kissing Colin's bloody face and wept again for his loss. Owen was killed in action on November 4, 1918, one week shy of the Armistice. He also deserved her tears, he whose life, like Colin's, was cut so short.

CHAPTER 34

On Sunday, December 8, Jenny didn't want to get out of bed. Couldn't the calendar have skipped this day? She forced herself to make a cup of tea. Tea was supposed to be soothing. Still in her pajamas, she stood in front of the closet, unable to decide what to wear or to think of any reason why she should dress today, of all days.

She went back to bed, taking her photo album with her. There weren't nearly enough pictures of Colin in it; he had usually been behind the camera, not in front of it. And how insufficient photos were – flat, two-dimensional portraits of a single moment and a single feeling which fell far short of the event they memorialized. Her mobile rang. She considered not answering, but it was Simon.

"I'd like to take you for dinner tonight."

"But it's way too cold. And it's my wedding anniversary."

"I know what day it is. Dress. I'll call by at seven." He rang off.

Did he know she wasn't dressed? No, he probably just wanted her to wear something warm enough. At least she had the rest of the day to figure out what.

They took the tube to Baker Street Station in central London and walked the remaining few blocks to Langan's Bistro, whose ceiling featured an unusual collection of upside down parasols. Jenny was amused to see many more wines on the menu than food offerings, although if she ordered the sirloin steak with green peppercorn and brandy sauce, she would be more than satisfied. Simon chose chargrilled swordfish. She listened while he discussed wines with the waiter and then was at a loss to know what to say. Colin should have been sitting across the table from her, enjoying his wine but not pouring her any because she was pregnant with his child.

When the waiter poured the wine, she blushed in response to Simon's toast, "To you, Jenny. You're lovely. Even if you are wearing only one earring."

He hadn't commented on her clothes – a dark blue dress with velvet trim on the collar and cuffs and a flowing drape that moved when she moved – but had somehow noticed she was missing an earring, although she had let her hair fall forward on the side of her face with the naked lobe. "The earring – it was found with Colin's personal effects. He must have had two in his pocket when the explosion occurred, but only one survived intact." She paused to settle her emotions and realized she had never seen Simon in a suit and tie. She was a little surprised by how handsome he looked. Remembering her manners, she answered with one of her own: "To you. May you stay safe. And may I see you dressed up more often."

The food was delicious, and she almost laughed when she saw the dessert: Mrs. Langan's chocolate pudding.

"I'm told it's legendary," Simon said.

It was tasty enough to earn that reputation, she decided, the chocolate oozing out of the confection and spreading across her plate. Simon accepted only a taste, content with black coffee. She added to hers the milk the waiter brought, warm milk to keep the coffee from cooling too quickly.

On the way home, she held his arm.

"You still miss him?" he asked.

"Yes, most of all at night. Simon, why did you do this for me?"

"Didn't want you alone," he answered.

"Thank you. You made a bad day bearable. My grief stalks me, but it was easier with you here."

He refused the coffee she offered him, citing early run in the morning, and turned to go.

The lump in her throat grew. "Simon, could you – I mean – no, of course you can't – you have Marcia – I'm sorry – I wish – you've done so much already – "

He stopped. "Jenny, what do you need?"

Her shoulders tensed. She looked away, then at him, and away again.

"Jenny?" he prompted.

"Simon – " Her voice caught. "Would you – hold me?"

He opened his arms, and she walked into them and gripped him tightly. After a moment his loose hug became firmer, he pressed his lips against her hair, and she struggled not to cry. He wasn't quite as tall as Colin, but he was solid. She felt his strength and knew she needed it. Feeling less lonely, she relaxed, and he stepped back.

In the morning she woke warm and sluggish. She hadn't been able to see his face, but the man in her dream had touched her just the way Colin had. The dream had ended, but the warmth between her thighs hadn't, and she was filled with longing and guilt at the same time, because she was alive and he wasn't.

CHAPTER 35

Sunday was the worst day of the week. And cold Sundays, like today, irritated Alcina the most. In the past she and Tony would have spent the morning in bed warming each other. He had been a good lover, not as selfish as some handsome men. Now he was a caged bird, his hair and brows as black as a raven's feathers. His thinner frame made his features sharper, almost predatory.

She looked no better. Her body now had angles where curves had been. Her hands were bony, and her fingernails more like talons than the instruments of seduction she had traced across Tony's chest and stomach.

She missed having a lover. She would even have welcomed Anatoli, Cecilia's fiancé. Sunrise, his name meant, and he had risen for her that Sunday. Her parents and sisters had gone to church, and he had arrived early for lunch. A little wine, a few whispers in his ear, and he had betrayed the woman he called his only love. Afterward she had never been able to understand what her sister saw in him. His thighs were soft, his attentions short, and his lack of skill in stimulating her annoying. His guilt had not unmanned him, however.

"He came, he left," she reported to her family with a sweet smile when they returned from the service. "Felt ill, I think." Cecilia had not been able to reach him until evening, but he had reassured her then with a host of flowery phrases. He had not confessed his infidelity.

Tony's advances had been adventurous, unpredictable, even aggressive. Until his prison sentence, he had never neglected her. She closed her eyes and imagined his beak-like nose brushing hers, his hands quick to strip her of her nightdress. He had slept nude. She now slept in warm nightwear to keep the chill of the cheap flat at bay.

CHAPTER 36

Jenny began her Christmas season with lies. She didn't want to spend the holiday in Texas. Her mother was entirely too cheerful, and her mother's insistence that she'd meet someone and marry again if she would just start dating insulted her. Had she thought so little of Colin that she was eager to replace him? She told her mother she was going to Kent. Then, knowing it would take too much energy to smile – smiles were no longer automatic – and more acting skills than she possessed to celebrate, she told Joanne that she would be in Texas. Who else would have expectations of her which she could not meet? Esther Hollister. She rang the bookshop and left a message that she would be gone over the holidays.

She didn't decorate for the holiday. Why put up a tree if no gifts from Colin would be under it? She didn't even hang the wreath on the front door. Christmas: a noun synonymous with birth, joy, and hope. She didn't need a reminder that her life held none of these.

Christmas shopping was an agony, because the Christmas music that filled the department stores spoke of merriment, anticipation, and faith for the future, the antithesis of what she felt, and because the person she most wanted to shop for was gone. Her Christmas gift to herself was more space in the closet, because she had decided to go through Colin's clothes. She kept most of his shirts, some of his ties and cufflinks, and all his handkerchiefs. The rest she gave to Oxfam and then regretted it. In the back of the closet she found the clothes she'd worn the day of Colin's death, the ones stained with his blood, folded neatly in a clear plastic bag. Beth must have placed them there. She knew she should throw them away, but she couldn't. She held the bag for a long time and then returned it to the closet unopened.

She missed Simon, although he was not hers to miss. Last year she had bought a gift for him, but in this year's desperate effort to downsize shopping, she hadn't.

A call from Colin's boss, Chief Superintendent Higham, surprised her. "The Commissioner would like to hold a memorial service for your husband on the date of his death," he said.

"But there has already been a memorial ceremony, and Colin was included in it."

"Yes, but this additional one we would like to hold would remember your husband only. With your permission, we'll plan the event, keeping you informed, of course." She thanked him, and after asking about her health, he rang off.

Christmas Day was chilly, the temperature hovering around fifty degrees Fahrenheit all day. She didn't bother to dress completely, and she was alone. "But it's my choice!" she said aloud, as if Neil Goodwyn were there, advising her to seek fellowship. Her parents had sent her a treasury of American music, and she selected the *Rhapsody in Blue* by Gershwin to play first. A rhapsody was one extended movement, the commentary said. This one had been composed early in 1924, before the Great Depression and between the world wars. There were blues in it but more – a contagious rhythm, an energy she saw as uniquely American. She didn't have the exuberance the piece exuded. What would it have sounded like if it had been written after 9/11? A longer blues section. More cacophonous chords. Rhythms disturbed to show urgency and panic instead of energy. An uncertain resolution.

A year ago Colin had been alive. They had spent

Christmas in Kent with both their families, and love had surrounded them. Love and more: laughter, delight in the excitement his niece and nephew had exhibited opening their presents, and hope in Colin's and her ability to begin their own family. He had given her a bracelet with jewels for charms: an emerald for her May birthday, a diamond J, an eagle with a sapphire eye, and two ruby hearts, one for each of their years together. It struck her now that never would another ruby be added to that bracelet; it was finished. But not complete, any more than her life was complete without the charm that he had added to it.

In her jewelry box – another gift from him – she saw the bracelet, and next to it, the single emerald earring that remained from the blast and that she had worn on their anniversary. Was she the delicate remaining gem, or was Colin, even in his death, more whole than she? It was Christmas, and she felt torn into pieces. She went to bed early in one of his shirts with the Union Jack cufflinks he'd been wearing when they had celebrated their engagement.

CHAPTER 37

She didn't leave the flat on Boxing Day, a secular holiday when in past times servants or those who were needy were given Christmas boxes of money or gifts. In modern times it most resembled the day after Thanksgiving in the States, when retail stores opened early, offered huge sales, and earned more money than on any other single day during the year. She had no shopping to do, however, so she slept late, not even collecting the newspaper until it was nearly dark.

When she read that a gunman in Hackney had fired on police and was being contained by them, she wasn't very interested, assuming the incident would end quickly. The next day, however, the standoff continued. Because the offender had barricaded himself in his first floor bedsit, dozens of people in the neighborhood had to be evacuated, and others had to stay inside or leave their homes only with police escorting them. It was colder than it had been on Christmas, with snow on the ground and gusty winds, and she worried about the armed officers who had to remain on the scene outdoors. Just stepping on her porch to get the newspaper had chilled her through and through, and the passersby, even with their heavy coats, hats, and scarves, looked smaller as they hunched forward against the cold. Byron had claimed that the English winter ended in July and began again in August, but T. S. Eliot had described the "very dead of winter," which she thought was more apt. Nature had no respect for people; rain and snow fell on the living as well as the dead. Was there snow on Colin's grave in Kent? If so, she was glad she wasn't there to see it.

News that the gunman had a hostage upset her. Who was he? How had he gotten himself into this mess? Why? The newspapers didn't say. The police were capable; surely they would be able to negotiate his release. Beth rang to tell her that Brian, Simon, and others were working seventeen-hour shifts, beginning either at five a.m. or five p.m., with an additional several hours to sort kit, be briefed, and drive to the site. The Technical Support Unit, or TSU, delivered a field phone, but the gunman, whom they now referred to as the "hostage taker," did not want to negotiate.

Days passed with no apparent progress. The police identified the gunman as a 32-year-old Jamaican named Eli Hall. The name of the hostage was not released. Reports said that he was alive and well, but Jenny worried all the same. He was being held against his will. Did he share her anger at the cruelty of fate? Which was worse, she wondered, having your life at the mercy of someone else's whim, or feeling, as she did, that her future would never be free from the grip of grief? "Time does not bring relief," Edna St. Vincent Millay had written. "You all have lied / Who told me time would ease me of my pain!" Darkness came early, both outside and in Jenny's spirit, and she retired to bed earlier and earlier, exhausted from the effort it took to trudge through her sorrow, which rose like floodwaters, steadily and inexorably.

By New Year's Eve, the media referred to the incident as the "Hackney siege." More shots were fired by the gunman on New Year's Day. Electricity was turned off to the gunman's flat. Jenny understood that the move was intended to make him so uncomfortable that he would come out, but she was concerned about the effect his increasing instability would have on the hostage.

In the mornings she read the *Telegraph*. In the afternoons she read the *Evening Standard* or watched the news on TV for updates. On January 3, the temperature began to drop. Even with heavy uniforms and woolen scarves around their faces, police had to keep moving to combat the cold. Officers deployed in pairs and swapped positions to remain alert. Regular deliveries of food were made to Hall and his hostage.

Jenny rang Beth. Nearly fifty officers were on the scene, Beth said, round the clock. Some nights Brian slept five or six hours on a camp bed at the base at Leman Street. When he did come home, he was worn out from the effort it took to maintain continual focus in the difficult conditions and convinced he'd never feel warm again. The marksmen had it worse, because they had to remain still for long periods. At least they were part of something, Jenny thought, and they had procedures to follow. She was isolated and had not found any way of subduing her sorrow.

On the eleventh day of the siege, the hostage escaped. Temperatures were now below freezing at night and not much above during the day. How long would the hostage taker be able to withstand the cold? She knew the police didn't want to kill him; they just wanted him to give up. "Give up!" she shouted as she read the newspaper accounts. "Show me that bad things can end well!" But still the hostage taker hid in his flat. He had blocked his window with a wardrobe and had only a narrow view of the outside world. Anxious to end the operation, the police placed a hose pipe on the roof and turned on the water to increase his discomfort. Jenny looked up. Her ceiling had no leaks, but her unhappiness far exceeded discomfort, and her world, too, had shrunk.

Still the gunman would not surrender. His behavior became even more erratic. He began firing indiscriminately on the police, who responded with CS gas, a non-lethal chemical irritant that caused the eyes to tear and the skin to burn. Jenny's eyes stung, too, and were red in the mornings from the colorless tears she had shed during the night. No more of this! she wept. Who was besieging whom? The gunman's flat was surrounded by police, but they were just as tied to the site as he was, and the siege was taking a toll on everyone.

Negotiations broke down entirely on the fourteenth day. Smoke was seen inside the flat. Because the police couldn't allow the fire brigade to enter a dwelling with an armed occupant, they used Hatton rounds or rubber bullets to break the windows. Armed officers then brought the fire under control but were not able to extinguish it entirely. Beth called Jenny to report that Brian had been one of those who had carried the heavy fire equipment in addition to everything else, but he was all right. Police speculated that Hall had set his furniture on fire to keep warm.

On the last day Hall fired three shots. A police marksman fired once. After again deploying CS gas, an assault team entered the flat and found him dead. The marksman's shot had hit him, as had a round from his own gun. Jenny wondered if the bullets had killed him instantly, or if he had bled to death in the dark, frigid flat, gradually feeling colder and weaker. Was that how her siege of sorrow would end? With her death? Would she then be an inconvenience to those who found her, the way the citizens in Hackney had complained about the gunman causing the extended presence of the police?

Following the siege, there seemed to be no news of consequence. The new year had come, but with it, no warmth, no sun, nothing to counteract her emotional undertow. When she woke in the morning, the fog of grief rested on her chest. She had become London weather: cold, cloudy, hazy, with precipitation likely.

CHAPTER 38

Alcina's anger, her silent companion, had not abated. Frustration had magnified it. Business at the bakery had been brisk over the holiday season, but her quarry had not appeared. A new year had begun, and she had had no forward motion. Her encounter had increased her confidence, and she hungered for another encounter, somewhere, anywhere. Her craving was almost physical, but food and drink did not satisfy it. She had felt it coursing through her veins, and she was greedy for more.

She knew she needed to develop patience, Tony told her so. "Timing is important," he said. "If you rush, you'll make a mistake."

"Like you did?" she snapped, causing him to scowl.

"Trust no one," he advised.

Had that been her mistake? She had trusted him, and look where that had led her.

"Plan everything," Tony added.

Yes, she was eager to progress, but she needed more information. Where did her target live? What could she discover about her routine? Eventually her enemy would enter the bakery, and when she did, Alcina would find a reason to leave for a few moments and follow her. If she hoped to succeed, she would have to make the most of chance meetings.

CHAPTER 39

The Hackney Siege had ended badly. Despite their best efforts, the police had been unable to resolve the conflict. Jenny knew that they would consider the entire operation a failure because it had not come to a peaceful conclusion. All would be affected, but the negotiator, who had had personal contact with the gunman, would feel deeply dispirited. The police, however, would move on to other engagements, while she was stuck on the same battleground, and no matter how hard she fought, grief refused to retreat. Another year without Colin? How could she love a world that he was not a part of? And why should she? The days ahead looked as bleak as she did. She hadn't worn makeup since her dinner with Simon early in December, and her hair obviously needed to be shaped and trimmed.

Something drew Jenny to the children's rooms. Rather than hiring someone to do the work, she and Colin had chosen the color schemes and wallpaper and finished them together. They had papered the rooms with hope, decorating one in blues and greens with a teddy bear border, because she had enjoyed the *Little Bear* books she had read to her brothers. The other showcased ducks – *Make Way for Ducklings!* she had exclaimed – with a yellow and orange background. They hadn't chosen furniture or names, although she intended to honor Colin's wish to continue his parents' practice of naming the boys with the letter C and the girls with J. When she had pasted the last strip in place, she and Colin had celebrated with a glass of wine and a toast to Little C or Little J. He had suggested that they do their part to make sure the rooms were occupied soon, and she had laughed and kissed him to start the process.

The rooms were empty. What should she do with them? Redecorate: The laughs and cries of children would not fill these spaces with life. She slipped her thumbnail under one low corner of the wallpaper and began to pull. The paper didn't release its hold on the wall neatly or easily. Repeated tears required her to start again every yard or so, and the wallpaper beyond the reach of her hands refused to cooperate. She stepped back. She had created a beast with multiple drooping tails. Hardly an auspicious start, and her concentration was gone. *Mañana:* Maybe tomorrow she would resume work. Maybe not.

Brian and Beth were expecting their second child. Beth was already eight weeks along, and they had gone home to tell their families. Simon had taken Marcia on a brief holiday. When Colin had had time off on gray days, they had gone back to bed after breakfast. Now she turned on the lights to chase the gloom away and wrapped a blanket around her shoulders to counter the chill. Always she was conscious of the days passing by, of the cruel countdown to February 23, the date of Colin's death. She wished for a way to escape or delay it. Maybe if she went back to bed – if she stopped leaving the flat – she could cause time to blur. She took her pillow from the sofa and climbed the stairs to their bedroom, hers and Colin's. She slipped off her jeans, sprayed a little of his after-shave on one of his shirts, and buttoned it up over her t-shirt. Wanting to fall asleep faster, she took a sleeping pill and then drifted off, thinking about her husband.

Awake she was dead to life, but in her dream she was vibrantly alive, and more important, so was Colin. They were on their honeymoon, and her skin was warm from the Bermuda sun. He was smiling at her, his most tender smile, the one that took her breath away because it said,

I'm going to make love to you now. "On the beach?" she laughed. "You're too beautiful to resist, and there's no one else about," he answered. Colin, his chest broad and strong, his body free of lacerations and trauma, holding her, kissing her.

When she woke, the day was still gray and hazy, as if the dawn hadn't wanted to come. No matter. She didn't care if it came. What was the daylight to her? She resented the hours she would have to wait until she could sleep again. She was slightly hungry. There wasn't much worth eating in her kitchen, but she lacked the energy and the will to bundle up and make the trek to Sainsbury's for more. She made do with dry cereal. If she could just shut out the distractions of things outside, perhaps she would dream of him again. She let the newspapers accumulate on the porch and turned off her phone, disregarding the message Beth had left about Jenny returning to help at school when the term resumed. The world was empty. She would not find Colin there, and she wanted so badly to see his blue eyes once more. Maybe grief wasn't such a bad thing. If it could cause her to dream of being loved, maybe she shouldn't want to let it go. When she dreamed, the days did not advance, the seasons did not change, there was no night or day. She turned off the lights downstairs. She straightened the sheets, fluffed the pillows. The flat was quiet, blissfully quiet. She took another sleeping pill and closed her eyes.

PART THREE

There is only the fight to recover what has been lost...
There is only the trying.

— T.S. Elliot

CHAPTER 1

It paid to be quiet. Sergeant Nick Howard learnt a good deal listening to others. From time to time he overheard bits of news about Jennifer Sinclair. "Never much food in her fridge. She's not looking after herself." "Beth hasn't seen her since before Christmas." "Her mobile's not working." Casey and Davies thought she was still having a rough go of it and were dead worried.

Howard had been assigned to her witness protection team, on a periodic basis only, and he hadn't thought much of it. Now the leader of an SO-19 specialist firearms team like Casey, he considered his role. Coppers were paid to respond to the needs of the public, but she hadn't requested assistance, and his skills didn't lie in public affairs. Leave it, he told himself.

Cathryn Donnelly, his live-in girlfriend, didn't agree. "You always wanted another chance to show your parents what they'd accomplished with you," Cath told him. "Just because she hasn't asked for help doesn't mean she doesn't need it. You know what grief is. But if you're to have any credibility, you'll have to tell her."

Years later he still didn't like speaking of it, but he knew what grief could do. Paralyse you. Eat you up inside if you let it. He could check on Jenny, see for himself. No harm in that.

"You'll go easy on her?" Cath asked.

"If I can," he said.

CHAPTER 2

Howard banged on Jenny's door. There'd been no answer to the bell, and newspapers were strewn all about her front porch. "Police!" he called. "Police! Open the door!"

Late morning, and she wasn't dressed. The bulky blue dressing gown she clutched around her dragged on the floor. Must have been Sinclair's. "Do you remember me?" he asked.

The witness protection officer with the dark hair and the darker stare who would never converse with her. He had more lines around his eyes than she remembered, but that grim mouth and forbidding expression: It had to be Icky Nicky, the one with no social skills. "Nick," she said slowly. "What are you doing here?"

"Sergeant Howard to you," he answered crisply. He held up a Tesco bag.

She frowned and leaned against the door jamb. "Groceries? I don't understand."

Her pupils looked normal in spite of her bleary eyes, but her speech was dull and her movements sluggish. He stepped past her into the flat. The drapes were drawn, and stacks of mail covered the dining room table. He headed for the kitchen and placed the shopping bag on the counter. The sink was filled with unwashed dishes. He opened the fridge. A glance told him that the milk had gone off; it was well past its sell-by. The cheese was mouldy. She had no bread. Good job he had come prepared. "I'll be making you breakfast," he said. He removed his coat.

Damn. He was staying. She followed him into the kitchen. "I'm not hungry."

"Sit." He found a skillet and unpacked his supplies. He rinsed a bowl, cracked two eggs into it from the box of six, beat them briefly, and poured them into the buttered pan. While they cooked, he rinsed a plate and fork and placed them in front of her. He scrambled the eggs until they looked rubbery and burnt them a bit on purpose. He wanted to get a reaction out of her. "Eat," he said, scraping the eggs onto her plate. He poured her a glass of milk.

"Go away," she whispered.

"When you've eaten."

"I hate scrambled eggs. Didn't your mother teach you to cook anything else?"

"My mum died when I was six."

No wonder he didn't know what TLC was. "What about your father?"

"I never knew him. Eat."

"Are you going to make me?"

He put the fork in her hand and closed his hand firmly over hers.

"No," she said. "I'll do it."

He released her and watched her take several tiny bites. The eggs were tasteless. He hadn't seasoned them. She pushed some of the mail out of the way, looking for the salt shaker. "Why are you doing this to me?" she asked.

"I've always been a bit bloody-minded."

No kidding. She took several bites, washing each down with a swallow of milk. She put her fork down. "What happened to you after your mother died?"

"I was put into care. None of the placements lasted for long. By the time I was ten, I'd taught myself not to care about anything or anyone. Then I was placed with the Thompsons."

"What did they do?"

"Saved my life." He paused. "Pick up your fork, Jenny."

She ate two half-hearted, slow bites.

"Two more," he commanded.

"Why?"

"The first rule of survival: eat."

She wasn't sure she cared about surviving, but something in his expression told her this wasn't the time to argue. She complied.

"That'll do," he said. She had consumed nearly half.

Sighing, she pushed herself away from the table but did not rise.

Her lack of spirit concerned him. "Mind if I have a look round?" He wanted to complete his assessment.

She hadn't liked him when he had guarded her in witness protection, and she didn't like him now. "Then will you go away?"

He surveyed the rest of the floor, including the loo. No drugs there. He headed downstairs. The rooms looked unused. Upstairs the master bed was unmade. Clothes were scattered about the floor. In the master bathroom, he found her sleeping pills. According to the date, there should have been many more in the bottle. One script was remaining. He removed one pill and left it on the shelf in the medicine cabinet. He put the bottle with the rest in his pocket to make it more difficult for her to refill. She would hate him, but he could handle being a target. The rooms beyond were evidently intended for children, but they were either unfinished – the wallpaper undone in places – or someone had begun to dismantle the décor.

While he had been upstairs, she had stretched out on the sofa in the sitting room. He thought better of speaking to her. No need for him to broadcast his plans.

He located her handbag on the table next to the front door. Not wanting to leave the flat unsecured, he took her keys with him and locked up after he left.

CHAPTER 3

The next morning, when Jenny didn't respond to the bell or his shouts, Sergeant Howard used her key to gain entry to the flat. She was waiting for him in the same robe.

"How did you get a key?"

"Took yours."

"You took my pills, too!" she said. "That's theft. I should call the police."

She was more alert than the day before. "Use your mobile then. Report me."

"It's dead."

"Use mine." He held it out to her. "I'll show the plods my warrant card and go home. They'll see the state of this place and call for a psych eval. You could be sectioned."

"What's that?"

"Compulsory psychiatric commitment."

She didn't want that.

He put his mobile back in his pocket and went into the kitchen.

"Are you going to give me a pep talk?" she asked. "Tell me to look on the bright side?"

She was angry. Good. "I'm not, no. Sometimes all you can do is weather the storm."

When he put the plate of scrambled eggs in front of her, she pushed it away. "I'm not eating this."

He raised his voice slightly. "You will."

"What for?" she cried. "It won't help! Don't you understand? All your orders – what are they good for? I'm alone! I just want to sleep, and you won't let me!"

He yelled back. "Damn it, Jenny, don't mess me about!"

In one swift motion she swept the plate of food off the table. "Go away! Just go away!"

He suddenly saw himself, an angry, desperate child striking out at everyone within reach, and he knew he needed to change his approach. He pulled a chair next to her and took her hands. "Jenny, quitting's not an option. For you or for me. I'm not walking away. I'll work with you." They were much the same words Mr. Thompson had used when he first arrived at the Thompsons' home.

She felt even worse. If Icky Nicky felt sorry for her, she must really be in bad shape.

"On the Job we're taught to take control of situations very quickly. If there's any possibility of armed resistance, we have to win. At the most basic level, surviving is winning. Being conscious and rational. That's what I want for you."

She just wanted to sleep and dream of Colin. When she woke, she lost him all over again, and the sorrow was deep and sharp.

"I brought milk yesterday. If you don't like my eggs, would you eat some cereal? We'll go to the market after."

"I don't have anything to wear. Clean, I mean."

"We'll tackle that next then." He made her a small bowl of cereal. While she ate, he cleaned up the mess from the eggs and brewed a cup of tea for himself.

When she finished, he watched her sort the laundry and start the first load. They worked together on the dishes in the sink. He found a bin bag and threw away the old newspapers and all nonessential mail. She folded the clothes when they came out of the dryer, her fingers lingering over Colin's shirts.

"Jenny, this sadness – you have to walk away from it."

"I don't know how," she sighed. "My life ended when he died."

"Head toward the glow on the horizon. It's there if you

look for it."

"There isn't any!"

"There will be. You're in a tunnel."

"Will the sadness go away?" she asked.

"It never goes entirely. But the glow gets larger."

"How do you know?"

"I just do." She looked knackered. "Jenny, I'll go to the market tomorrow. What would you like me to purchase?"

"Anything but eggs. Fruit? Cheese? Something sweet?"

He nodded. Before he left, he took one of her hands and placed a single sleeping pill in the palm. She closed her fingers over it and, after a moment, extended her other hand. "Please," she whispered.

"No," he said softly. "One will have to do."

CHAPTER 4

When Sergeant Howard arrived the third morning, Jenny was dressed, in a flowery t-shirt, a long, sloppy sweater, and a belt which held up her baggy jeans. She didn't want him to cook anything, so she ate some of the cheese and fruit he brought. He made tea for both of them.

"Tell me about the Thompsons," she said.

"They were an older couple. He was retired Royal Army, and she'd been a schoolteacher. Trouble started straightaway. I came home bloody from my new school and punched Mr. Thompson. Before he could punch me, you see." He shook his head, remembering the surprise he had felt. "He wasn't angry. In fact, the only time I ever saw him angry was when I upset Mrs. Thompson. Any road, he held me until I calmed. He called for Mrs. Thompson to clean me up. Then he sat me down and asked if I'd like him to teach me how to box."

He looked up at her. "He wanted me to be able to look after myself. 'Raw power is less effective than disciplined power,' he said. 'You need to have a target and aim for it. But first, son, you need to be fit.' He called me 'son' from the first day," he explained. "And he started taking me with him when he worked out at the gym."

"You needed a dad," she said.

He was silent, remembering his first boxing match. He

had trained hard. "I'm proud of you," Mr. Thompson had said. "Why?" he had yelled. "I lost!" Mr. Thompson had taken him by the shoulders. "Not in my book, son. Not in my book." And he had learnt that there were all sorts of victories. He cleared his throat.

He has been trained to be unflappable, but he's uncomfortable, she thought. It's hard for him to talk about them.

"Let's walk a bit," he said. "You'll need a coat. It's chilly." He wanted Jenny's appetite to increase and her depression to decrease. Cath had suggested that he get her moving.

Jenny found herself out of breath very quickly, but Sergeant Howard didn't hurry her. They walked as far as the entrance to the Heath. Today the Heath looked the way she felt: like an old woman. Her limbs were stiff, and her joints creaked, but some of the fog inside her escaped and became visible in the chill air. The winter wind slapped her cheeks, and she realized she was feeling again.

He didn't say much, and her curiosity about his life grew. "What was Mrs. Thompson like?"

"A real mum," he answered after a moment. "When I had nightmares, she was the first to come to me. At first she just woke me and held my hand. Later she put her arms around me. Mr. Thompson always patted my shoulder." He turned to face her. "Jenny, you need to stop taking sleeping pills."

"No," she objected, "I need them." With resentment she accepted the one sleeping pill he gave her before he left.

CHAPTER 5

"I'll cook today," she told Howard when he arrived the next day.

A good sign, he thought. Her hair wasn't as messy, and her clothes weren't untidy. She'd had pizza the night before. The box peeked out of the rubbish bin.

She made omelettes. He watched her crack the eggs with alacrity then beat them with a dash of milk and seasoning and more energy than he expected. She melted the butter, tilting the pan for even coverage before pouring the beaten mixture in. After a few minutes, she turned the omelette with one easy, fluid motion. It billowed up as it cooked. She slid the first one on his plate then repeated the process for hers.

He ate quickly, and she realized that she no longer thought of him as Icky Nicky. "The walk yesterday exhausted me," she said, "but I slept better last night. Are we walking again today?"

"If you don't mind it a bit wet," he said.

The rain was gentle and quiet, softening the landscape, and she wondered, as they walked, whether there was such a thing as gentle grief.

"On 11 September many women lost husbands. What do you suppose they were advised to do?" he asked.

She didn't answer, and he understood that he would

need to answer for her. "Remember them. But keep going. Don't let the bad guys win."

"Sergeant Howard, that's not enough!"

"It is for now," he insisted. "Thompson's Law: Things don't stay the same. Since they're already as bad for you as they can be, they're bound to get better."

They walked as far as Sainsbury's, Jenny bundled up and wondering whether she would ever find her grief as manageable as the puddles she stepped across.

Inside the store she selected croissants and challah bread from the bakery and several servings of frozen vegetables. All the meat was packaged for more than one diner, and she felt a wave of sadness wash over her. Sergeant Howard would leave when they returned to the flat, and the rest of the day would be interminable. It seemed incomprehensible to her that she would miss – of all people! – Sergeant Howard, but she was less lonely when he was there.

Her shopping completed, she tried to think of some topic that would engage him in a lengthy discussion. He answered her questions, however, with terse phrases. What could she do? Nothing on television would be worth watching. She didn't have the concentration to read. Yesterday she had sat in the living room for hours, first in one chair and then in another, restless and uncomfortable, waiting for the oblivion of sleep.

Why was she lingering when there was naught of consequence to see? "You're walking rather slowly," he commented.

She shrugged.

He carried her groceries back to the flat and watched while she put them away. He did not understand why she cried when he doled out her sleeping pill. Then he returned her keys so she could lock up after him.

CHAPTER 6

"Were you always a police officer?" Jenny asked Sergeant Howard over sausages and biscuits on the fifth morning.

"No, I was a soldier. I joined the Royal Army when I was eighteen." He remembered the smile on Mr. Thompson's face when he told him he wanted to enlist. "You're clever, strong, and quick, with eyes like a hawk's," Mr. Thompson had told him. "They'll be tough on you, son, but you'll do well."

He accepted a second cup of tea. "As soon as I could, I applied for Special Forces. Qualifying for the SAS, the Special Air Service, was the most difficult thing I'd ever done, but it was worth it."

"What motivated you? To push yourself so hard."

"I wanted to make the Thompsons proud. More than anything, I didn't want to fail. It was the only way I could show them they'd succeeded with me."

"They must be relieved that you're not in harm's way anymore. Do you see them often?" He was silent for so long she began to feel apprehensive. "Sergeant Howard – " Something in his expression made her stop.

He could no longer avoid telling her. "They're dead, Jenny."

She was stunned. "Both of them? What happened?"

"They died in a fire. Neither smoked, but their house was old. It burned to the ground. I returned from a training mission and was summoned by my supervising officer. 'They're gone, mate,' he said. All I have left of them – " he tapped his chest – "is in here."

She started to cry. "How did you go on?"

He saw the tears and knew they were for him, not for herself. "I didn't at first. I was gutted. Angry. Then I realised that they put a lot of effort into loving me. Helping me turn my life around." Jenny was stronger now. He hoped she was ready. His voice hardened. "Sinclair did that for you, Jenny. And you've made a mockery of it."

She was shocked by his sudden attack. "I don't understand," she stammered.

"Was his love real, Jenny?" He pressed on. "Did it matter to you? Did it change you? Then prove it. Prove it! And not just Sinclair. Others supported you, and you've made their belief in you a lie."

She was sobbing aloud now.

He watched her, recalling Mr. Thompson's strong arm around his thin shoulders, giving him comfort when he cried. He wanted to comfort Jenny – he wasn't as cold as some made him out to be – but his mission was not to teach her she could depend on others, as Mr. Thompson's had been. His mission was to teach her that she could manage alone. So he waited.

She began to remember, not what she had lost, but what she had gained. "Love lasts," Colin had told her once. "It survives the grave." He had been referring to his mother's love for his father, which had led her not just to marry him, but to follow him around the world on his foreign service postings and to make a life for herself after he died. Love, a divine gift, Colin would have argued, had given her the strength.

She remembered how amazed she'd been when he told her he loved her. How gentle and patient his courtship had been. He had given her hope and happiness. His love *had* changed her. She had healed, matured, blossomed. He would be grieving for her now, sad that she had let it all go. Disappointed because she had let the bomber steal a part of her.

She looked around the flat. She had tangible reminders of him: his framed photographs on the walls, clothes he had chosen for her in the closet, and engagement and wedding rings still on her finger. Sergeant Howard had nothing. "Tell me what to do," she begged.

"Make it your mission to get through one day. Then another. Then another. Do it until you don't have to prove it to yourself."

She swallowed hard. "Sergeant Howard, do you believe in God?"

"The Thompsons did. Mrs. T said that they thought God wanted them to help Him save one more. That's why they took me in when they were really past the age. And Mrs. T wouldn't have been at all surprised by how I met Cath."

"Is that your girlfriend? How did you meet her?"

"She was the fire brigade investigator. She determined that the fire had been accidental. Assured me that they died of smoke inhalation. Never felt the flames." He looked away briefly. "The fire started downstairs, late at night. They'd already gone up. They always held each other while they slept. As a boy I didn't understand it. Now I do." He paused. "Bad things happen, but God makes good come out of them. That's what Mrs. T believed."

"If I hadn't been raped, I would never have met Colin," she said slowly. "But his death? I think God has His work cut out for Him on that one."

When he didn't respond, she felt a flash of anger. "Aren't you going to answer?"

"The further I went in military service, the more I had to think for myself. Look after myself."

"But soldiers have – other soldiers! They're part of something, and they're not alone! I'm not a soldier!"

"You need to be. You're fighting a private war, that's all."

After he left, she felt bruised still from his words. He expected too much of her, but he was right about one thing: She had let people down. Colin had hurt her by dying, but she was hurting others by not caring about living – particularly Simon, who had always set high standards for her. She hadn't seen him in weeks. Sergeant "I-have-a-purpose-for-everything-I-do" Howard had recharged her mobile, a sure sign that he wanted her to use it. She flipped it open.

CHAPTER 7

Long after dark Simon Casey received Jenny's message on his voice mail, her voice so weak and shaky he barely recognised it. "Simon, I need – to talk to you. To tell you how sorry I am. Please." He wondered what for and rang her back to tell her he was on his way.

When he saw the tears on her cheeks, he took her in his arms. Her clothes were loose on her thin frame, and he wondered what had happened in the last weeks.

"Simon, I'm so ashamed," she cried. "I haven't been strong. Losing Colin – it hurt so much that I forgot to fight, and I didn't have the energy. I just wanted to slip away."

Dread tightened his stomach. In witness protection, things had got on top of her, but they'd been able to turn her round. He should have called by more often. He held her more firmly and felt her answering hug.

She released him first. "Tea?" she asked.

"No. Talk to me."

They sat down in the living room. "Sergeant Howard was here," she began.

"Howard? What did he want?"

"He gave me shock therapy, sort of. He took away my sleeping pills. He made me eat, the worst scrambled eggs in history. He made me walk. He made me angry, and he made me cry."

Simon's face darkened. "I'll make *him* cry."

"No, it was a good thing. He's had a really hard life, and he made me understand what I have to do: get through today. And then tomorrow. And then the next day. I've been on the dark side of the moon, and I need to face things now." She paused. "If you don't want tea, how about some wine?" She brought the bottle for him to open.

"Aren't you having any?" She held only one glass.

"No, if Sergeant Howard comes by tomorrow and finds me hung over, God knows what he'll do." She handed him the corkscrew and watched him use it to remove the cork.

"Jenny, why did he take away your sleeping pills?"

"He didn't trust me."

Simon took a long drink of the cabernet sauvignon. He should have been the one to intervene, not Howard.

"Simon, there's a plant – related to the primrose, I think – that can grow on rocks in terrible conditions, like frigid, oxygen-depleted air. It doesn't just survive, it produces flowers. I've always wondered how it does that. Does it have a relentless will to live or is it just too stubborn to die?"

He didn't like what he was hearing, and he hadn't seen a sign of the defiance which he respected.

"My mother always discouraged stubborn behavior, but maybe it's a good thing to be too stubborn to give up when life isn't what you want it to be. I need to find some of that stubbornness, because I'm alone so much of the time. Sergeant Howard wants me to do this by myself, but I don't think I can. I've been thinking about going back to Texas."

He refilled his glass, knowing as he did so that the wine would not ease the sudden ache he felt in his heart. "When? For how long?"

"Several months, maybe longer."

"I'd not like you to leave home," he said slowly.

"Simon, I don't know where home is these days. If I were a homing pigeon, I'd be flying in circles. And I can't ask you to take care of me. You have a demanding job, and you're in a relationship now."

Yes, with Marcia, who wanted more than a relationship. They'd had a brilliant time on their holiday, but she'd been at him since their return for a commitment he wasn't ready to give. He didn't want to jeopardise anything with her, however.

In the silence that ensued, Jenny felt lost. Simon had been her compass in witness protection, and in some ways, he still was, but it would be wrong to admit her need for him. She had nothing to give in return.

"I've missed our walks," he said finally. "We'll walk, shall we? At the weekend?"

When she took his hand in assent, he shifted his gaze from her eyes. He stood, needing to leave before he did something that would be wrong for both of them. "I'll ring you."

CHAPTER 8

Sergeant Howard brought her mail when he arrived the next day. "Jenny, you should open this," he said. "It's from the Commissioner."

The envelope contained the details of the memorial service to be held for Colin on the first anniversary of his death. She began to tremble. "I still don't understand why he had to die."

"Don't ask why. It'll drive you round the bend. And it'll not help to know. Ask what: What do I do now? And how do I do it?" That was the advice Mrs. T had given him when he asked why his mother had died. It's enough to know you're with us, she had said.

"What did you do on the anniversary of the Thompsons' deaths?"

"Cath and I visited the site. The Thompsons left it to me in their will, and we plan to rebuild there when we've saved enough. Then we took a short holiday." Cath had distracted him from his grief, promising not to put on so much as a pair of knickers all the weekend.

She held out the agenda. "Will you come? You and Cath?"

"If our schedules permit," he said. "In the meantime, get your trainers on. I have a car today, and there's somewhere we need to go."

- -

Jenny sat in the old gray Nissan and watched Sergeant Howard negotiate the streets out of Hampstead. She asked where they were going, but he didn't answer. When he reached the A1, he consulted the map. "To the M25, then past Potters Bar," he said to himself.

They rode in silence until he turned off the motorway. Then she saw the sign: RSPCA Southridge Animal Centre. "Where are we?" she asked.

He turned to her, and what passed for a smile crossed his face. "Hertfordshire. Shall we go in?"

She hesitated. Gruff Sergeant Howard had brought her to a pet place. She was surprised and pleased by his gesture, but a little nervous, too, not sure if she was ready to be responsible for another life. "Did the Thompsons – ?"

"They got me a dog."

She nodded. Inside they introduced themselves to the matronly-looking woman with short gray hair who stood behind the counter. "Edith Beasley," she responded. "Looking for a new pet, are we? We have some wonderful animals here ready for rehoming." She handed Sergeant Howard a set of forms to complete. He held them out to Jenny.

She felt a little shiver of excitement as she listed her name, address, and other particulars. At the bottom of the page was the question: Do you prefer a dog, cat, or other animal? Cats might be easier to care for, she thought, but they could be aloof. She checked the box beside 'Dog' and felt another little shiver. "May we see the animals now?"

"We'll just have a little visit first," Mrs. Beasley purred. She showed them into a small office and scanned the information Jenny had given. "Why do you want a dog, Mrs. Sinclair?"

"I'm a – " the word caught in her throat – "widow." It was the first time she had used the term aloud to describe herself. "I don't want to be alone."

"Are you looking for an animal to protect you?"

"That would be nice, but mainly I want to love him."

Anxiety had begun to defuse her excitement. What if Mrs. Beasley didn't think she was suitable? "There's plenty of space in my flat, and I'm not too far from Hampstead Heath. I'm not employed, so I have plenty of time for a pet." Not employed – that sounded bad. "But I can afford a pet. Really. I can give you financial information, if you need it."

"That won't be necessary," Mrs. Beasley said, "but we do require payment in advance."

Jenny wrote a check for the specified amount. "Could we see the dogs now?"

"Yes, we can conclude our interview after." She led them through a heavy door to a hallway with cages on both sides. "Don't try to touch any of the animals," she counselled. "If you see one you like, I'll bring him or her out to you."

Jenny walked slowly down the hall. She saw the puppies first, some of them bouncing off the floor with enthusiasm as she passed. The adult dogs were only slightly more restrained, terriers pushing their noses through the bars, spaniels wagging their tails, chows and Pekinese barking with smaller, shriller voices than the larger breeds. Only one dog was quiet, a large black Labrador who didn't even raise his head when she called out to him. She remembered reading about Winston Churchill's "black dog," his name for his depression. She had told Colin that her depression was a "black bear," because it was bigger and stronger than a dog. "Tell me about the Lab," she said.

Mrs. Beasley clucked her tongue. "He's obedient; housebroken; he sits and stays, that sort of thing; but he was abandoned, and he's not eating well yet. Grieving for his family, we think. Not the best choice if you're looking for a responsive companion."

We're alike, Jenny thought. He could be her mission, and she could be his. "Could I pat him?" she asked.

Mrs. Beasley opened the cage door and attached a leash to the Lab's collar. "Heel," she said, and he got to his feet and walked beside her, but his tail drooped, and he didn't hold his head up.

Jenny knelt down and held her hand for the dog to sniff. He had paws like a mastiff. When she touched his leg, he lifted it to the shake-hands position. When she took it, she smiled to herself: She was the one who was obedient. Wanting him to hear her voice, she told him how handsome he was. He was very still when she stroked his fur. "He's the one," she said. She would call him Bear.

"We'll need a further discussion then," Mrs. Beasley said, stepping forward to return the Lab to his cage. "Generally we make a home visit before placing an animal."

Jenny's face fell. "But – but – I've already named him! Can't I take him home today?"

"It's not our usual practice," Mrs. Beasley objected.

"Could I have a word?" Sergeant Howard moved a few feet away and beckoned to Mrs. Beasley. He took out his warrant card, explained quietly but firmly why Jenny needed to take the dog today, and promised to guarantee the quality of the home she would provide.

Mrs. Beasley seemed a little flustered by the sergeant's direct approach. "I see – yes – he'll not be the easiest animal to place – perhaps we could schedule a home visit in a few days," she stammered.

"Do you hear that, Bear? You have seen your last cage!"

Mrs. Beasley gave Jenny a sheet of printed instructions: *Caring For Your Dog*. She led him to the sergeant's car and watched while Jenny joined him in the back seat.

"Thank you, Mrs. Beasley," Jenny said, her hand on the Lab's head. "Come see us anytime."

"Thank you, Sergeant Howard," she added as they pulled away. "You knew I couldn't do it alone, didn't you?"

"I had my SAS mates and Cath," he answered. "And it's Nick."

CHAPTER 9

Jenny was alone in the flat with Bear. Nick had stopped at a pet store on the way back from Hertfordshire, and she had bought the highest quality dog food they sold, as well as bowls, treats, a leash, a brush, and a doggy bed. She put the bed on the floor in her bedroom and the bowls in the kitchen. Nick stood waiting in the living room, and she realized he had something to say.

"Jenny, there's more to do, but my leave's over. You'll have to take it from here. If you backslide, I'll hear of it." He returned the bottle which had held her sleeping pills.

He wasn't good at good-byes, but neither was she. A sudden regret seized her, for all the things she didn't know about this man and hadn't thought to ask. She had been so self-absorbed that she hadn't questioned how he had found the time to spend with her. She wanted to smile, to show him what his sacrifice meant to her, but her throat was choked with tears because she didn't feel happy that he was leaving. Breaking news, she thought: "Heart discovered in unfeeling officer." She hugged him, Icky Nicky who was no longer icky.

When she closed the door after him, she expected the flat to be quiet, but it wasn't: She could hear Bear breathing. She remembered waking in the night – when Colin was next to her – and being reassured by the sound of his breathing.

Many mornings when she woke, she knew without looking that he had gone to work because she didn't hear his breath. She would never forget that awful day in the hospital when his chest had been silent. She sat down next to Bear and buried her face in his fur. He didn't pull away, but after a minute she realized that crying was a terrible way to welcome him, so she wiped her tears away.

Simon answered her call after the second ring, alarm in his voice. "Are you all right?"

"Yes," she assured him. "Simon, I just adopted a dog, a big, black, sad dog. Nick Howard took me."

He wanted to shake Howard's hand. Jenny couldn't leave for Texas now. "He'll walk with us then," he said.

"See you Saturday," she answered and hung up. Then she made quick calls to her family, Joanne, and Beth to report the news. Her mother was a little disconcerted to hear that having a pet would prevent her from coming home.

She talked to Bear while she made his dinner, sprinkling a little garlic powder on top to make the food more appealing. He ate a little, but without the unrestrained gusto most dogs had for their food. He lapped some of the water and then stood quietly, waiting for her next instruction. She took him with her while she made her sandwich and watched television. She attached the leash to his collar before taking him downstairs to the backyard. At bedtime she led him to the doggy bed, but he remained standing. When she came out of the shower, she couldn't find him at first. He was lying by the front door, so she made a pallet for herself on the floor next to him, and since she hated seeing him on the hard floor, she put his bed there. With one hand on his side, she could feel him breathing as well as hear him, and for the first night in a long time, she didn't need a sleeping pill.

Jenny spent the next forty-eight hours trying to teach Bear to love her. She practiced all the commands with him – sit, stay, down, come – rewarding him with a treat for each correct response. She fed him and brushed him. Always she talked to him. At night she was still unsuccessful in getting him to sleep in his doggy bed in the bedroom, but in the morning he raised his head when she woke on her pallet, and in the afternoon his tail gave a half wag when she attached the leash to his collar. She hoped the exercise would improve his appetite; when Nick had made her walk, it had had that effect on her.

The third night Bear was sitting in the bedroom when she came out of the shower, so she moved his bed from the front door to the bedroom. He sniffed it, hesitated, sniffed again, and lay down. She felt like cheering.

She climbed into bed and listened. He was still there; she could hear him breathing. As she pulled the covers over herself, she realized she hadn't dreamed about Colin since Nick had first arrived. She was just as lonely for Colin as she had been before, but with Bear, less lonely in the flat. Was that progress? She didn't know. In an attempt to clarify her thoughts, she made a mental list: *Good Things That Have Happened Since Colin Died.* It was short: *I've discovered that Nick is a human being; I'm closer to Colin's mum;* and *I have a dog.* She fell asleep trying to think of a fourth.

The next day she double-knotted the laces on her tennis shoes and walked with Bear into the Heath past the bathing ponds. The trees' skeletal branches reached out but grasped nothing, and ice coated the leaves under her feet like the plastic slipcovers in photo albums. It had been warm when she had seen the ponds for the first time with Colin. Tears started to well up in her eyes, and she sat down on a nearby bench to recover. After a moment she heard a soft whine and felt a weight on her knee. Bear had rested his head there. She slipped off the bench and wrapped her arms around his neck, not caring what passersby might think. Progress, for Bear at least, but she realized how cold the ground must feel on his feet, and she felt guilty for thinking only of herself. She cut the walk short and led him back to the flat.

Later that afternoon Father Goodwyn came by. "I've not been able to reach you in some time," he said. "I've been concerned."

"You were right to worry," she answered. "I was really low."

And terribly thin. He'd not brought food this trip and wished he had. "Let's make tea," he suggested.

They both went into the kitchen. She set the water to boil then took milk from the fridge while he put the cups and spoons on the counter. "Jenny, you could have rung me. Even at night. In the Royal Army, I was available 24/7. Soldiers often sought me out at night. I've always wanted to be where I was needed most."

"Why did you leave?"

He smiled. "My wife and I wanted to have a family, and that's difficult to do when leaves are short and infrequent."

"Was she a soldier?" Jenny filled their cups and watched while he added milk and sugar to his cup. She squeezed a lemon wedge into hers.

"No, a flight attendant. It took awhile for our relationship to develop, partly because of her travel schedule and partly because phone service, where I was, was inadequate and unreliable. We're both very happy with our work schedules now."

They took their cups into the sitting room. "Are you often called away?"

"Not so much, but when I am, my wife, who understands service, holds things together in my absence."

She felt a wave of sadness. "I haven't held things together in Colin's absence."

"But you have a companion now, I see."

She told him about Nick Howard's intervention and introduced Neil to Bear.

"God often uses people to carry out His will," Goodwyn smiled.

Had He used Nick "it-would-kill-me-to-smile" Howard? And a dog? For the first time in weeks, she began to laugh.

CHAPTER 11

Simon had been curious about Jenny's dog. When he called by the flat for their walk, the dog had given a single restrained croak, as close to a bark as she had heard so far, she said. He was a handsome, well behaved animal and probably the reason she was less tense. She certainly smiled more frequently, and her story of "pleasing Mrs. Beasley," as she called it, had made him smile also. "The adoption center made a home visit," she said, "and I spent the entire time trying to send mind messages to Bear to wag his tail so they would know that he was happy with me." Those messages hadn't been necessary today; he wagged his tail at everything she said and followed her like a shadow. "I'm good at teaching creatures to love me, I think," she had said. Yes, both he and the dog had been quick learners.

On the serious side, she'd progressed. "I've discovered that after an avalanche, you can't dig yourself out," she said. "Nick rescued me, but my life is still so empty. Don't laugh, but I decided to beat this grief thing. Take the bull by the horns! I started to make a list of actions, but I couldn't think of any. And then I remembered what you always told me: that no one can do it alone and that the only way out is through. So I'm going to call Dr. Knowles, the psychiatrist."

He recalled Jenny, the victim, struggling to heal; Jenny the witness, the instrument of justice; Jenny the wife. Now she was Jenny the widow, struggling again. He wished there were something he could do. He rarely ate sweets but knew she loved them, so he stopped at a bakery on their walk back to the flat and bought her a chocolate croissant while she and the dog waited outside. The woman who sold him the pastry looked past him to the passersby on the pavement while he counted his change and scowled when he requested a napkin.

"All for me, Bear!" Jenny had exclaimed, explaining that chocolate wasn't good for dogs.

Special Forces operations and then SO-19 hours rendered it impractical, but he had always wanted a dog.

CHAPTER 12

Alcina had thought that she had her anger under control. She had thought that seeing her target would give her a measure of progress, of satisfaction. However, her target had not entered the bakery, and worse, her target had not been alone. Alcina was indignant.

The man had come into the bakery. Her target had waited outside with a dog, a big dog. Was it his dog? Her dog? It was essential to know. Alcina had seethed.

Because her target was not alone, Alcina could not follow her. The gathering of further information would have to wait. Alcina's frustration had mounted.

Was the man a friend or more? All her plans had centered on attacking a single target. Alcina's anger intensified.

The man made his purchase. Her target smiled at the man when he rejoined her. They left together. Alcina's rage boiled over. She wanted to crush something. She allowed one of the yeast rolls to fall onto the floor where she did her best to grind it into the tile.

CHAPTER 13

Sunday, February 23: the anniversary of Colin's death.
Jenny dressed carefully for his memorial service, wanting
to honor him, but the weather was so cold her uniform-blue
wool suit and white blouse were hidden under her heavy
coat.

Her parents were unable to attend, but her father
had sent her a long article about one of the individuals
highlighted in Ken Burns' video series on the American
Civil War. It told the story of a young Union Army major,
Sullivan Ballou, who had written to his wife, Sarah, a week
before the First Battle of Bull Run. In it he mentioned the
conflict he felt between love for his country and love for her.
Had Colin shared that feeling? Ballou was convinced that
if he were killed, he would whisper her name with his last
breath, and he had asked her to believe that the soft breeze
on her cheek belonged to him and that the air that cooled
her was his spirit. He had died on July 29, 1861, at the age of
32. Ballou's letter was beautifully written and very moving,
but Jenny couldn't figure out why her father had wanted
her to read it. Because he thought Colin had been loving and
eloquent? Or did he want her to believe that Colin's spirit
was alive? Didn't he know that the letter would break her
heart all over again? Colin's death had been too sudden and
unexpected for last words, and Ballou and Sarah had had

two boys. Although it must have been difficult for her to raise them by herself, she had not been alone in her years without him.

Joanne came to Hampstead, and the Commissioner sent a car for them. "I'm not sure I can do this," Jenny told her mother-in-law. "See the place Colin was killed. I'll probably cry in front of everyone."

"Anniversaries are difficult, aren't they?" Joanne answered. "The rest of the time we try to look forward, but anniversaries force us to look back."

Chief Superintendent Higham greeted them when they arrived at Oxford Street and escorted them around the corner to the exact site on Davies Street where the oval memorial plaque would be mounted. Colin's sister, Jillian, and her family arrived a few minutes later. Jenny felt damp like the weather, because her tears were just beneath the surface. She hoped neither she nor the skies would spill over. She watched the breeze ruffle the bouquet of flowers Higham had given her and felt warmed, in spite of the chilly temperature, by his thoughtfulness.

Police in cold-weather uniforms blocked Davies Street to through traffic. Beyond the barriers police cars lined the streets in every direction, and hundreds of officers stood shoulder to shoulder, removing their hats in a single gesture when the ceremony began. The customers at the Hog in the Pound peered through the windows, and pedestrians on the promenade across from the station entrance paused to listen.

The Mayor of the City of London spoke first, recalling the event as an example of the stalwart hearts of Londoners. The Chairman of the Police Memorial Trust read the citation, which carried Colin's name, the date of his death, and a summary of the incident which had caused it. His voice was a little unsteady on the final phrases, so he repeated them: "He gave all; he gave his best; he spared nothing." Jenny's tears began to press against her resolve to maintain control.

The Metropolitan Police Commissioner spoke at length about the threat Colin had faced and the additional threat every officer faced in a terrorist world. "At the critical moment, he did not falter," he said. He referred to Colin's sacrifice and the sacrifices all officers and their families made for the public good. Jenny swallowed hard, determined to stem the tide.

Father Goodwyn quoted Laurence Binyon, who had memorialised the fallen: "They shall grow not old, as we that are left grow old: / Age shall not weary them, nor the years condemn. / At the going down of the sun and in the morning / We will remember them." He then closed the service with prayer, asking that God equip all Londoners, civilian or civil servant, to face the days ahead with the strength and courage that Colin had shown when history had called upon him. Jenny knew that, until recently, she had not faced her days with strength and courage, and in a surge of grief the dam broke. She felt Joanne's arm around her shoulders and curved her arm around her mother-in-law's waist. Maybe grief shared would be grief halved.

A long line of officers came by to pay respects. Brian was there with Beth. Danny Sullivan and several of her other witness protection officers had attended. Nick Howard introduced her to Cath, a striking redhead, and asked about Bear. "He's fine," Jenny told him. "And thank you. Not just for Bear. For everything."

Simon stood to one side, finally stepping forward to give her a hug after the crowd thinned out. "He stepped up, Jenny," he said. "Showed us all how it's done. Be proud." He handed her a handkerchief, which made her smile because he never had any handkerchiefs.

After the service Jenny invited Joanne, Jillian, Derek, and the children to the flat for tea and tea cakes. She had ordered the pastries from a bakery on the High Street, and a thin olive-skinned woman with sharp features had delivered them and collected the payment. Bear, next to Jenny when she opened the door, had yawned at the woman and then made a single, short shrill bark. Jenny thought his reaction was a little strange. Bear rarely barked, and she hadn't known he could make that high-pitched a sound.

CHAPTER 14

At long last Alcina had the information she needed. The target herself had unwittingly provided the address, even the directions to the flat. Bitterness added an edge to Alcina's anger. The target's flat had multiple floors. Spacious for two occupants and annoyingly ostentatious for one. Much larger than the one she and Tony had lived in even when he was earning good money. The dog had been at the target's side when she opened the door to Alcina, so the dog lived there. There had been no indication of a man's presence.

An advance and a setback. Knowing where her target resided was a critical step forward. She would, however, have to figure out what to do about the dog. Was she equal to this? Yes. She would not be defeated by a mere animal.

In the meantime she would put her mark on trial, like they had done to Tony. Greek mythology told the story of the Greeks' siege of Troy, in which many forces had been involved. She was only one, but she could vary her type of attack and make herself seem plural. A quick solution was too easy; not wanting to tip her hand too soon, she would create fear through indirect contact first. Even small actions could be very satisfying. She would mount a sort of siege on her, repeated assaults over a long period of time. She couldn't cut off her supplies, but she could disrupt her life and destroy her peace. And that would give her time to decide how to deal with the dog.

When Tony was arrested, she had felt frightened and helpless. Throughout the judicial process, her helplessness had magnified, reaching an unbearable height with his conviction. Now, however, she felt powerful, powerful enough to succeed at a more complex challenge than she had anticipated.

CHAPTER 15

"Memorial Service Held for Slain Officer" and "City Remembers Met Hero," the headlines read. Jenny skimmed the articles and then the pictures, paying closer attention to the photos of Colin than the one of the plaque or the gathering of mourners at the memorial site. She studied each feature, willing the black-and-white image to glow with color and smile at her. Weren't memorial services supposed to help? She felt as if her scar of grief had ruptured all over again.

As she waited for her first session with Dr. Knowles to begin, she noted that he had added an aquarium to the reception area, but she wasn't entertained. She watched the fish swimming in circles and felt she had been doing the same since Colin's death.

When she entered the consulting room, she showed him the newspaper clippings. She hadn't seen the psychiatrist for over three years, since he had counseled her after her rape. What had been graying hair then was uniformly gray now, but the laugh lines on his face were still present, deeper even than before. She had often wondered how, when he dealt with anguish and sorrow every day, someone in his profession acquired laugh lines. When he finished perusing the articles, she began by questioning the idea of getting over Colin's death. "He was such a big part of my life. I'm not sure I want to let him go."

"Remembering him is positive," Knowles agreed. "Memories of lost loved ones can cause us to acknowledge them, to give tribute to their importance in our lives. However, I don't recommend focussing on regrets."

"Of course I regret things!" she exclaimed. "He was killed!"

"I'm referring to remembering the whole person, not just the way he died. I'd not like you to stay in the moment when you first heard he was gone or saw his casket buried. Jenny, memories are not intended to hold us back from living or to keep us in the same place. That's a sort of prison. Living in the past is not living. There was a British psychologist who claimed that 'All the fine art of living lies in a mingling of letting go and holding on.' I would agree with him."

"I can't forget those things," she argued. "They're part of me, and they still hurt."

"Yes, but you can limit the amount of time you spend thinking on them. Instead, seek a combination of negative and positive and gradually replace sad memories with memories of happier times. The author of *Peter Pan* said that memory gives us roses in December. I believe Colin would want you to have roses."

Red roses, she thought. Colin had known that red was her favorite color. "But all roses have thorns."

"Yes, that's the negative, but the flowers have greater importance. It is possible to enjoy them without being pierced."

"Then when will this grief end? It has been a year. Shouldn't I be doing better?"

"'Should' is not a word I like to use," he said. "Your grief experience is unique to you, and grief never ends completely."

"Are you going to tell me that grief is a journey? I hate that metaphor! I may be weighed down with 'baggage,' but in the real world other people are traveling, too. And when the trip ends, everyone gets to go home."

"Where is home for you now, Jenny?"

"It used to be the flat, because Colin was there. Now – " she thought for a moment. "I don't know."

Knowles nodded. "You've lost your sense of belonging.

That's a normal response."

"I always thought normal was supposed to be good!" she objected, letting her frustration show.

"Normal is neither good nor bad. But an important step in dealing with grief is to identify its components. Grief is a bigger word than it seems. It's more than just sadness; it's loss and can be a type of trauma. Many of the symptoms you experienced after previous traumas may return, because a new trauma can revive an old one."

"Or get mixed up, I think, because sometimes I dream about the man who raped me, but instead of attacking me, he has Colin's blood on his hands."

Knowles nodded. "Has your appetite been affected?"

"Why do you care about what I eat?" she asked, still feeling flustered.

Knowles smiled slightly, recognising her irritability as a symptom of her situation. "Because loss of appetite could cause you to confuse physical depression with emotional depression."

"I think I had both kinds of depression, until Nick Howard showed up. He's a firearms officer who filled in sometimes when I was in witness protection. One morning he arrived at my door with breakfast and made me eat. And later he took me to an animal center and arranged for me to adopt a dog."

"That's a very positive step," Knowles agreed. "Often grief causes us to subsume our social needs at a time when the friendship and acceptance of others is most important. Had you stopped eating?"

"Not consciously. I just didn't care about it one way or the other."

"Have your sleep habits been disturbed?"

"I had nightmares for a while." The dreams had stayed with her when she woke, stabbing her like shards from a broken wineglass. "After that passed, I couldn't get enough sleep. But now that I have Bear, I'm up and out at regular intervals."

"Do you feel personally secure in your flat, now that you are living there alone?"

She nodded. "Colin had an alarm system installed."

"Are financial considerations a source of insecurity?"

"No," she smiled. "I can even afford you. For a while, at least."

"Are there any other concerns you'd like to share?"

"After Colin's death, I withdrew for a while. Of course, the first few weeks, when I was in shock, people were with me, and there were things that had to be done. Since then, the reality of his death has hit me. I've felt overwhelmed. Grief hurts in so many ways."

"Grief doesn't always occur in a logical sequence, Jenny. Grief stages are often repeated. What are you feeling today?"

"Sad. Empty. I've lost my identity, my femininity. After I was raped, it took me a long time to trust a man's touch and even longer to love it. Colin was wonderful to me."

"You miss physical intimacy."

"Yes. Desiring someone and having someone desire me. That part of my life is dead now."

"Perhaps we could agree that your sexuality is in abeyance," Knowles suggested. "When a loved one dies, our lives go on, at first in part and later in full."

She shook her head. "No. Just tell me how to get through this. I want it to become history, for the horror and grief to fade and only the facts remain, like a chapter in a book I can set down and close. Not like a book that is still being written."

Knowles smiled at her impatience. It had been a positive as well as a negative in her previous therapy. "'How poor are they who have not patience! / What wound did ever heal but by degrees?'"

"*Othello, Act Two,*" she answered, a little surprised by his literary quote. Shakespeare had written more comedies than tragedies, but she had spent more time studying the tragedies and so-called histories than his lighter works.

"Acceptance is the first step," he continued, "acceptance of Colin's death and the feelings you are experiencing as a result, even acceptance of the time it will take for healing. I'd like you to pamper yourself a bit, for example, by indulging in a favourite food. And add some beauty to your environment, perhaps by purchasing a bouquet of flowers."

"But Colin should be doing that!" she exclaimed.

"No 'shoulds,'" he reminded her. "Simply tell yourself that he's not here, but he would want you to enjoy your life. I always recommend exercise, and your new pet will keep you moving. Also, occupying your time will help you. Find new activities you can enjoy, either by yourself or with others, particularly at the weekend or during holiday periods. Establish a routine. I want you to find ways to distract yourself from your grief so that you're not feeling it all the time. That will allow other emotions to come into play that may have been dormant."

A new list. She should have been writing all his suggestions down. "You want me to stay busy."

"Jenny, I'd rather you not focus solely on your loss. I wish I could take the pain away, but I can't. There are no easy answers here. Grief can't be hurried, but over time your feelings will become less intense. In the meantime I want you to know that I'll work with you for as long as you need."

No quick fix. That was right out of Simon's instruction manual.

CHAPTER 16

Alcina purchased several copies of the papers, clipping the picture of her target from each one. She taped them to the refrigerator, the mirror in the bathroom, and the back of the front door. She had long conversations with the snaps, sometimes laughing at the sad expression on her target's face and not at all disturbed that her subject did not answer her. She would have preferred colour photographs, however, and it occurred to her that if she purchased a camera – not in Hampstead, of course, where it would be too expensive – she could shoot pictures herself, of her target, her street, the building where she lived. The idea energised her, and she clapped her hands at her ingenuity.

The camera idea was only one of many. Her mind had become increasingly fertile, teeming with ideas which spawned more ideas. She had access to her target's porch and letter-box. What fun it would be to leave surprises there for her target to find, surprises that would shock and distress rather than delight. She began to scribble her ideas on bits of paper and then examined each one, trying to decide which would be most productive, attempting to put them in some sort of order. Some showed such promise that she could use them more than once.

None of her ideas, however, addressed the issue of the dog. Her target might leave the flat without the dog, but Alcina could not predict how frequently that might occur. The dog would never be out without her; hence Alcina could not attack the dog directly.

An indirect method of removing the animal permanently would have to be found.

"My terror campaign is about to begin," she said, her teeth bared, to the picture on the refrigerator. "I work in the suburb where you live. I am there six days each week. Many, many opportunities lie ahead of me." She stabbed one photo with a stiff finger. "One day I will catch you. I will have dealt with the dog, and it will not be able to protect you."

CHAPTER 17

The morning raid had ended earlier than expected, and Simon Casey's team were returning their kit to their lockers when a group of ARV (Armed Response Vehicle) officers entered to collect theirs.

"Beth's been dead worried about Jenny," Davies told Casey. "She hasn't seen her at school lately. Have you seen her?"

"She's not herself. Still sad-on most of the time," Casey answered. "Planning to see the shrink."

"Is that the bird whose snap was in the paper?" Abbott, one of the ARV drivers, asked in a loud voice. "Lovely."

Casey turned to look at him but said nothing.

"That's none of yours," Davies cautioned.

"Just needs a good poke, I'd say," Abbott continued. "Best cure for depression I know. All she has to do is drop her knickers and I'll set her straight."

Two swift, fluid steps, one well-placed thrust, and Abbott found himself on his knees, gasping for breath. "You bloody bastard," he hissed through his teeth, rage overcoming his surprise. "Can't take a joke!" When he got to his feet, Davies' arm across his chest restrained him.

Casey stepped back. The other members of his team stood beside him, curious and alert, none of them blocking his path. He waited, impassive, his arms loose at his sides.

"The calm before the storm, mate," Davies warned Abbott. "Leave it."

Abbott shrugged off Davies' arm and opened his locker. Casey closed his, very deliberately, and departed.

Later Casey berated himself. He shouldn't have let Abbott's remarks about Jenny get to him. He had been unprofessional. Couldn't he control himself? If a bloke commented inappropriately about Marcia, would he react in the same manner? Their fun times had been less frequent of late, both of them overworked, but he cared about her. Unlike Jenny, Marcia was on an even keel.

He had told Marcia about finding the sickly child in the closet. The team had raided an address where intel had thought drug dealing was taking place. They had found only a deceased female on the premises. They then heard scratching from the bedroom closet. He had never seen such hollow, sunken eyes or tiny wrists. The child wore stale and soiled clothes, but when he coughed, his breath carried a distinct fruity odor.

"Ketoacidosis," Marcia had said. "Symptom of starvation." She hadn't seemed troubled, and he had been puzzled by her matter-of-fact response. She hadn't asked what had happened to the child, but he had told her anyway. "We rang for an ambulance and Child Protection. Their officers sorted it."

Still no questions from Marcia. Perhaps she carried her professional objectivity a bit too far, but she couldn't do her job if she let every case affect her. Some insulation from the tragedies she encountered was necessary.

He had not spoken with her of his desire to have children, and he was a bit surprised that she had not raised the subject. He felt they were still in the early days of their relationship but knew she felt differently. Strange that she wanted a commitment before they had addressed this issue.

- -

Marcia saw the articles in the papers about the memorial service and asked Simon if he had attended. "I worked for him awhile back," he said. "Special assignment." He was always short on chat, only mentioning police incidents once or twice. She wondered occasionally if her muted responses increased his reticence, but off the job she preferred to focus on the lighter side of life. Keeping the conversation going almost by herself was no bother, as long as it led to laughter or lovemaking.

She knew that Simon believed that actions were a truer reflection of a man's intentions than anything he said. She agreed but missed the endearments Adrian used to whisper in bed. She had to admit, however, that in some ways Simon was more attentive to her needs than Adrian had been. Adrian's desertion of her still rankled; it coloured everything she had done since. Really, she should join AA: Actors Anonymous, for those who couldn't detach completely from their relationships with actors. Since he had left her, she'd had a tendency to hold onto things more tightly, although she tried to disguise it when she was with Simon, fearing it would cause friction between them. Holding back wasn't easy, but she felt she had to make their relationship work to prove that she was worthy of love.

Silly Adrian! He always wanted to be the centre of attention, even thought he was destined for greatness. "I was born with a stage name," he had crowed. "What could look better in lights than Adrian Hall?" She missed the night life; it was such a change from what she did during the day. Her work with patients – seeing the love some of them received from their families – made her long even more for that sort of connection in her own life.

Simon was more serious than Adrian had been, but she had been able to make him laugh. Adrian's unpredictability had been exciting. His work as an actor hadn't always been regular, and he tended to spend what he earned as soon as he had it, so she'd had to pitch in. She hadn't minded at the time, but she appreciated Simon, because he never expected it of her. When they went out, or on holiday, he paid for everything, which made her feel loved, whether he said so or not. Their best times, in fact, were when they were on holiday. It was the only time she had his full attention.

Simon's work was dangerous and required intense focus. She was a workaholic, and her high standards made her frustrated with a system that sometimes kept patients waiting and treated the physical disease with little regard for a patient's fears. Over the years she had developed a thicker skin, but some of the things she saw were so heartbreaking they still affected her. She and Simon were well matched; he had high standards also, although he handled the responsibility of life or death decisions better than she did. The autocratic nature of the A&E didn't bother her, because she was glad to leave those judgements to someone else.

They had been at each other lately. She had been busier than usual, and so had he, even at the weekends. Some weeks he worked eighteen-hour shifts. His leave didn't always coincide with hers. Perhaps a holiday would help, even a short one. And she needed to stop thinking about Adrian. She hadn't had as much as a postcard from him since he left for fame and fortune in New York, nor had he given her a forwarding address. Consequently she had had to decide, alone, to terminate the pregnancy.

CHAPTER 18

Alcina carried out most of her reconnaissance early in the morning, before first light. Each day on her way to the bakery she researched the neighbourhood of her target and on many occasions left evidence of her presence for her target to find. Although she rarely saw anyone during those hours, she didn't want to attract any attention so she didn't move quickly through the streets. She imagined herself not walking but gliding, and she was glad that she was alone. She laughed to herself. No one would suspect a lone woman. She was stronger alone. She was also less noticeable thin than she would have been had she been well fed. A shadow of her former self, she thought with a bitter smile.

She was a shadow, moving among shadows, hidden in shadows. The partial darkness camouflaged her as did her clothing, the charcoal greys and taupes she now wore almost as a uniform.

She considered the various meanings in her mind. A shadow, a cloud. Yes, she was a cloud, a dark spot looming over her target's life. She wanted to be as close as her target's shadow. She was also a shadow of potential violence, because one day she would shadow her and then strike. Contemplating that gave her a fierce joy.

Would her target get away? No, no one could escape a shadow. And when Alcina stepped out of the darkness, her attack would be so sudden that her target would be unprepared, defenceless. All the power rested with Alcina, *skia*, the shadow. Alcina, *skotos*, the darkness.

Jenny opened the front door to collect her newspaper and nearly stepped into a black mess on her front porch, ashes which the rain had turned into sludge. She was puzzled. To her knowledge, none of the other occupants of the building smoked, and they had their own entrance, so they couldn't have spilled their garbage by her door. Hoping it wouldn't hurt the flowers in the beds on each side, she hosed it into them.

The rain subsided enough for her to walk with Bear, but the streets were still wet, so she dried his paws before they reentered the flat. She prepared his dinner and then hers. Then she found the journal Simon had given her and sat down at the roll-top desk that had belonged to Colin's father. He had rarely used it, but she knew he had valued it because he had repaired and refinished it. She started a list: *Ways to Keep Busy.*

1. *Read Colin's books.* Could she learn to like science fiction? Maybe she should read C.S. Lewis' book on grief first.
2. *Listen to Colin's CDs.*
3. *Make his favorite recipes.* Roast beef and mashed potatoes. She had given up on Yorkshire pudding; hers was invariably as dense as a hockey puck and tough too.

4. *Walk Bear.* Really, he walked her.
5. *Walk with Simon.* He was so tired these days, sleeping at the base some nights because there were so many armed operations. It worried her.
6. *Visit tourist sites.* Alone? Yes.

Smiling, she added:

7. *Make more lists? Adopt more pets?*

She was spending less and less time at Beth's school and the Hollisters' bookstore. She had enjoyed her work at both places before Colin was killed, but his death had reshaped her. She needed a new direction, something that would occupy her time in a meaningful way. Simon would say she needed a mission. When Neil Goodwyn visited the next afternoon, she put the question to him. "What am I meant to do with my life?"

"That question indicates that a good deal of healing has taken place in you," he said. "You may be past what I call 'hard grief,' the initial shock and anger that accompanies the sudden death of a loved one. In the Army we called sudden death the 'short good-bye.' We couldn't make heavy weather of it because there was often no time for sorrow."

"Does grief end? I asked Dr. Knowles, and he didn't think so."

"I don't believe grief ends, but it can turn into 'soft grief,' the residue of what we feel at first."

She thought about the concept, hard and soft, like the difference between torrential rains and drizzles.

"Soft grief has the elements of acceptance and peace built into the sadness. Acceptance is a sort of letting go. It's not the same as starting over, because it precedes starting over."

How complex and tenacious grief was. "What did God expect me to do after Colin was killed?"

"To grieve deeply and to hold onto Him tightly," Goodwyn answered gently.

"Like falling into the deep end of a swimming pool and having to hold onto the side," she said slowly.

"Something like that, yes."

"I didn't do that. I sank."

"And God sent a lifeguard," smiled Goodwyn, remembering her description of Nick Howard's actions.

"And a life preserver," she said, thinking of Bear. "What does God expect me to do now?"

"To use what you learnt. Nothing is wasted in God's kingdom."

"But all I know about are grief, fear, and isolation," she objected. "That's not good news. And I don't see how they lead to a career of any kind."

"Don't forget hope and healing and victory," Goodwyn countered. "I am confident that you will find a way to communicate those."

Jenny wasn't so sure. She didn't feel healed, much less victorious, and hope was a dangerous thing. Even a thin flicker of hope hurt terribly when it was snuffed out. She didn't know what she dared to hope for now, and hope was just the first stage of the process, leading to – what? It was all a conundrum with no clues.

CHAPTER 20

"Do you have a support system?" Dr. Knowles asked at Jenny's next appointment.

"Yes, and I've neglected most of them," she confessed. "I withdrew over the winter. All I wanted was to sleep and dream about Colin. I took sleeping pills to sleep more. I slept through meals. I didn't break down; I eroded. Somehow the sorrow wore me down."

"And it was at that stage that Nick Howard intervened?"

"Yes. He's not very talkative, but even a short conversation with him wore me out. I fell asleep before he left, and he must have searched the flat, because he found my sleeping pills and took most of them away." Like a detective, she thought, remembering her husband and feeling a tightness in her throat.

"Did you want to die, Jenny? When you stopped eating and took drugs to sleep?"

She didn't reply right away, realizing that Nick Howard had protected her from herself. "I didn't think about it in those terms. I just wanted to dream of Colin. That was the only way I could be with him. I didn't stop eating entirely; I just wasn't hungry. And I didn't care whether I lived or not."

"And now?"

"I have Bear. I know it sounds silly, but it helps to be responsible for someone, even if it's a dog."

Knowles nodded. "He forces you to stay in the present. I would encourage you to do that also."

"But I don't want to, because Colin isn't in the present. I was planning to take some pictures with his camera – I thought I might feel closer to him if I adopted some of his interests – but there was still film in it. And when I had it developed, I saw a picture of the two of us, which made me miss him all over again. He was wearing slacks with a shirt and pullover sweater instead of his usual three-piece suit. He had his arm around me. I had on jeans, as usual, and a sloppy sweater, and I was leaning against him. I depended on him in so many ways. We looked so happy, and we were. We had no clue to what lay ahead. It's the last picture that was taken of him."

"When was that?"

"Christmas in Kent, 2001. My family was there, and my brother, Matt, took the shot."

"Photography could be a rewarding avenue for you to pursue."

Jenny shook her head. "It would take more concentration than I have right now, and staying busy isn't much help. I went to the Tate Britain, but I didn't have any insights. I liked Constable's paintings of the Heath, and Whistler was very particular about the frames which supported his paintings. I read all the commentaries and still felt like I was just spinning my wheels, because none of it made me less sad. Turner's paintings reflect his belief that we have no power over the things that happen to us. That's not encouraging. And I don't see how any of these activities help me to move forward."

"Recognising what you can control helps. For example, what you eat and drink, what you wear, when you sleep. Be proactive. When you walk, decide at the outset how far. Then consider your feelings. When sadness occurs, tell yourself that you've accepted it as a part of your life, but only a part. Limit your grief. Some persons allow themselves to experience their sorrow only for ten minutes in the morning and ten minutes in the evening."

He wanted her to be disciplined. Colin had wanted that

for her, too. He had thought that she'd be less impatient with his long hours if she occupied her time more productively, but when she did and he couldn't reach her during the day, he was frustrated: a real catch-22. There had been times when he'd been bothered with her complaints about the weather and once because she had taken too long to get dressed for a social event. She had discovered the hard way that he didn't think sandwiches were appropriate for dinner, although she had made them to avoid having to reheat meals he had been too late to eat on time. They had both raised their voices, and she had yelled, "Why did you marry me if you felt this way?"

His face had softened, and he had replied, the edge gone from his tone, "Because I loved you. And I still do. Sandwiches notwithstanding."

Her anger had evaporated, and she had embraced him, promising to reheat every meal with a smile. She heard Dr. Knowles' voice.

"Jenny, where are you?"

"Remembering," she sighed. "Colin's impatience. His moods. At the time I considered them flaws, but I would welcome them now. Why wasn't I more understanding? More patient? None of our disagreements seem important anymore."

"Jenny, every couple has misunderstandings. They're a normal part of dynamic human relationships. But I don't recommend dwelling on regrets. If you must, restrict the amount of time you spend thinking on them. However, in spite of these techniques, some days may still be more difficult than others. Psychological healing's not linear."

She gave a bitter laugh. "That's a nice way to put it. I think it's all capricious, like turning over your cards to see what you were dealt. One good day doesn't necessarily lead to another."

"Nor does a bad day lead to another," he said with a smile. "You are capable of dealing even with the bad days, Jenny."

"Maybe so, but I still wish you'd prescribe something to make it easier."

"Have you had any recurrence of your previous trauma?"

"No, my grief over Colin has forced everything else out, like a mutant alien fully occupying its host."

"You have, however, retained your sense of humour," he commented. "In view of the fact that you've come through a difficult time and seem to be functioning, I'd recommend against antidepressants at this time."

"So I have to tough it out."

"At this stage, that's best, I think. Change has to begin in the mind, and I think you've already taken the first steps."

- -

On the tube ride back to Hampstead, Jenny decided it was time to reconnect with family and friends. She resolved to invite Joanne to Hampstead for lunch and a day of shopping. She would phone her family and ask if they could come to London for Easter. The next time Jillian, Colin's sister, called, she would accept her party invitation. And Beth – she needed to see Beth and share her joy in her pregnancy. Just because Colin was dead didn't mean that she should treat everyone else as if they were. Filling her time like this wasn't very meaningful – it didn't address the long-term issues – but maybe it was a step.

Bear was happy to see her and even happier when she donned her coat and attached his leash to his collar. Lost in thought, she let him lead the way, and when she found herself panting at the top of Parliament Hill, she was a little annoyed with him. On their first walk in the Heath and many times since, Colin had taken her to Parliament Hill because on clear days it gave a spectacular view of London. She had purposely avoided it since his death. She found a bench near the summit and took a minute to catch her breath, closing her eyes against the sights they had seen together. Bear lay quietly at her feet.

A wisp of breeze caressed her face, and she suddenly became aware that the air around her was warm. Then she felt the scar on her cheek tingle slightly. Colin knew that the scar on her cheek bothered her. During lovemaking he had always caressed her cheek, either with his lips or the tips of his fingers, to let her know that it did not detract from her appearance. She sat very still, not wanting to break the spell of whatever was happening. Could Colin's spirit be alive, as Neil Goodwyn believed and Sullivan Ballou had hoped? Gradually, gently, the warmth receded. She clasped her coat around her, barely breathing, and waited. Bear nudged her foot with his nose. He was hungry. She was, too, and cold, but she didn't move. Darkness came, but the warmth did not return. With slow steps, she led Bear back to the flat.

- -

After dinner she plopped down on the sofa and picked up the C.S. Lewis book. *A Grief Observed,* he had titled it. He had monitored his feelings of grief as Dr. Knowles had suggested to her. Reading his bio, she felt an immediate connection with him. He had been seventeen years older than his wife. Colin had been thirteen years older than she was. Lewis' wife, Joy, had died of cancer after only four years of marriage. Not a sudden death, but a short marriage, like hers, with many wishes and expectations unfulfilled.

As she digested the pages, she remembered feeling the way Lewis had, the sudden tears, exhaustion so extreme that even the smallest chore seemed too hard. He, too, had wrestled with the platitudes of friends who intended comfort but missed the mark. He claimed that grief felt like fear. Was it grief, then, and not fear that made her nervous when she went out?

He referred to his relationship with his wife as a house of cards, because it had fallen so easily with her death. Colin had made her stronger; had her strength died with him? Was Lewis right? Was it all a house of cards? No, Nick Howard had proved to her that it was not.

She read on. "Passionate grief does not link us with the dead but cuts us off from them," Lewis wrote. That was true. When she'd felt Colin's caress on her cheek – if it had been Colin – she had been resting, not experiencing desperate sorrow. And in his own way, Lewis had felt the assurance of Joy's presence. Maybe her experience had been real.

He called his writing about grief, his "jottings." She had made lists to try to order her thoughts and feelings, to find clarity in the fog. Every time he described grief, it changed, he wrote. They had both recorded a series of still pictures.

Lewis' grief hadn't ended; he had just stopped writing about it, claiming that it was time for a "spring cleaning" of the mind. Was grief clutter? As spring approached, should she clear her mind? Not of Colin. Lewis had returned to teaching at Cambridge, but illness had intervened, and a short three years later, he had died. His book gave no clues about what she should do with the rest of her life.

On her Heath walks, she saw piles of debris beside many of the paths, evidence of forest control, and smelled the damp peaty aroma of decaying wood. If even the wild areas of the Heath needed clearing, possibly her mind did too. In several areas London plane trees had been uprooted in the hurricane of October, 1987. A year later new trees had been planted which were already tall. It wouldn't be sufficient then simply to remove deadwood from her life; she had to replace it with something.

Lewis had decided to focus on the two great commandments, love God and love your neighbor. If that meant setting aside his record of grief, had his book been nothing more than a crutch? Was she supposed to stop looking inside and direct her attention outward? If so, to what?

CHAPTER 21

Alcina pored over the directions that came with the camera. According to the tips for better pictures, photographing moving subjects was more difficult than recording still ones. She wasn't concerned about the quality or composition of her shots, however. Just the target. Bad shots of the target would mar her attractiveness, a welcome side effect and a prediction of what was to come. The camera as an instrument of prophecy. Excellent. She had not anticipated that.

First she would snap shots from a distance. Then, as she became more confident, she would move closer. The target focussed on the dog while she walked, paying no attention to her surroundings. She would not notice Alcina.

Her physical attacks would follow the same pattern: threats from a distance or while her target was not in the vicinity, then becoming more direct and immediate.

A festive season was approaching. Just the sort of thing that would be satisfying to disrupt. She would leave evidence of her presence. Then she would photograph it to savour later while she imagined her target's reaction. The camera: a more useful tool in her arsenal than she had expected. Well worth what she had spent.

The dog. She had still not decided how to deal with it, but she felt certain an idea would present itself.

CHAPTER 22

"Shock and awe" – what Jenny thought of as the American response to 9/11 but what was really the beginning of the invasion of Iraq – came and went. Prime Minister Tony Blair's speeches and the Queen's message to the troops, however, reminded her that it was a coalition effort, with the UK, Australia, and other countries participating.

She felt no awe at her country's display of military strength, only shock at the images on the news. Seeing her country assert itself should have made her feel powerful, but instead she feared what lay next. These bombings were only the beginning of the conflict. Lives would be lost on all sides.

In London, the police were on the alert for reprisals. Spokesmen insisted there was no specific threat, but the Commissioner brought in additional officers to patrol the city. That should have made her feel safer, but instead the news reports increased her anxiety. Ridiculous! she told herself. Terrorists wouldn't strike in Hampstead.

In contrast, she supported Red Nose Day for the first time. To raise money for Comic Relief, which used comedy to let people know about poverty in the UK and Africa, plastic or foam red noses were sold at Sainsbury's and other places. She purchased one but then wasn't brave enough to wear it. Her only comic relief came when she tried to imagine Simon with a red nose.

She was still preoccupied with her private battles, as she told Simon on one of their Heath walks. "I've been working with Dr. Knowles to cope better with my grief. I don't cry as much as I used to – most days I'm more like a drizzle than a downpour – but I'm still sad and lost. And I need to figure out what to do with the rest of my life." She smiled. "Besides walking with you and Bear. And taking pictures with Colin's camera. My camera now, I guess."

"What do you take snaps of?"

"Things that don't move!" she laughed. "And even then, my pictures are spectacularly dull. The camera and I don't agree on what will make an interesting shot. And I have less focus than it does. I'm still in kindergarten when it comes to photography."

"When I was a lad, I had a small camera," he said, feeling a bit wistful. "Photography's more technical and the equipment more advanced now. Keep at it."

She shortened the leash to keep Bear from bounding into the bathing ponds on their way back. Everywhere she looked, she saw new growth, which reassured her. "I love the Heath," she added. "No matter what the season, something is green, like fresh starts and new beginnings. And the daffodils are resplendent this year." She handed Bear's leash to Simon. "Winning over Bear was my mission for a while, but I think that mission is accomplished. You've won him over, too. He likes you."

When they passed the ponds near Highgate, Jenny saw the little boy with the blue eyes she'd seen in the fall. Even in his coat, he looked hunched over, and his face was thinner. She introduced herself and Simon to the child's grandmother, a Mrs. Dunaway fortunately not as thin as her grandson, and then talked to the child. "Do you like animals? Would you like to pat my dog?"

"He doesn't talk," Mrs. Dunaway said. "Hasn't since his mum was killed. He was in the house, but we don't know if he saw it happen or found her after. The police sent a special officer, someone trained to speak with children. She was ever so patient and nice, but she couldn't get him to say anything. He hasn't said a word since, not one. He eats what's put in front of him – well, some – he lets himself be dressed and bathed – but not one word. And not a tear. Not even at the funeral when the rest of us were beside ourselves. He just sat."

"Do they know who did it? Did they catch him?"

"No, their physical evidence didn't lead to anyone, and since Jack didn't speak..."

"Was he always quiet?" Jenny asked, feeling a little uncomfortable talking about the boy in the third person when he was there.

"No, the opposite. Playful, wasn't he just!"

He shut down, Jenny thought. She understood.

"His dad's in sales," Mrs. Dunaway continued. "He took some time off after, but now he's on the road again. Jack's an only child. He lives with us, with my husband and me."

Simon stood by her side, observing. Jenny liked children. She had wanted Sinclair's. "How old is he?" he asked.

"Ten plus," Mrs. Dunaway answered.

Jenny sat down next to him, picturing Nick Howard at this age, when the Thompsons had taken him in. "Jack, my name is Jenny, and my dog's name is Bear. He's really gentle if you'd like to pat him. You don't have to say anything."

Jack looked up, but he didn't move. His little body was caved in, like a puppet's when no one is holding the strings.

"My husband, Colin, had blue eyes just like yours," she said. "He was killed, too. I miss him, just like you miss your mum." She stood. "Being sad is okay. I'm still sad, and I'm a grownup." She waited, but Jack didn't respond, even to Bear's wagging tail.

"He's not meaning to be rude," Mrs. Dunaway said.

"He isn't rude, he's upset," Jenny told her. "I hope I'll see you again."

"We're here most days. My husband and I run one of the dry cleaners' in Highgate, and we take turns walking with Jack. We've been told that exercise might help, and being outdoors as well."

As Jenny and Simon walked away, she was reminded of the poem, "My Boy Jack," written by Rudyard Kipling after his son was reported missing in World War I. The Jack she had met was present in body but lost in spirit. Although Kipling's son was eventually declared killed in action, perhaps some hope existed for this boy. "It was such a sad poem," she told Simon, "because Kipling was afraid his son was dead."

He took her hand, and they walked in silence through Hampstead's narrow, winding streets. "Nice flowers," he said, noticing the fresh blooms on either side of her porch. "I see you've taken up gardening."

"Someone trampled on them. I had to replant them twice."

"Vandalism?" he asked.

"I found ashes on the porch, and on another occasion, coffee grounds. It was irritating."

"You should report it. There may have been other incidents in the area."

"Do you have time to come in? I'll make tea." He seemed relaxed today, comfortable and calm, and not as tired as he had been lately. He romped with Bear while she brewed, Bear giving a series of short happy barks and Simon laughing as he wrestled with him.

"Bear, sit," she said when she brought the tea. "Simon, sit," she laughed. She gave Bear a treat and poured their cups. "Tea is such a comfort. Sometimes I think I should stop drinking it as a habit and make a solitary cup and concentrate instead. You know, breathe in the aroma, sip, and think."

"I just want the caffeine," he confessed.

"Then you're missing out on the whole experience," she teased. "From the sight of the steam rising from the cup to the scent of the lemon, the pressure of the cup against your lips, the warmth and taste on your tongue, and the relaxed feeling it elicits: Tea massages your senses."

She had described drinking tea as a sensual experience. At a loss for words, he held out his cup for a refill and thought about how far she had come. When he was first put in charge of her protection, she was recovering from surgery and severe injuries. He had looked for signs of pain to treat, and there had been many. When she had healed somewhat and had become rebellious, he had looked for signs that she would do as she was told. When she got together with Sinclair, he had hoped to see signs of unhappiness, dissatisfaction, some hint that she could be interested in someone else, but there had been none. After Sinclair had been killed, he had looked for signs that she was still interested in living. Now she spoke of her lips and her tongue. Was she coming on to him? "You're waking up," he said, his eyes searching her face while trying to quell the rising hope he felt.

She nodded. "The other day I realized how soft Bear's fur is. And when I walk him in the morning, I smell the fresh bread at the bakery. Food has flavor again. The small miracles of life, according to Neil Goodwyn. And then I feel guilty, because I'm alive and Colin isn't."

He took her hand. "You're not meant to feel that. The guilt."

His hand was warm and firm. "That's what Dr. Knowles says. He wants me to forgive myself for being alive."

"I want that for you also, love," he said and saw her smile. He looked at the little dip in her throat just above her collarbone and then the faint scar on her cheek that put him in mind of how he'd come to know her. Her dark hair had a sheen to it, and the lace on her shirt did not completely conceal the skin underneath. "Jenny, I – " He stopped himself. "I should go."

On his way home, Simon was angry with himself. Speaking to Jenny about his feelings would have been wrong. He was spoken for. Marcia loved him, and he was quite fond of her. He wanted to love her. In time, he thought he could. Jenny still had one foot in Sinclair's grave. Just because she was showing signs of healing didn't mean that she was ready for a new relationship. Affection and trust from a woman didn't equal attraction and love. And nothing suggested that she would consider him as a potential partner when the time came. Sinclair had been a bloody toff, for Christ's sake. He could never fill those shoes.

CHAPTER 23

When Jenny saw Simon next, he was tense and troubled. "Look," he said, punching the newspaper with his finger. "It's three-and-a-half years on, and these officers are still on the hot seat."

She took a minute to skim the article. In September, 1999, two firearms officers had challenged a man who was reported to be carrying a shotgun in a bag. When he turned to face the officers and raised the bag, they fired, and one of the shots killed him. The bag was later found to contain a wooden table leg.

"There's going to be a new inquest," he growled. "Two years ago the Crown Prosecution Service declined to prosecute them. Another inquest could change that. It's rubbish. Bloody rubbish. I could spit feathers! We would all have done exactly as they did."

Bear pushed his nose against Simon's knee and whined.

"I don't understand."

He took a deep breath to calm himself and patted the dog's head. "One of the shots hit the suspect in the back of the head. Both officers insist that the suspect was facing them when they fired, but a new inquest means a new investigation. Anything could happen. Since the incident, the officers have been removed from operations. But we're all asking ourselves if this could happen to us. We face situations all too often where we believe we are at risk of injury or death. We're required to take decisions quickly. We can't be expected to sacrifice ourselves."

"And those who aren't in the line of fire – who have time to examine everything – review your actions," she said slowly. "That doesn't seem fair."

"And who have never been in our boots, because they either weren't police or weren't firearms officers. But that's the system," he acknowledged. "And it's not fair."

"I know what you need," she smiled, taking his hand. She rubbed his palm gently with both her thumbs.

He had himself well in hand this day. The black leggings she wore with her sweater hugged her lower frame but didn't affect him at all. When she placed his hand on her knee briefly to brush her hair behind her ear, he was still unmoved. When she picked up his hand again, her fingers felt unusually soft against his palm, but he forced himself to accept her gesture for what it was, an attempt at comfort from a friend.

"Maybe you should do this for me, too," she said after a few minutes. "The inquest into Colin's death is going to be held soon. I've had calls from the Coroner's Office, the Coroner's Court Support Service, and Chief Superintendent Higham. I've been told I'll be allowed to question the witnesses. I can't imagine why."

"Will you?"

Her smile wavered. "I don't think I'll be able to say anything at all." She shook her head briefly to clear the dread. "Simon, could I ask you – I've been worried about something."

He noted her anxious frown. "Let's hear it."

"I think I've changed since Colin's death. Neil Goodwyn comes by, Nick Howard had to jump-start me, and now I'm seeing Dr. Knowles. I was always proud of my independence, but I've needed so much help to get through this, and I'm afraid I've become weak and dependent on people."

He thought for a moment. "We've not walked in your shoes, have we? But leaning on others from time to time doesn't make you dependent; I rather think it shows judgement, knowing when you need help. When Burly's wife walked out on him – he's one of our SFO mates – we kept him with us, but on planning, not operations. He needed a bit less stress on the Job. No one considered him weak. After a time he returned in full."

"Do you think I'll go back to the way I was?"

"In my book you never left. You've made a life for yourself in a country not your own. You take your own decisions. Jenny, it was a shock when Sinclair was killed. It can't have been easy. You reacted. That's quite different to being helpless. You've come a long way."

She gave his hand a squeeze then released it.

He hugged her before he left but wished he had felt free to do more. Wished she needed him more. Sinclair's death had derailed her; now she faced reliving those dark days at the inquest. Memories flooded back of her previous courtroom experiences, when she had testified against the bastard who had attacked her and later against his thugs. He had been able to encourage her before each session and after as well. He could not be present to cushion her for this next ordeal. She didn't expect it of him. Why, then, did he feel that he had let her down? Both her and himself, actually.

With difficulty Alcina had been able to control her anger until she left Kosta's. A busy evening, many new customers, several large groups, but precious small tips, and she was tired. She closed the back door and then kicked it as hard as she could, nearly choking on the expletive she managed to whisper instead of screaming. By the end of the evening, both her feet had hurt, and now she would be limping to the tube station on one of them.

She hated Greek men, with their self-assured manners and easy laughter. She hated their wives and girlfriends equally as much for the way they talked down to her. She hated them for the food they left on their plates. She hated them for their designer handbags and matching shoes, shoes that were far more stylish than hers. Shoes that cradled feet that did not hurt from long hours of serving others.

At the tube station she was still on her feet. Through the turn stiles, down the escalator, across the walkways to the correct platform. There, at least, she sat for a few minutes waiting for the train. Once on her way, she rested again, but standing to exit the car was a painful shock. And in the morning she would have the long trek through Hampstead streets on her way to the bakery.

Leaving the tube station and approaching her flat, she saw a big bag of garbage which had fallen next to the skip in the alley. A small dog was rooting through it. A small, thin dog. Her feet throbbing, she stopped to watch it nevertheless. The dog was hungry. If she'd had food, even scraps, with her, she could probably have lured it into the flat. Then what? Confined it to her kitchen while she decided what to do with it.

A small dog was ideal. What worked with a small dog would work with a larger one like her target's. She would bring it bones and meat scraps from the customers' plates while she perfected her plan.

And in the meantime she would continue to remind her target that someone was watching her, someone who intended her harm.

CHAPTER 25

Easter was a paradox for Jenny. Her dad had an international driver's license, so he was behind the wheel of Colin's Audi, which Jenny had never driven, preferring to rely on public transportation. She navigated from the back seat, where she sat with Bear. Bear hadn't been in a car since Nick Howard had brought him home from the animal center, and Jenny was curious to see what kind of traveler he would be. She needn't have worried; Bear stretched out on the towel she placed on the back seat and promptly went to sleep.

They traveled to Kent to spend the holiday with Joanne, and Jenny felt most alive when she withdrew from the family group to sit by Colin's grave. Joanne had planted flowers near the headstone, and the bursts of color and green grass that covered Colin like a blanket spoke of life. It was sunny and warm, and Jenny shed her sweater and caressed the carved letters of his name. It must have been hard to chisel the letters so perfectly into the cold stone. For a minute she felt that she shared something with the chiseler, because Colin's death had resulted in something difficult for both of them, but the artisan had probably felt some satisfaction with his completed work, while the grief memorialized by the stone still chipped away at her heart.

She set the camera down, not sure why she had brought

it. She didn't want to document this site. She wanted to remember Colin smiling and happy, not hidden beneath layers of earth with a monument he would have dwarfed had he stood next to it.

She told Colin how much she loved him still. "I'll never forget how we met – and Colin, I'd go through it all again, the fear, the pain, everything, if I could just wake and see your face. And I feel so useless. I can't bring you back. I can't even avenge you." She described Nick Howard's visits and what a difference having Bear made. "It isn't the same, though. I used to sleep with you, and now all I have is a dog." She imagined Colin smiling. "I call him Bear, and I know you can understand why. He's here with me now, and I do feel less lonely. We'll be going to the Good Friday service soon – your mum said that Bear would be fine in the house while we're gone. I'll see you tomorrow."

In the morning Jenny's parents accompanied her to the Sinclair family cemetery. "Colin, my parents were here with me for a few minutes, but since I wanted to be alone with you, they've gone back to the house now with Bear. The sun is out again today, shining right on you. It's a beautiful morning. Is it always morning where you are? Never night?" She leaned against the headstone. "I had a really hard time for a while. When you died, the lights went out, and I wanted to step into the blackness with you. But I couldn't, because there was a small glow in the background that wouldn't go out. It had a voice, and the voice said, 'Choose life.' I like to think it was your voice, Colin. Anyway, I'm doing a little better now."

She took a deep breath. "Colin, the inquest into your death was held recently, and for the life of me, I couldn't figure out why. Chief Superintendent Higham explained that the purpose was to determine how, where, and when you died, but we already knew that, and the verdict, too: unlawful killing. When they read your post-mortem report, I had to leave the courtroom for a while. I know it's stupid of me, but I didn't know they'd done that to you, and I just couldn't listen to them describe all your injuries." She took one of his handkerchiefs out of her pocket and held it tightly.

"The whole thing was deceptive. The court was identified only by an innocuous black sign with white letters. No one wore robes or wigs. Even the judge – or whatever he's called – wore a suit, because he's a doctor in addition to his legal training. I wanted him to be old, like a family doctor, but he wasn't. And the hearing took all day."

She paused, trying to think of something positive about the experience she could recount. "There were a lot of witnesses, Colin, a tribute to the thoroughness of the Met's investigation. The coroner addressed us at the end, your mum and me. He acknowledged how difficult the proceedings were for family members and said we should be proud of you. We are, very proud. And he caught me in the hall as we were leaving to make sure I was all right." Enough about that, she thought. "Now for good news. Colin, Beth is pregnant! She's due late in August, and she's already showing. She says Brian likes her new shape because she has more curves. Would you have felt that way if I had gotten pregnant?"

After lunch she visited by herself again. "I'm busier now, but mostly it's just busy-ness. I need a purpose. Dr. Knowles suggested that I keep a journal – did I tell you that I've been seeing him? – and that made me sad, because you gave me one long ago, remember? And I've filled several since with my silly lists. Colin, Dr. Knowles says that I've confused grief and love, that they have become so closely intertwined that I'm afraid to let the grief go for fear the love will go with it. I know that holding onto grief isn't healthy and letting it go is, but I think that if I do, I'll feel unfaithful." That wasn't quite what she wanted to say. "Grief is a terrible thing, Colin. I don't want you to feel it. I want to make you proud of me, but I don't know how." She sat quietly for a few minutes, listening to the rustle of the leaves as the breeze caressed them. "It's peaceful here, Colin. Like being in church, sort of. I haven't prayed much since you died. Neil Goodwyn does it for me."

She looked up. A speckled brown bird was hovering overhead. Suddenly it dove past her, talons extended, and she realized it was a bird of prey, hunting. She stood up and shouted and waved her arms, but when the bird rose from the grass, it held something, something small, something wriggling, something still alive. Her intervention hadn't made a difference.

"Colin," she panted, "I feel awful. A kestrel – isn't that the bird that hovers before it strikes? – caught a mouse. It was a sudden attack. The mouse didn't know the kestrel was stalking it, so it couldn't get away. I was powerless to stop it."

She took a few minutes to catch her breath. "We can't keep bad things from happening, even to the people we love. Colin, I wish I could have! I wish I'd called you that day and delayed you, or done something to keep you from going to Bond Street, or – " Her voice broke. "When we were together and I wished for something, you always responded. I miss that so much, because even when you told me you couldn't grant whatever I'd wished for, I knew you wanted to, and that meant you loved me. Will you always love me? I'll always love you. I just wish I could show you." She closed her eyes, thinking it would be easier to hear his voice if he answered, but she heard only her agitated breathing.

When she visited after dinner, she was more calm. She tried to imagine her monologues as dialogues, waiting to give him time to listen and digest what he heard. "Colin, it has taken me a long time, but I understand now why you did what you did." She paused. "You had to take a stand against evil. You couldn't let the bomber win. Your instinct was to protect people, and that was one of the things I respected most about you. F. Scott Fitzgerald said, 'Show me a hero, and I will write you a tragedy.' I'll always wish you were with me, but I wouldn't ask you to be untrue to yourself. I still don't know what my life without you is going to look like, but I'm proud of you. Proud and sad at the same time, because we won't get to have a life together."

She shivered. "It's dark here, Colin. I don't like the dark, but I'm learning that even in the dark, I have memory of light. I hope you're in the light. And Colin – when they buried you, I made sure the dirt never touched you. I knew you would have hated that." She set her flashlight on the ground for a minute so she could button her sweater. "Your mum served a wonderful dinner tonight. Her dining room is my favorite room: It's elegant, like you, and I'll never forget eating there for the first time and how much bluer your eyes seemed, surrounded by the muted colors of the décor. Tonight I ate so much that I already feel sleepy. I wish you were here and we could crawl into bed together." She began to daydream. In the dark she could pretend that he would be beside her any minute, his chest bare, his arms reaching for her.

"Jenny?" someone called, startling her. "Jenny, are you all right?" It was her mother. "Jenny, it's chilly and dark out here. Isn't your flashlight working? Your dad's with me. Won't you come in with us and have something warm to drink?"

Jenny stood and stepped into her father's embrace. Someone was holding her, but not the person she wanted. She fought tears all the way back to the house.

In the morning she visited again. "Colin, I feel a little better today, and I just wanted to take a quick minute to talk to you before church. Could I honor you somehow? We both know I'd make a terrible police officer, so that's out, and I don't know if Sapphire uses volunteers. Do you think I need to be less specific?" She thought for a moment. "You helped people. Maybe I could find a way to do that. C.S. Lewis had his 'jottings.' Do you think my record of healing – my lists – could be of use to others? If I expanded them?" She smiled. "I can tell you think so. You always believed that good could come out of bad, didn't you? I'll think about it during the service. Easter is supposed to be about new beginnings, so maybe there will be a new start for me."

After church she brought Joanne with her. "Colin, I'm wearing the amethyst watch you gave me, the one with the purple hearts, to remind myself to be brave. I have to, because we're leaving this afternoon. I wish – I wish you were going with me! Or that you'd be waiting for me in Hampstead when I arrive. I miss you so much! I never had enough time with you. My parents are packing, but your mum's here with me, and Colin, since you died, I couldn't have made it without her. My mom doesn't understand all this as well as yours does. When I cried, your mum cried, too, and that made me less lonely. We're crying now, but we'll be all right. I don't want you to worry." She turned to her mother-in-law. "Joanne – Mum – it's like losing him all over again. How do you stand it?"

Joanne hugged her. "I feel the pain, and then I let it go," she said. "I let life go on."

CHAPTER 26

Eggs greeted Jenny upon her return to Hampstead. Not Easter eggs, however: These had been raw and the shells plain when someone had strewn them across her porch, and they had been there long enough to be rank. Her mother helped her clean the mess, and Jenny made a quick call to Constable Patrick Dugger at the Hampstead Police Station, wondering if she should have photographed the reeking refuse. Per Simon's instructions, she had reported the earlier incidents of vandalism to PC Dugger, who didn't look as if he were old enough to shave and hadn't quite tamed his curly hair. The small scar on his chin, probably from a childhood accident, nevertheless gave Jenny the feeling that there was a link between them. According to him, either the vandalism, which he called "criminal damage," wasn't widespread or others weren't reporting it. Probably teenagers. He encouraged her to be alert to anyone suspicious in the neighbourhood and, if she could, to pin down the time of day the incidents were occurring. He promised to have her street patrolled more frequently.

After seeing her parents to the train station for their trip to the airport and then returning home, she called Beth. "At first it was just annoying, but now I'm getting worried," she reported. "If this keeps up, I won't want to leave the flat without Bear."

Beth had news, too. "Simon took Marcia on another holiday," she said. "This time to Florida. Do you think they're getting serious? Florida's a real trip, not like popping over to Spain or France."

Jenny was startled. "I don't know," she stammered. "He never talks to me about her."

They exchanged Easter news. "Brian's mum couldn't stop feeding me," Beth lamented. "I was never allowed to get hungry. I think I doubled my weight in that one visit! My doctor'll not like it at all."

Jenny commiserated with her and then hung up, still surprised by the news about Simon and confused about why it bothered her. He had taken his girlfriend on holidays before. Maybe it was just because she felt particularly lonely, having left Colin in Kent and bidding her parents good-bye. She thumbed through the newspaper but couldn't focus on any of the articles. There were entirely too many ads for rings and other romantic jewelry. She tossed the rest of the paper aside and decided to go to bed early.

- -

Before locking her door in the morning she glanced up and down the street for anyone who looked questionable, but the street was deserted. Bear had loved romping and running in Kent, so she took him for a long walk on the Heath, which she had come to regard as a kind of oasis. The large houses of Hampstead always seemed to speak to her of families, but people often walked by themselves on the Heath, and the people who passed by didn't notice or respond to her sad face. On their outing she and Bear passed a mother with a little boy so new to walking that he wobbled with each small step. His progress could be measured, however, while she couldn't tell if she'd made any headway at all. She looked for Jack and his grandmother, wondering if he had made any improvement, but didn't see them.

Back at the flat, Bear had a long drink of water and then settled down for a nap in his bed. She felt tired, too, but not physically. The visit to Kent and her talks with Colin had taken a toll on her emotions. She understood that she could not hold onto him forever when he was not here, but she was not sure exactly what her next step should be.

She stretched out her left hand, admiring the rings Colin had given her. Her engagement ring had been his mother's, a delicate design with one raised diamond and several smaller ones surrounding it. He had insisted that her wedding band contain diamonds also. Taken together, these rings were a tangible sign of their love and their vows. "As long as we both shall live," they had pledged. But they weren't both living. Was it time for her to remove them? No. She still loved him. And he still wore his ring.

But they weren't still married. Were they? She slipped them off and inspected her hand: plain, bare. She didn't like it at all. If she didn't wear them, was it the equivalent of saying good-bye? She put them back on. Maybe she could spend some time each day without them as a way of adjusting. She could set the alarm clock for fifteen minutes in the morning and fifteen minutes in the evening. It didn't have to be an all-or-nothing decision.

CHAPTER 27

Morning dawned, and Jenny was eager for another walk with Bear. After breakfast, she opened her door, Bear beside her on his leash, and was greeted by another mess on her porch. Was it her imagination, or were the incidents occurring more often? She knelt down. Black rose petals? At least this cleanup wouldn't be as difficult as some of the others. She swept them into the flowerbeds. Should she go out? Yes, of course: Bear was with her. Nevertheless she stopped just outside the door and looked to her left and right.

It took them longer than usual to reach the Heath because Jenny slowed as she passed each home to determine if other porches had been similarly soiled. None had, on either side of her street, and the pots of flowers that many homeowners used to decorate their front entries were untouched. She and Bear entered the Heath from East Heath Road, and she had difficulty deciding which of the paths that snaked through the trees to take. She heard a man's voice behind her and stiffened, but he was addressing his companion: "The last time we were here, remember? So damp. So much nicer in the sun, don't you think? Hope it lasts." She waited for them to pass before turning back. In her distracted frame of mind, she could have become lost, and the Heath didn't have "Way Out" signs like the tube stations.

She stayed in the rest of the day, feeling alternately jumpy and then silly for being affected by the occasional litter at her door. As the police constable had said, no one had approached her directly, so there was no need to be afraid. Teenagers.

Late in the afternoon she was surprised to hear from the coroner, Dr. Millar, requesting her presence at a meeting to be held in his office. "We've begun a new programme," he said, "and we're seeking feedback from family members and witnesses with regard to its effectiveness." She made a note of the date, time, and location.

She was still uneasy when Simon came by after dinner. "It's beginning to feel personal, and I can't figure out why. Does someone want to frighten me? And why me? Anyway, PC Dugger probably thinks I'm losing it. He'll call his report, 'Continued Cleanup Unhinges Hampstead Woman.'"

Simon smiled and accepted the beer she offered.

She poured a glass of wine for herself and sat down in the armchair across from him. "Don't these situations usually escalate?"

"Take Bear with you when you go out," he suggested.

"I do, but I can't take him everywhere. Simon, I want a weapon."

"Best if you leave the weapons to the professionals."

"I've fired guns before. Rifles. My dad used to hunt."

"No, Jenny. It's not allowed."

She set her glass on the table. "Simon, why did you go to Florida?"

Her abrupt turn of subject startled him a bit. "What?"

"Florida. Beth said you went to Florida. Why?"

"For a holiday," he said carefully, aware of the edge in her voice. Bear heard it as well and whined softly.

"With Marcia?"

Damn Beth. "Yes."

"For how long?"

"Jenny, that's none of yours."

She released her hold on Bear's collar and folded her fingers into fists. Bear whined again. "You took her to *my* country!" she cried, her eyes blazing.

"I'll have none of this, Jenny," he said, his voice cold and firm.

"Why there? Of all places! Wasn't France romantic enough? Or Italy?"

Where was she going with this? And why?

His eyes were an uncompromising blue, his nose a little wider than the classic Greek profile, and his upper lip slightly narrower than his lower. When he was angry with her, as he was now, both lips became equal candidates for the Thin Feature of the Year. And he was tan, from the Florida sun, which made her madder. "Damn it, Simon, how could you?"

He stood suddenly, and Bear barked. "I didn't come here for this, Jenny!"

She also rose to her feet, her chin uplifted, her shoulders raised, leaning forward slightly on the balls of her feet. Was her posture intended to make her look tall and imposing? If he hadn't been so angry, he'd have laughed.

"What did you come for? What do you ever come for? Why do you bother?" she yelled over Bear's howl.

"Leave it, Jenny!" he shouted back.

"No, you leave it! Just leave! Go away!"

He slammed the door behind him, and she burst into tears, shocked at her own behavior, frightened by his, and unable to understand why she had caused it on her birthday.

- -

Simon reached the tube station in half the time it usually took, but his increased pace didn't ease his temper. Why had Jenny gone off on him like that? He'd done nothing to warrant her anger. And it wasn't like her, being stroppy. The sterling silver bookmark he'd brought for her birthday was still in his pocket. He'd had the top engraved with her initial, a floral *J,* so he couldn't return it. Bloody hell.

The Florida trip with Marcia hadn't gone as well as he had hoped, although Jenny couldn't know that. He had wanted to relax, reconnect, recharge. Marcia had wanted to make plans. Since their return, his schedule had been grueling. He had no patience with Marcia's demands. And now Jenny. He was most comfortable in situations where the rules of engagement were clear. With women they weren't. Perhaps he should quit the lot of them.

- -

In the morning he had a voice mail from Jenny. "Simon, I don't know what came over me. Anyway, I'm sorry."

The next day she left another. "I was out of line. It was my birthday, but that's no excuse. I'm ashamed. Please forgive me. I miss you. Bear misses you."

On the third day, her message was: "Simon, I'm tired of these one-sided conversations, but I'm not going to grovel." There was a pause, then she continued. "Yes, I am. Please call back. You mean a lot to me."

He didn't delete her calls, instead listening to each one more than once. He heard something in Jenny's Texas drawl that he had never heard in Marcia's voice: need. No longer exasperated, details of her appearance came back to him, her pearl cross swinging free from her shirt when she leant forward, the tiny diamond studs in her ears, her bare wrists and – hands. She had not been wearing her rings.

CHAPTER 28

Alcina had always loved being photographed. Many times when Tony was earning good money and she had both the figure and the clothes to attract the attention of other men, she had wished someone with a camera would step forward to record her appearance. Now, with Tony in prison and her life in such difficult straits, she rarely felt attractive. Fortunately that mattered less to her than it had before. Her focus – she smiled grimly at her word choice – had changed.

It was important to have goals in life, and she had one. The dozens of photos she had taken with her camera recorded each element in her siege, as well as snaps of her target with and without her dog, her target's house, her target window shopping, with carrier-bags, on the High Street, in the rain. Generals planned each attack, didn't they? Kept track of each outcome? They gathered intelligence to increase their chances of success. They sent spies behind enemy lines. She was doing the same. Her map of her target's neighbourhood marked each home, its entrance and exit, the driveways with walled fences, and the trees or other places that would conceal her. She varied her approach, the frequency of her strikes, and her method. She was thorough and proud of it.

At Kosta's she continued to open the wine bottles before bringing them to the tables so she could have a little taste of the beverage. She deserved a reward for her persistence, her ability to carry through. Each small swallow was her own private celebration of the actions she had taken and a toast to the ones she would take in the future. Actions that were hers and hers alone.

She had also begun collecting scraps for the dog. Unfortunately most nights there was no sign of him when she neared her flat, but she left the food near the skip where she had first seen him. Perhaps if he found it, he would stay in the area. She would have to win him over, of course, and then find a way to disable him that would work equally well with her target's animal. She had been successful so far in everything she had attempted; she would be in this also.

CHAPTER 29

"Mrs. Sinclair," the coroner said, "thank you for coming." He gestured to one of the empty chairs in his office. "My name is David Millar. Would it be acceptable to you if we addressed each other by first names during this interview?"

Jenny wasn't sure she wanted to be on a first-name basis with a coroner. "Where is everybody? I thought you wanted me to attend a meeting."

Millar smiled and shook his head. "I'm sorry if I didn't make myself clear. Where possible, I'll be handling the interviews individually. We don't want one person's opinions to influence another's. We're mailing the survey to those persons who live an inconvenient distance away or who cannot leave work for a non-compulsory summons. If you'll have a seat, we'll begin by completing a brief questionnaire."

The British plural, she thought, understanding that she, singular, would answer the questions. Her name, contact information, inquest she had attended, specific role at the inquest, and types of assistance given by the Coroner's Court Support Service (CCSS) representative were the preliminary queries.

"Tea?" he asked when she handed him the form. "I can have my secretary bring you a cup."

Every inch of his desk was covered with files and stacks of documents, and her paperwork would just add to the disarray. Personally, however, he was very neat, with close-cropped dark hair, straight brows, and long, slim fingers. He was preternaturally pale, and she tried not to think of the work that required him to be indoors. "No, thank you."

"If you'll indulge me, then, I'd like to give you a little background. Coroners are one of the oldest offices in English jurisprudence, dating from September, 1194. To become a coroner, one must have both medical and legal training and at least five years' experience."

Another old English tradition, Jenny thought, but a fairly young proponent: Dr. Millar was just in his early forties. Maybe it would help if she thought of him as an officer of the court rather than someone who investigated death.

"Unlike other courts, however, we have not had witness support service until January of this year, a critical lack, I believe. Most individuals who attend a coroner's inquest have had previous contact with the legal system, and their demeanour here may be coloured by those experiences."

"You expect them to be upset."

He smiled briefly. "Exactly, yes. This jurisdiction is the first to provide any sort of support to those who may be called, and we feel very strongly that the sooner we can demonstrate its value, the more likely replication will be." He peered under the edges of several stacks of papers looking for a pen. "Now, may I ask – which CCSS services were the most helpful to you? You ticked several boxes on the page."

"It was reassuring to be contacted by them ahead of time so I knew what to expect and what not to expect. Being shown the layout of the court helped, too, but the most important part was the volunteer's quick response when Colin's – my husband's – injuries were being detailed. She escorted me from the court and stayed with me until I felt strong enough to go back."

He looked up from his note taking. "Other thoughts?"

"It was strange to appear in a court that didn't try to dispense justice."

"You're correct. We don't assign blame. Our brief is to determine who the individual was and how he or she died.

We seek to provide answers to some of the questions that loved ones have. In some cases that information leads to criminal prosecution and accountability, but homicides are not the only cases we hear. Violent or sudden death can also result from road traffic or industrial accidents or suicide."

"Your title is Dr. Millar. Did you ever practice medicine?"

His jaw tightened briefly. "Yes, I had a surgery – what you would call general practice, I think – for some years before returning to school for legal training." He looked down at the query form. "I see that you did not question any witnesses or make a statement to the court. May I ask why?"

Because it seemed anticlimactic. Because it wouldn't have changed anything. Those answers would show disrespect for his job. "No," she said simply and then regretted her lack of cooperation. He was much less brusque out of the court setting.

"My apologies," he said immediately. "I didn't realise the interview would distress you."

"I didn't, either," she said. "My husband has been gone over a year, but sometimes it's still hard."

"Of course. We'll stop here for now. I may, however, have further questions in the future. If so, may we contact you, Jenny?"

"Yes, Dr. Millar," she answered as he nodded his head in regretful acceptance of her use of his title. Why, she wondered as she took the tube home, would a doctor seek a job where he couldn't heal? And train for a legal job where justice was not the goal? And was this support project his only way to minister to the living? Being a coroner was a dead-end job if ever there were one, but she shouldn't have given him a hard time just because she hadn't heard from Simon.

CHAPTER 30

All relationships had their ups and downs. Consequently Simon made another effort to reconnect with Marcia outside the bedroom. In bed she was responsive and he more than pleased, but physical satisfaction didn't last long. If they were to become permanent partners, as Marcia wished, he needed to feel close to her in other ways as well. She'd let her blonde hair grow longer, giving her a youthful innocence which appealed to him. He liked her confidence and her irreverent sense of humour, but lately it seemed that for every step forward, they took one or more back.

They'd bought a quick meal at the chippy across the street and washed it down with bottles of Peroni which she kept on hand. Now she was kneeling on the floor thumbing through her DVD collection.

She spoke with him only occasionally about her work, although his experience as a Special Forces medic had given him some understanding of the pressures of her job. She rarely asked him about his. "Let's leave work at work, shall we?" she said. Tonight, however, he needed to relate a recent incident which still disturbed him, when a German ex-Special Forces bloke had threatened to kidnap his baby if his ex-girlfriend didn't allow him to see her.

"She refused, and he produced a firearm. Somehow she fought herself free and rang the triple nine, but the baby was left in the house with the suspect."

She looked up. "So – your team was called to handle it?"

"The ARV guys – armed response officers – arrived on the scene first. They surrounded the house and waited for us. But the German started acting very matey with them. He was chatting and even offering them tea when we arrived. We reinforced the perimeter and prepared to begin negotations. Suddenly two ARV officers jumped over the fence and attempted to floor the suspect. Two big, burly coppers against one skinny German. No contest, right? Wrong! He fought them off and started to retreat to the house, where the baby was. We heard a single shot, then a loud crack. The lives of our fellow officers being at risk, Davies and I knocked down the fence to assist them. Suspect arrested, baby safe, fortunately."

"Happy ending then," Marcia concluded, still preoccupied with the videos.

"Not exactly. The ARV guys reported that the suspect had produced a pistol from a pocket and pointed it at them before firing to his left instead. The bullet went right through the fence next to where Davies and I were standing. The local super commended the ARV guys for bravery and for bringing the incident to a quick conclusion, but the SO-19 chief inspector ripped them. Took them off Ops. Too right! No one would have wanted to work with them."

She frowned. "Why? They showed initiative, didn't they? They took charge."

He tried to stem his impatience with her civilian view. "Their tactics were unsound, unplanned, and unnecessary. You do not rush a suspect who is armed, and this suspect was violent and trained as well. And there was the baby to consider." He'd been glad to hear their dressing down. Wished he could have had a part in it.

"But, Simon, it all worked out."

He took a deep breath, not understanding her lack of concern for the baby, for Davies, or for that matter, for him. "Their job was containment. Ours was resolution. The ARV guys could have been killed. Davies and I, even standing behind the fence, could have been also. Bloody fools, both of them."

"You're rather inflexible," she remarked.

"I have to be. You know what firearms can do. There's no room for compromise. Their actions were rash and irresponsible. The unit has no room for blokes who want to be heroes. They deserved their reprimand."

"It seems to me they just made a mistake, were a bit overeager. Were they new on the job? And you said the German was friendly."

"If we'd met the German in the pub, we'd have been mates after a few pints, but the moment he used a gun to force himself on his ex, he became a suspect."

A tense silence settled between them.

"I'm glad you're all right," she said, almost as an afterthought.

Wanting a connection, he tried again. "Rough day?"

"No more than usual." She paused. "What are you in the mood for?" she asked, referring to the videos. "Something with skin?"

On most nights, that would have done nicely. Now, however, something was missing. His conversations with Jenny made him uncomfortable at times, but they had created a bond of trust between them. "Not tonight. Early run tomorrow. I'll give you a hand with the washing up before I go," he said, changing the subject, but not before thinking that Jenny's reaction to his story would have been different altogether. He would have had her full attention. She would have expressed fear for his safety, perhaps even questioned him about how often such risks occurred. She would not have had Marcia's sense of detachment. She would have taken his hand. Just his hand – but it would have been an indication that she cared. Some blokes wanted a partner who didn't worry overmuch, but expressing no concern at all? He shook his head but could not rid himself of his dark mood.

CHAPTER 31

Alcina was angry. Tony didn't want to hear about her plans. He cut her off when she tried to tell him. Said none of it made any difference. She heard the scorn in his voice. How could he? Didn't he see how much it all mattered to her?

She had wanted to discuss with him the problem of the dog. Tony had dismissed it immediately with insulting laughter and a brisk wave of his hand. She had been speechless. She had thought the topic would interest him. He hadn't been interested in any other aspect of her life lately, and she had no desire whatsoever to hear about his difficulties. He was sheltered at the government's expense, fed regularly, and exercised. She was the one who had to try to make ends meet in spite of exhaustion and strain.

She cut their session short and stomped all the way to the tube station. On the train she continued to seethe. It cost Tony nothing to spend time with her, while she had to pay for her transport and use — no, *waste* — precious energy making the trek to see him. She tried to recall the last time he had smiled at her and could not. She cursed him, unaware that she had spoken aloud until several people — *men*, even — moved away from her.

She exited the train and climbed the steps to the street. On her way home she made a new resolution: If Tony wouldn't help her, she would help herself. And another: If he wouldn't encourage her, she would encourage herself. She stood as tall and as straight as she could, forcing her shoulders back and her chin up. Then she whispered to herself, I am strong. I am determined. I am confident. She smiled. She felt better already.

CHAPTER 32

Out of the blue Simon called Jenny, asking if he could call round. She hesitated. It was late, she was ready for bed, and his voice had an edge to it. "Are you still angry with me?" she asked.

"It's done and dusted. Our row. But I need to see you, and I'm on my way."

She hastily shed her nightgown, pulling a t-shirt over her bare chest and slipping on a pair of jeans.

He banged on the door instead of ringing the bell. "I want to come through," he said in a loud voice.

She stepped back, her feet cold on the wood floor.

"I've been down the pub with Davies and some of the others. We had a rough one today. I could do with a pint." He followed her into the kitchen.

She handed him one. "What happened?"

"Man in Southwark threatened his wife. Damn it, we were boots down as soon as we heard and we were too late. When we made entry, he'd already killed her."

"Simon, come into the living room and sit down with me."

"Not possible to sit."

"Simon, please stop pacing! You'll spill your beer."

He paused, looked at it as if he had forgot he had it, then drained it. "Another, if you will," he said and resumed his activity.

She had never seen him so upset. Wishing she could help but not knowing how, she brought him the beer and asked, "Simon, would you like something to eat?"

He shook his head. "No joy in food at the moment." He took a long swallow. "He slashed her, stabbed her, then slit her throat. He butchered her! Her blood was everywhere. Kids were huddled in the corner but not out of reach of it."

The color drained from her face. "There were children?"

"Young ones. A boy and a girl. In shock, I'd guess."

"What about the husband?"

"Alive, I'm sorry to say. Dropped the knife when we came in so no threat to us. Then tried to tell us he had to do it, she deserved it, her fault, never his. All bollocks." He drained the last of the beer and held the empty container out to her.

"Was this the worst thing you've seen?"

"All the ones with sprogs are the worst. They hit you hard."

She took another beer from the refrigerator but sat down on the sofa, not wanting to hear more but knowing he needed to tell it. "Simon, whoa. Please. You're making me dizzy. You'll have to sit down if you want this one."

He joined her and reached for the beer.

"Was Brian there?"

"Yes, the entire team. Davies will be glad to see his family tonight." He held the beer to his lips. "Three attacks. One would have done! He killed her over and over." He downed the beer in several long swallows then fidgeted with the empty bottle.

Afraid he would drop it, she took it from him and set it on the table.

"It was a bloodbath," he continued. "Our best wasn't good enough. I just want to forget it."

"How do you forget things like that?" She put her hand on his knee to still the drumming of his foot.

"Sometimes you can't." He put his arm around her and pulled her close.

It had been so long since a man had held her. She closed her eyes. His mouth found her mouth, not with a gentle kiss but with the kiss of a man who was hungry. She tasted the alcohol on his breath and didn't care, kissing him back. When his hand moved across her chest, she knew she should stop him, but she didn't. Then she felt his hand under her shirt. A moan escaped her when his fingers found their mark. If her lack of a bra surprised him, he didn't show it. He didn't speak. She didn't think, just responded, her kisses more fervent than before. When he reached for the zipper on her jeans, she didn't pull away. Breathing hard, he pushed her back on the sofa, fumbling with her clothes and his own. She lifted her hips so he could remove them then again to press against him. Awash in sensation, she wanted to know his touch, his smell, more. She wrapped her arms around his neck.

He moved against her, faster and faster, his breathing coarse and rapid. "Jenny," he mumbled before going still.

For a long moment she lay with her lips against his rough cheek, feeling like a woman again, waiting for her heart to return to its normal rhythm, before the shame engulfed her. "Simon," she choked. "Get off me. You have to leave."

Still dazed from what he had drunk, he pushed himself to a sitting position and looked her up and down. "Jenny, my God. Bloody hell. Sorry." He reached for his trousers.

She covered her naked half with a pillow from the sofa. What had she done? How could she have let this happen? She had never been so immodest and impulsive, and she wished that he could dress as quickly as he had undressed.

"Jenny – "

"Just go," she whispered, trying to blink back tears. "Go away."

He was out of the flat before he had laced his boots.

When the door closed behind him, she called out for Bear. "Where were you?" she demanded. "You could have bitten him, or even me, for that matter!" She cried for her lack of fidelity to Colin, in his flat, without love. She had felt shame before; for a long time after her rape she had felt it, until therapy had taught her that there was no need for her to feel responsible for another's action. This time, however, she could not escape the fact that her action had been the cause. Simon had been drunk, but she had not been. There was no excusing her behavior. When eventually she was able to move, her remorse followed her into the shower, into bed, and through the night.

PART FOUR

All changes...have their melancholy; for what we leave behind is a part of ourselves; we must die to one life before we can enter another.

— Anatole France

CHAPTER 1

His mind clouded with fog, Simon Casey wasn't certain at first if he were awake. Then he moved, felt his head pound, and knew that his dry mouth and stiff limbs were no dream. He was lying fully clothed on the bed in his small plain Ruislip flat. He took a shallow breath and immediately regretted living above an Indian restaurant. Although weak, the stale smells from the previous evening's cuisine threatened to turn his stomach.

Gradually the events of the previous day came back to him. The raid. The dead woman. Her children, covered in blood and fear, cowering in the corner. The man who had caused it all. Bastard. The anger he still felt at him made his stomach lurch. Best if he didn't move much yet.

To a man the team had felt it. No one had voiced it, but they all knew the pub was their first stop when the shift ended. Like the others, he had ordered his next pints before draining the ones in front of him. Somehow he had got home.

He groaned. No, he'd made a stop on the way. This time when he moved, he welcomed the pain in his skull because he remembered going to Jenny's, needing to forget himself. He blinked. The light coming through the window struck his eyes. He closed them but still saw what he had done. Used her.

He tightened his stomach muscles in a vain attempt to

stop the nausea. Marcia. He had betrayed her, not thought of her once when he was with Jenny. He could not continue to see her now.

As slowly as he could, he eased his legs to the edge of the bed and lowered his head between his knees. With his eyes closed and his breaths shallow, he managed to remove his boots. How could he have been so bloody daft? He had thought of nothing save his own need, and now Jenny would hate him.

He stripped off what he could on his way to the shower. Still feeling unsteady, he leant against the wall and waited for his stomach to calm and his mind to clear while the cold water washed over him. He had broken bridges before but rarely looked back. Regrets? Not many. Waiting as long as he had before defending his mum when his dad abused her. Allowing excessive focus on self after his Shakyboats injury. Being unwilling to accept Rita's love and comfort.

One more. Not speaking up to Jenny about his feelings for her when she was in witness protection, when he and Sinclair had been on equal footing.

He gritted his teeth against the bile in his throat and removed the few remaining pieces of clothing. He and Sinclair had never been equals. Sinclair had wealth and breeding, a stable family line. He, Casey, had nothing. Once Jenny had begun to heal, however, she had seemed glad for his presence. Perhaps as an American she was less concerned with family class.

But he had taken advantage of her. She would no longer welcome him in any part of her life.

Finally he could stand erect. He shut off the water. Could he keep down some Paracetamol? He had to try. He towelled himself off and swallowed a dose. Jenny. His memory of the event was less clear than he would have liked, but she had responded. Hadn't she? At the least she had permitted it. She had made no move to stop him that he could recall.

He pulled on his sweats and laced his trainers. The outside air was cool. He stretched.

After, however, she had been distressed. Of course she had. She would never forgive him.

He began his run, his head pounding with every step he took. What to do? What to do? Nothing. Leave it. He felt a new pain, this time in his heart. Never see her again? Abort the mission? He had never left a mission unfinished.

Correction: This mission he had never well and truly begun. He had stood by while Sinclair won her over. Married her. He had contented himself with second place. Just as well. She was angry with him and rightfully so.

She had been angry with him on another occasion – her birthday. He had never known the cause of it, but later she had rung him to apologise. He could do as much. Make certain she was all right. But to what end? She would not trust him again.

Finally he reached a rhythm in his stride. A solo mission, a mission he could not train for. A mission with strategy but no tactics. A mission with no weapons, no gear, no action plan. A mission with scant chance of success. A word from Jenny could end it, blow him out of the water.

Little to lose then.

CHAPTER 2

Simon had insisted on seeing Marcia but hadn't said why.
"No kiss?" she asked when he arrived.

He leant forward and brushed her cheek with his lips.
"Your sister here?"

"Abby's on travel with her job. Drink?"

He followed her into the kitchen and opened a beer for
her but didn't accept one himself.

"What's so important that you needed to see me
straightaway?"

"I need a word." He shuffled his feet slightly. "I'm fond
of you."

"That's a lukewarm declaration," she said.

"Mars – Marcia – "

She frowned. Why didn't he want to use her nickname?

"You deserve better."

She felt tendrils of dread begin to line the pit of her
stomach. "Better than what? We had fun in Florida, didn't
we?"

"Yes."

Since she never cooked, having a small kitchen hadn't
bothered her, but now the walls seemed to be closing in. She
went into the sitting room and sat on the edge of the sofa. "I
don't understand then."

He didn't sit. "I've given you all I could, and it's not

enough," he said, an unusual gentleness in his voice. "For either of us."

He was ending it! Shock unbalanced her, and tears stung her eyes. "That's it? Can't we even talk about this? We're good together!"

Regret and concern filled him. They'd had the occasional spat, but he'd never seen her cry. "You are not at fault here. That's all I can say."

"Don't touch me," she objected when he tried to take her hand. "You're only making this harder."

He put his hands in his pockets.

A rush of anger flushed her face like a sudden fever. "You bastard!" she swore. "Why are you still here? What are you waiting for?"

He was silent.

"I just called you a bastard. Aren't you going to yell back?"

He'd been called worse, and he didn't want his last words to her to be hurtful. "I respect you, Marcia, and I'm sorry."

He turned to go, and she knew better than to stop him. She realised she still held a drink she had yet to take a sip of. She took several long swallows, but they failed to eliminate the emptiness she felt, nor did they dispel the spreading sadness. Had she asked for too much too soon? She had felt an urgency to make this relationship work. He had never told her he loved her, however. She had told him, and now she wondered if it were true.

She looked about her. The pastel colours which had seemed subtle when Adrian was a part of her life had become drab after he left. Wanting a symbol of a fresh start, she had repainted the flat with bold hues, goading her sister into helping. Brightening the walls had not brightened her life, however. It had taken Simon to do that, and now he was gone. Why had she thought that changing her surroundings would affect her in any meaningful way?

She took a shaky breath and finished her beer, feeling her anger and her energy drain away and with them, her tears. She knew she had never broken through Simon's reserve, but she had held back as well, not wanting to risk everything again the way she had with Adrian. If Simon had suspected it, he had been kind enough not to say so. What a pair we were, she thought, both of us wanting to have the best without giving it.

Now what? The sitting room, the dining room, the kitchen: All appeared garish now, all mocked her. Should she paint again? If so, a neutral shade like ecru or ivory. If not, drink until the colours blurred? No, that would jeopardise her effectiveness at work. She needed her wits about her there. Her work – the only thing she had given her best to since Adrian had left. At the end of the day she still had her pride in her profession and her commitment to it. Unlike the men in her life, nursing had been good to her.

CHAPTER 3

Forty-eight hours passed. Jenny hid in the flat, forgoing Bear's walks, just letting him into the back garden when he needed to go out. She was angry at Simon and angry at herself. She had wanted a man's touch so badly that she hadn't shown even a veneer of resistance. She was also angry at whoever kept leaving nasty things on her front porch, this time a torn garbage bag which had leaked down the porch steps, too.

When Simon called on the third day, she didn't answer. He left a voice mail: "Jenny, I want to see you, and I'll not take no for an answer. Ring me back."

She didn't.

His second message was also unyielding: "I know you've got your mobile with you. If you're not home, I'll wait."

What did he want from her? More of the same? She didn't want to see him. When the doorbell rang, she debated not letting him in.

"Jenny!" he called. "It's important!" He pounded on the door. "I'm not leaving until we've spoken."

She cracked open the door. "What do you want?"

"To chat. Just to chat," he said. "I want to make this right. May I come through?"

"Have you been drinking?"

She was wary. Not surprising. "No," he answered.

"Jenny – about the other night – I needed a distraction from the day's events, but what I did was wrong." He pushed the door fully open and stepped past her into the sitting room. "You have every right to be angry with me."

She watched Bear press his nose into Simon's hand, his tail wagging. "Bear, come," she called sharply, irritated that the dog was glad to see him. When he reached forward to take her hand, she pulled away.

He raised his hands in compliance. "Would you sit with me?" he asked.

On the same sofa where it had happened? Was he kidding? "No." She kept her arms crossed and watched him seat himself cautiously on the edge of the sofa.

Her dark face and defensive posture were not good signs, but she had not prevented him from coming in. Not an auspicious start, but it could be worse. "Jenny, I've broken it off with Marcia."

"Why?"

"You're the one I want," he mumbled.

"What? I didn't catch that."

He'd spoken too softly. He cleared his throat and repeated his words. "Jenny, when things turned pear-shaped on the Job, you were the one I needed."

"No, I wasn't! You just needed sex. I could have been anyone."

He shook his head. "I came here for support. When we make entry on a raid, we see horrific things. We rely on our training and do what we have to do. But later – when the incident is over and the adrenalin is gone – we've got to deal with the pictures that are still in our heads. That's why I came to you. We've always been able to talk with each other, haven't we?"

She didn't respond.

"Jenny, I didn't plan what happened. Usually I can keep work and play separate. The other night I couldn't. But Jenny – " He shifted his weight, still not comfortable. "I would have stopped. You've got to believe me. A word from you."

"I should have stopped you, but you should never have

started. And now I'm angry at myself, too. I never thought I'd be anyone's one-night stand."

"You're not."

"Really? What would you call it?"

"A mistake. Jenny, when my father drank, he did things he regretted. I swore I'd not be like him, but sometimes I am, although I don't want to be. I used you, and I shouldn't have done. I'm not proud of what I did."

Neither was she. She sat down in an armchair across from him and, sick with shame, covered her face with her hands.

"Jenny, would you tell me – " He wished he could see her.

His voice was gentle, and she bit her lip, hard, to keep the tears from coming.

"Why did you give it to me?"

She closed her hands into fists and tried to steady her voice. "Simon – the alcohol – that may have been a factor for you, but it wasn't for me." She choked back a sob. "I'm so lonely. When you kissed me, I wanted you – so much! – but afterward I felt even lonelier."

That hurt. No man wanted to hear that, but he should have expected it. He'd had her, but he hadn't made her feel loved because he'd taken, not given. "Jenny, look at me. I can make things right between us."

"How?" she demanded, her voice shaky in spite of her resolve. "We can't go back to the way we were."

He moved to the end of the sofa and reached across the void to take her hand. "Jenny, I – " He took a deep breath, then another. He'd not felt nerves like this in a long time. "I want us to be a couple. I want to be with you in every way, but I'm willing to proceed at your pace, whatever it is." He had his work cut out for him, because he wanted to win, not just her desire, but also her love.

She stared at him. "I don't know what to say. This is so sudden!"

"No, Jenny," he said softly. "It's not. I've fancied you for a long time."

She felt his fingers massaging her palm, and the ache in

her chest eased. "Simon, you're important to me, and when I didn't hear from you, I felt like I didn't have a friend in the world, but – this is a lot to take in. What we did – I can't – I don't know if – "

"Don't answer now," he interrupted. "There's just one thing I need to know. Where do you stand with Sinclair? If you're grieving still, I'll respect that." He caressed her ring finger. "You're not wearing his rings."

"I couldn't put them back on after what we did." She paused. "I'll always love him. I still miss him. But he's gone, and I know I have to accept it. I'm trying. Somehow I have to make a life for myself. I just don't know what that life is going to look like."

Nothing so far had put paid to his hopes. She hadn't said she hated him or never wanted to see him again. "Fair enough. Jenny, about my schedule. I have three weeks on. The number of ops determines my hours, but eighteen-hour days are common. Then a week spare, when I'll likely be called out, a week of training – sometimes we're even called out from training – and a week's leave, not necessarily in that order. You'll not be able to reach me directly, but I'll ring you whenever I can. If it's not every day, don't think I've changed my mind about you. That's not going to happen. On my leave weeks, it's down to you how much time we spend together. For the rest, I'm asking you to trust me. I'll not be playing away. Not seeing anyone else," he added, to make his meaning clear.

She had never heard him make such a long speech, this man she knew in so many ways and yet did not know. That, and everything he'd said and done since he arrived, surprised her. "Are you briefing me?" she asked, trying to smile.

Her sense of humour intact: good. He smiled back. "I like to keep all members of my team fully informed." He drew her to her feet. "I'd like to see you tomorrow. Shall I take you for dinner?"

Bear jumped up, expecting them to take him for a walk. "Bear, sit!" she snapped. She felt flustered by both of them. "That's awfully short notice."

"With my schedule I can't plan too far ahead."

"What else are you planning?"

"Just dinner. Nothing more."

"Promise?"

"Yes. Tomorrow then? I'll collect you at eight." He wanted to kiss her but didn't want to pressurise her in any way. In the end he lifted her chin and hoped she'd meet him halfway. She didn't.

CHAPTER 4

Jenny spent the day waiting for the hour of eight to arrive, her stomach unsettled, unable to concentrate on anything for very long. Simon had been an important friend in her life for a long time, but now the parameters of their relationship had shifted dramatically. He had apologized; he had explained himself; but was that enough? Should she call and tell him not to come? If she did, what would he do? What exactly did he want from her? He was a man of direct questions but usually indirect answers, yet he had told her that he wanted them to be a couple.

Would he make a pass at her? He had last night, sort of, and it hadn't been very satisfying. She hadn't allowed it to be. Would he want to kiss her tonight? Was that what she wanted? She thought about his mouth, smiling, moving closer to her, and realized it was. But why? She wasn't looking for an intimate relationship. How could she, when she was still in love with her husband? Now she was about to have her first date since Colin's death, she wasn't sure she wanted to go, she didn't know what to wear, and she didn't know how to act.

Simon knew. He greeted her by kissing both her cheeks. He had dressed for the occasion, wearing a sports coat, slacks instead of jeans, and a button-down shirt. He complimented her on the colourful blouse she wore with her dark pants. He brought her a bouquet of flowers. Tough, terse Simon with kisses and flowers: a paradox that would take some time for her to get accustomed to. Would he want to hold her hand? She picked up her purse and folded a light sweater over her arm so he couldn't.

"There's a small Italian restaurant just off the High Street," he said as they walked. "I booked a table for us."

The restaurant looked small from the street but extended though one long, narrow room. She stiffened when she felt his hand on the small of her back, having to remind herself that he was simply guiding her to the table. They were seated near the brick bar in the back. He ordered a half bottle of the house wine and poured more in her glass than in his. The tables were so close together that she could hear the couples around them engaged in conversations, but she felt tongue tied. Over the top of her menu she could see numerous pictures of movie stars in black frames. The soundtrack from *The Godfather* was playing. Not a good omen. She spoke to the waiter, ordering bruschetta with diced tomatoes, goat cheese, and basil. She perused the rest of the menu. Every pasta dish known to man was listed, but feeling rebellious, she eventually chose a walnut and apple salad and steak with potato gnocchi. He ordered a bowl of cream of sweet potato soup, mackerel, and vegetable risotto. Now only a vase with two red tulips separated them. The table was small, and she felt fenced in, her chair against the wall. They had not spoken to each other since their arrival.

The bruschetta came. Between bites she sipped her wine, once, twice, a third time, racking her brain for something they could talk about and irritated because he wasn't helping. "Simon, do you feel as awkward as I do?" she finally said. "I don't know what to say to you. I'd read the menu aloud, but the waiter took it away."

A pained expression crossed his face but he didn't look away. "We could speak of our families," he suggested.

"Then it'll have to be yours, because you know all about mine. You don't talk about your parents much, particularly your father."

He sighed, reached for the wine, then changed his mind.

"He wanted to be a football player," he said. "My mum said he was agile and quick but too small. When he didn't make it professionally, he became bitter. He finally got a job working on boats. Repairs, refinishing, and the like. He was good at it, good with his hands, but he didn't like it. He was paid on the Friday, and he drank most of what he earned before he came home." The waiter arrived with their food, interrupting him.

She picked up her salad fork. "And?" she prompted, a little surprised to find that she was curious to hear more.

"He was an angry drunk. My mum took the brunt of it. Fortunately she'd gone back to nursing after my brother and I were born, so we were never hungry, but I was too small to defend her, and I hated that."

"Your parents aren't still together, are they?" Her steak was delicious. She knew she should tell him but didn't want the compliment to give him the wrong idea.

He shook his head. "The boatyard changed hands. His drinking had caused his work to deteriorate, and the new owners weren't willing to keep him on. His behaviour got worse. One weekend I took him on. He was bigger and stronger, but I was sober and more determined. He jeered at me when he left. Said I'd end up just like him." He had finished his soup and nearly cleaned his dinner plate.

"What happened to your food?" she asked. "Did you inhale it?"

He put his fork down. "Sorry. Habit from Special Forces days. Eat fast, and never leave food." He downed his wine in one swallow, gave her a regretful smile, then set his glass aside and refilled hers.

Half her food was still on her plate. She ate quietly, realizing that some of their rapport had returned. She wondered whether the wine or his company had relaxed her. "You were the cop even then," she commented.

"Something like that, yes."

"Did you ever want to be a doctor?"

"Not an option. When I joined the Royal Marines, I wasn't certain I'd take to the medical training, but it enabled me to be useful. I'd still rather hold a rifle than a scalpel, though."

He paused. "Dessert? They have chocolate pudding on the menu."

She smiled. He knew her preferences. "Too heavy. My meal was more filling than yours. I'll have the lemon sorbet."

He ordered coffee for both of them. "Still using your camera?"

"No, I discovered I wasn't going to be the next Ansel Adams. My pictures would be a good cure for insomnia."

When the waiter brought the sorbet, she gave Simon a taste. "How old were you when you had your first car?" she asked.

He wasn't bothered by her questions. Dating curiosity, he hoped. "I didn't have any money until I joined the military, and then, not much. And there's good public transport here. Didn't need my own vehicle until I became a police officer. How about you?"

"I was eighteen. In Texas people don't walk anywhere if they can help it. If we could drive up to the dinner table, we would." A shadow crossed her face. "I think I'm addicted to walking now. When Colin died, I needed the outlet. Walking and tea are universal palliatives. Americans are poorer for not making them a habit."

He settled the bill. "Ready to go?"

Suddenly nervous, she wished she had another cup of coffee. "Not quite." She took a sip of the water in the bottom of her glass and tried to think of another topic. "Have you ever ridden a horse?"

He hadn't.

"Or ice skated?"

"No, have you?" he asked.

"Not very well," she confessed. "I fell down. A lot! The only thing spinning was my head."

"Not much call for winter sport in Texas," he guessed. "I've snow skied, however. Learnt in the Special Forces." He paused. "Jenny, we've finished our coffee, not to mention everything else on the table. I think it's time for us to go." He held her sweater so she could slip her arms into the sleeves but didn't take her hand.

She was pensive on the slow walk back to her flat. "We're

very different, Simon. Our family life, our education. I'm afraid of everything, and you're not afraid of anything."

He was afraid she'd not come to love him, but he didn't contradict her. "We have a good deal in common, actually. We've both had missions that kept us from our families. We've both suffered combat injuries. You have drive, and you're independent and resourceful. We like physical activities. Besides, we've already lived together, so I know we're compatible."

Compatible? He was way ahead of her. "In witness protection? That's hardly the same thing."

"More's the pity," he teased.

She was quiet, not sure how to respond to his flirting. They were approaching her flat, and she didn't know what he was going to do. "I feel like I'm walking on uneven ground," she said. "You don't stay with women for very long. Are you going to love me and leave me like you did your other girlfriends?"

He took her hand. "I'll not leave you. I've no exit strategy."

"Even if I get mad at you and tell you to go away?"

"No."

"What if you get mad at me?"

"We'll sort it."

He hadn't hesitated in his responses. "Simon, you're so definite in the things you say. I probably won't get pregnant, but if I did – "

"I'd want you to tell me."

She stopped and tried to read the expression on his face. "Why? It's my body."

"Yes, but what's inside would belong to me also."

"But – "

"No buts. Promise me, Jenny."

"Okay. Yes." She hung back, nervous about what he would do when they reached the door.

"Take it easy. I'm not coming in. Jenny, I've – " He cleared his throat. "Been with other women. But you should know: I've been careful, and I'm healthy."

She stared at him. What did he expect her to say? Me, too? It was all too embarrassing.

He broke the silence. "I'd like to see you tomorrow, if that's acceptable."

"Simon, I'm still ashamed of my mistake."

"No need for that, Jenny. But it's down to me now. And you can trust me."

She looked at him, dressed up, hands at his sides. Usually he was good at concealing his feelings, but now she saw hope on his face, and her heart softened a little. "Come by late in the afternoon. We'll take Bear for a walk, and then I'll make dinner."

"Will you give us a kiss, Jenny?"

She froze. Although he had used the polite plural, she felt sure he wanted more than a kiss on the cheek. And then what?

He waited until she put her hands on his chest before bending down to meet her. It was not what he would call a proper kiss. He forced himself after to step back.

CHAPTER 5

Jenny watched Simon carefully over the next several days, but there was no sign of the Simon who had drunk too much and come on to her. He seemed to respect her still, in spite of what she thought of as their disastrous coupling. Nor was he the old Simon. This Simon kissed her when he saw her, held her hand while they walked, and brought her little gifts, which pleased and embarrassed her and made it hard for her to stay angry with him. "An orange!" she exclaimed. "Why an orange?"

"For your health," he answered.

"Then we should share it." She removed the rind and fed him some of the sweet, juicy sections.

He watched her while she ate, wanting to kiss her for another taste of the fruit.

"Orange you glad you're here?" she asked with a smile.

Laughing and groaning at the same time, he gave her a kiss – a quick one, because he didn't want to push her – to show her that he was.

Another day he brought her a chocolate éclair, and yet another, a sprig of lavender. On Sunday he brought a kite, and they took Bear with them to the Heath. She watched his fingers as he tied the string and adjusted the reel. The kite rose as they ran, and she felt her spirits rise. "Simon, that's what I want," she called. "To rise above everything but still be connected. I want to fly and be tethered at the same time."

"That's what love is," he called back.

She nearly stumbled, she was so startled by his romantic response. Some time later he reeled in the kite, and they headed back to the flat for supper. They worked well together, she thought. While he chopped the vegetables for the salad, she boiled water for the fettucini and sautéed garlic, green onions, and chicken strips.

"Are you trying to make a chef out of me?" he asked while he worked.

"No, I don't go for lost causes," she laughed. "Being a prep cook will do." She added seasonings and a few dollops of cream cheese and mixed her ingredients together. "We're having a tossed dinner."

He smiled and tucked in. "I ran into Hunt at Leman Street not too long ago," he said between bites. "He asked after you."

Jenny remembered the brash young officer. He was the type to lose at strip poker on purpose, certain that displaying his physique would have a good result. He had shocked her at first with his outspokenness, and it had taken some time for her to adjust to him. Later, however, he had become a bridge for her to the real world, where people wouldn't be as kind about her appearance as the rest of the protection team had been.

"He hasn't changed. Still overimpressed with himself. He was nearly ticketed from drink driving recently but talked his way out of it. The traffic officer was female."

"Is he married?"

Simon added a bit more shredded parmesan to his fettucini. "No, but he has a girlfriend, he says. Not sure how long it will last, because he puts it about a bit. More than a bit, actually." He could tell from her frown that she wasn't sure of his meaning. "He wants to bed every woman he meets," he explained, "and to hear him tell it, when he uses the macho armed police approach, he's usually successful. That same traffic copper paid him a visit at home when his girlfriend was out." Hunt had described with enthusiasm his sexual prowess, but Simon rephrased for Jenny. "He was near consummation when his girlfriend came home unexpectedly."

"She caught them in the act?"

"Nearly caught him," Casey admitted. "The copper was still clothed but wasn't in uniform, so Hunt spun some tale about her being a nurse visiting someone in the area who saw him collapse after a run. He was so pale that his girlfriend believed it."

"Are you trying to restrain a smile?"

"It would have been funnier, actually, if she'd well and truly caught them. But blokes like Hunt – they have more luck than they deserve. He always was a loose cannon."

"Were you like that?"

He paused. "In my younger days I looked for opportunities, yes, but I had no home life to risk."

"Weren't you ever serious about anybody? Before Marcia?"

"Yes," he nodded, "but it's been a good while."

"When you were in the Special Forces?"

"Yes, I had someone to come back to then."

His answers were short, as usual, but at least he was answering. "What happened?"

He put his fork down for a moment to let her catch up. "I was angry. I drove her away. After my injury. When I realised I couldn't requalify physically for service."

"Why? You weren't mad at her, were you?"

"No, at the world, but she got the brunt of it." He remembered Rita crying that his life wasn't over, he was still in one piece, he wasn't paralysed, and he still had her. At the time it hadn't been enough. "I didn't want comfort. I was that angry." He saw the concern on Jenny's face and knew he needed to get the conversation back on an even keel. "I regretted it later, but she had found someone else. Since then I like to think I've learnt from my mistakes."

"What are you looking for now?"

He chose his words carefully. "Most of the blokes I work with are risk takers. The risks they take in their personal lives don't signify because they put the Job first. On the

Job we train to minimise the risk, but we can't eliminate it entirely. If I let my concentration waver during an op, I could endanger not just myself but every man on the team. Depending on the nature of the op, perhaps members of the public as well. So for that time the Job comes first. I've no choice. Any other time, I'll do whatever it takes to be with you." He smiled and picked up his fork. "Like Davies with Beth. He's loyal to her because he loves and respects her."

Jenny had given herself smaller servings, but he was nearly finished anyway. "He's a good man."

Simon nodded. "I don't want the wild life. I want what he has."

Jenny blushed slightly and didn't answer.

"My leave's over," he told her as they were washing up. "I have to parade early tomorrow, and I'll not be able to see you for a while."

"Simon, what you do is so dangerous. Please be careful. It's okay if you don't think about me."

"I'll be all right. Our scenarios are approved by our supervisors. I'm trained for what I have to do. I'm armed and all kitted up." He tried for a lighter tone. "Besides, I can always send Davies in first."

"I don't want anything to happen to him either," she said.

"Nor do I. Jenny, my military training taught me to be aware of my surroundings. And if I can survive SBS ops, I can survive life on the Job."

Colin hadn't survived, and the depth of her anxiety for Simon surprised her. "Will you call me when you're finished? So I know you're okay? I don't care how late it is."

Her concern warmed him. "Promise," he said and collected another kiss. It was the first time she hadn't just accepted his move but had responded by kissing him back.

CHAPTER 6

Day one of Jenny's twelve days without Simon dawned. He had explained to her that a seven-day week was followed by five days on duty. He wouldn't be coming by every night, and she was curious to see if she would miss him and if so, how much. Meanwhile she located the journal he had given her and titled a new page, *My Options.*

Should she take up a musical instrument? Sign up for drama lessons? Learn to paint? She could learn to sew. No, sewing involved more pinning, cutting, and ironing seams than actual stitching. She still had nothing on her list. She could join a gym. She walked regularly with Bear, but she felt sure that Simon would approve of additional exercise. *Gym,* she wrote.

Learn to cook better was her next entry, but Simon wasn't particular about food. *Gardening?* Dull, but growing vegetables would be useful at least.

Bird watching? The Heath attracted all kinds of birds, birds of prey like kites and osprey as well as a number of varieties of ducks and geese. Shore birds migrated through the area. Colin had pointed out the resident species to her, robins and starlings, the noisy jays and magpies, robins, wrens, and woodpeckers. He had even identified, with a straight face, the great tit, which he considered misnamed since it was only 5-1/2 inches long. She had been unable to restrain her giggles when he told her that although tits in the wild fed on insects and seeds, in captivity they were attracted to nuts. He hadn't really been a bird watcher; as a result of his profession, he had simply been aware and informed about his surroundings. Watching birds didn't appeal to her. Besides, her bird watcher stereotype involved balding rotund men and women with flyaway gray hair.

A new idea came to her: *Learn a foreign language.* To pass the time in witness protection, Simon had tried to teach them Italian, with varying success. She had thought the language beautiful, almost musical, but none of them had been very serious about the lessons. The travel phrases had seemed useless to her. Brian had been preoccupied with cooking terms, and Danny only wanted to learn romantic phrases. She'd forgotten most of the vocabulary for money, weather, and food. She'd have to start over, but Waterstone's would have an Italian dictionary. Learning something new would be a way to look forward.

Still needing a longer list, she set the journal aside and went downstairs to collect the newspaper. Maybe she could find some additional ideas for activities in its pages. Not today, however: Someone had cut it into shreds which had blown across the front garden and down the walk. She sighed. That meant another call to PC Dugger. Would teenagers have done this? So early in the morning? If not, it was more than a prank. She gathered what she could and disposed of it, then checked to be sure the doors and windows were locked.

Upstairs again, she answered a call from Dr. Millar requesting her assistance on compiling the results of the first group of questionnaires.

"It would be unethical for the CCSS to evaluate themselves," he said, "and my staff is overworked already."

"Don't you need someone with credentials to do this?" she asked.

"At this stage you'll do," he said.

She heard the smile in his voice.

"Since you're coming from Hampstead, perhaps you'd like to spend several hours here each time. I don't imagine the work will take more than a day or two to complete. May I count on you?"

"I don't do mornings," she said. "How about Thursday and Friday afternoon? I can give you a little time next week, too, if necessary."

He thanked her and rang off.

She returned to her list. In ordinary circumstances a new relationship would be time consuming, but Simon's schedule precluded that. However, she was now less anxious about his physical expectations of her. He had been restrained; he had not pressed for more than a kiss. She laughed at herself. Whether he had intended it or not, he had whetted her appetite a little.

Was he in love with her? Surely it was too early for that, and he had only used the word once, indirectly. Instead he'd said he fancied her. What did that mean exactly? He'd fancied Marcia but had broken up with her. He wasn't careless with words, and he'd said he needed her and wouldn't leave her. That sounded like a commitment, the lack of appropriate romantic vocabulary notwithstanding.

Everything about their relationship was strange. It had begun in witness protection, when she needed his medical help but didn't want it because she was scared of him. Next had come their often adversarial relationship during the healing process, punctuated with what she had considered his unrealistic expectations of her. When she finally came to trust him and rely on his support, an unlikely friendship had been the result. Danny and Brian had been like brothers, but Simon had never fit into that category. After her return to London, they had kept in touch. He'd been attentive, often advising her when she asked for information or guidance. A colossal lapse of judgment, and now they had to start over. They couldn't be friends; he wanted more. And she had no idea what she wanted. She missed him, but at the same time she was a little relieved to be out from under his scrutiny.

She looked down at her lap. She hadn't made much progress with entries in the journal. She focused her mind and added: *Writing.* She smiled, wondering what Simon would think if he received a note from her. She knew he lived in Ruislip, but not his address, and she had never seen his flat. "A second storey with one bedroom," he had told her once. "Indian restaurant on the ground floor, proprietor and his wife on the first. I fall asleep to the aroma of exotic spices and wake to the smell of stale exotic spices."

Writing, not correspondence, she reminded herself. "Ham & High," the weekly periodical that covered events in Hampstead and Highgate, had a health column, but it only covered physical health news. Their "submit a story" option requested ideas from subscribers for stories their editorial staff would pursue. She felt sure that her experience of grief and recovery could be helpful to others, but it didn't seem to fit any of the "Ham & High" formats. It wouldn't be an intellectual exercise because she couldn't write from a reporter's point of view.

Perhaps she should return the C. S. Lewis book to Esther Hollister and ask for her suggestions. Because Esther believed that people had relationships with books, she liked to encourage what she called the "get acquainted" stage in her bookstore. Accordingly, her shop was cozy, with plenty of places to sit comfortably. Esther liked to get to know her customers, believing that in the long run that made everyone happier, she with more sales and her customers with the confidence that they were welcome to browse as long as they liked.

In the past books had helped Jenny to see beyond herself and her experiences. She smiled, thinking of Esther telling her, "I'm certain you can find some friends on my shelves." She grabbed a sweater. She'd take Bear for his walk, have a light lunch, then spend the afternoon with Esther. No, first she'd have another cup of tea and try to talk herself out of checking the doors and windows again.

Hoping to see Jack again, she guided Bear past Parliament Hill to the paths near Highgate. He was there, with his grandfather this time, the remains of a picnic spread between them. Jenny introduced herself to Mr. Dunaway, who appeared to have been the primary consumer, and then spoke to Jack.

"Bear and I are glad to see you."

Jack looked at the dog and then at Jenny and frowned slightly.

She laughed. "I bet you're wondering why I call my dog, 'Bear,'" she said. "Because after my husband was killed, that's how big my sadness was: bear-size. It helped me a lot to have a dog. Do you want to know why?"

She saw a slight nod. "Because I can talk to him and I know he won't tell anybody. Would you like to try it?" She stood and gestured to Jack's grandfather to step away with her. "Bear, stay."

She and Mr. Dunaway watched Jack from a short distance. After a few minutes, Jack lifted his hand, and Bear began to wag his tail. Jack froze, but Bear nudged Jack's hand with his nose and continued wagging until Jack stroked his head.

"He needs a dog, doesn't he?" asked Mr. Dunaway.

"It might help," Jenny agreed. "But ask the animal center to make a home visit before you take Jack to choose one. Otherwise they might not let him bring the dog home right away, and that would be awful."

Bear's head was now resting in Jack's lap, and Jack was bent toward him. Jenny couldn't tell if he were speaking: She couldn't see his lips. There was, however, the ghost of a smile on Jack's face, and that made her smile.

"Could I – about your husband – " Mr. Dunaway stammered, running his hand through the few strands of hair that remained on his head.

"He was killed last year," Jenny answered. "It was sudden and a terrible shock. We didn't have any children, and I had pretty much given up on life when a friend took me to an animal center north of London. None of the cute, lively dogs appealed to me. Bear had been abandoned, and he seemed as lost as I was. We needed each other, and having something to take care of has made a difference in my life." She again thanked Nick in her mind for pulling her back from the brink and stepped closer to Jack, in case her information had made Mr. Dunaway uncomfortable.

"Jack, would you like to give Bear a snack?" she asked. "I have some in my pocket."

Jack hesitated briefly before opening his hand, and Jenny put a small bone-shaped treat on his palm.

"Bear, say please," she said, and the dog gave a short bark before nibbling what Jack offered. Jack's smile widened. Jenny glanced quickly at Mr. Dunaway, who had taken a handkerchief from his pocket and was blowing his nose.

"First smile since," he choked.

Jenny knelt down. "Jack, Bear and I have to go now, but I'll see you again soon. Okay?"

Jack nodded, and Mr. Dunaway touched her shoulder briefly before turning to the boy. "Let's see what your grandmother would think about getting a dog, shall we?"

Jenny waved to them both and headed to Waterstone's. An Italian/English dictionary and a workbook on verb conjugations would help her start her review of the language. And maybe she could find something appropriate for Jack.

CHAPTER 7

His name was Agabio. He had been the last to leave the table at Kosta's, having spent the entire evening eating and drinking with the other patrons. He had noticed Alcina early on, or so he said. His friends had women to go home to, but he was in London on business and would be alone in his hotel room. He would be honoured if she would accompany him for an after work drink.

She was tempted. His Greek name meant "of much life, with vigor," and she knew in reality he was offering much more than ouzo. For many months she had been enlivened only by anger. She had felt like a soldier but not like a woman. Tony would not know what she did with Agabio. If she were careful, Kosta would not know. She had been sneaking the occasional illicit swallow of his alcohol for months now, and he had not discovered it. Now she was glad; the sips this evening had relaxed her, made her feel more attractive than usual. Released a hunger, however, she thought she had repressed.

Agabio was not unattractive. His hair was as dark as Tony's, but the resemblance ended there. Physically he was no match for Tony when Tony was at his best, but now no woman would look twice at Tony. Agabio's wide shoulders and wide smile caused her to swing her hips and smile back. He was older than Tony, but he had been free with his money during the evening, treating his guests to extra drinks with enthusiasm and leaving her an unusually large tip.

Later she wondered why she had done it, what had caused her

to lose focus. He should have been christened Arcario, or "without grace," because he had been clumsy from drink. He had seemed nice enough at the beginning, calling room service for wine and cheese and pouring her the first glass, even reciting a flowery Greek toast to her. The hotel room had been large and nicely appointed. His advances, however, when they came, had been less than polished, and the affable manners he had demonstrated at Kosta's had deteriorated into brusque directives. Nothing she wouldn't have done, but she did hate to be told what and how. Why had she thought that those big hands and thick fingers would be tender? He had satisfied himself but taken no steps to satisfy her. Attractive? No man was as attractive after sex as before. He had then fallen into such a heavy sleep that she suspected him of using more than alcohol.

She had no intention of staying with him until morning. She had had enough of his coarse dominance, seen enough of his wide belly and what lay below it. The trains didn't run this late, so she took some money from his wallet to pay for a cab. Nothing more than he would have given her had he been awake, she was certain.

Rousing herself to arrive early at the bakery in the morning would be more difficult than usual. She had not been drunk, but she had imbibed more than she generally did and stayed awake longer. Why, she asked herself again, had she succumbed? His awkward, inconsiderate performance could be attributed to alcohol abuse, but her behaviour could not. She hoped his London business was complete, that he would not return to Kosta's. She had no desire to see him again, in the restaurant or outside it. He was a reminder of her weakness at a time when she needed to be strong. It was dangerous to set anger aside, even for a little while. And if Tony no longer believed in her, it was essential that she believe in herself.

CHAPTER 8

"You're looking well," Neil Goodwyn remarked as Jenny admitted him to the flat.

To help the time pass until she saw Simon again, she had invited the chaplain to stop by. Now he followed her into the kitchen while she heated the water for their tea. In the months immediately after Colin's death, he had visited her often and was well acquainted with the contents of her cabinets. He set two cups on the counter.

"I'm starting something new," she said. "A relationship with Simon Casey. I'm not too sure about it, but he says he's interested in me. Do you remember meeting him? He was one of my protection officers. The one who had been in the Special Forces before joining the police."

"Wasn't he the young officer who was with you after Colin was killed? You've known him for some time then."

While the tea steeped, she took cream from the refrigerator for him and sliced a lemon for herself. "He was a medic but had to retire after a serious injury. Fortunately he passed the Met physical, though."

"I often worked with medics when I was a Royal Army chaplain," Goodwyn recalled. "Sometimes I was only allowed as close to the front as their station. They never seemed to mind my prayers. And occasionally I assisted with some of their treatments."

"Why did you want to be near the front? Weren't you scared?"

He watched her prepare the tray and carry it into the sitting room. "I was the most frightened when I was near the front line but also the most useful. I never felt brave. I did learn how to say the world's fastest prayers. And to pray when my mouth was dry! Often prayers were interrupted by gunfire, explosions, or screams. I learnt to pick up where I had left off."

She poured his tea first.

"I prayed for soldiers I knew precious little about, to honor them, their service and their sacrifice. I was rarely able to follow up with them, however, because deployments – and lives – ended. There's more balance in the work I do now because I can take the time to allow relationships to develop." The cream he added to his tea cooled it, and he drained the cup quickly.

"Was it a difficult adjustment, returning to civilian life?"

He smiled, remembering. "It took time to realise I wasn't in a war zone. I didn't need to ride with a convoy to be safe, and long stop lights didn't endanger me. Besides, it is so much cleaner here! The dust and sand soiled everything, and the desert was merciless, almost as hostile as the enemy. Storms brought stinging sand, rain, and sometimes even hail. I welcome the rain we have, gentle and cleansing." He held out his cup for another serving. "Enough about me. Tell me about Simon."

"It's silly, but I feel a little guilty, wanting to have a relationship with another man. My life with Colin was so short, and I can't stop loving him." She set her half-empty cup on the tray. "I'm two different people at the same time. I know I can't bring Colin back, but I'm not sure whether I'm ready to leave him behind. If I can't, then I can't offer Simon a whole person. And I'm not sure I want to anyway, because he has a dangerous job."

Goodwyn smiled. Jenny's disclosure had highlighted so many issues. "You'll always love Colin, and no one will ask you to stop. Fortunately our hearts are big enough to have all sorts of loving relationships, because this new relationship doesn't erase what you experienced with Colin. However, I believe you're engaged in a sort of tug-of-war, because you know that Simon is vulnerable in spite of his experience and training. Jenny, there is risk of some sort in all relationships."

She laughed. "No kidding! I could use some advice, though."

"Your relationship with Colin didn't develop overnight, did it? Give this one some time. The feelings we have for others rarely stay the same. You've had good reason to trust him. Like my soldiers, you've had to live life faster than many people. Now, however, you can slow it down a bit."

After he prayed and left, Jenny took Bear for a short walk. Because Brian was on the same schedule as Simon, she and Beth had planned to meet for dinner at the Café Rouge in Pinner.

- -

Jenny took the Metropolitan Line north from Finchley Road and left the train on the sixth stop. She reminded herself to look for a white awning with a cherry-red storefront above it. The few outside tables and chairs were unoccupied.

"Where's Meg?" Jenny asked Beth, who had arrived first. The waiters were busy, and it was a few minutes before they were seated.

"Staying with my neighbour," Beth answered. "It's her bedtime soon, and this way I won't have to hurry home. Are you having your usual?"

Jenny smiled. The Baguette Rouge, ribeye steak on a toasted bun, was her favorite. "No, I had beef this weekend. I'm going to order the chicken. Beth, you look wonderful. You're glowing from head to foot."

"I'm 6-1/2 months along," Beth said. "Always hungry, and you can tell I rarely deny myself." She checked the blackboard for the daily specials. "Good – they have cream of asparagus soup today. I'll have that and rocket salad with grilled chicken," she told the waitress.

Jenny ordered a glass of wine with her baguette. She

was eager to tell Beth her news. "Simon and I – we're dating, sort of."

"It's about time!" Beth exclaimed. "He's been mad about you for years."

Jenny blushed. How had she known? "You never told me!"

Beth smiled. "There was no point, was there? You were in love with someone else."

The waitress brought her wine and Beth's water. "Still, it can't be true."

"Jenny, he's been seeing you whenever he could as long as I've known you. Blokes don't do that unless there's an agenda. They don't have women as friends."

Maybe that was why Colin had always been suspicious of him. "Those months in witness protection – we talked about a lot of things, and there were times when I felt really close to him. But he never said anything, and he's had a whole host of girlfriends."

"He spoke through his actions. Besides, you were with Colin."

"What do you think happened with Marcia? He went with her for a long time."

Beth made room on the table for her salad and soup. The waitress went back to the dumb waiter for Jenny's sandwich. "They were two people together for the wrong reasons, I think. She was on the rebound from another relationship, and he was trying to prove to himself that he wasn't in love with you."

In love with her? If that was true, had she been so wrapped up in herself that she was unaware of what was happening around her? She knew Simon's standards, his drive, his likes and dislikes. They had transitioned easily from the witness protection relationship to friendship. How had she missed the point when that friendship had become something else? "He hasn't said he loved me."

"Of course he does! The question is, how do you feel about him?"

Jenny had barely begun on her baguette. "I'm not sure," she said. "I respect and trust him. So many times he's used his military knowledge to help me. But everything about this caught me off guard! First we were fighting, and then he was telling me about a raid that upset him, and then – " She took a sip of wine and decided not to tell Beth about their sexual encounter. "He told me he wanted us to be a couple, and he explained his schedule to me. I always wondered why he was free at different times, and I didn't realize Brian was gone so much. How do you stand it?"

"I miss him, and he's not home enough for me to be bored with him. I think it's made us closer, because we really value the time we do have together. And on his off weeks, it's our honeymoon all over again, except for those times when he's called in, of course. And unless I'm still angry because I've hardly seen him for weeks and don't want anything to do with him! Wouldn't you love having a honeymoon every six weeks?" She laughed at Jenny's obvious embarrassment.

"Simon and I aren't anywhere near that far along," she protested.

"Just don't let him get away," Beth advised. "You could do worse." She paused. "There's something you need to have a think on, however. On Brian's ops weeks, he's not even home long enough for a good night's sleep. If you're going to make a go of this with Simon, you'll have to be willing to look after yourself a good deal of the time. Their work is stressful. He'll need you to keep your end of things running smoothly. And it's hard on Brian, not being able to be here if I'm having trouble. He wants to fix things, and I want him to, but he can't. Many relationships – including marriages – don't survive. One of Brian's mates was married to a woman who resented his commitment to the Job. She paid him back by being unfaithful. I admit I occasionally resent the amount of time the Job takes. When we were first married, we had to start over sometimes to reconnect with each other. Not everyone's cut out to be a copper's wife, but you know that."

"I always believed in the importance of what Colin was doing, but it was still hard sometimes, dealing with the long hours he worked."

Beth nodded. "And odds on, Simon will be on duty on calendar holidays and special occasions. I've got used to celebrating my birthday on different days each year."

"Do you worry about Brian's safety?"

"More than he does, actually. He always tells me how well-trained they are. And he respects Simon. If I didn't have my teaching and Meg to occupy me, I'd worry all the time. But there you go."

Stay busy, in other words, Jenny thought. That had been one of Dr. Knowles' recommendations for dealing with grief. Clearly having a relationship with Simon wasn't going to solve the problem of what to do with her life. After her visit to Waterstone's, she had stopped by Hollister's Books, but Esther had been away on a book-buying trip, so Jenny hadn't been able to get any suggestions from her. Instead she'd walked through Keats House, feeling safer indoors than on the sidewalk and struck by the contrast between the brightness of the rooms today and how dark it must have been in Keats' time, when it was lit only by candles. Keats had been worried about money, his health, and the success of his poetry, yet he had written some of his most beautiful verses while residing there. Proof that it was possible to rise above your circumstances, she supposed. The poet had fallen in love with Fanny Brawne; maybe a relationship with Simon was just what she needed. If it was a relationship. If she could be sure it was love. "Do you really think he loves me?" she asked.

"Not a doubt. Now what's for afters?"

"Nothing for me."

"Jenny, I need a partner in crime."

"Then order a slice of pie, and I'll take a few bites."

Beth summoned the waitress and requested the custard tart with strawberries. "Jenny? If you're not going to finish your baguette, could I take it? When I get hungry later, it would be just the thing."

"It's all yours," Jenny smiled.

"What did I tell you? I wasn't joking about my appetite!"

CHAPTER 9

Several days passed, Jenny discovering each morning that her newspaper had been destroyed. Now she had a strong feeling of apprehension when she opened the front door, and sure enough, it was warranted. Another slashed issue. Maybe the vandal wasn't harmless. Maybe he was a stalker, and she had been singled out for some reason. She was glad Bear was beside her. Bear: *un cane,* a dog. *Un cane nero,* she thought, reminding herself that in Italian the adjective often followed the noun. Bear, her protector, who sniffed the porch as she locked the door and startled her with a low growl.

She would stop delivery of the *Telegraph* for a while. She wouldn't stop reading it, however. She could purchase copies either from the newsstand on the High Street or the one near the Hampstead tube station. Unlike the presses in Texas, in London the Saturday newspapers were larger than the weekday editions and the Sunday larger yet, and she wanted to keep up with events.

The next edition of "Ham & High" was available, so she found a bench and thumbed through the local periodical. An article reporting recent rapes in the Hampstead and Highgate area disturbed her. Was her vandal a rapist? Would his actions toward her escalate? He had already raped several women, none of whom could give a good description of him: average height, wearing sweatpants and a sweatshirt. He had grabbed them from behind. One had felt stubble on his cheeks, but he had told all of them not to look back, and they hadn't.

When she stopped by the police station to tell PC Dugger about stopping the newspaper, she asked what he knew about stalkers and rapists.

"Stalking is a form of threatening behaviour," he said, "but physical harm's not usually associated with it. Mostly stalkers want to frighten their victims, not harm them."

"But not always?" she persisted.

"Usually stalkers engage in mental assaults as opposed to physical or sexual assaults," he replied, looking uncomfortable. "Most are male, but there's no evidence that your incidents of criminal damage come from a stalker, much less a rapist."

She didn't press him any further.

"Bear, let's walk – *camminiamo* – to the park. *Al parco.*" Simple sentences, a pitifully slow start, but a start nonetheless. *Un inizio.* And something to think about besides her vandal. Or stalker.

The Heath was beautiful in the morning, the dew still damp in some places, making the leaves shine like new pennies. She found a bench midway through her trek and watched children – *bambini* – climb in the trees with low branches. She took the Italian dictionary out of her pocket. She didn't know the words for tree or branches. Or stalker. She sighed. Her life was out of balance. Too much time, too little purpose. Too much Simon, then too little Simon. Too much confusion in her feelings, too little clarity. She would discuss it all with Dr. Knowles during her afternoon appointment. She headed back to the flat, stopping by the Hampstead gym on her way to purchase a trial membership and arrange to join an exercise class. Maybe she could make friends with some of the other participants.

The psychiatrist rarely kept her waiting, but on this occasion she had more than enough time to waver in her resolve to tell him everything about her relationship with Simon.

"Sorry," he said when he opened the door and invited her into the consulting room. "I had an emergency."

"Were you able to help?" she asked.

"I believe so," he smiled. "And now, how may I assist you today?"

"I think someone is stalking me, although so far the local police officer – Constable Dugger – calls it criminal damage." She described the ashes, trampled flowers, and shredded newspapers she had found on her porch. "I didn't mention it to you before, but since several women in my general area have been raped recently, I'm wondering how afraid I should be. What do stalkers want? PC Dugger wasn't specific."

"Stalkers tend to be angry individuals," Knowles replied. "Their anger can take any one of a number of forms. Extreme cases involving violence do occur, but they are relatively rare. Women who have been assaulted by a former partner are most at risk for violent behaviour."

Simon would be glad to hear that. Simon. She wasn't ready to talk about him yet. "Can you give me more details?"

"Some stalkers are predatory. They plan to attack the person who is the focus of their anger. Others are resentful. They want revenge for a grievance which may be perceived, not real. Do you have a safety plan?"

"I have Bear," she said. "And since the vandalism started, I've tried to be more alert to my surroundings, but I can't look in all directions at the same time."

Knowles nodded. "Damaging property can lead to more serious behaviour. You're wise to proceed with caution."

"I even pray for rain, to reduce the likelihood of an attack."

A silence fell. Jenny was aware that Dr. Knowles was waiting for her to continue. "I went to Camden Market the other day," she said, knowing she was still procrastinating.

"And?"

She had worn her rattiest jeans and taken plenty of cash, since most shops didn't accept credit. "The vendors there hawk everything from belts and buckles to shirts and scarves, jewelry and ceramics, as you probably know. But I bought a prism. I wanted to see rainbows." *Arcobaleni,* she thought. "Even with all London's rain, I seldom see one."

"Why is that important?"

"Because I want to believe that something beautiful lies ahead for me. When all the storms are past."

"Are you in a stormy period now?"

Damn. It was silly to postpone it any longer. "Sort of," she said. She took a deep breath and blurted it out. "I slept with Simon Casey."

"Tell me about it," Knowles nodded.

She was distracted by his frown. The bottom half of his face remained neutral, but there was a definite contracting of the skin between his brows. "Do you think less of me?"

"Do you think less of yourself?" he responded.

"I'm disappointed in myself. It wasn't even a date!" She described the circumstances. "And I'm a little worried. There was no romantic prelude and not much foreplay. He didn't have to do much to seduce me. I just – capitulated. Am I so lonely – so desperate – that I would have responded to anyone?"

"You didn't think about stopping him?"

She blushed. "I didn't think at all."

"Jenny, I'd like you to look at this experience without judgement. Simon is not unknown to you. He's someone who protected you, who looked after you during one of the most difficult periods in your life."

"That's true, and he has kept in touch with me off and on ever since I came back to London."

"He's not just any man then, is he? You have reason to trust him. I gather you weren't frightened at any time?"

She shook her head. She had been frightened by how good it felt – even though he wasn't Colin – but she didn't intend to say that. And their encounter had only briefly shaken her trust in him.

"Were you angry with him?"

"Yes, and with myself, but fortunately I didn't get pregnant."

"Have you seen him since this event?"

"Yes, he came by and apologized. He felt responsible. He wants to have a relationship with me."

"Based on sex?"

She blushed. "I'm sure he wants sex to be a part of it, but he said he'd wait. He had some time off last week, and he came by every night. He brought me little gifts. He hugs and kisses me but in a restrained way. Now he's back on duty, but he calls when his shifts end."

Knowles smiled. "Perhaps it's time you examined more closely your feelings for him."

She thought for a moment, then smiled as she realized that her face probably wore the same frown she'd seen earlier on his. "I never thought I'd say this, but I'm attracted to him. I felt so guilty and ashamed afterward, though, and I don't want that. Beyond that, I just don't know."

"Relationships are always in flux. Give yourself some time to adjust to the change in this one. I must, however, caution you. It would be unfair to place the burden of your grief recovery on a single individual or new relationship."

"I don't understand."

"Some individuals may seek a new relationship as a way of avoiding or escaping grief, but a new relationship in and of itself will not heal you."

She thought for a minute. "I don't think I'm doing that," she said slowly. "I didn't seek him out, and I'm not looking for anyone to take Colin's place. A part of me will always love and miss Colin, but I can't have a life with him."

Knowles waited for her to continue.

"I'm not avoiding the past, but when I'm with Simon, I'm not thinking about it, and that's a good thing, isn't it? You didn't want me to focus on Colin's death all the time, remember?"

He nodded, glad that she was verbalising her thoughts.

"Being with Simon doesn't take away the grief. I wish it would, but I don't expect it to. It just helps me adjust my thoughts. And besides – "

Knowles saw the corner of her mouth curl into a smile.

" – since I don't know where this relationship is going, I'd be crazy to depend on it to solve my problems."

"I agree," he laughed. "And I must compliment you. You've made significant progress, because you are no longer experiencing grief alone. You are now capable of allowing other feelings to come into play, not to replace your sorrow but to exist in balance with it. Your sense of humour, for example."

"So I shouldn't feel ashamed?"

Knowles shook his head. "No, but I would like you to remember that you are in charge of your body. Use it consistent with your values, and you'll not have cause for regrets."

CHAPTER 10

At the SO19 base on Leman Street, Brian Davies searched for Simon Casey. Davies didn't miss the Specialist Operations base on Old Street. They had outgrown it, and the base at Leman Street had been modified to meet their specifications. It even had a lift, although none of them would have been caught dead using it. Only the suits needed help getting from one floor to another.

He didn't find Casey in the basement checking his kit nor in the gym. Not surprising. When they worked as many eighteen-hour days as they had recently, no one had the time or the energy for additional exercise. The canteen was closed. He finally caught him up in the team briefing room on the SFO floor. Whiteboards covered the walls, as well as maps and team assignments for the next day's operations. The power point projector was dark. Casey was thorough, always checking every detail. He should have come to the briefing room first. "Goodnight," he heard Casey say before he snapped his mobile shut.

"Jenny?" Davies asked. "Beth told me you were seeing her."

Casey waited, silent.

"Are you sure about this, mate? She's fragile. She's already lost someone, and he didn't exactly have a dangerous job. You put yourself in harm's way every day and she knows

356 | NAOMI KRYSKE

it. How's she going to handle that?"

"She's stronger now. She'll deal."

"She lost it after Sinclair's death."

"She had a rough patch, that's true, but she came through. She always does."

"And if she doesn't – second thoughts?"

"No. I'll take what comes."

"Beth and I – we look out for her."

Casey recognized the warning. "I'll not hurt her. Furthest from. And she'll be stronger with me than without."

"You'll go easy, won't you, mate? Give her time if she needs it?"

Casey was quiet again, his fingers playing with the coins in his pocket. "Longest single mission of my life," he confessed. "Easier for me than for her, but I'll not pass on it. Not this time. I'm playing for keeps. No matter how long it takes."

"Good luck then."

"I'll need it," he acknowledged. "There's risk. No guarantee things will go well." It was possible, of course, that he'd already lost, but he'd not admit that to anyone.

CHAPTER 11

Alcina's frustration led to anger. Her target's porch held no newspaper. How dare she interrupt her satisfaction?

Each day the knife had felt more comfortable in her hand; each day she had plunged it more confidently through the printed pages. It was only a small knife, borrowed from the bakery, but it was sharp and had served its purpose well. The baker had not missed it. He had many others.

She slammed her fist on the table. It was not enough. The cat-and-mouse game she had been playing was no longer enough. She wanted to see the effect her actions were having. Did her target know she was marked? Was she afraid with each coming and going? Did she look over her shoulder, examine the face of each person that passed by? Start at every sound?

She rose and went to the refrigerator, examining the photographs closely. She recalled the power she had felt when she was behind the camera capturing her target. Now, however, the snaps highlighted her failure because none of the pictures showed signs of unease in her target. Why? Because she still had the dog. The animal was present in every photo. He, too, was her adversary. It was time for her campaign against the dog to begin.

CHAPTER 12

With Simon's schedule so demanding, the work at Dr. Millar's office was a welcome distraction for Jenny. She didn't see the coroner on Thursday; he'd been chairing an inquest, and his secretary had made a space for her in the conference room. On Friday he brought her tea and a biscuit and expressed his appreciation for her cooperation. "Shall I see you Monday?" he asked.

Simon would be working long hours next week, too. "Why not?" she answered. Coming to the coroner's office hadn't been as creepy as she had feared, and if she put in some time early in the week, she would be able to finish the project before Simon became available.

Would it be awkward when she and Simon saw each other again? He called regularly, but she heard the exhaustion in his voice, and their conversations were too short for her to feel that they'd connected with each other. Big operations were inherently dangerous, but even too many routine raids could exhaust the officers and increase their risk. Some nights Simon didn't take the time to go home, sleeping at the base instead. And no operation involving firearms was routine. Beth had told her that on big jobs, an ambulance was on site, but Jenny didn't find that reassuring.

The exercise class wasn't working out, either. Yet. Literally, it was, of course, she thought with a wry smile, but the trainer wasn't nearly as fit as Simon, and one of the women had warned her about him. "He comes on to all of us. Don't sign up for personal training with him unless you're looking for a fling. His!" She hadn't really made friends there because the other women were in a hurry to leave. They had children to pick up from school and husbands to prepare dinner for, which made Jenny feel lonely as well as tired. She walked back to the empty flat with hours to fill until bedtime.

On Saturday she attended a cocktail party at Derek and Jillian Horne's. Colin's sister had included her on her guest list several times before, but Jenny hadn't felt social. Now she was desperate for diversions. She considered what to wear. She knew Jillian would be clad in something that complimented her blonde hair and highlighted her blue eyes. Not wanting to be outdone, she tried on several outfits but found herself wondering what Simon, not Jillian, would think of each one. At last she chose a long cotton skirt and a blouse with blue flowers that could have been inspired by a watercolor painting, their shapes relaxed and their edges slightly blurred.

The Hornes had a generously stocked liquor cabinet and a plethora of elegant hors d'oeuvres. *Pâté de foie gras* filled miniature tart shells, and caviar on narrow slices of tomato was graced with a light, creamy sauce. Jenny particularly liked the salmon with cream cheese and rocket on cheddar scones.

Jillian had received a bequest from Colin's estate, and from the appearance of the flat, she must have spent the entire sum remodeling it. The hardwood floors shone, and Jillian had purchased new, contemporary furniture with clean lines and understated colors.

Derek Horne's honey-colored hair and round lenses gave him an owlish look, but as he filled her wine glass, he gave her a less than reserved smile. "I began the party before the guests arrived," he confessed.

Jillian introduced her to everyone by saying, "Jenny was married to my brother," which stopped all conversation temporarily as the guests tried to navigate their way around the awkwardness, because they all knew Jillian's brother had been killed and how. Once the topic was safely skirted and the conversation on safer subjects, Jenny breathed a little easier.

"She's from Texas originally," Jillian added breezily, which helped a little, and Jenny was able to dispel many of the myths that had arisen concerning her state. She was more comfortable, however, drawing out others. She missed Colin, whose superior social skills had enabled him to put others at ease even when they discovered he was a police officer.

As the party progressed, Jenny became increasingly sad. She hadn't seen the blockbuster movies or enjoyed the latest play or attended the opera, and the two sleek male guests who competed with each other in keeping her wine glass filled seemed so innocent that she felt herself aging on the spot. They were talkative, glib even, and elegantly attired, but should she be impressed because they were comfortable at a cocktail party? Simon felt no need to fill the air with meaningless chatter. She even found herself appreciating his indifference to what he wore. As soon as it was socially acceptable, she said her good-byes to Jillian and Derek and took the elevator downstairs to ask the doorman to call a cab for her.

Seeing Jillian and Derek's flat had given her an idea, however. Maybe she should make some changes to hers. Colin's framed photographs still hung on the walls, and although he had been a good photographer, most recorded places she had never been. She could look for some paintings or prints which spoke to her and added color. She could consider replacing some of the furniture, or at the very least, adding accent pillows which coordinated with the artwork. She didn't want to make the flat fancier. On the contrary, she liked the relaxed warmth of Brian and Beth's house, less pretentious than Jillian and Derek's and so much more inviting.

Another item for her list, and one that could be time consuming. When she reached home, she would add it to her journal and then wait for Simon's call and the reassurance that he had made it through another day safely.

CHAPTER 13

Jenny's work at the coroner's office continued. She saw Dr. Millar only briefly on Monday, but on Tuesday he visited with her long enough for her to observe his gentle sense of humor. During the inquest he had often been forceful in his questions, but one on one he was patient and unfailingly courteous, leading her to conclude that he must have had a wonderful bedside manner as a doctor. "The results of the survey are overwhelmingly positive," she reported. "Some of the respondents had to wait years for the inquest and were surprised that they were still so deeply affected by the proceedings. The understanding of the support service volunteers meant a lot to them."

"I'm glad your husband's hearing was held sooner than that. I hope it gave you some closure."

He had such sympathetic brown eyes that she hated to disagree. "A psychiatrist told me once that feelings don't end. I think that means that closure never comes."

"Of course," he conceded. "The end comes for the deceased but not for those who remain behind. I apologise."

"No problem. By the way, I'll have the survey results ready tomorrow."

"May I take you to dinner then as a way of thanking you? I realise that I have you at a disadvantage: Because of the way we met, I know far more about you than you do about me. At dinner, however, I'll subject myself to your interrogation."

- -

Dr. Millar, whom Jenny thought she should now call David, rang for a taxi to take them to an Asian restaurant not far from Paddington Station. She ordered fried rice with beef and shrimp. David selected one of the vegetarian dishes, explaining that he didn't eat anything with a face, and chose a bottle of wine.

"No wonder you're so slim," she said. "Is your wife a vegetarian, too?"

He paused briefly before responding. "I haven't seen my wife in over fifteen years," he said. "She wasn't a vegetarian then, but neither was I."

"But you still wear a wedding ring," she stammered. "What happened to her?"

He didn't answer until after the waiter had poured the wine. "She disappeared. I don't believe that she deserted me; we were happy together, and nothing was missing except her purse, keys, and the clothes she was wearing. The police, however, suspected foul play. Because I was a doctor, I could have disposed of her, they thought. I was their main suspect."

"What did you do?"

"I closed my medical practice and studied law. I wanted to know exactly how the system worked in case I ever needed to defend myself. The detective sergeant on the case still checks in with me periodically, but her body has never been found."

"What was she like?" Jenny asked and then regretted using the past tense.

"A free spirit," he smiled. "Spontaneous, disorganised, somewhat impulsive, generous with her time and affections. I've asked myself many times if there were any signs of a mental illness that I missed, if she could have wandered away and forgot herself, but the answer is always no. She was young, that's all."

Jenny's entree was similar to Chinese food but a little spicier. They both ate quietly for a few minutes. "No wonder you haven't experienced closure," she said finally. "For you nothing has ended."

He nodded and refilled her wine glass. "She may still be alive. I live in the same house in case one day she finds her way home."

"Like Matthew Arnold, you're 'still nursing the unconquerable hope,'" she quoted.

"I prefer Shelley: 'To love, and bear; to hope till Hope creates / From its own wreck the thing it contemplates...'"

No one except Colin had quoted poetry to her, and now it came from a man who did not even know he was mourning. She felt a sudden stab of sorrow for both their losses.

"I don't mean to make you sad," he smiled. "My life's not completely empty, you know. I believe in the worth of the work that I do, and if I may make a brief confession to you, I have not been entirely faithful to her."

"Don't you want to move forward? Get off the merry-go-round?"

The waiter inquired about coffee or dessert, but Jenny declined both, and David provided his credit card.

"There's always the chance that one of these days I'll meet someone who'll show me how," David said. "Jenny, it could be you. We enjoy each other's company, I believe, and it's possible that a fondness could develop between us."

"But – you're still married," she objected.

He smiled gently. "I've shocked you, I see. I apologise."

Shocked and appalled her. "David, I can't give you what you want. That has to come from inside you. And besides, if I fall in love again, I want all a man's love. I certainly don't want to play second fiddle to a ghost."

"Some wi – " He stopped and corrected himself. "Some women enjoy a physical relationship which doesn't require them to commit themselves. Both parties can benefit."

Anger propelled Jenny to her feet. He had almost said widows. *Widows.* He was in a unique position, coming into contact on a frequent basis with bereaved women. "Thank you for dinner, but it's time for me to go home."

He stood. "May I escort you to the tube?"

"No," she said, grabbing her purse.

"I'll ring you in a week or so."

"Don't bother," she answered, but she was already nearly out the door when she spoke and didn't know or care if he heard.

On her way home she became increasingly angry. He had spied her vulnerability and preyed on her emotions in the most callous and calculating way she could imagine. That speech about his wife – had she really been missing for years? – must have been successful in the past. He had not touched her once, wrapping his proposition in apparent manners and restraint, when in fact all was a lie. When Simon had come on to her, he had been deeply disturbed by an incident. He had acknowledge his inappropriate behavior and wanted to make amends. He was willing to let her set the pace. Was she, however, consigning him to second place?

CHAPTER 14

Much had changed in Alcina's life. She, who had never been interested in any sort of cooking, worked at a bakery, where she had become fascinated with knives. She, who had always loved fancy clothes, now dressed plainly. Clothes she would have discarded before, she now wore, to blend, to look unremarkable, and in her nondescript disguise to provide a layer of protection for herself, a sort of armour.

The baker and his wife trusted her now; they had given her a key to the bakery. She could come and go as she pleased. She had a hideout if she needed one.

Yes, much had changed in Alcina's life. She, who had never liked animals, now had a dog. She had brought food to the alley where she had first seen it and left the food for the dog to find. Once she had seen it emerge from the darkness as she was turning away. Several more feedings had resulted in the dog eating while she was still present although distant. Finally it had come close enough to eat even when she did not move away. She had been patient, waiting until she was sure it would not run away from her. Then she had thrown a towel around its head and taken it home with her.

There were places in her flat for the animal to hide, but that did not concern her. She had no intention of bonding with it; she simply needed it to come into the kitchen to eat and drink. When it did, she blocked its escape. Cleanup in the kitchen would be less difficult.

She would grind the meat scraps she had saved from Kosta's. It would be easy, then, to add the rat poison.

CHAPTER 15

Jenny didn't hear from Simon until after dinner on Friday, when he asked if he could call by for a few minutes.

"Yes," she said and felt her stomach skip. Would he kiss her when he saw her? On her cheeks or on her mouth?

When he arrived, he pulled her close and kissed all three places.

She held him tightly, relieved that he was there. "Are you hungry?" she asked as she released him. "I could make you a quick omelette."

He made tea for both of them while she beat the eggs, diced the ham and onion, and shredded the cheese. He told her what he could about the operations his team had undertaken during the week, emphasising the skill and professionalism of his team members and omitting any mention of the unforeseen circumstances they'd had to overcome. He listened as she told him about the chopped up newspapers and agreed with her stopping delivery for a while. He took his plate and cup into the sitting room, remembering to give her the small gift he had brought.

She joined him on the sofa, tucking her feet beneath her. "I don't think I've ever received such a thin present," she said as she opened it. "A bookmark! With my initial. Simon, thank you, but what is the occasion?"

"Just glad to see you," he said between bites.

"When did you have the time to buy it?"

"I've had it for a while."

For how long? she wanted to ask but didn't. When he finished eating, she cleared his plate. "More tea?" she called from the kitchen. She almost said *tè* but decided to keep her Italian study a secret for a little longer.

He didn't answer; he had fallen asleep on the sofa.

She sat down across from him, wondering what to do. If she woke him, he would apologize and leave, and she didn't want that. After watching him breathe for a few minutes, she brought a blanket and covered him. She had often felt cold on the leather couch and thought he might too. Extinguishing the lights, she climbed upstairs to her bedroom, the silver bookmark in her hand. She was unable to concentrate on her reading, however, wondering if she should have told him about Dr. "I'm-a-wolf-in-sheep's-clothing" Millar.

- -

Simon woke, taking stock of his surroundings before he moved. He was at Jenny's flat, and his watch told him he'd slept over six hours. His internal clock had woken him at three a.m., close to the time he'd been rising for work the last twelve days. He swung his feet to the floor and considered his situation. She had given him a blanket; probably not angry then. She had welcomed him warmly to the flat, but that did not mean she would welcome him to her bed. He paid a visit to the loo. A new toothbrush lay beside the sink. She wanted him to stay, he concluded.

He cleaned his teeth and thought some more. He had showered before he left the base. She would be warm and soft. He would wake her gently, hold her gently. He wanted to know her every curve, what touches excited her and where. He was still knackered, but he could perform if called upon. More important, he was sober. He would go only as far as she wanted him to do. He caught sight of himself in the mirror and shook his head at the reflection. Exhaustion must have addled his brain. He splashed cold water on his face. Stripping to his pants, he stretched out on the sofa and covered himself with the blanket. Restraint was called for. Better if he didn't move too fast. Better if he waited for her to come to him.

CHAPTER 16

In the morning the smell of fresh coffee woke Simon. He pulled on his shirt and trousers. Jenny was in the kitchen, in jeans and a t-shirt with a trio of hummingbirds flying across her chest. Lovely.

"I'm not much of a breakfast person, but I have orange juice, the kind with juicy bits, as you Brits say. And bread and marmalade. I've never gotten used to your custom of eating beans for breakfast," she said, accepting a quick kiss on each cheek. Colin had always chosen to kiss her scarred cheek first to let her know he still thought her pretty, but Simon never differentiated, as if the scar weren't there.

"Just coffee. Sorry about last night. I didn't intend to fade out on you like that."

"No problem," she answered. "Can we spend some time together today?" She told him about her plan to begin to make changes to the flat. "When Colin and I were first together, I thought the flat was a little stark. I wanted to soften it, so I put some pastel pillows on the sofa, flowers on the dining room table, and fruit in a bowl on the kitchen counter, but it was still Colin's flat. Now I want to make it reflect a little more of me. Bear's paws have scratched the leather on the sofa, so I should probably replace that, but I thought I'd start with new pictures. Do you hate shopping, or would you like to come with me?"

"Yes to both," he smiled. "But I'd like to make a run by my flat for a change of clothes first."

"While you do that, I'll put something in the slow cooker for dinner," she said. "After we're through shopping, we'll have most of our meal waiting for us."

"Do you have what you need? No incident of vandalism doesn't mean no danger. I'd not like you to go out."

"I won't," she said and locked the door after him. While he was gone, she diced carrots, onions, and a bell pepper, and placed them in the pot with beef tips, seasonings, and broth. Had she locked the door? She had. She made a tossed salad to accompany the stew.

Still with time to fill, she realized she could do a little research on her grief book before he returned. She sat down at Colin's computer. No, hers, she reminded herself. He had bought a newer and faster one after their marriage, and she had been the primary user. Now she was the only user.

The internet had a wealth of information about grief, she discovered. All the sites agreed that it was okay to cry. A quote from Washington Irving touched her: "There is a sacredness in tears. They are not the mark of weakness, but of power...They are the messengers of overwhelming grief... and unspeakable love."

She read further. Depending on the source, grief could have four, five, seven, or even ten stages. She decided to combine them into three, because she hadn't been aware of the finer points of grief when she was experiencing it. And ten stages? That was discouraging.

The first stage she called, *Disbelief*. It had felt like shock, when she had understood intellectually that Colin was gone but had felt numb inside. Then periods of numbness had alternated with periods of intense sorrow.

That had led to her second stage, *Despair*. With the numbness gone, her grief had been raw. That phase had been complicated by loss of appetite, trouble sleeping, and exhaustion even when she had slept. She had been an island besieged with waves of anxiety, anger, and guilt. She had withdrawn.

In her final phase, *Determination,* hurt had still been

present but it was hurt tempered by hope. She had begun to believe that a productive life might be possible for her, however unclear it seemed. Then Simon had reentered her life in a dramatic way and changed everything. He would be back soon. She logged off the computer and set her notes aside.

They started their excursion by walking down to the charity shop on Finchley Road and then on to the Oxfam on West End Lane. Neither had any pictures that appealed to either of them, so they worked their way back, stopping in small art galleries to peruse the paintings and the prices. Jenny was surprised to discover how well Simon could describe each painting they saw.

"In the Royal Marines we were taught to observe. Lack of attention to detail could cost a life."

"Do you still watch people like that?"

"Yes, it's useful in the work I do." He paused. "When you're afraid and don't want others to know, you press your hands into your lap. If you're about to cry, the right side of your mouth turns down before your left. When you find something funny, your eyes laugh first."

"That makes me feel like a specimen."

He laughed. "It's not like that. When I've a bit of down time, I like to think on you, that's all, and it helps to recall you clearly."

Was that love? she wondered.

"I also know that you study me when you think I'm not looking."

She blushed, because she had. She had examined his strong face and felt reassured. She had concluded that the parts of him she couldn't see were strong too. She knew what the tightness between his brows meant and how his smile softened his usual stern expression. His left eye squinted more than his right. She took his hand and found the callus he had on his thumb. "If something happened to you, I'd want to remember everything about you," she said softly.

That called for an embrace and a kiss, but he limited himself to slipping his arm about her waist and drawing her close.

She smiled up at him before turning back to the paintings on display. "I have to confess – I know more about what I don't want than what I do. No paintings of fox hunts or sailing vessels. No still lifes. No photographs. Nothing too abstract; I want some color but not only color. The next shop will be our last."

"Fancy this one, Jenny?" Simon asked after they'd browsed for a few minutes.

She joined him and smiled. He had called her attention to a watercolor painting of a white bird rising effortlessly through the night sky, the tips of its outstretched wings tinted silver. Occasional small flecks of orange and blue represented the stars, but one's eyes were drawn to the bird and the ease of its ascent.

"Reminds me of a phoenix. Of you, actually."

"Why me?"

"That was our code name for you when you were in witness protection. Because phoenix is the name of a constellation."

"Who came up with that?"

He didn't respond right away.

"Simon – did you?"

He nodded. "And Sullivan thought you could rise from the ashes, so we agreed on it."

"Then yes. That's the one I want," she said. "And it's already matted and framed, so we can hang it immediately." She peered at the tag. "Not too expensive, either."

The gallery owner was glad to process her credit card and wrap the painting for them. Simon carried it for her, and together they surveyed the walls of the flat to determine the best spot, both agreeing that it was striking enough to occupy the space over the fireplace. "Thanks for being so patient with the shopping," she said. "I promise I won't take you shopping every time we're together."

The shopping hadn't been a bother. She had been so serious in her quest that he'd been able to focus on her without her being aware of it. He'd liked the exercise and the way her hand found his while they walked. He was happy for any sign of affection on her part.

They ate in the sitting room, Jenny having declared the dining room table too big for just two people and wanting to sit somewhere with a good view of the new painting. "Is it a dove, Simon? Doves mate for life, I think."

"What if their mate dies?" he asked. "Birds don't have long lives, do they?"

"Several years, maybe. But since the desire for reproduction is strong in wild creatures, they try to find another mate."

"Are you a wild creature, Jenny?"

She laughed. "No, I'm domestic."

"Are you looking for another mate?"

His earnestness surprised and flustered her, but at least he hadn't asked about her desire for reproduction. "I don't want to be alone the rest of my life," she said slowly. "I miss – I miss everything that goes with loving someone, the tangible and the intangible. I miss being loved, knowing a man is coming home to me, having him beside me at night. I miss feeling safe." She sighed. "There's a rapist in the Hampstead/Highgate area. I felt safe last night, when you were here. Thanks for not leaving."

His face tightened. "Tell me."

"PC Dugger doesn't think he's my stalker. And Dr. Knowles told me to be cautious but didn't seem concerned. I'm still nervous, however."

"Jenny, I'll stop the night with you again if you want me to do."

"I can't ask you to do that without – "

"No strings," he said firmly.

She was quiet for a long time, but she couldn't seem to keep her hands still until he grasped one. "I'm confused," she said finally, looking at how neatly her small hand fit into his palm. "About how I feel, I mean. I don't want to slip into a relationship with you because you're around and it's convenient. I want to make a conscious choice. And I want to prove to you, and to myself, that I'm strong enough to handle things when you're not here. So you won't worry about me when you're working."

"Tomorrow then." He leant forward to kiss her and was

encouraged when one kiss turned into two, and then three, because she didn't pull away.

"Come for brunch," she said.

CHAPTER 17

On Sunday Jenny realized that despite their time apart, she and Simon weren't starting completely over. Their awkwardness behind them, they had reestablished their easy rapport. He seemed increasingly relaxed and more than amenable to whatever she wanted to do. For brunch she made pancakes with maple syrup and fresh fruit, and he laughed at her attempts to flip the pancakes and catch them in the pan. After their meal, she gave Simon the leash, and they took Bear for a long walk.

On their way back, they stopped to watch other couples go by, some calling out to their unleashed dogs, others with children in hand or in a stroller. Jenny surveyed the expanse of green but didn't spot Jack or his grandparents. Joggers passed by, heading toward Parliament Hill and the oval track beyond. Just seeing them made Jenny feel tired. She sat down under one of the plane trees and leaned against its knobly trunk. Simon joined her, as did Bear, his head resting on her knee.

"In spite of its plainness, I always liked Colin's flat," she said, "because it was his. A man's flat – no frills – but comfortable. Its similarity to the protection flat made it seem safe. His stamp was everywhere: the photographs, books, all a reflection of him, a record of where he'd been and what he'd done. Gradually I made my presence felt, but after he died, he was everywhere in the flat. I was the one who ceased to exist; the flat shouted that he was there, which really hurt, because, of course, he wasn't. Now, it just holds memories, the way postcards do, and the memories don't hurt. In a way they keep me connected to him. But I think it's a good thing that I'm ready to make changes, don't you?"

The breeze was ruffling her hair, and he wanted to press his lips against it. For starters. "It's a step forward, love, and I'm glad to be a part of it."

She leaned her head against his shoulder. "Me, too, Simon. I'm glad you're here. Next time we walk, let's take the Frisbee. Maybe we can teach Bear to catch it. Or at least retrieve it." She smiled suddenly. "If not, I will."

When the sun began its retreat, they brushed the grass from their clothes and headed back to feed Bear and reheat the leftover stew for themselves. Jenny knew he would leave after supper, and she found herself dreading the moment. "I don't want you to go. I'll miss you," she murmured.

He went to her, put his arms around her as she sat, and kissed her. "It'll not be for as long this time," he said. "I'll ring you each night if I can."

She lifted her face for another kiss and then rose to lock the door after him. She cleaned up their dishes and poured a glass of wine for herself to settle her nervousness about whether the door was really locked. She took it into the sitting room where she could see the new painting.

Emily Dickinson had written a poem entitled, "'Hope' is the thing with feathers." How did the lines go? "That perches in the soul / And sings the tune without the words..." She couldn't recall any more, but maybe it was enough.

Hope, Dickinson evidently believed, lived inside us. Jenny thought that her hope had died with Colin, but perhaps it had been present all along. A sleeping bird would give no sign of its presence, but when Simon kissed her, she felt the flutter of its wings, so maybe hope was awakening, just as the bird in her painting was rising in the night sky. Gravity notwithstanding, birds didn't just rise; they soared. They sang. Could she rise above the gravity of grief? Could hope lift her?

Carl Sandburg had also written a poem about a bird, a little white bird that you could hear – and feel in your heart – but not see; a little white bird that caused you to pray, to feel safe, to feel strong. He had called the little white bird, love.

Hope and love. These weren't equivalent, but they were connected. She looked at the painting and thought about Simon for a long time.

Monday and Tuesday passed quietly, but the sight that greeted Jenny when she left the flat Wednesday morning stunned her. Spatters of red paint like a Jackson Pollock painting contrasted sharply with her blue front door, and florid script proclaimed, *Liar!* She sank to her knees, her arms around Bear's neck, and tried to slow the racing of her heart. When she was able to stand, she brought Bear inside with her and called PC Dugger. "It's a personal attack," she told him after describing it, "and I don't know why. I'm not frightened, though. I'm not."

Dugger was on the scene within the hour. "Paint's dry," he observed. "Mrs. Sinclair, I can no longer consider this a case of criminal damage. It's malicious. I'll be ringing detectives to speak with you. They may want to photograph this, so I'll have to ask you not to remove it just yet." Before he left, he made certain her doors and windows were securely fastened and locked.

Jenny sat down on the floor next to Bear and waited. She still hadn't resumed regular delivery of the *Telegraph*, so she couldn't use its headlines to distract her. She didn't have the concentration for anything more, even checking her e-mail or using the internet. Music? Mozart would be soothing, but she felt too heavy to stand up. She wished Simon were with her. He would know what to do; and even if there were nothing to do, she would feel safer, but Beth had warned her that she needed to handle things without him. When Bear whined at the door, she let him out briefly in the back. Lunchtime came and went. She was not hungry. Just before tea-time, PC Dugger called.

"Two detectives from West Hampstead are on their way to see you," he reported. "I've met with them and given them your case history. DS Wyrick and DC Mackeson. They'll identify themselves when they arrive."

When Jenny answered the bell, she saw two men in suits with their warrant cards open for her. "Detective Sergeant Stephen Wyrick," the taller man said. "My colleague, Detective Constable Graeme Mackeson. May we come in?"

"Yes," she said. "I'll make tea."

DC Mackeson accompanied her to the kitchen. "May I be of any assistance?" he asked.

Mackeson's five o'clock shadow nearly obscured the cleft in his chin. He was a burly man with thick dark hair and brows, and she didn't think china cups would be safe in his grip. She nodded toward the cabinet which held the mugs. He selected the Union Jack mug and one covered with Flanders poppies. "I'm not familiar with this flag," he said, holding a third mug.

"That's the Texas flag. I'm from the Lone Star state."

DS Wyrick had stepped into the sitting room and was quietly inspecting his surroundings. "You have an upstairs as well?" he asked when they joined him, Mackeson carrying the tray.

"Yes," she answered, wondering why that was relevant. While Mackeson resembled a good rugby player, DS Wyrick looked like he needed the tea cakes she served with the tea. His hair would have been gray if he'd had any, and his gaunt frame exacerbated the lines in his face.

"May we have a look round? To rule you out, you understand."

"That's insulting!" she objected. She watched Mackeson set the tray on the coffee table. Wyrick nodded at him, and in three strides he closed the distance to the guest bath and entered. Wyrick mounted the steps. "Bear, come," she called and wrapped her fingers in his fur.

Mackeson returned first. "What's down?" he asked.

"Guest rooms, and below those, the garage."

He stepped away, light on his feet for a heavy man. She could hear Wyrick's footsteps moving upstairs.

"Do you live here alone?" he asked when he reentered the sitting room.

"Didn't your search answer that?" she retorted. "When you see empty rooms, can't you connect the dots?"

"Large flat for one person," he commented.

"Do I have to talk to you?" she asked, trying to keep her outrage under control. She had been married to a policeman. Didn't they know? How could they possibly suspect her of anything?

"It's in your best interest."

"If you thought I might be making this up, why did you bother coming?"

"It is our duty to respond to each complaint," Wyrick answered in a near monotone.

When Mackeson came back, she picked up the teapot and then replaced it, realizing that its weight would not still the trembling in her hand. "You'll have to pour," she told him.

"Having tea's the best part of this job, no mistake," Mackeson said, filling their mugs and biting into one of the tea cakes. He seemed oblivious to her distress.

Wyrick sipped slowly. "A police officer by the name of Sinclair was killed just over a year ago. Were you acquainted with him?"

Jenny squeezed her hands together in her lap. "He was my husband."

"I'm sorry for your loss." He gestured to Mackeson, who downed his tea quickly and opened his notebook.

"He wouldn't have appreciated your approach," she said, still angry. They were sitting in her flat, drinking her tea, with what she considered a marked lack of concern. Was this case not important enough for them? Did they think her safety was a waste of time?

"Perhaps not," Wyrick answered, "but he would have

understood it." He cocked his head slightly at the DC.

Mackeson reviewed the incidents of vandalism one by one, but she had nothing to add to the details he covered. "Do you know what time of day these occurred?"

"I saw them when I left the flat in the morning. There were no new ones when I walked in the afternoon."

"Some time during the night or early in the morning," Mackeson said, making a note in his book. "And you have no idea who could be behind this?"

She shook her head. "I'm a low-profile kind of person."

Wyrick sat very still, seemingly detached, his face neutral but his eyes watchful.

"Have you noticed anyone in the neighbourhood hanging about? Who looked as if he didn't belong? Or noticed anyone staring at or following you?" The pen appeared small in Mackeson's mitt.

"No."

"Do the other residents of this block have any reason to be unhappy with you?"

"Not that I know of. Their rent hasn't increased."

"You're the owner of this block of flats then?"

"Yes."

Wyrick stirred. "The person who painted your door considered you a liar."

She pressed her lips together and did not reply.

"When have you lied, Mrs. Sinclair?" His voice was gentle, the way a knife appears to be gentle when it cuts through soft butter.

She looked at her clasped hands, angry with herself because she couldn't keep them from shaking. "When I told PC Dugger I wasn't afraid," she whispered. "Because the stalker's behavior is escalating, and a rapist is out there. They could be one and the same."

Mackeson's eyes widened. "We'll take that under consideration," he said. "Mrs. Sinclair, I'd urge caution on your part. You'll want to lock up after us." He pocketed his notebook and pen.

She stood slowly, still angry and not reassured by his police language. She'd heard the word "caution" before. What did it mean exactly? Did they all have a limited vocabulary? And did they really think she wouldn't lock the door? She wanted to lock them out.

"A photographer will call by in the morning," Wyrick added. "He'll not disturb you. And we'll send some uniformed officers to search for the paint can. Mackeson and I may have a few more questions for you tomorrow."

After they left, she clipped Bear's leash to his collar. There was time for a short walk before dark, and she let him set the pace as they headed toward the Heath. She regretted the destination. The Heath was no longer a haven. She had to pass wooded areas to reach the open spaces, and she felt exposed and vulnerable. She remembered Simon telling her once that the barrage of heavy artillery which preceded the Battle of the Somme in France in World War I could be heard on Hampstead Heath. Now, however, the danger was not across the English Channel but in Hampstead itself. Even if she and Bear stuck to residential streets for a while, that would not guarantee safety. Would she know when the threat came? Even with peripheral vision, she didn't think she could see enough of her surroundings. What she could see nearby – the details of grass and leaves – appeared to be safe, but who could say what lay in the distance? The Heath was no longer a landscape of refuge and renewal.

On the way back she purchased a large pizza to take with her. With tonight and tomorrow's dinners provided for, she wouldn't have to shop for groceries. She rummaged in the garage for something to tape over the accusing word on her door, finally locating some butcher paper and masking tape. Then she called Neil Goodwyn and asked if he could be with her when the detectives returned. "Two against one doesn't feel fair," she said. "I know they're supposed to be on my side, but they have such a terrible bedside manner that it's frightening. I just want to even the odds a little."

When Simon called, very late, she could hear the exhaustion in his voice, so she minimized the events of her day and asked about his. When she hung up, the flat seemed unnaturally quiet. Maybe she'd feel less alone if there were other voices around her. She found Colin's radio and turned the dial to a twenty-four hour station.

CHAPTER 19

It was like conducting a symphony, Alcina thought. When she raised her hands, the paint splashed, and she heard the clash of the cymbals, marking the end of a musical movement.

Overnight, an interlude, deceptively quiet, but not a rest. She rarely rested completely. She worked late at Kosta's and rose early to slip through the Hampstead streets on her way to the bakery.

The next morning a dissonant horn sounded in her ears as she rent the paper covering her message, announcing that her statement could not be sabotaged nor silenced. The knife had felt good in her hand, strong and pure. Knives were good for all sorts of things. This one had gone deep, scarring the door beneath, like plunging it deep enough to strike bone. A short movement but a powerful one, its theme clear.

She needed to be strong, and she needed a success because she had failed with the dog. After eating the food with rat poison, it had lost its appetite. She had been unable to tempt it to eat again. She had waited to see symptoms of physical distress, but for several days it had simply been lethargic. Finally one morning before she left for the bakery, she had noticed some slight muscle tremors and heard a weak cough. When she had returned after the night shift at Kosta's, its breathing was rapid and then stopped altogether. She had thought she would feel some sense of victory, but the entire episode had been anticlimactic. And there had been no blood.

Perhaps this method would have failed with her target's dog as well. It was well fed, which made it hard to be certain it would have eaten what she left for it.

She thought idly about using the knife on the carcass, but she didn't want to touch it. She wrapped it in a towel and disposed of it. As she did, she repeated her mantra of success to herself, first softly and then with more strength and purpose. Yes, I am strong. I am confident. I am determined.

She would find another method to deploy against her target's dog.

CHAPTER 20

Jenny woke with new resolve. She wouldn't let the two detectives – the West Hampstead Humanoids, she had dubbed them – unnerve her. She had done nothing wrong. Colin had outranked both of them. Simon possessed skills they didn't. And Neil Goodwyn was planning to stop by after lunch and wait with her until they arrived. *I bastardi,* she thought with clenched teeth, guessing that the Italian was a cognate for the English word "bastards" and promising herself not to say either in front of Neil.

She had a light breakfast and called for Bear, who growled as they stepped outside. When she turned to lock the front door, she understood why, and the shock made her knees weak: Someone had slashed through the butcher paper with such force that there were deep gouges in the wood beneath it. Feeling the first stirrings of panic, she sat down on the steps and put her head between her knees. Then she began to count to slow her heart. She took Bear into the garden in the back and watched him romp for a few minutes. No walk today.

When Father Goodwyn arrived, he expressed his concern. "The force and frequency of these episodes are increasing." The doorbell rang, and he clasped her hand for a quick prayer.

She let the detectives introduce themselves to Father

Goodwyn. DS Myrick raised his eyebrows slightly at the presence of the priest. "We've all the snaps we need," he reported. "In view of the new damage to your door, I must ask you again if you can think of anyone who desires to scare or harm you."

She shook her head.

"You should tell them, Jenny," Goodwyn said gently. "It may not be relevant, but they should have the opportunity to decide."

"Tell us what, Mrs. Sinclair?" Wyrick's eyes flickered, and she realized that she had aroused his interest, at least slightly.

"I want to know if you're going to help me. If you still think I could be the wrongdoer, then I'm not going to say any more."

"We'll do what we can," Wyrick assured her, unable to keep the impatience from his voice.

She sighed. Police-speak, but it would have to do. "In 1998, six women were raped and murdered in London. A seventh was attacked but did not die. A man – " she couldn't bring herself to say his name – "was convicted of the crimes and sent to prison."

"Cecil Scott," Wyrick said. "The 'carpet killer.' I recall the case. One of the victims was from Camden."

"Several attempts were made on the life of the seventh victim."

"Jenny – " Goodwyn began.

"The attacker was killed in prison."

"They need to know, Jenny," Goodwyn said again.

DC Mackeson looked from one to the other, not certain where the conversation was leading.

"What do we need to know?" Wyrick pressed, giving her his full attention for the first time.

She opened her mouth to speak, only to close it and shake her head. She gave Goodwyn a pleading look and then turned away.

"What Mrs. Sinclair is having difficulty telling you is that she was the seventh victim," Goodwyn disclosed.

Mackeson gaped at her. Wyrick allowed himself a rueful

smile. Every time he thought he'd seen it all, something came along to prove him wrong.

"I have assured Mrs. Sinclair that there will be no need for her to recount what she experienced at the hands of that monster," Goodwyn stated.

Against her will, Jenny began to tremble. She had recovered; she had put it behind her; she had gone on with her life. Why did it still have the power to hurt so much? She felt someone take her hand and knew it was Goodwyn. "He was killed in prison," she repeated. "After that there weren't any more attacks. This can't possibly be related. Can it? Can it?"

Wyrick rose to his feet. "This information puts your incidents of criminal damage in a new light. We'll need some time to review the facts of that case before we speak with you again." He paused. "Mrs. Sinclair, can you recall the name of the senior investigating officer on your case? I'd like to contact him."

So would I, she thought, and swallowed hard. "Detective Chief Inspector Colin Sinclair."

Her husband – something else he hadn't expected. "Is there someone who can stay with you?"

"I'll advise Mrs. Sinclair on that point," Goodwyn answered.

Jenny watched the two detectives take their leave. "I have Bear," she said. "And leftover pizza. I'll see Simon tomorrow night or Saturday. I just want to cover the door with fresh paper, and then I'll lock up for the night."

Goodwyn held the paper while she taped it in place. "I'll ring you tomorrow," he said.

CHAPTER 21

"About your door – I peeled the paper back," Simon said when he came by late Friday night. "You didn't tell me how nasty it was. Protecting me?"

"Yes, sort of."

He didn't know whether to be pleased or angry. He didn't want her keeping things to herself.

"And trying to act more British," she said, failing to smile. "You know, stiff upper lip and all that, but I'm not sure I'm succeeding. Whoever did it must be really angry. He didn't just cut the paper, he dug into the wood."

He held up his Bergen. "I'm prepared to stay, if you need me to do."

"For now, I just need to be held. I feel like I'm swimming in muddy water; I can't see where the danger will come from."

He sat down on the sofa, and she rested her head against his shoulder. It was odd to be close to a man who wasn't Colin. Odder still, feeling like she fit there. "Simon – even with your arm around me, I can't seem to get close enough to you to feel safe."

"I can think of a way for us to be closer," he smiled.

"I'd be using you, and that would be wrong," she answered.

"Jenny, I'd never mind."

She laughed in spite of her tension.

"In a love relationship, people have sex for all sorts of reasons, and it's not wrong."

"Is that what we are? A couple in a love relationship?"

"I hope so," he answered.

Dr. Millar hadn't offered her a love relationship. How different he and Simon were! "I like the sound of that. But I need to be sure, and I'm not, yet."

"I'll bunk on the sofa then. And tomorrow I'll repaint your door."

She kissed him, went upstairs, and for the first time in forty-eight hours, turned off the radio. When she put on her nightgown and climbed into bed, she began to wonder what would have happened if she had invited him upstairs. Would he have been as tender with her as Colin had been? He hadn't been rough when he'd taken her on the sofa, and even drunk, he hadn't hurt her. He'd known he was with her, because he'd said her name.

He was a mature man, experienced with women. Would her body satisfy him? What if it didn't? In witness protection he'd treated her wounds. He knew the scars were there, but it was different when you had a personal relationship with somebody. Wasn't it? She felt suddenly shy.

CHAPTER 22

In the morning Simon found a brush and a can of blue paint in the garage, but no wood filler. "Any extra toothpaste? I'll use that instead."

Jenny applied masking tape to the door knob, letter box, and hinges, and then watched while he worked. "Where did you learn how to do this?"

"After my dad left, I had to do the repairs. I learnt as I went along."

"You're good with your hands."

He stopped and smiled at her. "I like to think so."

She blushed.

"If I stopped coming on to you, you might think I'd changed my mind," he said, surveying his work. "We'll let this dry. If it needs another coat, I can apply it tomorrow. In the meantime, I'll wash the brush if you'll make some fresh tea. I'd like to have a word with you about something."

They sat down together on the sofa, and Jenny poured cups for both of them.

"Jenny, you're safe as long as you're with me, but I can't be with you on a regular basis." He leant forward. "I don't want to alarm you, but some precautions are in order."

"Simon, why are you so concerned? No one has approached me directly."

"Violence usually escalates. A weapon was used on the

newspapers, most probably a knife of some sort, and now on the door. A knife is a very personal weapon. That changes things."

His matter-of-fact voice frightened her more than an urgent tone would have. "I feel so helpless. Is there anything I can do?"

"Be unpredictable. Take different routes to the Heath or walk somewhere else. Stay alert. Be aware of what's going on around you. Sometimes what you sense matters more than what you can see. Don't discount your intuition."

"Simon, you're scaring me."

"Not my intent. Shall we walk Bear this afternoon?"

They took an extended walk. She led him up Heath Street past La Gaffe and into Whitestone Gardens to show him her favorite bench, a wooden structure with two huge, articulated hands suspending the plank between them. "Look, Simon – even the fingernails are carved into the wood. It's a metaphor for all the people who supported me during my grief."

He nodded, his eyes taking in the surroundings. The street was nearby, but trees made the site too secluded for his taste. He took her hand. "You mustn't come here without me," he said softly. "It's too closed off. Someone could attack you, and no one would see."

She paled and sat down suddenly.

"Sorry," he whispered.

She leaned forward and put her arms around his waist. "Simon, I feel so small."

He stroked her hair. "I remember one op," he began after a moment. "We were almost to the extraction point when a sudden storm broke. Not much cover for us; just tall grasses whipped by the wind. Rain beat down on us and we knew the copter couldn't approach. In the scheme of things, we didn't signify. Nor did the mission we'd risked so much for."

She looked up, wanting to see his face. He rarely mentioned his Special Forces experiences. "What did you do?"

"Nothing to do but wait. Our rations were nearly gone. Contact with the enemy was less likely in that weather, but they'd have more time to catch us up."

"Did they?"

"No. Weather must have discouraged them or erased our tracks." He sat down next to her. "It was the first time I felt alone on the team, however. We couldn't move closer together; bad for security. We couldn't even risk calling out to one another."

"So you waited by yourself."

"Yes. The storm was loud and seemed long. In the sudden quiet after, the sound of the rotors was nearly deafening but more than welcome. The skies were completely free of clouds. CAVU, we called it: clear and visibility unrestricted. Only then did we know that we'd all made it."

"After hurricanes," she said, "the Texas sky seemed so bright. I remember the relief we felt." She paused. "I wish my storm were over, but it isn't. We'd better go."

On the way back to the flat, he ordered Chinese food to cheer her up. They took it home with them. After their meal, they cuddled in front of the television, commenting on anything and everything but the threat that loomed in the background.

"Would you like a goodnight kiss?" she asked, not waiting for him to answer.

He responded by pulling her close. "If you keep on kissing me like that, we'll have a very good night indeed," he said when she paused. "I'd like to do that. Make it a good night for you." He slipped his hands under the back of her t-shirt and heard a sharp intake of breath. Not certain whether that meant yes or no, he waited.

"Simon – Simon – " she whispered. "You're not making it easy for me."

"If it's difficult to hold back, perhaps you shouldn't," he suggested and felt her tense. Reluctantly he let his hands fall. "It's all right, love. Best if we wait until it's right for both of us. But if you change your mind, you know where to find me."

- -

For the first time in many months, a nightmare woke Jenny. Even after she opened her eyes and surveyed her surroundings, she couldn't shake the intense fear. Pulling a robe around her, she went down to the kitchen to make herself a cup of hot chocolate. The milk hadn't even scalded when she heard Simon's voice from the sitting room. "Are you all right?"

"Simon, weren't you sleeping?"

"Thought I'd watch the street for a bit. Why are you up?"

"I had a bad dream."

"Tell me about it."

She poured the hot milk into a mug and mixed in a generous amount of chocolate syrup. "Someone I couldn't see splashed my shirt with red paint. But it wasn't paint, it was blood. I was terrified."

"Better now?" he asked as she sipped the cocoa.

"Yes." She smiled. "Chocolate always helps. Would you like some?"

"I'll make tea."

She watched while he set the water to boil and placed a tea bag in the Big Ben mug. "I've never seen you without a shirt," she commented when he joined her.

"Shall I dress?" He had kept on only a pair of jeans.

"No. I like what I see." His work required him to be strong, and he was, as Beth would say, seriously fit. He had, after all, been a combat swimmer.

"There's no law against touching," he smiled, and watched her blush, confirming his suspicion that she'd thought of it.

She laughed but didn't answer. He finished his tea, and she tried to focus on the syrup that had sunk to the bottom of her mug and not his bare chest.

"Shall we say goodnight again?" He stood and held out his hand.

The hair on his chest was ginger, not dark. She rested her cheek against it and closed her eyes. She felt his arms close around her and his lips on her hair. "One kiss is not going to be enough, but more than one, and I'll have a hard time falling asleep," she whispered, as his mouth found hers.

"It's your call, Jenny." He made the one kiss last as long as three, holding her head gently in his hands and then nuzzling her neck.

Her neck shivery, she wanted him to take the next step – to push her robe and pajama top out of the way and caress her chest. All she had to do was place his hand where she wanted. He would do the rest. But when would he stop? Would he think that a green light on the next step was a green light to the final step? What would it mean if they proceeded to the end without declaring themselves? Would the relationship last? Colin had made it easy for her by acknowledging his feelings early on. Simon had done the same himself, sort of – he had said he wanted them to be a couple. But he hadn't specified what that meant exactly. She sighed.

"I've a pence," he whispered in her ear.

"For my thoughts?" she smiled. "That's not nearly enough."

"I can bid higher then."

She leaned forward and brushed his nose with hers. When she kissed him gently on the lips, he responded in kind.

"Something you want, Jenny?"

She pulled away slightly. She had always been too impatient for her own good. Her body was saying, "Why wait? You know you want him. You won't regret it." But she had. What had Dr. Knowles advised when he had counseled her and Colin? Something about nothing being lost by waiting. That an investment of time at the beginning of a relationship would pay dividends later. That implied that she could mess things up if she hurried. "Simon, I'm not teasing you. I just – I want – but – I'm not – ready," she said finally.

CHAPTER 23

Simon was so quiet on Sunday that Jenny began to wonder if she'd offended him. In the morning he put a second coat of paint on her front door. In the afternoon they took Bear for a walk, Simon glancing up and down each street they passed on the way to the Sainsbury's on Finchley. "I'd like you to get some groceries in this weekend," he said. "The fewer trips you make without me and Bear, the better." He waited outside with Bear while she chose what she needed.

"Should I stop going to the gym? I have to walk there by myself because dogs aren't allowed in."

He nodded. "It would be best."

After dinner he sat down with her on the sofa and spoke to her again about her safety, which really made her nervous.

"Next weekend I'll teach you some basic self-defence moves. Between now and then, I want you to prepare yourself mentally. When my team plans an op, we get our minds straight first. We don't ask ourselves if we can be successful, because we know we can be. We only ask how. On the Job we can't afford to lose. We have to win every time."

"Have you been thinking about this all day? I was afraid you were quiet because I disappointed you last night."

He smiled briefly. "You've never disappointed me. Now listen up. Repeat after me: I am alert. I am prepared. I know

I can win."

She obeyed.

"I can win in any circumstance, over any opposition."

He waited while she echoed his words.

"I can survive. I did before, and I can do it again." She faltered.

Hoping to relax her, he began to run his fingers across her palm.

"Simon, how do you know all this?" she asked. "Did you ever need to psych yourself up?"

He took a deep breath. "A while ago, yes. When I was first in the Special Forces and sent to the Persian Gulf. Prior to Desert Storm." He stopped.

"Simon, I know you're uncomfortable, but please tell me." She smiled. "Should I massage your hand?"

He appreciated her humour: a good way to control fear. "I had some anxiety about my ability to perform under fire, so when I loaded my magazine, I named each round with what I thought I needed. Strength. Endurance. Calm. There were others. When I had a few ops under my belt, I boiled it down to mindset. My gear was in order, and I was physically ready. So it all came down to a constant state of mental readiness."

"I understand."

"Focus, Jenny," he said gently, "and repeat the exercise." He nodded when she finished each phrase. "Think of a time when you felt strong, and then say it." He waited.

"I can't think of one," she said after a few minutes.

"You graduated from uni."

"That doesn't seem significant now."

"You married."

"I felt happy then, but it was taken away. I think I'm only strong when I'm with other people. Like you."

"Then say it with a bit of anger. Next week we'll work on the tangibles."

CHAPTER 24

Sunday. No prison visit today; visits had to be scheduled ahead of time, and Alcina had forgot to do it. The bakery was closed, but she had gone to Hampstead anyway. Usually she arrived in the half light of dawn and wore colours that blended with the shadows that still remained from the night. Her anger burnt brightly, but nothing else about her could be allowed to shine.

Hoping to catch a glimpse of her target, however, she had made the trip in the daylight. She had spent hours watching her target's flat, from one vantage point and then from another, but her target had not appeared. A wasted trip. She had wanted to see her target's face, see lines of tension there in addition to the scar. The scar didn't detract enough from her appearance; it was too easy for her to hide by tilting her head and letting her hair swing forward. How satisfying it would be to give her some wounds that were more difficult to conceal. And at the end, wounds that would never heal.

Until then, caution was the order she intended to follow. She was unused to weapons. She had had to train herself. It had taken time for her to learn to hold the knife like an attacker, to grip it tightly, to take decisive strokes. It had been difficult at first to control her breathing, to keep her approaches silent. She had closed her shades and practiced in her flat, pacing back and forth with the knife in her hand, stopping suddenly to slash things. Pillows had been too soft, books too hard. It hadn't taken her long to talk herself into using Tony's stuffed armchair as a target, because he had deserted her, betrayed her trust. She pinned snaps of her target to the chair and refined her aim. Newspapers had some substance to them also. Like human flesh.

Jenny didn't see Simon until Friday evening. "I'm happy to see you, even if you do look like last week's news," she said.

He held her briefly. "Our spare week, and we were just as busy as we are on our regular ops weeks."

She had expected a greater show of affection and now wasn't sure what to think. "Have you eaten?"

"Fish and chips on the way here," he said, "but I'd like a cup of tea. Then we'll start work." He'd spent his down time during the week trying to think like her stalker, asking himself how he would attack her. He had concluded that his first step would be to waste the dog. As long as Bear was with her, she had a line of defence, but he would have felt better if she had a police dog, capable of responding to commands at a moment's notice. And she could not seek cover or conceal herself while walking him.

"Every man has vulnerable points," he began, having downed his tea in three swallows. "His eyes, his bollocks, and his knees. Your goal is to deflect an assault by striking hard and fast, to give yourself time to get away."

His gravity was sobering. After a week apart, she needed to reconnect with him. He had given her only a perfunctory kiss when he arrived.

"Hampstead streets aren't usually deserted, and you'll have Bear – " or so he hoped – "but I'd rather you be overprepared than underprepared."

"Bear's been weird. He barks more than usual, and when we go out, he growls and sniffs all around the porch."

"He's picked up your stalker's scent." He had her stand in front of him, while he pantomimed both frontal and rear attacks in slow motion, guiding her responses. "Watch my hands, Jenny. Are they high or low? Which one do you need to block?" He nodded. "Well done. Let's try it again." He stopped. "I know you're right-handed, but you need to use both hands. Got it? Tomorrow we're going to speed everything up."

"Simon," she said in desperation, "could you stop and hug me for a minute? To remind me that we care about each other?"

"Sorry," he said. "I'm still in team leader mode."

She walked into his open arms and stood on her tiptoes to kiss his cheek and his mouth. The firmness of his embrace was reassuring.

When she stepped back, he began again, narrating each move and gradually increasing his aggressiveness.

"Whoa!" she exclaimed. "You scared me that time."

"Training only works if it's taken seriously," he said. "You need to be able to react even if you're frightened."

"What's that?" she asked, hearing a repeated beep.

"My pager." He stepped aside and made a brief call. "Just an update," he reported. "Where were we?"

"Finished with the physical drills," she said, crossing her fingers behind her back.

"What's your mindset then?"

Relieved, she repeated the "I can" phrases he had taught her the weekend before, first in English, then in Italian, watching his eyebrows rise. "*Sono vigile. Sono pronta. So che posso vincere. Posso vincere della circostanza, contro dell'opposizione. Posso sopravvivere. Ho sopravvissuto già, e sopravvivrò un'altra volta.*" She paused, waiting for his response. "My grammar's probably wrong."

"*Che sorpresa,*" he said after a moment. "Are you taking a class?"

"No, just seeing how much I can learn on my own."

"There's my girl," he said and kissed her. "*Brava*."

Their other activities over the weekend paled next to Simon's focus on teaching her to defend herself. On Saturday the drills were longer and his moves more sudden. "Your resistance needs to be stronger and faster," he scolded. "Don't worry about hurting me."

On Sunday they shopped for groceries, and he quizzed her as they wove their way through the streets. "The person who just passed us by: Was it a man or a woman? Approximate age? Hair colour? Can you describe what he was wearing? Who is behind us?"

His questions unsettled her, and she lost her balance and stumbled while trying to watch everyone around her. When they returned to the flat, he led her in yet another round of exercises, insisting that her week without incident was no reason for her to let her guard down. "Keep exercising. Try to walk a bit farther or faster. Being physically fit will give you an edge. Complacency is your enemy."

He ignored her pale face and continued. "If an attack comes – " For her benefit, he forced himself to say "if" although the stalker's use of the knife had, in his mind, changed the equation to "when" – "you'll have little or no warning. You'll be frightened, possibly confused. Remember to breathe to calm yourself, in through your nose and out through your mouth, deep, regular breaths. Slowing your breathing will slow your heart rate, lower your blood pressure, and correspondingly, slow any bleeding. Get in the habit of taking water with you when you go out. Drinking it after an incident will help your body rid itself of stress."

"Then I need some water now!" she said. "You've been Drill Sergeant Casey all weekend. I never got to spend any time with relaxed, funny, sexy Simon, and I miss him!"

He realised suddenly that he had focused on the threat and neglected the woman. He put his arms around her and held her.

His embrace was a little too tight, and she knew he was afraid for her, even if he didn't say so. Her own fear grew, and she squeezed him back. "I wish you could be here all the time! Since you aren't, I wish I were fearless, like you."

"I'm glad you're not. Don't want you reckless. If you're a bit wary, you'll be a good deal safer." He loosened his grip slightly. "Jenny, dealing with a threat isn't always about superior power. It's about being smarter. I'd not like you to go out after dark," he added. "Even with Bear. Promise."

"Simon, I promise, but – next weekend – can we find time for something besides self-defense? Anything."

"Promise."

She smiled. "We're making promises to each other. I like that."

He liked it also, very much.

CHAPTER 26

Best leave he'd had in a long time. Three times the dreaded pager had called Simon back to duty, but the rest of the time he'd spent with Jenny. He had taken her flowers Friday night; hadn't even mentioned self-defence until Saturday. He'd gone through the drills with her daily, remembering to reassure her after each session. He couldn't press her as hard as he did his team, and at the end of the day he feared the drills were too little, too late. She hadn't sufficient reps, and she hadn't responded well to his unexpected moves. She needed to practise when she was tired and when distractions disrupted her concentration. He rather doubted that she'd react quickly enough when the time came. Her attacker would be taller, stronger. Her only edge – if it could even be considered one – was her desire to live.

He led a team of capable, professional men. They were all trained to take control quickly in any situation, for their own safety and the safety of those they encountered. In his personal life, however, he could not assert himself in the same manner. He couldn't mandate Jenny's love, he had to win it, in a hearts-and-minds op of the most delicate sort. And as in any hearts-and-minds action, what one did was more important than what one said. In any case he planned to proceed with some caution, not wanting to cause her to say no.

He noted some signs of progress. She was more affectionate and more responsive to his advances, particularly after their picnic with Davies and his family. She had been surprised by how comfortable he was with Davies' daughter, Meg, and how much Meg liked him. "I looked after my brother," he had told her. "As you did with yours."

They had lunched on the cold cuts and rolls that Jenny brought, with croissants from the bakery in Hampstead for the adults and decorated cookies for Meg. Then he and Jenny had taken Meg to the slide to give Davies and Beth a bit of time on their own.

On their way home after, Jenny had surprised him with her sombre mood. First she'd told him she was writing a book about grief. A workbook, she called it, because healing was hard work. He hadn't known what to say but hoped it would be healing for her. Then she mentioned children. "I couldn't conceive with Colin. If you want a family, I'm the wrong girl for you." He had tried to buoy her up, telling her he was certain she was the right girl and that he had his own shortcomings. It was a package deal for both of them.

On Thursday morning they went downstairs, intending to take Bear for a walk, when he heard her cry out. Someone had pushed a snap of her through the letter box, a distance shot with her torso slashed, and she was shaken. He took her by the shoulders and at his urging, she repeated what she called her mantra: "I'm alert. I'm ready. I know I can win. I can win in any circumstance, over any opposition. I can survive. I did before, and I can do it again." He was proud of her.

The receipt of the photo, however, necessitated a call to the detectives. She introduced him when they arrived. "Simon was one of my protection officers."

"Where's your nick now?" the DS inquired.

"Leman Street," he answered, wanting the detective to get the message. Jenny had told him how they had treated her.

"Did you handle the photograph?" the younger one asked. They both nodded.

"In the event that there is another, I must request that

you touch the edges only," DS Wyrick commented. They concluded from the clothes Jenny was wearing that the picture had been taken some time ago, while the weather was still cold. They questioned her, somewhat gently, about her contacts with men since Sinclair's death.

"None," she said, raising her chin.

Simon was glad to see her sign of defiance, however slight.

Wyrick rephrased. "Do you have any casual male acquaintances who may have misread your friendly nature?"

"I'm not friendly with strangers," she answered. "But there was a man recently who made me feel very uncomfortable."

"And that would be – ?"

Wyrick had asked the question, but Simon wanted to know also.

"Dr. Millar, David Millar. The coroner at Colin's inquest. I agreed to help him with some paperwork afterward. When I finished, he took me to dinner and played on my sympathy. He said his wife had been missing for years. He implied that he was lonely."

All three men waited for her to continue.

"He was a reptile. He wanted sex with no strings, and I don't. I walked out on him."

"Was he angry?" Wyrick asked.

"He was passionless."

"Description?"

"Brown hair, brown eyes, medium height, slim, and pale as an insect that lives under a rock. And he knows that I live alone, and where."

"We'll look into it. We've begun a preliminary review of the Scott case," Wyrick added.

Both he and the DC glanced surreptitiously at the scar on her cheek, but Jenny didn't miss their brief looks. "Are you on my side now?" she asked.

"I can assure you that we are," Wyrick answered. "We haven't the manpower for surveillance, but we'll have a car drive by periodically. We have questioned your neighbours and requested that they be alert for any suspicious-looking individual." When they left, they took the photo with them.

"Jenny, I need to know more about this – reptile – you mentioned. Did he hurt you?"

She shook her head. "Simon, he never touched me. I spent several afternoons in his office compiling the results of a survey to evaluate the Coroner's Court Support Service. When my work was finished, he invited me for an early dinner, to thank me, or so he said. That's when I heard the sob story about his wife. He still wears a wedding ring, so when he suggested that if I entered into a physical relationship with him, we could become fond of each other, I knew he wasn't offering anything I would value. And I had no desire to become his latest infidelity."

He waited a few minutes before speaking but was unable to curb his anger completely. "Jenny, someone is threatening you. You should have told me about this bastard."

"You were exhausted when you called, and I was ashamed. And Wyrick and Mackeson are the detectives."

"Excuses, Jenny."

"Yes, you're right, but please don't be mad! He made you look really good."

"How's that?" he asked, curious in spite of himself.

"Because you care about what I need and want. And right now I need a hug."

Finally he smiled. "Come here to me then." He collected a kiss also.

- -

The next morning when he woke, he found Jenny asleep, fully dressed, in the armchair across from him, a blanket over her shoulders and lap. "What's this?" he asked her. She didn't admit to fear, saying only that her senses were in overdrive and she wanted to be closer to him. He made her smile by noting that she'd missed her mark by a few feet. Then she reminded him that she was still scarred from Scott's attack and shy as a result. When he got over his surprise – why would she be concerned about scars on her chest and abdomen if she weren't considering letting him see them? – he told her that he didn't give a toss about them. "You don't expect them to slow me down, do you?"

During a Heath walk with Bear, they'd seen Jack Dunaway, the sad little boy Jenny had told him about, with a Jack Russell terrier, a small, compact white dog with one black eye and one tan. According to his grandmother, Jack still hadn't spoken, but she reported that his appetite and activity level had improved. When Jack threw the ball, the terrier had bounded after it, and they'd heard what sounded like a hoarse cough from Jack. "It's his laugh," Mrs. Dunaway explained. "Made me weep the first time I heard it. The counselor says his speech will return." Jenny had been delighted, and he had enjoyed seeing her smile.

Later that day during a cuddle on the sofa she had slipped her hand under his shirt and then unbuttoned it before kissing his chest. He had taken that as an invitation to explore what was under hers with his fingers and his mouth. When he put his hand on her stomach, however, she'd placed her hand over his. He preferred to think her gesture wasn't a "no" but her way of saying, "Not yet." He wondered then what she was waiting for. Was she afraid of pregnancy? An issue easily enough solved. Was it her monthly? If so, he could understand her shyness. Had his drunken action scared her? Should he ask? No, asking could be construed as pressure. Sometimes things worked themselves out. He knew what he wanted: to make love to her sober, taking the time to savor each sensation, his and hers.

Perhaps his job schedule was the roadblock. The more time they spent together, the closer they became. Then days would pass when he couldn't see her, and she'd be tentative again. He knew he was asking her for a good deal of trust, but he believed, given time, she would be confident of him.

Providence! Teresa, young, cheeky Teresa, dropped a loaded tray at Kosta's. A wine bottle spilled and six glasses shattered on the tile floor. Teresa, who received from the customers admiring glances which should have been Alcina's, although she no longer cared about causing them. Teresa, withering under Kosta's ire, because the wine had been one of their more expensive burgundies. The shards caught the light and reflected it, much as the ideas bursting in Alcina's brain. Like diamonds, she thought, dangerous little blood-red diamonds that would lie seductively on her target's porch and slice into the dog's feet.

Of course she offered to clean up the mess, and it was all she could do not to laugh aloud while she worked, sweeping the precious jewels into a thick sack she could take home with her. Teresa was very grateful for her assistance, apologising over and over, and Alcina found that funny also, because Teresa was the one who had helped her. Other glasses, dishes, plates, could be made to fall. Things were always breaking in a busy kitchen, and Alcina would collect all the broken pieces. Then – when she had enough – she would send her target the message: You are vulnerable. You will be easy prey for me now.

A rush of excitement spread across her chest. She had stepped from a dark tunnel into a blaze of light, light that spelled the successful conclusion to her plans, light that proclaimed, Victory! Should she use the larger knife? For weeks she had admired its graceful shape, sometimes caressing the blade with the tip of her finger. She would sheathe the knife in her target's body, a sudden strong thrust to start, others to ensure success. She would not gloat; she need not linger. Her satisfaction would be complete. Her work would be done.

Jenny hated to see Simon's leave week end. In spite of the interruptions – he had been called away several times, teaching her that no plans were sacrosanct – they had become closer. They'd enjoyed doing simple things, laughing and talking while they walked, throwing the Frisbee, playing catch with Bear, and stopping at the Hampstead Creperie for a savory snack or dessert. The more fun they had together, the harder it was to see him go. She'd felt safe with him beside her, and although she knew that his job called him to protect others, she dreaded his return to full-time duty and her corresponding heightened vulnerability. She'd miss him physically in other ways, too. He had kissed her, caressed her chest, then stopped, his forehead against hers. She had heard his heavy breaths and knew he had heard hers. His fingertips had skimmed her lips, making them tingle. She was in a quandary, not wanting him to stop but relieved when he did.

She resolved to keep busy. She reviewed her Italian, spending some time with the new visual dictionary she'd purchased. Then she set the book aside and found some blank paper. She had decided to call her workbook, *Working Through Grief*. She intended to encourage her readers to keep a diary as a way of clarifying their thoughts and feelings about the loved one they had lost and then, over time, releasing those feelings. She would begin with a short narrative and then include portions of her lists as examples as well as spaces for the readers to make their own entries. Although she hadn't realized it at the time, her lists had helped her to mark her progress.

One chapter would cover things people said and did that weren't helpful and things that were, followed by a contrast between what she had expected the grief experience to be like and what it really was. Another would discuss grief support. Hers had come from individuals rather than groups, but the concept was no less valid. The issue of what to do with your loved one's possessions should be addressed. Perhaps she should call it, *To Discard or Not to Discard.* Another chapter could explore what grief and loss had taught her. She had only hoped to get through it, but there had been valuable life lessons along the way.

A new list – *Ways to Assert Yourself* – could be useful.

1. *Give yourself permission to grieve in your own way and at your own pace.* Simon had done that for her, understanding that the grief journey had no timetable.

2. *Find someone who understands what you're going through.* Colin's mother, Joanne, had understood. She'd have to tell her about the project.

3. *Associate also with people who aren't grieving, even if they don't understand.* Simon, Beth, and others had distracted her from her grief and kept her connected to the normal world.

4. *Keep moving.* Her endless hours walking on the Heath had also given her brief respites from grief. They had kept her away from the flat Colin wasn't coming home to and made the weight of grief less heavy when she returned. On the Heath she had pretended for a time that she hadn't lost anybody and felt less guilty that her heart was still beating when his wasn't.

5. *Regrets are normal.* She hadn't loved Colin perfectly, but she had done her best.

Thinking of Nick Howard and Bear, she added:

6. *Healing may come from unexpected sources.*
7. *Do your best to keep dates and places from having power over you.* She had been captive to the circumstances surrounding Colin's death. It was more important to give significance to the places he had lived and the special occasions they had shared.

More research would be necessary, however, for the workbook to be complete. Did men grieve differently than women? She wished she had asked Colin more about how he'd dealt with his father's death. However, both Dr. Knowles and Neil Goodwyn could share information with her. Then she called Colin's sister, Jillian, to arrange a lunch date. Jillian had lost a parent and a brother. She might have some valuable insights.

Looking for additional paper in Colin's roll-top desk, she found an old notebook with a list entitled, *Things I Learned from Colin's Mother.* She had made the entries after their first meeting, when Joanne had talked about the many adjustments she'd had to make as the wife of a foreign service officer, but some of the items seemed just as relevant now to the grief process. *Family matters most. Having friends helps. Be resourceful. Take the long view. Starting over is a part of life and not necessarily a bad thing.* Jenny would include them.

C. S. Lewis, she remembered, had written about a spring cleaning of the mind. By the calendar she was well into the summer – July 4 had come and gone, and once again she had missed the annual five-mile walk on the Heath to benefit breast cancer – but she had begun the process already without realizing it. In spring cleaning, people discarded items that weren't needed and kept the ones that were. Grief was a familiar skin she needed to shed. Her feelings of grief for Colin had been so intense and consuming that they had shut out other feelings. She knew now that letting her grief for him go didn't mean letting her love for him go, and she understood that if she didn't let grief go, she wouldn't be able to let other feelings in. The sorrow of his loss, her fear of a future without him: These were cobwebs she should sweep away. The army of feelings associated with despair had camouflaged her feelings for Simon until recently. Now she wondered what it would be like to wake in the morning with him beside her. To open her eyes and see his chest rising and falling and hear his breathing. Or would he rouse first? Would he want her, and wake her gently, the way Colin had? Of course, if he were in her bed in the morning, he would have been there the night before, too. She sighed. She wanted more than one night and one morning; she wanted a whole succession of them, and that meant a commitment. And commitment, to her, meant expressing love.

On one off-duty weekend, Brian had a cookout for some of the firearms officers, those on Simon's team and others from a team on which Brian had served previously. Beth was eight months pregnant, but she was a good hostess, holding two-year-old Meg's hand while introducing Jenny to the men and their significant others. Simon knew all of them, but Jenny had a hard time keeping the names straight, since Brian and Simon referred to them by their nicknames and Beth had used each man's given name.

Donny Miller was called "Sleepy," but his date, Kaye, sexy in heels, tight gray jeans, and a lemon yellow belt, kept his eyes wide open. "Moe" – Miles? – invited Brian to compete in a best-of-five arm-wrestling duel, Moe's well-developed chest and shoulders straining his t-shirt. "The two muscle bosuns," Simon explained. "Watch Davies play him. He'll lose the first two to make him complacent, then overwhelm him three straight for the win." Among the viewers, only Moe's wife, Laurie, bet on him. While Moe was bald with barely the suggestion of a mustache, Laurie had long wavy brown hair. Where he was hard, she was soft: her figure, the colors she wore, and the voice that was lost in the noisy cheers the others raised for Brian.

When the din subsided, the statuesque Georgina McGill confessed to Jenny that she'd loved her husband Hugh the first time she saw him. "I was attracted first to his dimples, but he was wearing kilts, and when he moved, I saw that he had such beautiful – legs!" she laughed. "And now I'm expecting. Hugh and I both have children from our first marriages, but this will be our first one together." Jenny waited to feel the familiar pang of regret that she and Colin had been childless, but it didn't come. Instead she felt relaxed, enjoying being included in Georgina's confidences.

Nick Howard and Cath were there, Nick greeting her but making no reference to his intervention in her life, perhaps as much to maintain his privacy as hers. Both Ed Burleson, a divorced father of two from another team, and the single Aidan Traylor, his hair dark as coffee grounds, flirted with her when Simon stepped away to help Brian with the grill. "I'm single again," Ed told her, his smile creasing the laceration on his cheek, a jagged line that stopped and started, running across his cheekbone, past his temple, and into his hairline.

"We tossed a coin, and I won," Aidan added. "If you and Casey don't make it, I'm next in line. Glad Pilsner didn't show; we'd have more competition than we could manage."

"And Dyer," said Ed. "He's so chatty, we'd never get a word in."

Jenny laughed, feeling more comfortable with the easy camaraderie among the officers than she had at Derek and Jillian's party. Somehow Meg wasn't intimidated either, running past the throng of heavily-muscled men who crowded the house and finding her father, who was the tallest. Perhaps their regular training gave them a sense of the physical space their bodies occupied, because they all seemed to be both confident and relaxed, and there were no wasted movements. When she mentioned her observations to Simon, he smiled. "We're confident because we know we're good at what we do, and we're relaxed because we don't have to prove it to anyone. And we don't do it alone."

On the drive home she asked him about the wound on Ed's cheek.

"Training injury," he said.

She hadn't known that injuries occurred while they were

training. "Did someone shoot him?" she asked, her voice rising. "Do you use real bullets when you train?"

"For some reason we were using frangible ammo that day. It's made from ceramic," he explained, "so when it hits a plate, it fragments. Unfortunately someone's round fragmented and hit his cheek."

"Not just his cheek – his head! He could have been seriously injured!"

"He wasn't. He laughed about it later. He'll tell you himself that it wouldn't have happened if he'd been where he was supposed to be."

"Simon, he could have been killed!"

He glanced at her, concerned by her reaction. "Jenny, most training injuries usually amount to nothing more than a sprain or strain from physical activity."

She didn't answer. The next time he took a glimpse in her direction, she was looking out the window, and he couldn't read her expression.

Inside the flat she kissed him once quickly then stepped back. "Simon, I don't want to see you again. And don't call me anymore."

He was stunned. "What's this about?" he asked.

She wouldn't face him. She was gripping one hand with the other, her knuckles white.

"Jenny? Did I do something wrong? Or not do something?"

A quick shake of the head.

"Look at me, Jenny. I've got a right to know." He took her by the shoulders and saw that she was on the verge of tears. "Now, Jenny. Tell me!"

"I'd rather end it now than lose you," she quavered. "I can't – couldn't – not again – "

He understood. Burly's injury had cycled her. He pulled her to him and held her firmly while she wept into his shoulder. Part of him was encouraged by her fear for his safety. Another part recognised that he needed to help her control this fear or his mission was lost. "Sshh," he soothed. "Injuries are rare. And serious injuries even more so."

"But – but – you were hurt not too long ago."

"A few sutures. Minor, really." He drew her down beside

him on the sofa. "Jenny, listen to me. We live in a dangerous world. It's far more likely that I'll be injured in a traffic accident than in training or on the Job. And for that matter, you could be. A Hampstead driver could lose concentration or look away at the wrong moment or hit the accelerator instead of the brake. We know someone is threatening you. Should I break it off with you because something could happen to you?"

Her eyes were wide. "No," she whispered. "Please don't do that."

He hugged her in relief then sat back. "What shall we do about this then?"

She didn't know. What would Dr. Knowles say? Or Neil Goodwyn? Trust in the future? "Maybe – take one day at a time?"

"Works for me," he smiled. "When I ring you in the evening, I'll tell you that I'm all right and you can tell me the same."

"Simon – if I tell you I'm sorry, will you kiss me?"

He heard another sort of concern in her voice and knew that the crisis was past. "I'll kiss you with or without," he said and did. "No worries, Jenny."

- -

Simon's ops weeks passed slowly, and regardless of his reassurance, she worried. Part of her didn't function until she received his calls in the evening. In addition, photographs of her continued to arrive, unnerving her a little more each time, because the more recent ones hadn't been taken from a distance. She practiced her mental readiness by repeating the "I can" phrases Simon had given her, but she couldn't do the physical drills by herself. The stalker knew where she lived, so she couldn't hide from him, and changing her appearance wouldn't help. On their walks Bear padded along silently, and she listened for footsteps other than her own. Every sudden noise startled her, even the normal ones: the ring of a cell phone, the rustle as a bird flew from one tree to another. What was safer, sitting on a bench where she could survey her surroundings or keeping on the move? She felt on edge, and the alternating bursts of sunshine and showers didn't ease her mood. She and the atmosphere were both unsettled. She couldn't concentrate, so she didn't refer to the Italian dictionary in her pocket.

She began to sit in the living room by the bay window, because it gave her the best view of the street, to watch the people who passed by. Did the tall man slow his steps when he neared her flat? Was he the one? Why did the stocky man glance toward her door? Sometimes an entire hour elapsed while she scrutinized the sidewalk and the street. Not many cars drove by, but she didn't think her stalker would come by car. In a personal campaign, he'd be on foot. She didn't mention her surveillance to Simon when he called, just reported that she'd given the pictures to the two West Hampstead detectives. When she hung up the phone, a sudden gust of wind made the windows shake, and she wondered if her fear had infected the flat, making it tremble with her. She remembered the lines from Shakespeare's *The Tempest* and recited them aloud – "Be not afeard; the isle is full of noises, / Sounds, and sweet airs, that give delight and hurt not." – but she was still afraid.

She missed the way Simon touched her. When they were together, he often rested his hand on her shoulder or waist. They held hands while they walked up and down Hampstead's small lanes. When she showered, she wished that his hand held the soap. He could cover her scars with the suds. And close his eyes. Sometimes she dreamed that he was kissing her and woke wishing it hadn't been a dream. Still, she held back. She didn't want their physical relationship to escalate because of her desire or her fear; she wanted love to be the motivator. She knew she wanted him; but didn't most things begin with some kind of desire? She had made English literature her major because she wanted to study English writers, particularly the poets. The more she studied, the more she had come to love their ability to paint visual pictures, to put so much meaning into each carefully selected word, to touch her emotions through black print on sterile white pages. Love had followed desire because she had given it time to grow. Given the number of divorces among firearms officers, it must be difficult maintaining relationships, but she thought it was even harder building one. Simon's schedule was punishing. They spent far more time apart than together. He was attentive when he could be, but if he loved her, why didn't he say so?

The second week in August, Beth gave birth to a baby boy. At 6 pounds, 12 ounces, Robert William Davies wasn't a small baby, but when she and Simon visited, Jenny thought he looked tiny in Brian's arms. "Are you going to call him Bobby or Billy?" Jenny asked Beth.

"Robbie," Beth said.

He'll call himself Rob when he gets older, Jenny thought. She remembered her college boyfriend Rob, killed in a car accident. At the time she had thought she would never get over it, but now she could think of him without tears and be glad that Beth and Brian's son would have such a good strong name.

"Would you like to hold him?"

"Oh, yes."

Simon watched an expression of wonder cross Jenny's face and felt something tug at his heart. He stepped closer to her and put his arm around her. "Isn't he wonderful?" she whispered. "You both are," he answered.

Jenny smiled up at him and then gently placed Robbie in his arms.

Beth watched the two of them and wondered how Jenny could question Simon's love for her and how she could doubt her love for him. The usually-stern Simon smiled when he was with her, and she seemed happier and more relaxed than she'd been in a long time.

"I brought a baby gift for Robbie and a big-girl gift for Meg," Jenny said. "And a casserole for you to put in your freezer. I'm a little nervous bringing anything I cooked to Brian, but you can eat it as a last resort."

Simon transferred Robbie to Brian, and he and Jenny left shortly thereafter. She had given Simon the keys to Colin's car, and on the way home, she snuggled close to him. "I'm so happy for them," she said.

"Jenny, if you – married again – would you want to have children?"

"I'm not sure I can," she said. "You know that."

"Would you want to try?"

She paused. "I can't answer that without talking about Colin," she said, wondering if that would offend him.

He gave a slight nod. "Let's hear it then."

"When we married, I thought I couldn't possibly love him any more than I did at that moment. But I was wrong, because our love grew. Each experience we shared, each issue we faced, brought us closer. I thought that having his baby would give me a way to love more of him, even though you know in your mind that the baby will grow to be his own person. But he or she will have characteristics of the person you love." She paused. "Colin's love made me feel like a new person. Love is healing and powerful. It's so powerful it really can create a new person. I wanted to experience that. I think I might feel that way again, but I'm afraid of the medical part. I'd hate to have to go through all that again."

"Afraid of anything else?" he asked, hoping for an issue he could resolve.

"The stalker, of course," she admitted, "but only when I'm not with you. I used to be afraid of anger, but you taught me that anger is a normal human thing and that it doesn't have to be destructive. Colin and I had disagreements, but when we worked them out, we felt stronger, like nothing could come between us for very long. And then he died."

"Nothing to be afraid of in disagreements," he agreed, choosing to focus on the positive and not on Sinclair's death. "Just something to be sorted."

"Yes, and I read something recently that gave me hope:

'No heart is as whole as a broken heart, and no faith is as solid as a wounded faith.' I hope it's true."

"You're certainly stronger than you used to be."

"Simon, could I tell you something? Something else serious?" She put her hand on his thigh. "Because I feel really close to you right now."

"If you'll keep your hand there," he said with a smile.

It was a moment before she spoke. "I believe in God now," she said quietly.

"Because of Davies' baby?"

"Partly, because people can't make anything that perfect by themselves. None of the things people make last. Cars, trains, planes, they all depreciate. Deteriorate."

"Sometimes relationships last, Jenny."

She snuggled closer. "Simon, what do you think love is?"

"Commitment."

She thought so too. "Are you committed to me?"

"Yes." He paused. "Jenny, what else made you believe in God?"

"Father Goodwyn, because he's so sure, but mostly because Colin's spirit is alive, and if that's true, there has to be a God."

"How do you know that?"

"Because I felt it, one afternoon on the Heath. It wasn't the breeze or something gone haywire with my nerve endings. It was his caress on my cheek, it was feeling suddenly warm on a cold day, it was feeling inside the way I always did when he touched me."

He was silent, trying not to feel jealous of a dead man.

"Do you think I'm weird?"

"Jenny, I – " He struggled to find the right words, knowing she had told him something very close to her heart and the wrong response could drive her away. "I think you've experienced something most people haven't. If it brought you comfort, I'm glad."

"Simon, I wish you weren't driving right now, because I want to kiss you."

"I'll collect that kiss when we get home," he smiled, his envy gone. "And Jenny – I'm inclined to agree with you where Davies' baby is concerned. He's perfect. *Perfetto*."

CHAPTER 31

Simon's third week on operations began, and Jenny, following his recommendation to vary the times she left the flat, prepared to take Bear for a late morning walk. Bear was always excited by the prospect of going out; he ran toward the door as soon as he saw the leash in her hand. When she opened it, he bounded onto the porch and into a pile of broken glass. Pieces flew everywhere. He yelped and whined, becoming agitated and slipping as he tried to escape the pain in his paws. She stepped toward him, crying, trying to lift him off the glass, wondering if it would cut through her shoes. He was heavy and in motion, and when she finally got her arms around him, she sat down in the doorway with him in her lap and sobbed from shock and fear.

"Get a grip!" she said aloud to force herself to focus. "You're not hurt, but he is." She laid him down just inside the door and knelt next to him to inspect him, talking to him in a soft voice to soothe him. Glass was imbedded in his fur, and the blood on his paws kept her from seeing clearly how badly he was hurt. "Stay," she said and opened her cell phone to call for a cab. "It's an emergency!" she wailed to the dispatcher. "I need to take my dog to the vet immediately. Please send someone strong enough to help me lift him." She couldn't get to the cab unless she cleared at least some of the glass from the porch, so she pushed it to one side with her foot. Then she waited, stroking Bear's ears and hoping the action would calm them both.

The cab driver, an older man with an obvious affinity for beer, took a blanket from his trunk and placed Bear gently on top.

"Are you all right, Madam?" he asked, and Jenny realized her clothes were stained with Bear's blood.

"Yes, yes, let's go," she urged.

When they arrived at the veterinarian's office, he carried Bear from the car inside. "Shall I wait for you?"

"No – I don't know – it could be awhile," she answered.

"I'll park nearby then until another call comes through," he said.

The vet, a round bearded man with gentle hands, cleansed and examined Bear's paws. "Some of these cuts are rather deep," he said. "I'll need to anaesthetise him while I suture them. Perhaps you'll wait outside? I'll call you in when I'm done."

When one of his staff brought Jenny a cup of tea, she stopped pacing and sipped the warm liquid. Then she called Detective Sergeant Wyrick to report the incident, giving him her phone number and location.

The wait seemed interminable, and the news, when the vet returned, was not good. "We'd like to keep him overnight," he said. "I've sutured and dressed the wounds, but he's in a good deal of pain, and his movements must be restricted. Injuries of this sort can take a month or more to heal. Would you like to see him?"

Jenny thought she had never seen anything more pitiful. Bear was too groggy even to twitch his tail, and all four paws were heavily bandaged, three of them also with splints. The fur with the glass in it had been shaved away, his cuts had been dressed, and he wore a wide plastic collar around his neck.

"The Elizabethan collar will prevent him from licking his paws," the vet explained. "The splints keep his foot pads from spreading and reopening the cuts under his weight. Of course, he'll be off his feet entirely while he's here. When you take him home tomorrow, you'll need to clean and dress his paws. We'll instruct you. He should be on his feet as little as possible – only when he goes outside – and then with a sandwich bag taped in place over each foot. That should reduce the possibility of infection."

"May I sit with him for a few minutes?"

"Most certainly."

She leaned over to rest her head against his fur, whispering in his ear to tell him what a good dog he was and how much she'd miss him even though it was only for one night. When he licked her hand, she began to cry from the unfairness of it all. Was the broken glass meant for her? Who could be so cruel as to injure an innocent animal? "You didn't sign on for this, did you, Bear? I love you. I'll see you tomorrow."

She was surprised to see DC Mackeson waiting for her in the reception area. "I've come from your flat," he said. "Wyrick and I thought you might need some transportation home. We'd rather you not walk by yourself. And I'll give you a hand cleaning up the glass."

It struck her then how vulnerable she was and how determined her stalker was. This attack had required careful planning and the willingness to inflict pain. It would be a long time before Bear could accompany her on any outdoor errands. She was either grounded or exposed.

"Thank you," she said, glad it wasn't Sergeant Wyrick, even though her attitude toward him had moderated to some extent. "I'll tell the cab driver he can go."

When Simon called late that evening, she told him what had happened and how guilty she felt. "I wasn't paying attention," she confessed. "I should have restrained him, made sure it was safe, but I wasn't expecting anything like that, and I was thinking about you."

"I don't want you going out alone."

"When I pick him up tomorrow, I'll call a cab again. There's a wagon in the garage I can line with towels and use for a bed. Then I can wheel him from room to room so he can be with me."

"I'll be with you in forty-eight hours," he promised.

"That can't come too soon, Simon. I need you. I don't mind admitting that I'm scared."

He was apprehensive also. Now that the stalker had taken out her dog, she was next. Any weapon she carried could be used against her, and there was no meaningful way he could protect her while he was on duty.

CHAPTER 32

Alcina carefully sharpened her knives. She needed the stone only for the knives, because her anger had honed her. She stroked each blade against the oiled block, first one side, then the other. It didn't produce a loud sound, nor would there be a sound when the knife of her choice split her target's skin. She hadn't yet decided which one to use. Each had its assets.

Keeping her knives sharp would make them more effective. Sharp. She let her mind caress the word and felt strong. For knives, of course, sharp meant cutting or piercing, but even her tongue could have a cutting edge. Her mother had chided her for it. Not her fault; entirely the fault of her sisters, because she had learnt it from them. Her father, on the other hand, had complimented what he called her sharp wit, which she took to mean, superior.

Sharp. Sharpshooters had sharp eyes. Tony had been called sharp because he was quick to understand and take advantage in a situation. Therefore, to be sharp was to be successful. In prison, however, he had lost his edge. He was dull, and she had cut him out of her life.

She was now the successful one. She and her knives.

CHAPTER 33

The argument between Jenny and Simon began Friday night as soon as he arrived.

"Jenny, I want you to go away for a while," he said, reaching down to pat Bear but not taking the time to sit.

She stared at him. "I've been waiting all week to see you and you want me to leave?"

"You could visit your parents, perhaps."

"I don't want to go to Texas," she objected. "With such short notice, they'd ask questions. I told them I had some problems with vandalism, but not about the stalker. And even if I could get a flight, it would cost an arm and a leg."

"Kent, then," he pressed, still standing and facing her.

She shook her head in frustration. "Why? It won't do any good. When I come back, the threat will still be there."

"Jenny, I want you safe. Out of harm's way."

"Then get me a gun!"

"Jenny, no. We've been through this."

"How about a knife? A combat knife."

"Out of the question," he insisted. "You've not been trained in combat."

"Then what? More self-defense drills? I know I'm not very good at them, but leaving Hampstead isn't the answer. Besides, Bear needs me." She moved away from him and sat on the sofa.

He followed and sat beside her. "I need you as well, Jenny."

She raised her chin in defiance. "That's not fair! I need you, too, and you're never here! And you're asking me to choose, and I won't."

"You're already choosing. Just tell me how getting yourself hurt is going to help either of us."

"I won't get hurt," she protested. "I'll stay indoors. Honest."

"Dammit, Jenny! I wish you weren't so bloody stubborn!"

Her throat tightened. Was he mad enough at her to leave her? She wanted him *in* her life but not running her life. She raised her voice to his level and forced the words out. "I could say the same about you! Just stop it! Stop acting like a policeman! Taking over! Why do you always have to win?"

"Because I'm fighting for your *safety*! If I lose, you lose."

"What are you trying to say? If I get hurt, what will you lose?"

"Don't turn the subject, Jenny."

Why didn't he tell her that he wanted her safe because he loved her? Those words would have changed everything.

He leant forward. "Jenny, we have to sort this out. Get it over and done with."

She gave a quick shake of her head. "There's nothing more to say."

Her brow tightened in anger, she was still lovely. Her shoulders were hunched forward, her face pale. She's afraid as well as angry, he thought. He sighed. "I'll make some tea." He returned in a few minutes with the teapot and two cups on the tray. "I've sweetened yours for you," he said, "but you'll have to unclench your teeth to drink it."

"I realize tea is good for a lot of things, but do you really think it will help end this argument?"

He wanted to kiss her mouth open, but the tea would have to do the job. "Unfold your arms and have a swallow." He waited until she had taken a few tentative sips. "How did you feel when Bear got hurt?"

"Guilty. Frightened."

"And when DC Mackeson took you home from the vet's:

Why do you think he did that?"

She hated the patient tone he used when he had to explain the obvious. "He didn't want me to walk home by myself."

"Think this through with me, Jenny. Why would an overworked copper take the time to drive you?"

She lifted the teapot to refill her cup, but it was still almost full. She replaced the teapot. Her shoulders slumped. She had no way to defend herself against his inexorable logic. "He thought I was in danger," she said in a small voice.

"Right. Jenny, when the stalker damaged your property, I was concerned. But when he injured your dog, your risk rose to a new level. If he truly wants to harm you, taking out Bear is a necessary step. And it's another two weeks before my next leave." He had her bang to rights, and she had to know it. "Jenny, there are two ways to deal with a threat: direct action, which means eliminating the threat, or indirect, which means lessening it. We can't take direct action because we don't know who's behind this. As for the indirect – why do you think I wanted you to memorise those confidence phrases? Be unpredictable? Be aware of what's around you? Be trained in self-defence? A threat can be minimised by mental and physical preparation."

Her hand was trembling as she reached for her cup. She changed her mind about picking it up. "Simon, are you too mad at me to hold me?" she asked.

He moved closer to her and put his arms around her. "I'd not like anything to happen to you, love."

She leaned into him. "You think it will, don't you?"

"I'm trained to plan for the worst case."

"Could – could we compromise?"

"Tell me what you have in mind," he answered, relaxing his embrace slightly.

"Could I wait until Sunday to go to Kent? And come back next weekend? And will you call me while I'm there?" She searched his eyes.

He would be with her at the weekend, but the following week she would be unprotected. Unless – "Didn't Sinclair have a retired copper look after you that time you were in

Kent? When you were still in danger from Scott?"

She leaned back and looked at him, nodding. "Yes. His name was MacKenna, I think. I remember how trim he was: his beard, his mustache, his movements, even his speech. I could never engage him in a regular conversation, and he never looked at me directly. He was always watching everything around me."

Alert to any threat: good. "Then we'll take Bear to the vet tomorrow. I'll put you on the train to Kent on Sunday. And while you're gone, I'll contact MacKenna and arrange for a meet. He could shadow you when you go out. Provide a bit of security for you and some peace of mind for me." Her face was still tense. "Sorted?"

"Yes, but – Simon, I wish I had something of yours to hold onto. I don't even have a picture of you."

"I've one of you," he admitted. "A wedding snap. Davies brought it to me."

"But – that was – "

"A long while ago, yes. I wasn't lying when I told you I'd fancied you for a long time." He paused. "You have – " He stopped again. It came out as a whisper. "My heart."

She couldn't speak. She rested her head against his chest and listened to his heart. Beating for her.

CHAPTER 34

Jenny had mixed feelings about her time in Kent. Once she arrived safely, she'd been relieved, happy to leave her fearful feelings behind her. During the daylight hours, she was glad to be there. Colin's mother, Joanne, drew Jenny into her flurry of activities, and the time passed quickly. They spent a day shopping in Ashford, although fortunately not together, because while Joanne bought clothes for her grandchildren, Jenny tried on lingerie, following Dr. Knowles' suggestion that she pamper herself a little. Her new lace bras and panties felt soft against her skin, and she wondered what Simon would do about the delicate fabric when he discovered it. Returning to the house, they searched through the attic for items to place in the rummage sale to be held at Joanne's church. She helped Joanne pick flowers for the Thursday evening vespers service and cook for the weekend bake sale.

At night Jenny was lonely. Joanne's house was much larger than Jenny's flat, and their voices seemed to echo through the empty rooms. Despite being an early riser, Joanne preferred dining somewhat late and then retiring to bed shortly afterward, leaving Jenny, the night owl, to spend the rest of her waking hours alone. She curled up in the leather recliner in the library and read excerpts of poetry from the numerous volumes there. Reflecting one evening about Wordsworth's "Intimations of Immortality from Recollections of Early Childhood," she agreed that only children considered themselves and their worlds immortal; adults learned that everything died save truth. Yet Wordsworth's verses weren't depressing. On the contrary, several lines summed up what she felt: "What though the radiance which was once so bright / Be now for ever taken from my sight, / ...We will grieve not, rather find / Strength in what remains behind..." Wordsworth had used what he learned from grief to love life more. She hoped that her grief workbook, although nowhere as eloquent as the poet's lines, could encourage others to move forward from suffering to faith in whatever life still held.

Simon's calls were brief and businesslike. He had contacted Sean MacKenna and met with him one evening when his team had completed their work earlier than usual. After Jenny returned to Hampstead, MacKenna would provide soft surveillance during the day, observing the flat and shadowing Jenny from a distance whenever she went out.

Simon was mission-oriented, she knew that, and he was very concerned about her safety. He was attentive when they were together and spent as much time with her as his job allowed. He was capable of tenderness. Before he had sent her to Kent, he had massaged the tense muscles between her shoulders, stroked the back of her neck, and then brushed it with his lips, but he had not said anything. Her body was ready to love him; in her heart she was beginning to love him; but her mind told her to wait until he declared himself. She didn't want a casual affair. His nightly calls, which were likewise short of endearments, did nothing to dispel her doubt. He claimed to miss her, but his voice spoke more of fatigue than of longing.

She and Simon had been seeing each other since before the summer began. He had given her time to work out her feelings for him, and also important, to experience how his schedule would shape their lives. Beth had made it clear that SO19 wives had to accept, respect, and share the sacrifices their husbands made for the Job. Jenny had known when she fell in love with Colin that she would live in England, not in America, but she had never seen that as a sacrifice. Colin's long hours on the job had sometimes caused problems between them, but she had never been able to imagine him doing anything other than policing.

Simon's police service could drive them apart unless she embraced it as fully as he did. In the past he had spoken of operations with an "acceptable risk." Was that what he was taking with her? Wanting her eyes to be open before he made a commitment? Or was he confident that she could rise to the challenge of dealing with his erratic schedule? As always, instead of using words like "sacrifice" to tell her what his work was like, he preferred to let actions and experiences speak for themselves. His integrity wouldn't allow him to deceive her; therefore words of love from him meant commitment. She couldn't love a man if she didn't respect his life, and she had a deep respect for everything Simon stood for.

She found some time each day to visit the family cemetery where Colin was buried. She leaned against his headstone, tracing the letters that were carved there and then closing her eyes to absorb the peaceful atmosphere. The only sounds she heard were the rustling of the leaves through the trees, an occasional bird singing, and her voice as she spoke to her husband.

"Colin, I'm writing a book about grief, a workbook to help people who have lost a loved one. I told your mum about it, and she had some wonderful suggestions. I think she was pleased, because I'm going to dedicate it to you."

She smiled to herself. "That's kind of a backward compliment, isn't it? Thanking you for something you accomplished through your death. But you always did believe that good could come out of bad, and I hope this book will do that. Anyway, I'm going to have it printed myself. Thanks to you, I can afford it. I'm going to give the first copy to Neil Goodwyn because he has helped me so much. And then I'm going to give away the others to anyone who needs them."

She didn't tell him about her stalker, though, and

she waited until her last day in Kent to mention her new relationship with Simon. "I'm seeing someone, Colin," she began, "and I'm falling in love with him. I'm going to tell your mum, but I wanted to talk with you first. Do you want to know who it is?"

She paused, knowing that she had delayed the news as long as she could. "Of course you want to know. Your inquisitive nature was one of the things that made you a good detective, wasn't it?" She took a deep breath. "It's Simon. Don't be mad – when you were jealous of him in the past, there was no reason. He was just a friend to me then, and I was always faithful to you in every way. I didn't know until recently that there was anything more in his heart. And a part of my heart will always belong to you. I'm going to give him the rest, but I haven't told him yet."

She sighed. "It isn't the same, Colin. I'm older and sadder than I was when I fell in love with you." She gave a rueful smile. "I know the expression is older and *wiser*, but I'm not sure I am. Anyway, we need each other, and he's good to me. Can you – " Her voice faltered. "Can you be happy for me?"

She felt the skin around the scar on her cheek begin to tingle, then her lips, and finally the tips of her fingers. Gradually the sensations lessened until none remained. Her chest tightened, and tears rose because she knew he was letting her go. She wasn't going to say good-bye to him, however; that would be like pretending that he had had no impact on her life, and she couldn't do that. Instead she sat for a long time next to him, not hindering the gentle tears which fell upon the earth which covered him. Even without good-bye, it was the end of something.

Her target was alone. Alcina was certain of it. She had seen blood on her porch, dark drops of blood smudged like wine. It had to be the dog's blood. Her heart leapt: Could her target have been injured as well? She tried to slow her excited breaths and think things through. Her target would have worn shoes, so an injury, if any, would have been slight. Good. She wanted to inflict harm on her target directly, not cause it through an impersonal method.

Alcina hadn't danced since Tony's arrest. Now, however, she needed some way to express the fierce joy she felt, because she was no longer a follower. No, she was the leader of this rhythmic action. And the weight she had lost over the months of training had made her lighter on her feet, quicker as well, yet stronger, because her energy was focused on a single, powerful outcome.

She laughed aloud and began to sway from side to side.

Extending her arms, she admired the continuous line from her shoulder to the tip of the knife she held. She imagined the blade catching and reflecting the light, glowing as if alive. Bending this way and that, letting the knife wave gracefully in the air, she choreographed her deadly sinuous ballet. One two three, a turn, a dip, a twirl, one two three.

She continued the dress rehearsal, confident in her starring role. Her entrance would be sudden and strong, with no lines necessary because the knife would speak for her, piercing again and again.

One, her target unarmed; two, without warning; three, unable to alter the result. Thrust two three, thrust two three. Thrust two three, thrust two three. Victory was certain.

Jenny stepped off the tube platform at the Finchley Road station on Saturday looking smaller than Simon Casey remembered. He gave her a brief hug and kiss and told her he'd give her a proper kiss when they got home.

"I don't want a proper kiss," she said. "I want improper ones and lots of them."

He laughed and steered her out of the station. At the flat, however, they took only the time to leave her holdall before heading to the vet's to collect Bear. They had barely settled the dog when they left again to purchase groceries. It was evening before she thumbed through her mail. "Strange," she said when she saw the plain, unaddressed envelope. She tore off one end, removed a short strip of black ribbon, and held it up for him to see. "How creepy!"

It was a death threat. "Have you received others?" he asked, trying to keep his voice light. She would have need of him, but they would both have to rely on MacKenna.

"No, and it doesn't have my name on it. Maybe it isn't meant for me."

But it had been pushed through *her* letter box. "Set it aside for the detectives," he advised.

They were beside each other on the sofa, but she was jumpy, changing the subject frequently and occasionally losing her train of thought. "I told Colin's mum that I was seeing someone and we were pretty serious," she said. "Did I overstate things?"

"Not at all. How did she react to the news?"

She smiled. "She was glad."

Joanne hadn't been surprised, however. She had told Jenny that Colin had suspected Sergeant Casey's feelings for her went beyond friendship. "I was afraid that Vi's unfaithfulness would cause him to doubt you – once bitten, twice shy, you know – but he trusted your love. When he added up everything you'd given to be his wife, he just didn't think it would be possible for you to betray him. And he was well aware of your sergeant's sense of honour. So there's nothing to cast a shadow on the happiness you feel now." Jenny had embraced her.

"I told my parents, too. That I was seeing someone."

"And?"

"Mixed reaction. Happy I'm not alone but sad that I didn't find someone in Texas." She shook her head to clear her mind of the memory. Her mother had been decidedly unhappy. "Simon – when I'm in Kent, I visit Colin's grave. I talk things over with him, sort of. I told him that you're the reason I'm doing better, and he – he let me go."

She wasn't smiling. He took her hand, not certain what she meant. Was she telling him there was room in her life for him? He cleared his throat. "Are you done then? With grief?"

"Dr. Knowles says that grief never stops entirely, but life – a more normal life – returns. I don't feel normal, but maybe that's because of the stalker. Do I need to meet with Mr. MacKenna?"

Fortunately not, because he wouldn't have wanted her to hear their conversation. MacKenna, a slender man with streaks of grey in his hair and beard, had understood immediately that once the dog was removed, she was next. "He's been sufficiently briefed," he answered. "He'll be on the job Monday. You'll be able to go out whenever you wish."

"What if I want to go to Ricky to see Beth? Will he wait for me the whole time at the tube station?"

"Jenny, I'll give you his mobile number. You can ring

him when you're returning. When you're in Hampstead, he'll be nearby, but it wouldn't be wise to approach him."

She wriggled out of his embrace and sat up. "I have to look like I'm not being protected, is that it? Wouldn't it be easier just to paint a target on my chest?"

She was more apprehensive than he had realised. "Not to worry, love. He'll be close enough to protect you and catch the baddy as well."

Sunday brought more of the same. She broke off the self-defence drills and leaned her head against his chest. "I need a break. Tea?" When she went into the kitchen to make it, her hands were shaking. "Where are you off to this week?" she asked. "Do you have to go? What if I need you? Oh, damn, I spilled the tea."

He put his arms around her. "Sshh," he said softly. "You remember: It's my training week. You'll be all right. I'll ring you each night."

"I can offer better accommodations," she said in a lighter tone.

"Too right. I don't like being so far away, but the following week I'm on leave. Time then for me to protect you myself."

"I wish – " she began and then stopped. Wishes were fantasies. The danger was as real as Simon's embrace and more enduring.

- -

To borrow one of Simon's words, Jenny felt their weekend had been "unsatisfactory." She had been eager to see him – she had wanted kisses that would distract her from her situation – but when they were alone at the flat, she couldn't forget that danger was imminent, and she couldn't relax. He'd be away all week for training, which wouldn't help her, while she'd be bait for the stalker, like the rabbits they used to make greyhounds run faster. She felt like running. She felt like screaming!

He'd led her through the self-defense exercises on Saturday, but on Sunday she'd stopped trying to defend herself and held onto him, fighting tears and asking if the stalker would have a gun. He hadn't scolded her. "Not likely," he had replied and kissed her hair. She loved it when he did that; it was the kind of thing a guy would do only if he loved you.

She looked at Bear. He had a sad face in the best of times, and now he looked positively mournful with the cone around his neck, a symbol, she thought, that the stalker had won the first round. As he hobbled around in his bandages, she wondered if she'd look like that – or worse – in a few days. Knowing that Mr. MacKenna would be in the background somewhere didn't give her a warm and fuzzy feeling. She was still exposed. The stalker would be bigger and stronger than she was. What if Mr. MacKenna weren't fast enough? What if she were killed before she and Simon had confessed their love for each other? Would Simon grieve for her the way she had grieved for Colin?

- -

Believing it was always better to get the lie of the land before a job began, Sean MacKenna recced the Hampstead site. From where he stood, he could see the entrance to Mrs. Sinclair's flat easily. He rolled himself a cigarette and watched Sergeant Casey and Mrs. Sinclair arrive with the dog. They were preoccupied with the animal and didn't see him.

Before he left the area, he'd identify possible hiding places and escape routes as well. He already knew the closest cross streets and most direct way to the High Street. He had located the Hampstead nick and Royal Free Hospital.

A weapon could be concealed in an assailant's clothing, in a briefcase, or even within a folded newspaper. The weather being warm, bulky clothes would stand out. The High Street had two newsstands; Finchley Road, one. He'd purchase a newspaper himself each morning, from a different vendor, taking time to observe other customers. Did they appear to be heading toward a commercial location or traversing neighbourhood streets?

Three tube stations served Hampstead. He'd spend some

time observing the flow of persons from each one. He had been advised that Mrs. Sinclair did not go out at night; the attack would therefore take place in the daytime.

Sergeant Casey had requested nightly updates. No problem; he'd ring the sergeant on his mobile.

Poor little lady, losing her husband like that. She was alone and vulnerable, but he'd look out for her. He leant on his cane and finished his cigarette. It was good to be on the Job again.

CHAPTER 37

Alcina felt certain that her campaign was entering its final phase. Her target must know that she was not safe. At the very least the dog had been injured. It was no longer capable of defending her or disrupting Alcina's plans. The attack could come soon. Alcina had prepared well, and she would be ready.

What should her approach be? Should she knock her target down first, then attack her while she lay on the ground at her feet? She liked that image, her target writhing in fear and pain on the dirt. Perhaps she should practise that scenario. No, she would have to bend so far down to strike her that the force of her thrusts could be compromised. And her target could strike back before she had a chance to sink the knife in her flesh. She could curl up to protect the most vulnerable spots on her body. She could attempt to crawl away.

No, Alcina would strike her as she stood. If she fell to the ground wounded, so be it, but the first blow would come when she was at a convenient height for the knife. Her target was small and weak, inferior in stature as well as strength. All Alcina had to do was let her hand fall. The knife would gather momentum as it drew closer to her target's body.

The key: She had to be ready to act at a moment's notice, whenever the opportunity presented itself. For the best chance of success, not the High Street or other busy footway but an isolated spot with no one around to respond to screams, to intervene in the attack, to aid her target in any way. Many of the neighbourhood streets in Hampstead were quiet, with little or no traffic either in vehicles or on foot. Alcina had done her homework. She knew where those streets were. She knew who, what, why, and how. The only question in her mind was when.

CHAPTER 38

On Monday Jenny traveled to Rickmansworth to spend time with Beth, Meg, and Robbie. From the Hampstead tube station, she took the Northern line – which didn't connect directly with Ricky – in the wrong direction and transferred twice to the Metropolitan line at Bond Street – but she felt safer. The Hampstead station was closer to the flat, hence less time walking without Bear, and since she had to change trains, it could be harder for the stalker to follow her.

Like Hampstead, Ricky had bakeries and restaurants on the High Street, but Ricky had many more charity shops and a large Marks and Spencer department store, too. Jenny picked up Chinese food from a restaurant not far from the train station, knowing she and Beth would enjoy it and Beth could use the leftovers later instead of having to prepare a new meal. Past the car park, a tunnel led to a tree-covered walkway. On rainy days she appreciated the protection it gave her, and on warm days it was cool beneath the arching branches. Now, however, she knew that Simon would see potential villains lurking among the trees, and she doubted that Mr. MacKenna had followed her from Hampstead. Had the stalker boarded the train and kept her in sight? If she needed the police, officers from the Met would not respond to her 999 call. She was in Hertfordshire, the domain of the Hertfordshire Constabulary. She walked quickly to the housing area that lay just beyond.

After greeting Beth, she played with Meg to let Beth rest when the baby slept. When Meg took her afternoon nap, she was tempted to nap, too; she hadn't slept well after Simon had left on Sunday, but she had come to help Beth, so instead she did laundry, folding the clothes which Beth had left in the dryer and doing an additional load of children's wear. She didn't dwell on her stalker situation with Beth, just mentioning that Simon had hired a retired copper to keep an eye on her. On her way home, she rang Mr. MacKenna to let him know when she'd be arriving and at which station. "Quiet day, Mrs. S.," he reported. "No one neared your flat." She didn't see him when she arrived. She knew better than to look for him, but if she couldn't see him, could he see her?

Monday night she tossed and turned. During one wakeful episode she made herself a cup of tea, hoping it would warm the unseasonable chill that ran through her bones but not surprised when it didn't. Neither did the extra blanket she put on the bed.

On Tuesday, wanting to encourage and congratulate Jack in some way, she called Esther Hollister at Hollister's Books for a gift suggestion.

"What kind of dog did he adopt?" Esther asked. When Jenny responded that it was a Jack Russell, Esther exclaimed, "I've just the thing! *Jack Russell: Dog Detective* is the first of a series of books by Darrell and Sally Odgers. He'll love it! Shall I send it for you?"

Jenny thanked her and arranged payment. She realized that she'd never told Esther about her grief workbook and resolved to give her a copy when it was printed. Then she grabbed a sweater and walked just far enough into the Heath to sit on one of the benches with vistas of open spaces around it, the better for Mr. Mac to see her. She wished Bear were with her, but his paws were still healing, and three of the four were still bandaged. Under the gunmetal skies she thought, no, obsessed about Simon. She removed her journal from her purse and titled a new page, *Simon: He loves me, he loves me not.* He had called her "love" for as long as she could remember, but she knew he didn't mean anything by it. A common form of address, it was used by cab drivers, cashiers, and others with customers. Some British men called every woman they met, "love." Maybe her loneliness caused her to hear it differently now. She didn't enter that habit in either column.

However, her relationship with Colin notwithstanding, Simon had taken her places, calmed her fears, and helped when she had needed him. He kept in touch. When Colin was killed, he had come to the hospital, taken her home, and stayed until family arrived. He had held her when she cried and been patient with her grief. He called her flat, "home." He stayed there and respected her boundaries. He was loyal and attentive: "constant as the Northern Star," as Shakespeare had said. She smiled. She had never thought a Shakespearean passage would describe rough-edged Simon. He hadn't attended her wedding, but she thought she knew why, and he had a photo of her that had been taken there. He had said that he was committed to her. He had told her – somewhat haltingly – that she had his heart. She entered all these in the positive column. On the negative side, there was only one item: *He hasn't told me he loves me.* He had told her she was the one he wanted, but not the one he loved. He had said that he wanted what Brian had. That meant marriage and family, didn't it? And in her book that added up to love. Did it for him?

Colin had been more verbal, giving her words of love and encouragement and then following them up with loving actions. However, when she added it up, the *Simon loves me* list was overwhelming, with so many actions over such a long period of time. She was probably being unreasonable, but she still wanted to hear him say the words.

The days without incident made her more afraid rather than less, and her dreams reflected her fear. In one of them, on a dull overcast day, she stood perfectly still, but the wolf turned in her direction anyway, mouth open, teeth bared, snarling and slathering. He howled once as he loped toward her, and suddenly a whole pack of wolves, gray as the clouds, appeared behind him. A bite wasn't a superficial wound; it was a mouth full of sharp blades that would sink deep, rend, and tear. Her muscles were paralyzed, locking her in place, and still the wolves came, an entire horizon of them. She screamed, heard barking, and woke, realizing it was Bear who had saved her from the dream's end. She cried out for Simon, who was not there, and stammered through her "I can win" mantra. She hadn't practiced saying it when she was in Kent, and her heart wasn't in it now. Hearing the wooden phrases didn't make her feel more secure. She thought then about Father Goodwyn, who had often encouraged her to pray. She tried the Lord's Prayer, but that didn't answer the mail, except for the verse, "Deliver me from evil." Finally she just asked God to keep her safe. And when daylight came and she was still awake, she asked Him again. And when her morning tea didn't chase away her exhaustion and fear, she simply prayed, "God, please."

On Wednesday she limited her errands to the Finchley Road side of Hampstead, shopping at Sainsbury's and buying pizza from Domino's. After locking the door and setting the alarm, she still needed to relax, so she opened a bottle of wine and poured herself a glass to drink with the pizza. When she drank a second glass, she realized that it had been months since she'd seen Simon drink more than one beer or one glass of wine. She should add that to her *He loves me* list.

After dinner she reviewed her progress on her grief workbook, spreading the pages out on the dining room table. She had a title page, acknowledgements, and dedication. She added Shakespeare's quote from *Macbeth* to the introduction: "Give sorrow words; the grief that does not speak / Whispers the o'er fraught heart and bids it break." She had made extensive notes for the chapters, including fragments of poetry to highlight each section. Some organization and transitional sentences were needed, as well as a conclusion. What message should the conclusion convey? Acceptance and hope, certainly, but who was she to recommend acceptance, when she still railed at the injustices of life?

Then she wrote a note to Colin's solicitor, instructing him to modify her will. She wanted the grief workbook to go to Joanne, who would be able to complete and compile it, and Colin's Audi to Simon. In a postscript she mentioned Bear. Simon was her first choice to adopt Bear, because the dog knew and liked him, but if Simon's lifestyle precluded having a dog, then perhaps Brian and Beth would take him. Bear would love being part of a family. If both those options failed, she asked the solicitor to query Joanne, thinking of the fields and forests around her Kent home that Bear could explore.

After Simon's call on Wednesday night, she still felt down. There was an ache deep in her chest, not like the tightness she felt when she was afraid. Could she have caught the flu? She stretched: no aches in her arms or shoulders. She held her breath: Her heart had its normal rhythm. She closed her eyes and imagined hearing Simon tell her that he loved her. The ache eased slightly, and she knew that he was what she needed. If the stalker killed her before he told her, would his chest ache like this? "Stop these morbid thoughts!" she scolded herself. "Focus on what you can do!"

Tomorrow she'd mail the letter to the solicitor and then go by the bakery on the High Street. Buying some chocolate croissants would give her a lift; chocolate always did. "God, please," she prayed and waited for sleep to come.

Jenny felt lethargic when she woke late Thursday morning. Bear seemed sluggish, too, still moving slowly on his hurt feet. When the water finally boiled and her tea was ready to drink, it didn't energize her. Deciding what to eat and what to wear was a chore. When she left the flat after lunch, she felt a pronounced chill in the air. By the time she thought about returning for a jacket, however, she was already at the bottom of the hill and dreaded walking back up. Maybe the cold would enliven her.

It was warm in the bakery, which further magnified her torpor, and she was disappointed to find that they had sold all their croissants, even the non-chocolate varieties. The tray which usually held the chocolate éclairs was empty, too. She considered the other chocolate selections. A chocolate cake would be too rich. Her choice was limited to dark chocolate cookies with raspberry filling or shortbread cookies with a dollop of milk chocolate frosting on top. Indecision paralyzed her, and she had to overcome a sudden shyness just to tell the tall woman with the black hair, the baker's assistant, to help the next customer. What to buy? Maybe a cream puff with hazelnut filling. Or two. She could make a cup of hot chocolate to go with it. The tall woman stepped away, a strange smile on her face. Jenny paid the baker for her selection and watched him wrap it for her.

Outside the bakery she stood still for a few minutes, puzzled by her feeling of uneasiness. Maybe Simon's self-defense exercises had made her paranoid. Were there any other purchases she needed to make? It was silly to have left the flat for only one item; she should have planned better. The first day this week when she might get a glimpse of the sun, and she had nowhere else to go. On a warmer day she might have found a bench on the Heath and had a mini-picnic, but not today. She sighed, remembered the letter she wanted to mail to the solicitor, crossed the street, and trudged past Waterstone's on her way to the post office. She placed her letter through the slot and doubled back past the Community Market, slowing to admire its mouth-watering display of fresh fruits and vegetables. She paused briefly at the Hampstead Florist, whose merchandise was also set outside to tempt passersby.

- -

As Alcina left the service counter, she whispered her declarations of power: "I am strong. I am determined. I am confident." Stripping off her apron in the back room, she added one more: "I am ready." She heard the baker call, "What are you doing? We have customers." I am doing what I planned to do, she thought to herself, her excitement rising. She exited the back of the bakery and hurried through the alley to the High Street.

Her skirt had large pockets, and its fullness concealed what she carried in one of them. At first she didn't see her target. When she spotted her on the other side of the street, she slid her hand into her pocket and rested it on the blade she had selected. Her target was coming in her direction but was distracted by the fruit and flower displays.

Alcina watched her target pass the markets and approach Perrins Lane. When her target turned onto Perrins, Alcina exulted. Her target was moving away from the busy High Street into the housing area. She was not looking in Alcina's direction. Her target was on her way home, and Alcina knew exactly which streets her target would take to get there. Her months of reconnaissance and research were about to lead her to victory. Not long now. Not long now. She quickened her steps.

- -

When Jenny reached the intersection of Perrins Lane and Fitzjohns Avenue, she had to wait until traffic eased before crossing Fitzjohns. Fitzjohns connected her to Ellerdale. A few more blocks, and she would be home. She smiled, remembering her first days in Hampstead: She had had to keep to the main streets then. Now she knew all the quieter, less populated streets where she could focus on her own thoughts while she walked.

She heard rapid footsteps behind her and from a distance a man's voice – Mr. Mac? – yell, "Run!" She turned and saw the woman from the bakery, her olive face contorted, a large knife held high in her hand. There was no time to step aside; the woman was nearly on top of her. Automatically Jenny raised her right arm to block the attack, but the woman kept stabbing at her, screaming something unintelligible and grazing her forearm. Blood welled up through her sleeve. She couldn't fend the woman off, and still the knife was coming. Jenny panicked. If she turned to run, she'd be stabbed in the back. If she didn't, she'd be slashed in the face. If she tried to dodge the assault, she could lose her balance, fall, and be mutilated. She reached with both hands to grab the blade, one fist squeezing tightly over the other, her teeth clenched vainly against the pain, the sharp, shocking, screaming pain. The woman was so strong that Jenny wasn't sure her two hands would be sufficient defense against her, but if she didn't hold on, the woman would overpower her and kill her. She could feel the pain weakening her grip; she hadn't the energy to cry out or think what to do next. In her peripheral vision she saw Mr. Mac running toward her, his cane extended. He swung it with both hands at the back of the woman's legs. The woman cried out, fell to her knees, and released her hold on the knife. He slammed his foot into her back, and she lay writhing and shrieking on the stone sidewalk.

"Shut it!" he yelled at the woman on the ground, forcing one of her arms behind her back and using his knee to pin her down more effectively. "Mrs. Sinclair! Mrs. Sinclair! Are you all right?"

Jenny was too dazed to answer. Her knees felt weak, and she sank to the ground, still gripping the knife in her hands.

She's a rabbit in the spotlight, MacKenna thought. "Mrs. Sinclair," he said firmly. "You can put the knife down." He leant toward her. "My handkerchief's in my front coat pocket. Take it and wrap it round your hand." Her reflexes were slow. "My pocket," he repeated. "Well done, Mrs. S. Well done."

Blood soaked through the handkerchief and dripped onto her clothes. She saw Mr. Mac on his mobile phone, giving their location to the dispatcher and requesting police assistance and an ambulance. Then she heard him speaking to Simon. "It's done, and she's all right. It was a knife attack. Wounds not life-threatening, but we'll have her tended to. Catch us up at the Royal Free."

The first officers on the scene cuffed the woman, who glared at Jenny and refused to speak, not even to give her name. They then photographed Jenny's wounds, hastily rebandaging her hand. More officers arrived. She looked at their earnest faces and cried while Mr. Mac identified himself and described the incident. He knew it all, her circumstances, every incident that had preceded this one, and the names of the West Hampstead detectives.

Jenny cried because she didn't understand why this strange woman hated her enough to try to kill her, because it seemed that all her clothes were destined to have bloodstains on them, because she couldn't stop crying long enough to thank Mr. Mac, and because, even surrounded by police and medical personnel, she felt alone without Simon.

"The sergeant's on his way," MacKenna told her.

That didn't stop the shaking, and she wasn't able to give much of a statement to the patient officer with the notebook. "She works at a bakery on the High Street, but I never did anything to her! She attacked me, and I tried to defend myself. That's all I know."

The ambulance ride to the Royal Free Hospital was short, but the wait at the Accident and Emergency unit was long. Mr. Mac filled out the forms and then waited with her, reminding her gently to elevate her arm. Still her wounds throbbed, and what little energy she had, drained away. Every time someone came through the revolving door, she looked for Simon, but she was called to the examining room before he arrived. She felt a little faint, so she lay down on the examining table. The doctor, a redhead who looked as if he didn't have time to eat, cleaned and anesthetized her wounds. "A few pinpricks," he said matter-of-factly, suturing her hand first. "The palm of the hand is a high tension area. Sutures will need to remain for ten to fourteen days. Keep it dry the first twenty-four hours. Cleanse and apply antibiotic ointment twice a day after. Blot dry. Paracetamol should be sufficient for pain when the anaesthesia wears off." He cleansed and began to suture the gash in her forearm. "Sutures needed for only eight to ten days on your arm. For less scarring, these sutures can be removed early. Keep the wound closed with steristrips. When I apply the bandages, you'll be good to go."

"I'll need to have a look first," a voice Jenny loved said. It was Simon, his warrant card held out for the doctor to see. "Not to worry. I'll not contaminate the sterile field."

Tears of relief rose up suddenly and rolled down her cheeks. She struggled but couldn't sit up. "Simon, it was a woman!"

He bent over to kiss her. "I know, love. Safe as houses now. Well done." He gripped her unsutured hand, more tightly at first than he had intended. "Not a good idea to move at the moment." He looked up at the doctor. "She cries when she sees me coming. Must be a symptom of something."

She couldn't stop. "I want to thank Mr. MacKenna," she wept.

"I've spoken with him."

"He – he – saved my life, Simon!"

He smiled. "That's not the way he tells it." When the doctor had bandaged her wounds and given her a tube of the ointment, Simon helped her sit up, keeping an arm around her waist. "Take a moment. You may be lightheaded."

She clung to him, unable to stop sobbing in spite of her relief.

"Breathe," he advised and waited for her to calm. "Think you can manage a motorcycle ride home?"

"No! Don't let go of me yet."

"No rush. Stay as long as you need," the doctor said and departed.

Simon took advantage of the privacy and put both arms round her, afraid he was hugging her too hard but hearing no objection from her. After a few minutes, her trembling subsided, and he tied his leather jacket round her and steered her outside. "Hold tight to me with your good arm. I'll go slow."

At the flat, he settled her with a cup of tea before asking, "Jenny, why didn't you run? MacKenna said he shouted to you."

"There wasn't time! And you never taught me to run."

He should have. "And why did you grasp the knife?"

"That wasn't very smart, was it? I panicked. I was afraid she'd cut my face, and I just couldn't let that happen again. But she was so strong! I think I should've been lifting weights."

He leant forward to kiss her. "I'm proud of you, love. You acquitted yourself well. More than, actually."

"Why?" she cried. "I couldn't keep her from cutting me!"

"You reacted quickly. You defended yourself. Now let's get some food into you so you can take the Paracetamol."

"I'm not hungry. And I don't want any pills. It doesn't hurt as much now."

It would, he knew, so he rummaged in her kitchen, finding pizza he could warm. While they waited, he examined her for signs of post-incident tension, running his hands over her jaw, temple, neck, shoulders, and back. "Deep breaths," he said, and massaged her shoulders until he felt her muscles relax.

While he served the pizza, she waited with Bear, her companion in bandages, and wondered what had become of her cream puffs. After the meal and medicine, she curled up next to Simon on the sofa, her head on his chest. "I want you to hold me and never let go. Do you have to go back?"

"Not until my leave's over," he said, resting his arm on her shoulder.

"I'm glad. And Simon – I prayed this week. That I'd be safe."

He was quiet for a moment. "I prayed also," he said softly. "It's my guess the man upstairs heard us." When she didn't answer, he noticed that her eyes were closed, and her breathing was regular and slow. The natural letdown he had expected. As gently as he could, he gathered her in his arms and carried her upstairs. She looked small on the master bed. He pulled the comforter over her blood-stained clothes and bent to kiss her lips. An unfamiliar emotion tightened his throat. He stretched out beside her on the bed and put his arms around her, being careful not to put any pressure on the bandages. She murmured something he couldn't catch and nestled against him. That same strange feeling made his eyes sting, and he pressed his lips against her hair. Yes, he had prayed.

CHAPTER 40

The flat was quiet when Jenny woke, her hand throbbing. With it came a stab of fear until her surroundings and the smell of coffee registered. Simon was there! And Bear, licking her uninjured hand now that she was awake. She kicked off the comforter and realized she was still wearing yesterday's clothes, wrinkled and bloody. Her last memory was of feeling warm and safe in Simon's arms as he carried her up the stairs. Needing his embrace, she tried to dress quickly but found that she couldn't. Her bandaged hand was next to useless. She managed to slip into a clean pair of jeans. Getting a t-shirt over her arm and hand took a little longer, and because she didn't want to wear anything red, she chose a shirt with embroidered bluebells. She went to find him, with Bear close beside her all the way.

"Knackered and upset," she heard him say to his mobile. "Yes, sutures in her hand and arm, but it could have been much worse." He looked up and saw her. "Thanks, she'd like that. My best to Beth," he said and ended the call. "That was Davies. My team's been phoning about you. Any discomfort? The second day's the most painful."

"No kidding!" She had a lump in her throat and put her good arm around him. "I wish I could hug you the way I want to."

"Not to worry. I'll take your hugs any way at all."

"It hasn't sunk in yet, Simon – that I'm safe."

He continued to hold her. "That'll come. In the meantime, I'll bring your meds and some orange juice and toast, and I'll scan the newspaper I bought."

"I need to feed Bear."

"Already done."

She released him and watched while he poured the juice, shook the pain pills out of the bottle, and handed them to her. He joined her on the sofa, opened the paper, and spread it on his lap, smoothing the pages. She sipped the juice and waited for the toast.

He finished his quick read just before the bread popped up in the toaster. "I've been manning your mobile," he said as he slid the toast onto a plate with butter and jam. "I rang Padre Goodwyn, who sends his best. And the two detectives you're so fond of will be calling by soon to speak with you."

That made her smile. He was referring to the Humanoids, although her dislike of them had eased slightly. "They probably want my statement. I didn't give the officers much information yesterday."

She finished her juice, nibbled the toast, and then made herself comfortable on the sofa, putting a cushion under her injured arm to keep it raised. Bear was at her feet. She ended her call to Father Goodwyn just before Simon answered the door and admitted DS Wyrick and DC Mackeson.

"Do you feel up to a little chat?" Wyrick asked.

"Yes, and I think I have as many questions for you as you have for me," she said.

Mackeson took out a tape recorder and made the introductory remarks, and Wyrick asked her to describe the previous day, beginning with her departure from the flat. The dynamics between the two men had changed, Wyrick taking an active rather than a supervisory role and conducting the entire interview himself. He interrupted her several times to clarify details in her narrative. She related each movement, having to stop occasionally to regain control of her emotions. "I don't know why I'm so shaky," she said by way of apology.

"You've had a very frightening experience," Wyrick said.

"Take a moment to collect yourself."

The usual phrases, Jenny noted, but nevertheless she found them comforting.

"Slow breaths," Simon advised.

She nodded. "I was startled and confused. I couldn't imagine what she had against me. I thought she was going to kill me. And without Mr. MacKenna, she would have." She turned aside for a minute. "Simon, I watched her hands. That's why I was able to deflect her initial attack. And I used both hands to defend myself, like you told me to."

"Did she say anything to you?" Wyrick asked, redirecting her attention.

"Nothing intelligible. She screamed at me. But there's something weird about her. I saw her from time to time at the bakery, but I've never really met her. Yet I could swear she was wearing my ring. On the hand that held the knife. I saw it when Mr. MacKenna pinned her down. Her right arm was stretched out on the ground."

Wyrick's eyes narrowed. "Can you describe it? We have an itemised list of the personal effects she was wearing when she was taken into custody."

"Three small pearls on a gold band. The initials "RAM" and "JCJ" are engraved inside. My maiden name was Jennifer Catherine Jeffries."

"When did you lose that ring?"

"September 14, 1998: the day Scott's men kidnapped me. I was wearing it when I left the hotel, but not when the police found me, whenever that was."

"Thank you, Mrs. Sinclair," Wyrick said.

Mackeson made concluding remarks and stopped the tape recorder.

"Now I'll tell you a bit about your assailant," Wyrick continued. "She's Greek. Her name is Alcina Michalopolous. You'll recall that Anthony Michalopolous was convicted of false imprisonment and conspiracy to rape in your case. He is her husband."

Jenny shivered, remembering his menacing face. "I testified against him. He must have taken my ring and given it to her."

"That's entirely possible," Wyrick said.

"Is he out of jail? Did he put her up to this?"

"He is still incarcerated. We've not yet spoken with him. She could be acting either on her own or on his behalf. Interviews with her have thus far proved unsatisfactory."

"She rants in Greek when she speaks. The rest of the time she's silent and withdrawn, according to the custody sergeant. No eye contact whatsoever. A real nutter," Mackeson added bluntly.

Wyrick frowned. "That's not a legal opinion, you understand."

Casey had been watching Jenny's face. "Enough for today," he said.

"Of course," Wyrick relented. "I'd just like you to know that we've apprehended the man who was committing rapes in this area. He made the mistake of attacking an undercover policewoman." He stood and nodded at Mackeson. "We'll need to speak with you again in a few days, Mrs. Sinclair. Shall we say Monday?"

Casey showed them out and joined her on the sofa. "Now I want you to tell me about it. The unofficial statement."

She leaned against his shoulder. "It was like a series of still photographs. The knife held high enough to catch the sunlight; the notches in the blade; her knuckles gripping the shaft. Her face distorted with anger; her brows black; her eyes wild. In her black clothes, she looked like a devil woman, and she towered over me." She took a trembling breath. "Every time I close my eyes, I see the knife. Stained with my blood. And I'm scared all over again."

"Steady on."

"Behind her was a birch tree with leaves a vivid green and thick ivy on the trunk. A fat fir tree crowded it. I wasn't aware of much else, just the death image and the trees, the life image." She swallowed hard. "Simon, I thought I'd be carved up on that Hampstead sidewalk and never see you again."

He'd had a similar fear. He bent to kiss her, letting his eyes rest on hers first.

She looked back. His blue eyes were warm and his lashes

so blond they were almost transparent. He kissed her slowly, gently, almost reverently, his lips barely touching hers. Was this his way of telling her he loved her? She whispered his name, and he gradually pulled her closer. She could feel his rough skin against her cheek and his chest pressing on her chest. She didn't want to cry; she wanted to kiss him back with the same kind of tender devotion, but he had touched something inside her that she could express only in tears.

He chuckled softly and drew back, kissing her wet cheeks and then massaging her unbandaged hand.

"Sorry," she said, watching the circular movement of his thumb against her palm and thinking of all the times he had comforted her with that gesture. She knew now that it was a caress, and it had been for a long time. Love in another language.

"Not to worry. Bound to happen."

She laughed. What she called "Simon-speak" had broken the spell, but the feeling she had inside didn't dissipate completely. "Lunch?"

"I'll rustle up something, and then we need to tidy up," he said. "Davies is coming by later to make dinner, and some of the chaps are bringing things."

He made sandwiches while she warmed some soup, and after a light lunch, she cleared her workbook pages from the dining room table while he "hoovered," as he called running the vacuum cleaner. Realizing she needed to clean herself up, she went upstairs to shower and wash her hair, using the small garbage bag he had given her to cover the bandages on her right arm and keep them dry. Bear followed her everywhere she went, and she stopped from time to time to kneel down next to him and run her good hand across his fur.

Brian and Beth arrived first. "I wanted to see if you were all right," Beth said. "Are you? You're all bandaged!" She gave Jenny a gentle hug.

"I came to see about Casey," Brian smiled, his arms holding a grocery bag. "He went ballistic yesterday when your man called." He leant forward and kissed her on both cheeks.

"Where are the kids?" Jenny asked.

"A neighbour's watching them," Beth answered. "It's so good to be out! But we have to be back before Robbie gets hungry."

Miles and Laurie Watkins came next, bringing a large salad and a dessert. "You should move to Truncheon Alley where you'll be safe," Miles said.

"Where is Truncheon Alley?" Jenny asked.

"In Hayes," Laurie answered. "But don't believe a word of it! A lot of coppers live there, but none of them are home long enough to make it safe."

The McGills had taken advantage of the extra day off for a quick trip to Scotland, but Clive Hewlett and his partner had picked up a vegetable platter at Marks & Spencer. "We saw Donny and Kaye choosing cookies," Lucy said. "Here they come."

"Nice flat," Aidan Traylor said when he arrived. "Stay on her good side, Casey." He held a case of lager. "I was the slowest and the lowest this week on every drill," he confessed. "This is my penance, but if Pilsner comes, it won't last long. He's quiet until he has a pint or two under his belt. Then he'll bore you with his Army stories."

"I heard that," objected Ross as he entered the flat. "Casey looking after you well enough?" he asked Jenny and snapped his fingers in mock regret when she answered in the affirmative.

Brian was already in the kitchen, and Jenny went to help him find the skillets and saucepans he needed. "We all know Casey's no cook," he said, "and you're down for the count, so we thought we'd help out. Besides, we got an extra day off because of you. Where's the paring knife? I need to dice the onions." He opened one of the drawers and removed a larger knife. "We'll need this one as well. For the bread."

She paled and felt slightly faint, having to reach out to the counter to steady herself.

"Casey!" Brian called. "Seeing the knife upset her."

Simon stepped into the kitchen and put his arm around her. "In Davies' hands it's a tool, Jenny. That's all it is." He guided her out of the kitchen.

"I know. I know. I'm so embarrassed," she whispered, not wanting to leave his embrace.

"No need," he said softly. "All friends here."

Aidan hadn't brought a date, so he agreed to be Brian's prep cook. "He doesn't let her out of his sight, does he?" he remarked to Brian.

"Casey has a long history of protecting her," Brian answered.

Jenny sat on the sofa with Beth and Laurie, taking deep breaths and trying to focus on the easy banter among Simon and his team. "Thanks for doing this," she said.

"We look out for each other," Beth answered.

"But I'm not really an official part of this group," Jenny commented.

"In Simon's eyes you are, and that's all his team need to know," Laurie added, trying to coax her long locks into a casual ponytail. "But tell me: did a crazy woman really attack you? Why?"

Jenny could smell the garlic and onions that Brian was sautéing. He must be making meat sauce for spaghetti. "She's been stalking me for quite a while, but it's strange! I never thought it was a woman." She gave a brief description of the incidents.

"Where's your dog?" Laurie asked. "Do you still have him?"

"He's upstairs," Jenny said. "He still has to stay off his feet most of the time, and I wasn't sure how he'd react with so many people. Should I set the table now?"

"If we let you do it, Simon will be after us for sure," Beth laughed. "Come on, Laurie. We'll need trays for the ones who won't fit at the table and have to eat on their laps. Then we'll gather everyone and serve the salad."

Jenny saved a spot next to her for Simon and accepted very small servings, knowing that with only her left hand functional, it would take her twice as long to eat half as much. Miles kept everyone entertained with what seemed an endless supply of jokes and funny stories, including one about a training exercise with the MSU. "The Marine Support Unit," he explained to Jenny. "We were well into it when we got a call that a man had jumped off a bridge. We kickstarted the launch to get as close to the victim as we could, and one of us leant so far over the side of the launch that we had to hold his ankles. He grabbed the man by his hair. 'This is your lucky day,' he said, but the man came out of the water cussing a bloody streak. He didn't want to be saved!"

"You should've thrown him back," Casey laughed with the others.

Aidan countered with a story of his own, ending with a punch line that was even funnier delivered in his wry, understated tone. Ross Pilner took full advantage of every lull, relating some of his more interesting Army adventures, or "misadventures," as Aidan called them. Pilner's tattoos peeked out from under his t-shirt, but Jenny thought they weren't the only sign of how he felt about his military service. Even amid the humor, his pride showed through.

Jenny slipped off her shoes and leaned on Simon, enjoying the raconteurs but more tired than she had expected to be.

Davies watched Jenny. Like Casey, he had learnt to recognise signs of exhaustion or pain when he was on her protection team. Now he noted that her smiles were slower in coming and weaker when they did. "Time to go, mates," he said, rising to his feet.

Beth and Laurie put the leftovers in Jenny's containers and everything else in the dishwasher. Then it seemed that everyone left all at once.

"I made her laugh," Miles commented to Simon. "My mission, right, mate?"

"Never let it be said that I didn't do my part," added Pilner. "She's a good audience."

"Delicious as ever," Jenny told Brian.

"Glad to do it, JJ," he answered. "Glad you're okay."

Aidan hastily finished his bottle of lager and gave her a wave.

"Tea?" Simon asked after everyone had left. "Then I'll change your dressings."

"No tea. Just TLC," she smiled. She watched while he worked. "Simon, I can't remember anything the doctor said to do. I'm glad you know. And Simon – I felt part of a community tonight. More than I did when Colin and I socialized with his colleagues. You work with a nice bunch of guys."

"Being in harm's way together bonds you," Simon explained.

"It bonded us, I think," she agreed.

He nodded. "This stalker thing – it's been worrying for both of us." He taped the last bandage in place.

"I hate for this day to end," she sighed. "I'm worn out, but having you here has been wonderful."

"Past tense?"

"No, present and future, I think." She leaned forward to kiss him. "Goodnight." But it wasn't a good night. In every dream a knife suddenly appeared, shocking her: mutated from what she thought was a pen on the desk, hidden in her purse next to her keys, camouflaged among the twigs on the Heath. She woke repeatedly trembling and shaking, wanting him desperately. He was downstairs; just a few steps, and she could be in his arms, where she would forget all about knives. She needed him, but that meant she was more concerned with taking than with giving. Then in a flash she understood why he had gotten drunk and made love to her after the bloody scene his team had encountered. Sex wasn't the issue; engaging in something so compelling that it drove the shocking images away was. His need had overcome his reason. All these months he had been trying to make it up to her, and now the shoe was on the other foot. If she allowed her need to direct her actions, what would the result be? Would she regret having intimacy with him before they had declared themselves? Need was not the same as love. Was it a part of love? She was afraid to go to him, because if she did, she would not be strong enough to hold back.

CHAPTER 41

On Saturday Jenny resolved to make headway on her grief project while Simon went to Ruislip to collect some clothes from his flat. He had smiled approvingly when she showed him her progress. "Looks like you have a mission."

She glanced at her final chapter: *Conclusion.* That was the wrong message. Grief didn't end; it metamorphosed.

While Jenny was in Kent, Colin's mother had spoken frequently about her husband, Cam, and what she had learned from his death. "There are things you can't see if you look too hard," she said. "You have to look past them. Cam taught me to look beyond pain to love and trust."

"What about Colin?" Jenny had asked. "Did his father teach him something, too?"

"Colin died childless, as you know, but when his father was dying, there was a time when Colin was the parent to us all. That experience connected us in a new way."

"But Colin's death was so sudden," Jenny said. "He had no time to teach me anything."

"Look at his life then," Joanne had recommended.

The events of the past few days had caused Jenny to look back, to remember how she'd met Colin and how their relationship had progressed. He had told her he loved her long before he had any expectation that she would respond. Love triumphs. That was his faith and the way he had lived his life. His last act, before his death, had been one of love, purchasing emerald earrings for her when there was no occasion on the calendar. Love was his legacy, and she was not honoring it. Life was too short to withhold love from those around you. If she hadn't learned anything else from Colin, she should have learned that. Not telling Simon she loved him because she wanted to hear it from him first was selfish and silly. "Sorrows are our best educators," Lord Byron had written. "A man can see further through a tear than a telescope."

She crossed out the title, *Conclusion,* and wrote in, *Legacies.* A legacy could be emotional – a relationship healed, a family brought closer, a misunderstanding clarified – or spiritual – the inspiration of a loved one's faith – as well as tangible. A dying person could leave multiple legacies, as Colin had. And legacies survived the person who had bequeathed them and therefore embodied hope. She spent over an hour rewriting the final chapter, but still something was missing. She began a postscript.

Grief is like a newborn baby whose needs require around the clock care, and you carry your grief close to you because babies can't walk. Then the child grows into a terrible two-year-old, whose tantrums you can't control. Gradually the child's increasing independence allows you brief respites. Adolescence comes, and with it, times when you are separate from your grief. Finally adulthood arrives, and although you will always have a connection with your child, your grief demands very little of you, just the occasional recognition of its presence and meaning.

She smiled ruefully. She, who had never conceived, had borne a child after all, just not the one she had wanted.

Grief never goes completely, she continued, *because love doesn't end. The hold that grief has over you lessens but never disappears. A wise friend told me once that there's a glow on the horizon that you can't see when your grief is most powerful. When your grief begins to ebb, even just a little, the glow is visible, but only if you look for it. Each time you see it, the glow will be larger. Remember to look.*

Then she realized that she needed to address the issue

of faith and its relationship to grief recovery. Some days she still felt her faith was as frail as a butterfly's wings, but Father Goodwyn had assured her that doubts were a normal part of everyone's faith journey. "God is faithful," he had told her once and then demonstrated that trait by visiting her regularly. He believed that God was a part of healing, no matter what kind of hurt had caused it, and now that she had some perspective, she believed it, too. This chapter – should it be near the beginning or near the end of the book? – would have to be phrased just right in order to communicate to those whose faith was delicate as well as those whose faith was more confident. She wrote, crossed out, rewrote, considered, and finally prayed that she had achieved the right tone.

Her work completed, she checked the mail. An official-looking letter had been delivered, notifying her that Colin had been awarded the George Medal posthumously, for valour above and beyond the call of duty. An awards ceremony would be scheduled at a later date, but a description of the medal was included: a silver disc with the words, The George Medal, on the top edge. St. George on horseback slaying the dragon appeared on one side and a picture of Queen Elizabeth on the other. The medal was suspended on a red ribbon with five narrow blue stripes. She felt both proud and sad: proud because Colin's action had indeed been brave and sad because that same action had taken him from her.

She set the letter aside and made herself a cup of tea to soothe the pangs of grief it had engendered and to calm the butterflies in her stomach while she waited for Simon. When the tea didn't help her nervousness, she wondered if she'd have the courage to tell him what she wanted to tell him in spite of the upset of the past few days.

He came in with a smile. "I bought some croissants at the bakery," he said.

"*The* bakery?" she asked. "Where the devil woman worked?"

He laughed. "She never did the baking."

"Simon, thank you." She let herself be distracted by his

thoughtfulness and didn't verbalize her feelings. Later, when they stood side by side in the kitchen boiling fresh pasta and warming the spaghetti sauce, she again postponed her declaration, focusing instead on how safe she felt when he was around. When he changed the dressings on her arm, she watched his hands and wished he were touching her in other places, but still she didn't speak. If she told him, would he make love to her right away? Was that what she wanted? She wanted to be free of bandages, but if she waited that long, his leave would be over and her opportunity lost.

She prolonged her good-night hug with him and went to bed berating herself for her cowardice. God, help me to be braver tomorrow, she prayed. And please take the nightmares away.

On Sunday he helped with chores around the flat, and she thought about what her life would look like if he weren't a part of it. Bleak. Desolate. By mid-afternoon, she was so frustrated with herself that she was on the verge of tears. She was sure Father Goodwyn noticed it when he came by to hear about the capture of the stalker, because instead of praying for healing, he prayed for her to have peace.

"Fear is tenacious," he said. "Sometimes it clings to us even when the threat is gone."

"No kidding! She's in custody, but I've still been a basket case since the attack."

"It will lessen."

"He should have prayed for me to have courage," she confessed to Simon after Father Goodwyn left.

"Why, Jenny?"

"If you'll pour me a glass of wine, I'll try to tell you."

After she had taken several long swallows, he gently took the glass away from her. "Tell me," he said firmly. "You've been jumpy all day."

She reached out and took his hand instead.

"Now, Jenny. Out with it, whatever it is."

She hadn't heard his saying-no-is-not-an-option voice in a long time, but it calmed her, because it came from a man who always knew what to do. "I have something to ask you first," she said. "Why do you put up with this arrangement?

Me upstairs and you on the sofa down here?"

"You know why," he said, wondering why she was asking. "When I drank too much and went too far with you, I abused your trust. The only way I know to get it back is to let you call the shots. For as long as it takes."

She started to speak then stopped and took a deep breath. "I think it's been long enough."

Her round-about way of communicating confused him. "What exactly are you telling me, Jenny?"

"I wish you would talk about your feelings. You don't do that much, I understand that, but – but – don't you see? Words matter. To me. I hope they do to you, because I've decided that even if you don't speak up, I will."

Feelings. Words. Speak up. Was she – did she – " Did I hear you right?"

She raised his hand to her face and rested her cheek against it. "Simon, I – I need you, and I want you, and – and – I love you! And I'm all mixed up, and if you don't love me back – " Her voice caught in her throat and tears welled up. "I don't know what I'll do."

His heart skipped a beat, and he crushed her in a tight embrace, unable to say anything.

"Simon, breathe! And say something!"

He was still silent.

Her tears spilled over. "If you love me, now would be a good time to say so!"

She was the first woman who had told him she loved him and cried at the same time. "Jenny, Jenny, don't you know?" he whispered. "Don't you know me?"

"I need to hear it. If you do. Please."

"Jenny – " His voice broke, and he tried to steady himself. "Love. Yes," he managed to say.

He felt her hand on his cheek and her lips at the bottom of his chin. He relaxed his embrace slightly and bent down to meet her. They were the most passionate kisses she had given him, and in a flash he understood. For Jenny, love was the key. He should have known. "Love," he repeated. "More than."

She smiled up at him, feeling joy and relief in equal

measure. "Did I surprise you?"

"Yes, very." He kissed her once, twice, three times, stopping in between to smile back. "What do you want to do about it?"

"I want a do-over. I want us to be together, but I'm not feeling very sexy, and I'm afraid the attack has ruined things. Maybe a fresh start will help."

He thought for a moment. "Tomorrow, then, after the detectives are done with you, we'll go away together. Replace a bad memory with a good one." He kissed her again, long, slow kisses on her lips and then her neck. He ran his hand slowly across her chest. "Are you sure you want to wait? Because for me, the where doesn't signify. Only the who."

She leaned against him, wanting him to continue but wanting even more for him to understand. "Simon, I need to tell you something. I know why you did what you did when you were drunk. Because – because the other night – I wanted you to make love to me, just to take the fear away."

"Jenny, you could have come to me."

"I almost did. I wish I had. Unfortunately," she smiled, "I was too sober."

"And now?"

"I'm still sober!" she laughed. "But I'd love to go away with you. Somewhere I've never been. Away from Hampstead. Away from this flat."

He released her. "We'll sort the rest later then. I have some calls to make. Where do you board Bear?"

"I never have."

"The vet's then."

"I'll pack. Anything special you want me to take?"

"Surprise me."

All evening he was unusually affectionate, spontaneously embracing her and even wrapping the dish towel around her waist to pull her within range of his kisses when they washed up. "Jenny, why did you wait to tell me?"

"I wanted you to tell me first. Yesterday, while you were gone, I realized it didn't matter who went first. Why hadn't you told me?"

"It's difficult. I haven't said it much."

Something in the way he said it made her wonder if he ever had, but that didn't matter now. His arms were around her.

"But I do," he whispered. "More than you know."

"I wish I didn't have stitches. I wish I could make love to you without a handicap."

He kissed her injured hand. "We'll make do," he said.

CHAPTER 42

"Wakey, wakey, Jenny," Simon called. "The suits from West Hamp are calling by."

She opened her eyes to see him standing by the bedroom door, fully dressed. "So early?"

"I rang them," he said with a smile. "Said you were leaving town today. I've already taken Bear to the vet's. And it's not early."

She had slept longer than she intended, probably because the danger was past and because she and Simon loved each other. So many issues resolved. "Where are we going?" she asked, sitting up.

"Lovely place in Kent. Far enough from London that I'll not be called in. No more info until we're on our way."

She showered and dressed as quickly as she could and went downstairs for her cuppa. In anticipation of the visit from the detectives, Simon had made a full pot. The *Telegraph* was on the table, the date listed under the masthead: *Monday, 15 September 2003*. "You're good for me," she said. "Yesterday was the fifth anniversary of my attack, and I was so focused on telling you I loved you that I forgot."

"And now?"

For a long time fear had clung to her like barnacles on a ship's hull. "I remember the dark, cold room, the anger of my attacker, and the fear. But for the first time I'm free of the feelings that went with the events. I think I've finally moved on."

"Well done," he said and bent down to kiss her.

"Mmm," she whispered. "So much nicer to think about what's happening now." She had barely finished her tea when the doorbell rang.

"Thank you for making time for us," DS Wyrick said when they arrived.

"No tape recorder?" she asked DC Mackeson.

"The purpose of our visit is to take a second series of photographs of your injuries," he answered, holding up a camera. "And get your signature on your statement."

She sat on the sofa to read the typed document. DS Wyrick remained standing in the dining room. "It's all correct," she said after a few minutes, "but I'm right-handed, so I can't sign it. Aren't there some police phrases you can use? 'Because of the nature of her injuries, Mrs. Sinclair could not affix her signature to this document. She gave her verbal assent to its accuracy,' or something like that?"

Mackeson smiled. "That'll do," he said, adding the sentences in longhand and leaving space for his and Wyrick's signatures as witnesses. "If you'll remove your dressings, please."

Simon stepped forward to loosen the tape that held the bandages in place. "You're healing nicely," he said.

"I don't think a palm reader would agree with you," she smiled. "Look: The knife severed my life line."

"Perhaps it's a new life line," he countered. "I'll cleanse and rebandage these before we leave."

While Mackeson took the shots he needed, she thought about the wounds the camera could not capture. Wyrick seemed to be inspecting the pages of her grief workbook which were spread out on the table. "We're ready," Mackeson told him.

"Please help yourselves to tea," she said. "I'm not very good at pouring with my left hand."

Both men seated themselves and filled their cups. Wyrick sipped his and then began. "We have a very complete statement from Sean MacKenna. You were wise to enlist his assistance. And we've spoken with the baker who employed Mrs. Michalopolous. She was a bit moody, but he had no reason to distrust her. She didn't seem to mind coming in very early, so we believe that the incidents occurred in the early morning hours. She also had a night job as a waitress at a Greek café. Her employer there reported that she was becoming irrational and unpredictable. The café, however, is in another part of the city, much closer to her flat."

"Her flat," Mackeson echoed, rolling his eyes.

"Yes, we've had a look at it," Wyrick continued. "We found a number of disturbing items there, including newspaper clippings of your husband's death and memorial service and dozens of photographs of you, many defaced. She possessed additional knives, both smaller and larger than the one she used to attack you. An upholstered chair with your snap attached to it was cut to pieces. We found rat poison, which we believe she would have used against your dog if the broken glass had not been effective."

Jenny felt suddenly weak. She set her teacup down quickly and shook her head, as if to rid her mind of the information she had heard. "She practiced attacking me?"

"She didn't use a moving target, and she didn't expect you to defend yourself," Simon said. "You were more than a match for her."

Wyrick nodded. "In short, we believe that she became fixated on you after her husband's conviction and incarceration." He leant forward. "We'll gather the best evidence we can, but a psychological evaluation will determine if she's fit to stand trial. Significant evidence does exist of rational planning, and I'm certain that will be taken into account. I'd like to see her charged with psychological harm as well. There's legislation that addresses that issue. Unfortunately, her defence counsel will oppose any sort of trial. I can't guarantee that you'll see justice done. I'm sorry."

"I'm not," Jenny said. "I've been there and done that. All I want to know is whether I'll be in danger from her again."

"Very unlikely," Wyrick assured her. "We'll be informed

of her status, but she'll not be released."

"Was it my ring?" Jenny asked. "The pearl one I saw her wearing?"

"Yes, exactly as you described it," Wyrick answered. "I'm afraid we'll not be able to return it to you for some time, however."

"I don't want it back," she said. "I just thought it was a piece of evidence that shouldn't be overlooked."

Wyrick consulted his notes. "With regard to the coroner, David Millar. We made contact with the Surrey detective who investigated the disappearance of his wife. Not a shred of evidence existed against Millar. According to him, they had just returned from a very enjoyable holiday visiting inns and antique shoppes between London and Wales. He went to work and assumed that she was home with post-trip chores. Nothing was disturbed in the home. A load of laundry was found in the washing machine. Millar was completely cooperative with the officers. Although Mrs. Millar's friends suggested that she was not as happy in the marriage as he claimed, no motive for his doing away with her was ever uncovered. Millar's lack of distress was suspicious, but he maintained that his belief that she was still alive mitigated excessive emotion.

"His reasoning notwithstanding, the Surrey officers felt that Millar was too calm. The home was too tidy. All documents and papers were in order. Mrs. Millar had not been seen by anyone other than her husband for some time prior to the holiday. He had ample opportunity to dispose of her on their automobile trip, for which he could not provide an itinerary. Clearly he was not involved in your attack, but the case in Surrey remains open." He closed his notebook.

"Maybe those detectives should see if any of the widows who appeared in his court have disappeared," Jenny said with a shiver.

"Indeed. That concludes our official visit." Wyrick stood and gestured for Mackeson to do the same. "Mrs. Sinclair, I have a question of a more personal nature. The material on your dining room table: What is it, and from where did you obtain it?"

She raised her eyebrows in surprise. "I guess you could say it came from my grief experience," she said. "I lived it. Then I wrote it, with additional thoughts, in the hope that it might help other people."

"What are you planning to do with it?" he asked.

"Print and distribute it, why?"

Wyrick glanced back at Simon and Mackeson, who were conversing about something they both found humourous. He cleared his throat and looked away briefly. "My wife," he said and stopped.

He's uncomfortable, Jenny thought, which means he has feelings. She felt a pang of guilt for calling him a humanoid.

"She has cancer," he said quietly. "She couldn't tolerate the last medication they gave her, and as a result, her prognosis is not good. I'm afraid I may have need of your writing in the not too distant future. I'll remit whatever is required."

"Sergeant Wyrick, I'm so sorry," she said. "I should have copies available in a matter of weeks. And there's no charge."

"You'll ring me then, when it's ready?"

"Yes, I will."

"Thank you." He looked again at the other two men. "Mackeson!" he called. "We're keeping Mrs. Sinclair from her holiday."

Mackeson joined him, and the detectives left. Simon turned to Jenny. "We'll have a quick lunch, then I'll replace your bandages and load your things in the Audi. Our drive will take several hours."

- -

Jenny was confused. Simon had driven the Audi out of the garage, but he wasn't accelerating, and he was going the wrong way. "Simon, where are we going? This isn't the way to Kent."

"We have a stop to make first. Somewhere you need to go. Trust me."

He headed down Ellerdale and stopped where Ellerdale curved, right where – "Simon, no. Please, no," she begged. "I just want to get away and forget."

"Not going to happen if we don't do this. Jenny, the attack took place in your neighbourhood. You can't avoid these streets." He stepped out of the car and opened her door, extending his hand. "We'll do this together."

She gripped his hand, but he had to pull her to her feet. She felt too lightheaded to stand straight. She felt his arm, firm around her waist.

"Breathe," he said. "Count and breathe in, count and breathe out."

"One," she gasped. "Two. Three. Four. Simon, why are you doing this to me?"

"Because facing your fear is the only way to cut it down to size."

"Five. Six. Don't let go."

"Look, Jenny," he said gently. "It's just a street."

She straightened slightly. The faint feeling had passed.

"Are these the trees you described? The one with ivy on the trunk? And the fir?"

"They must be, but – they look so ordinary."

"Exactly. Easy peasy. And the pavement?"

She looked down. "No blood stains. I might never have been here. But I know now why she seemed so tall. The street goes uphill. I was below her."

He relaxed his grip on her waist. "We'll walk to Fitzjohns, then back. So you'll know you can do it."

She held his hand to make sure he walked with her. She remembered how absorbed in thought she had been, not concentrating on each step as she was now, but when her feet crossed the spot where the attack had taken place, she felt no panic, just the deep exhaustion that came with long sought after relief and a corresponding gratitude for the man next to her who had engineered it. She put her arms around him. "I'm okay, Simon. Thank you."

He kissed her lightly. "Off to Kent then."

CHAPTER 43

Simon Casey paced. When they arrived in Kent, Jenny was chuffed about their suite in the hotel, exclaiming over the fireplace in the room, the huge footed bathtub in the adjoining room, and the flat screen TV they could see from the bed. Hotel d'Italia: She liked that also, the paintings of Tuscan landscapes on the walls and the promise of Italian cuisine. She'd showered before leaving Hampstead, so she'd kicked off her shoes and said she only needed to freshen up. He wasn't certain quite what a woman meant by that, but he'd always thought it was a shorter process than a shower, so he told her it sounded good to him. While he waited, he wondered: Should he order champagne?

He stopped pacing and thought back. She'd held the map and navigated while he drove through London, but when he turned onto the A20, she'd fallen asleep, knackered, he guessed, from the emotional hurdles she'd had to clear recently. No matter; he knew the way from there. From the A20 to a ramp, then a roundabout, and he was on the M25. Past Sevenoaks, she woke. "We'll arrive in about twenty," he told her, glad to see her smile. The check-in process was efficient, and they were escorted to their room. More smiles.

He shrugged out of his shirt. He hated waiting. On the Job they planned, they got kitted up, they were transported, and then they waited. Time slipped away while they listened for the "Go! Go! Go!" that would signal that the mission was on. The real work began then, the movement of the team, the short bursts of intense action. He had learnt to accept the waiting, but he had not learnt to like it.

He found himself pacing again and realised that she'd been in the loo for more than a few. He didn't hear water running. He approached the door and knocked lightly. "Jenny? You all right?" When the door swung open, he saw her sitting on the edge of the bath, still partially dressed, her face pale. "What's this?"

"Simon, I haven't changed my mind, but – I'm a little scared. My heart's going a mile a minute."

He sat down next to her and put an arm around her. "No need for fear. We've already been together."

She leaned into him. "Yes, but when we – we – you didn't stop to look at me, and we didn't even take off all our clothes, and – "

"Full stop, Jenny."

"But I have scars and bandages, and I want you to think I'm beautiful, and I don't want to disappoint you, and it matters so much more now!"

"Jenny, a line here and there doesn't signify. Not to me." He thought for a moment then asked with a smile, "How do you know I'll stop to look this time?"

She appreciated his attempt at humor, but it didn't calm her. She put his hand on her heart to show him what she still felt.

He didn't speak right away. "My first jump," he began. "I was afraid I'd not hear the crack of the chute when it opened, my heart was beating that loud. And I'd closed my eyes as tightly as I could." He paused. "Preparation is the key. Preparation of your mind and preparation of your equipment."

"How do I prepare my mind?"

"You already have. Your mindset – ours, actually – is love." He moved his hands to her shoulders, felt the tension there, and gently kneaded her muscles. After a few minutes he moved her blouse out of the way and kissed the places his fingers had touched, then the sides of her neck and her ears. "Waiting to jump is harder than jumping, but when it's time, we'll jump together," he said.

"You won't let me go splat?"

That made him smile. "No. Just close your eyes and hold on."

She put her arms around his neck, and he carried her to the bed. "No worries, love. When I first met you, your wounds hadn't healed, remember? But you looked lovely to me even then. Nothing's changed, except I think you trust me a bit more."

That brought a smile to her lips: a Simon Casey understatement.

When he saw it, he leant over her and kissed her, softly, tenderly, then waited, his lips less than a breath away from hers.

She felt her anxiety ease, only to be replaced with an entirely different kind of tension. She kissed his mouth, his rough cheek, his mouth again. She no longer cared what he saw; she wanted him to know how much she loved him and she couldn't show him with her clothes on. "Simon, I think my equipment is ready," she whispered.

Who needed champagne? He began to remove the rest of her clothing, one piece at a time, kissing what he uncovered, whispering her name, wanting her to feel loved. She was slim, shapely, even lovelier than he remembered. The reconstructive surgery she'd had on her shoulder had minimised the damage there, and the scars on her torso were no more than thin threads against her pale skin. He saw the contraceptive patch on her abdomen and felt a pang of regret. Best to be safe, of course, but if she fell pregnant, she would need to stay with him, and he was not yet sure of her.

"You might want to lose your jeans," she said into his ear.

He stripped off and kissed her again. He heard a squeal. "Simon, I'm ticklish."

Resolving to locate all those places in the days ahead, he resumed his lovemaking. The soft sounds she made were like extra kisses, and she surprised him by humming slightly as she pressed her lips against his skin.

He was over the moon: The woman he loved was naked beneath him, her mouth open for his kisses, her heels digging into his backside. No more holding back, no more waiting. "Jenny," he gasped.

She clung to him, managing to tell him how overwhelming she thought it was and how much she loved him. When he started to shift his body to one side, thinking he might be too heavy for her, she tangled her legs in his and begged him to stay with her a little longer. He did, pushing her hair out of her face and giving her light kisses. Serious kisses followed. She sucked on his tongue, and he felt his groin tighten again. "I can't get enough of you," he said. When she called his name, he was beyond words. His body alone would have to tell her how much love he felt.

She had forgotten how much she liked feeling a man's weight. When he finally rolled to his back, she felt exposed, vulnerable, bereft. Needing to prolong their feeling of closeness, she turned on her side and put her head on his shoulder and one arm across his chest. "Simon," she whispered, "I've had feelings for you for a long time. I just didn't know what they were. I wish – I wish it hadn't taken me so long to realize I loved you."

He chuckled softly. "Two of us then."

"I didn't think I'd ever fall in love again, and certainly not with another policeman. Your work is far more dangerous than Colin's was."

He heard what she had left unsaid. "Jenny, I'm trained. Armed. Briefed. I don't go in alone or without intel. And now I've the best reason in the world for being careful."

"We'll have to make each day count." She ran her fingers across his chest. "You didn't like me at first, did you?"

Women always wanted to talk after sex. For the first time it was no bother, no bother at all, because it kept her close to him. "When we met, how I felt about you wasn't the issue. Your health and safety were. But you didn't think much of me either, as I recall."

"I was afraid of you. You were so direct, so unyielding, and you never smiled."

"And now?"

"I feel like I've come home." She snuggled closer. "Simon, are you happy?"

He'd not have used that word to describe himself until now. "Yes."

"How did you find this place? Did you choose it because of my interest in Italian?"

"Rang my mates. Davies knew about it. His folks had been here."

"So they all know we're here?"

"And what we're doing," he smiled. "Traylor bet that I wouldn't let you out of the room. Davies bet that I wouldn't let you out of bed."

Blushing slightly, she kissed him. "Simon, what do you love about me?"

He thought for a moment. "Your resilience. Your smile. Your defiant chin. Your ability to surprise me." With a mischievous smile he added, "Your shape. When you were in witness protection, I very much liked watching you work out."

She swatted him playfully. "You told me those exercises were physical therapy!"

"For you they were. For me they were entertainment." Her skin was soft, warm, and smooth. He didn't want to move away from her, but the time was late, and he wondered if she were hungry. "Are you ready for room service?" he asked.

She couldn't restrain a giggle. "I think I've already had it," she said.

Laughing with her, he reached for the In Room Dining menu on the nightstand.

After reading through the extensive offerings, she decided to try the breaded cheese risotto appetizer followed by a Caesar salad and pasta with Bolognese sauce, all items she could manage with one hand.

"No dessert?" he asked.

"Maybe later. What are you having?"

"Crab and spinach risotto and cioppino di mare. And champagne." He pulled on his jeans and watched while she donned a tank top and knickers.

When their food was delivered, she inhaled deeply, enjoying the aroma of the Italian herbs, and realized that happiness had a smell, something that floated on the air that you breathed. During her marriage to Colin, happiness had filled the flat, as if fresh coffee were forever brewing or prime rib roasting. Her happiness with Simon was an unexpected joy, like turning a corner and finding that the bluebell buds had burst into bloom and were surrounding her with their fresh fragrance. But floral aromas faded. She wanted happiness that would cling to her so strongly that its scent would remain on her clothes no matter how many times she washed them. Indelible.

He ate slowly, enjoying his meal but distracted by her scant dress. After they finished the Italian delicacies, she cuddled beside him. Her knickers were black. Lacey. "You're overdressed," he said.

A slow smile spread across her face. "What are you going to do about it?"

"Rise to the challenge."

- -

Jenny dreamed that Simon was kissing her neck and her cheeks. A good dream, for a change; she'd had a bad one she wanted to forget. This wasn't a dream, however. She was awakening, very slowly, from a deep sleep. He was clothing her with kisses. Her body heavy, she felt his hands, warm on her skin. "Don't you ever sleep?" she murmured.

"Not when I've something better to do." The caresses continued. "But you don't have to move. Let me do the work."

How could he make her body feel so good when she was too tired to open her eyes? Finally she stretched and turned toward him. It was all the invitation he needed. He took her as lovingly as he had prepared her. "Oh, princess," he whispered. "I missed you."

"Princess? I'm a commoner."

"Not to me."

She felt as if he had given her insides a soft squeeze. She

rested her head on his chest, felt his arm encircle her, and fell asleep to the lullaby of his heart.

CHAPTER 44

Simon woke first and looked over at Jenny. He had often tried to imagine what it would be like to kiss her. And more. Many times he had wished that he, not Sinclair, had been the one to teach her to trust a man with her body. He had wondered if her rape still affected her, if there were any residual effects. He'd seen one: She'd left the light on in the loo, explaining that she didn't like being in the dark. No bother for him, of course. He'd wanted to see as he touched her and as she touched him. She hadn't donned her nightdress, but he would not have objected. Whatever she wore could be removed easily enough when the need arose.

He smiled, remembering her initial shyness. Once under way, however, she had been eager. Amid the passion, he had wanted to know her preferences, and she had said, "Again," when he demonstrated her choices, and then, between breaths, "Both!" He had laughed then, as he had when she had named in Italian the body parts she knew and made up names for the ones she didn't. As their lovemaking became less hurried, she had queried him as she touched him, wanting to please. He'd wished he had the words to tell her what she meant to him, but he was struck silent.

He folded the bedsheet back slightly, admiring her shape, naked except for the bandages on her hand and arm. They put him in mind of her recent danger and his possible loss, and his heart skipped a beat. If he lost her now, when they had been together for such a short time – he didn't want to think on it. Perhaps he should engage MacKenna on a regular basis! Again he was reminded of Sinclair, her shock and grief at his death, and the special ability she had to recover from the worst life threw at her.

Even after the night they'd spent together, he couldn't quite believe she was in his bed. She was lovely with her lashes closed and her face relaxed. Once past her shyness, she had been lovely in passion also, a mature woman showing no restraint, her hair falling forward as she moved above him. Once during the night, however, he had woken to her cries of alarm. "Sshh. I'm here," he had said. "Bad dream?"

"What's wrong with me?" she'd asked through her tears. "I'm with you, and I'm happy. Why would I have a nightmare?"

"You've had a rough go of it. Someone tried to kill you less than a week ago. You'll not forget that so soon, but you're safe now." He'd held her until she calmed. When she slept, he caught a few himself then washed up.

Now he ran his fingers across the wrinkles the bedclothes had made on her skin.

Her eyes opened and rested on him. It had been a long time since a day had dawned like a promise. A smile played around her lips. "I thought you'd be running," she teased.

"Not today, princess."

"What would you like to do today?" Silly question, she realized. He had shaved and applied aftershave.

"Kiss your shoulder, your knee, and everything in between."

She smiled again. "What would you like me to do?"

"The same."

CHAPTER 45

Jenny and Simon stayed in Royal Tunbridge Wells all week, and as the days passed, the knife attack gradually lost its hold on her emotions. Only once did he see her trembling. She clutched him and cried briefly, then apologised, which wasn't necessary.

"Simon, I wish you had a gun."

"No need. I have other ways of subduing an aggressor."

"Your Special Forces training?"

"Yes." He reminded her to breathe the way he taught her, which seemed to help. He didn't know what had triggered the episode.

One night he took her to Thackeray's, a restaurant where the novelist's home had once been. She was shocked by the prices, but he talked her into ordering the roast partridge soup and platter of lamb, explaining that he had quite a bit of money saved and he could provide for her in every way. He chose a starter with crab and avocado and the panfried sea bream for his main. They shared the dessert sampler.

On another evening they went to Sankey's, a casual brasserie and oyster bar where she lost count of the number of oysters he consumed. "Did it ever occur to you that you're eating the whole animal?" she asked. "All its little systems."

"I'm not squeamish," he laughed. "Are you? I see a few oysters in your seafood spaghetti."

"Touché," she answered. "Simon, we've both been through so much. It has taken us a long time to get here. Don't you wish life could be easier? I need some time without crisis or trauma. A dull life."

"No such thing," he answered. "Life's a series of challenges. Whatever happens – high tide, low tide – we have to push through. Sometimes we have a chance to catch our breath or get a second wind, but where life is concerned, we can only make things between us easier. We haven't any control over the rest."

Up and down the narrow streets they walked, exploring the shops and cafés and sometimes reaching for each other's hand at the same time. In a jewelry store in the Pantiles, where the promenade was paved with tiles, he encouraged her to select something to remember their trip by. She chose a gold watch with a narrow band and a diamond chip to mark each quarter hour. "So I'll know when it's time to make love," she teased. They didn't visit any of the museums or galleries, but one afternoon they spent some time in an aviation bookstore. She watched him peruse the shelves and remove a volume. He opened it and ran his fingers down the table of contents. It seemed an intimate gesture, his fingers against the print. She thought about where he had touched her and how she'd felt and, wanting him again, she stepped closer and slipped her hand into his back pocket.

"What are you playing at?" he asked quietly, a bit surprised.

"I'm not playing."

He looked up and saw her blushing. "Let's go then," he said with a smile, closing the book and taking her hand. They hadn't gone far when the overcast sky opened up and a light shower began to fall. "We'll run between the drops," he said, not wanting to take the time to unfold the umbrella.

They dashed to the hotel, the rumbles from above making them increase their pace, the raindrops dancing around their feet and beading on his cheeks as well as hers. Had she felt less desire, she might have laughed at his moist freckles, but she had her arms around his neck almost before he locked the door. He kissed her there, standing up, and his breath in her ear excited her. They didn't make it to the bed, and she was glad. She hadn't wanted to wait. "You can go back to the bookstore now," she said, and they both laughed.

He found a hospital nearby with an A&E where the doctor replaced the stitches in her arm with steristrips. "When it's time, I'll remove the sutures in your hand myself," he said. "Just takes scissors and tweezers." Then he kissed her still bandaged hand and confessed that he had been afraid he would lose her.

While she was basking in his love at night and his presence during the day, he seemed to have an agenda. Over dinner one evening he mentioned his work schedule and asked if she thought she had adjusted to it. On another he asked whether she wanted him to come to Hampstead each night when his work was done instead of waiting to see him at the weekends. She reached across the table to take his hand when she said yes. He always seemed to be touching her somewhere, her hand, her shoulder, her waist, as if to make up for all the times when he couldn't. When she told him she loved him, he responded with physical expressions of love and closer approximations of the three-word phrase she hoped to hear but still stopped short of spelling things out exactly. As the days passed, the actual words became less important, because the tender tone he used when he called her "princess" seemed to say it all. Then one night in bed he whispered, "*Ti amo.*" In Italian it only took two words to say, "I love you," but it was ten times more romantic.

All too soon, it was Sunday and time to check out. He closed his holdall. She put the last few items in hers and looked up at him. "I don't want to go home," she said. She had fallen asleep each night with his arms around her and woken each morning in his embrace. Her nightmares had abated. She felt loved, satisfied, and safe.

He had never been particularly attached to places. As a Royal Marine and later a Special Forces operative, he had always been on the move. "Home's where you are," he said.

She smiled. "But I don't want this to end."

Nor did he. He moved beside her and took her hand.

"Could we do this again sometime? Go away somewhere

and make love the whole time?"

"Sounds like you want a honeymoon," he said, holding his breath. "Would Italy do for you?"

Her eyes widened. *He has thought about this.* "But – honeymoons come – after – "

"Weddings, yes. I can manage that," he said carefully, watching her.

Her smile made her whole face light up. "Promise?"

"*Prometto.* I promise," he said, bending to kiss her. Mission accomplished.

THE END

ACKNOWLEDGEMENTS

As Sergeant Casey would say, no mission is accomplished alone. Soldiers are trained, briefed, supplied, and transported. In my world I was advised, encouraged, and reassured as I put words on paper. My thanks to Phillip Hagon QPM, Commander (Retired) Metropolitan Police Service, who continues to be a source of information and inspiration. Bill Tillbrook, Chief Superintendent (Retired) provided positive feedback and support. PC Ian Chadwick (Retired) and PC John Eaton (Retired) gave me behind the scenes glimpses of firearms officer operations and lifestyles. Detective Inspector Heather Toulson added background and insight into the work of SOIT officers. PC Rob Jeffries (Retired) at the Thames River Police Museum shared his extensive knowledge of the history of the river police.

My family's delight upon hearing that the story which began in *The Witness* would continue carried me through times of doubt. David and Joel Dunham of Dunham Books brought my mission to a successful conclusion. And as always, thanks to my readers (particularly my husband Larry and my son Jeff), whose constructive criticism made *The Mission* a better book. Any errors, whether intended or not, belong only to me.

ABOUT THE AUTHOR

Naomi Kryske was educated at Rice University, Houston, Texas. She left Texas when she became a Navy wife. Following her husband Larry's retirement from the U.S. Navy, she lived on the Mississippi Gulf Coast until Hurricane Katrina destroyed her home and caused her relocation to north Texas. *The Mission* is the second of a series of novels set in London (*The Witness* is the first), involving the Metropolitan Police, and exploring the themes of trauma and recovery. In 2008 she was awarded a grant from the Melissa English Writing Trust for *The Witness*. She is an active Stephen Minister.

Visit Naomi on the Web at www.naomikryske.com and on Pinterest at www.pinterest.com/NaomiKryske.